CLAIMING HER

CLAIMING HER

Marilyn "Mattie" Brahen

WILDSIDE PRESS

CLAIMING HER

Published by:
Wildside Press
PO Box 301
Holicong, PA 18928-0301
www.wildsidepress.com

DEDICATION

To Ray Bradbury, friend, extraordinary writer, mentor and benefactor of Mr. Electrico's blessings. Your encouragement and faith in me are my blessings.

To Hannah M.G. Shapero, friend, artist, my first reader and surprise copy-editor, whose father, Harold Shapero, is a composer of classical music. Thanks for helping me portray Terence in a more realistic fashion.

To Ben Jeapes, friend and writer, whose editorial guidance was both brilliant and gentle with understanding and insight.

To Lynn W. Perkins, friend, artist and encourager, whose superb cover illuminates *Claiming Her*.

To my father, Irvin Wm. Brahen, my mother, Sarah Snyder, and my sister and brother-in-law, Michelle and Larry McHugh. They helped me to stay grounded in the real world, while building my creative ones.

To my son, Brian Octaviano and his family for teaching me that youth need not always follow in the parents' footsteps, as Hermann Hesse's novel, *Siddhartha*, so eloquently expresses.

To my friends, Linda and Ron Bushyager, for your "tech support" and your loving generosity. And to the Philadelphia SF, F & H Writer's Workshop, many thanks.

With much love to my husband, Darrell Schweitzer, who helps me to control the fictional worlds that bang at the doors and windows of my mind, asking to be let out, who insists that they (and I) be patient, while properly shaping them.

A creative life is sometimes a river flowing onward. It is sometimes a railway station, where you sit dejectedly, thinking you have missed your train, but there is always another train. And so I thank Elizabeth Counihan, editor of *Scheherazade* magazine, for suggesting I send *Claiming Her* to Ben Jeapes, and I thank Ben himself for having faith in the novel and me and helping me to make it the best it could be. And I thank John Betancourt of Wildside Press, my publisher, for being there for me.

This novel is dedicated to all of you with much love.

-1-

I developed, early on, psychic powers, becoming a spiritual medium in a world that seems afraid not of death, but of life after death.

I met many non-mortal people, seeing them in dreams, sensing them while awake, people whom I had to pretend weren't there, weren't real.

But when he came back to claim me in this lifetime, I was twenty-three, ignorant of my spiritual past, and psychically naive, for all that I thought I knew.

I had just given birth to my son seven weeks before, in the cold gloom of mid-January, 1971, and still felt extremely sore. Daniel, a strong but cranky baby, had finally quieted down enough that afternoon to take his nap. I took advantage of his sudden silence to also lie down and rest. Thoroughly exhausted, I drifted into twilight sleep, wafting in and out of consciousness, my body numb, as if I'd been drugged and anchored to the bed.

It was then that I felt a dark presence, a brooding mind seeking my acknowledgment, yet deliberately cloaking his identity from me. I knew the presence to be male; he projected a possessive sensuousness towards me which was distinctly and proudly masculine.

I couldn't visualize him. He kept that well-hidden. I struggled to wake up, fighting the power he emanated. My mind came awake, but my flesh still failed me, woodenly immobile against the cool sheet.

I sank back into sleep for what seemed a scant few minutes then truly awakened.

Rising easily now, I found my body mysteriously healed, the soreness and aches conspicuously gone.

I checked on Daniel. He slept on, his small chest rising and falling evenly with each tiny breath, a cherub with dark brown hair and eyes, his skin smooth and golden-peach, having none of the blotchiness so common among infants.

The dream disturbed me. I knew the dark presence had been real, invading my awareness, briefly controlling my psyche, and then releasing me.

At first I wondered if it had been Terence, up to his old tricks. A mischievous British spirit with long blond hair and pale blue eyes, he had been in my life as guide and friend for three years now. Yet all my instincts told me it had not been Terence, but a personality distinct from any spiritual being I had known.

I made a cup of coffee and sat sipping it, while Daniel still napped.

I had married his father one year ago. Terence had been wary of the match, but I, needing mortal warmth and love as much as the next woman, thought Richard Warren would be the emotional and intellectual companion my love colored him into. How strange that I, who could see so accurately as a clairvoyant, had fallen so far beneath the mark in my mortal judgment.

Richard and I had dated for two years. I found his sandy red hair—much lighter than my own and richly waved, his startling blue eyes and his slim muscular body extremely attractive. He had been open-minded toward my psychic beliefs and shared my other interests. Terence grumbled throughout this time, but couldn't pinpoint the reasons for his distrust and reservations toward Richard, and so I discounted his advice. Looking back, I often wondered why the Creator sent me spirit guides, since I so rarely took their advice. I've since learned that this response by young Earthly charges is quite common and a constant complaint among guides.

Richard's past was glamorous to my unexperienced mind. Although he read and enjoyed learning, he found college boring. He dropped out in his second year and joined the Merchant Marine. He loved being a sailor, becoming rugged and seasoned after three years at sea.

Although we were both originally from Philadelphia, we met in New York City. Richard had returned there to regain his land legs and further his education, working days as the manager of a sporting goods store and attending NYU at night, working once again towards a degree in engineering. I was five years younger than him, living in the Big Apple for the sheer adventure of it, employed as a typist at a CPA firm and living at the Simmons House, a women's hotel.

We were married in a civil ceremony, which only my parents attended, my mother disappointed that we hadn't let her plan a larger wedding, my father more than happy that we hadn't and trying to be cordial to Richard, whom he didn't quite trust to do right by me. Richard's parents were also not pleased with his marrying me, a non-Catholic; they sent their regrets and excuses and a small cash wedding gift.

Richard and I, both bravely and foolishly, ignored these early warning signals. We had just moved in to our furnished apartment in Queens, New York when I became pregnant four days past our wedding night. My pregnancy strained the marriage. Richard reacted sullenly, angrily, as if I had deliberately and prematurely foisted parental responsibility upon him. He didn't register for the next semester of evening courses, insisting that they cost too much with our baby on the way.

Our financial stresses increased. The sporting goods chain Richard worked for closed down his store, laying him off. The unemployment checks only lasted six months. Our son Daniel arrived in an emergency ward, the hospital writing me up as a Department of Public Welfare patient, but treating me well.

Now our rent was overdue, our food was low, and money nearly non-existent. Richard's attempts to find work failed. Sales jobs, it seemed, had become competitive and scarce.

Depression had vied with my aches and soreness before the dark spirit interrupted my rest. Now, feeling immeasurably better, I decided to confront Richard and rectify our difficulties, a plan of escape coming to mind.

Richard came home that evening, flung off his winter coat, and grunted a perfunctory greeting at me.

"Where were you?" I asked.

"At the billiards parlor. I stopped in to play a couple of games and lost track of the time." He bragged happily about some greenhorn he had bested there. I half-listened, as usual, to his pool hall exploits.

He took a second breath between his boasting. I jumped in. "Richard, can we drive out to Philadelphia this weekend? I'm really homesick. I want to visit my parents."

He rummaged in the refrigerator. "Did you make anything for dinner?"

"There's some tuna salad. I never know when you're coming home, so I didn't cook anything. Not that there's much in the freezer. Just a roasting chicken. Can we go home this weekend?"

He pulled out his wallet to check its contents. "Hmmn. There's still enough left of our emergency assistance check. It shouldn't take too much gas, and the car's running okay. Yeah, we can go."

"Good. I'll call my parents to tell them. We'll stay overnight to Sunday."

Richard heaped tuna salad onto a slice of bread and cut up a tomato. "Fine. I'm going to go down to the welfare office on Friday. See if they can't sign us up for food stamps, maybe a monthly check until I get work. How's the kid been?"

"Sleeping now. He was cranky most of the day, but I managed to get him down for a nap, and napped myself during it."

"Mmn." Richard wolfed his sandwich down and began fixing a second one. "Do we have anything to drink?"

"Iced tea." I poured him a glass. "I'm going to take a shower now.

I'm pretty worn down."

"Mmn." He reached for a book he'd left on the table earlier, reading as he ate.

The shower warmed me, almost felt like a caress against my naked flesh. I washed my hair, rinsing off the shampoo and soap, then toweled dry and blow-dried my hair, taking pleasure in its soft auburn sheen as it fell on my shoulders.

I watched myself in the mirror, taking a strangely clear, critical notice of my features—bright brown eyes, small rounded nose, heart-shaped face accentuating both cheekbones and a chin which dimpled—and found it pretty. This appraisal—so rarely did I judge myself narcissistically—caused a small smile to play at the corner of my lips, as I studied my mirrored self. For just an instant, it seemed *someone else* cracked that wry smile. I turned away abruptly, troubled, from my reflection, and busied myself, pulling my dry hair back in a band, wrapping the ponytail in a fat roller to curl it.

In the bedroom, I put on a soft flannel nightgown, then tiptoed into Daniel's room. He still slept peacefully. He would probably wake for late night feeding, but I, for now, could get some sleep, too. I left the door slightly ajar to hear him if he awakened.

The covers of my bed hugged me, as if a strong arm had been laid protectively across me. I welcomed the nurturing sensation, feeling as cradled as Daniel in his crib. I wondered if Terence was perhaps sending some optimism to me psychically. But he, whose presence I can normally sense, as a bright flash commands attention, had been conspicuously absent all day.

I was nearly nodding off when Richard climbed onto the bed, his shifting of the mattress jarring me. As I leaned into the pillow, slipping back to sleep, the touch of his hand on my back intruded again. His fingers traveled downwards to my buttocks.

"You awake?" he whispered.

I pretended sleep.

His hand continued kneading the cheeks of my rear. "Leigh Ann? Are you that sleepy?" His tone presumed my response.

I turned wearily. "You want to make love." It was a statement.

"Do you?"

"Mmn." Perhaps it would make things better. Anything was better than making him angry. My refusal would do that. It would be a sullen anger, as usual, accompanied by further late night returns and his flimsy excuses.

He bent down to kiss me, and I returned his kiss. I still had feelings for him; they just weren't always very good ones. Talking hadn't helped. Perhaps sex would. Sex as the healer.

He spent scant time in foreplay; I was young, requiring little to ready me. Entering me, he worked his body above me, bent to his own satisfaction. Waiting patiently for him to climax, I gained some pleasure from the act itself. But he seemed to be having some difficulty; perhaps it was the six weeks of abstinence following Daniel's birth. I became bored beneath him, wishing he would finish and let me return to sleep. And then a small wail filtered in, picking up volume, and becoming frantic cries.

"The baby," I said, my body stiffening beneath Richard.

"The baby can wait," he said between thrusts, panting. "He has to learn to sleep through the night anyway."

I touched his arm, then pushed gently. "He's an infant. He might be hungry or wet. I have to get up."

Disgruntled, sighing, Richard withdrew himself and rolled over.

I got up and went into Daniel's room. He lay on his back, squalling heartily, his small face reddened from his exertion. "There now, it's okay. Mama's here." I picked him up, and held him as I checked his diaper: not the problem. Cooing and stroking his back, I went to the kitchen to heat his formula. His caterwauling had lessened; occasional bursts of baby indignation would issue from his lips, punctuated by silence. I tested the milk on my wrist, heated it a minute more, and retested it for warmth. Sitting on the chair, I offered Daniel the bottle. He took it eagerly, but drank only about one-third before pushing it away. "All done? That's Mama's angel." I took the dish towel off the table and laid it across my shoulder, lifting Daniel against it to burp him. He let out an enormous gas bubble. I continued rubbing his shoulder lightly; he fell asleep against me.

I sat there, savoring the silence, and was only half-aware of a figure, seen peripherally, entering the kitchen archway.

I looked toward the entrance, expecting Richard.

No one was there.

—*Terence?*— I thought, but couldn't sense his bright aura.

—*No,*— said a voice not physical, sounding like a whisper in my inner ear.

I responded with my own inner voice: —*No?*— And more cautiously: —*Who is this?*—

At first, just silence, outer and inner. Then, —*One who's waited. For you. Waited far too long, but willingly.*—

I attempted to probe the spirit, to pick up his appearance. He blocked me, but not before I visualized coal-black, opaque, almond-shaped eyes. They seemed to have neither pupils nor whites.

Only a wall of black, and I knew instinctively I could not see through them to the core of his soul. That, too, he had blocked.

I shivered, the kitchen suddenly cold, sitting there in my nightgown with Daniel asleep against me.

This spirit frightened me. I had neither courage nor curiosity to probe him further. My mother, who also had the psychic gift, had warned me of its dangers shortly after my first clairvoyant experience.

I had just turned eleven. My father, mother, sister, baby brother, and I were picnicking in the Pennsylvania countryside and decided to tour a nearby eighteenth century manor. I had spied a small girl, silent and alone in an upstairs alcove, dressed in period garb. She gazed directly at me, but no one else in the tour group, descending a staircase, seemed to notice her.

The tour ended in a drawing room below, and there on the wall above a fireplace was a portrait of the girl. When I questioned having just seen this child, Mother hushed me, making light of my comment.

Even during the drive home, she refused to discuss it, my father silencing me further with his admonition to "learn the difference between imagination and reality." It was only later that night, when Mother entered my room and sat down on my bed to talk, that I learned the psychic facts of life.

Rule 1 was never assume other people will believe the supernatural, let alone in your psychic ability. Rule 2 was to keep a sharp yardstick of judgment and control during any seemingly psychic incident, to rule out physical and psychological causes and stay in charge of the experience. And Rule 3 was to keep a Godly light—an aura of protection against evil—around oneself whenever dealing with the spirit world.

Mother admitted to her own psychic talent and warned me that my father had not a shred of belief in any of it. And so we became our own secretive, helpmate society, Mother and I. My sister, at six years old, was still too young for us to tell if she'd inherited the trait. As it turned out, she hadn't, and since then Ginnie and I have had long sisterly talks concerning the paranormal, agreeing to disagree, but twelve years ago, Mother deemed it wise to keep Ginnie well out of it. And now, as that brooding male spirit flitted purposely about me in the kitchen late that night, I fervently wished my mother were with me. Even Gin's blunt skepticism would have been welcomed if it served to drive him away.

I clutched Daniel to me and began to mentally build a halo of protective light around both of our bodies. Auric colors, invisible to the mortal eye, surrounded us, blue, gold, and white. The spirit made no move to interfere with my psychic defense. I sealed the auras and felt immensely calmer. I stood up to take Daniel back to his crib.

The spirit's psychic voice intruded again, soft now, soothing, but carrying a possessive, chauvinistic edge. —*I would never harm you, nor your child. Nor would I allow any other to harm you.*—

"Who are you?" I whispered.

The velvet tone of his answer almost stroked me. —*One who loved you long ago and has returned.*— I sensed a wistful smile, a small, upward turn of his lips.

I gave no answer, unwilling to involve myself until *he* gave more answers. I knew he was the same spirit who had earlier disrupted my rest, still slightly sinister in manner and aspect, and I put no trust in him at all.

I laid Daniel down in his crib, and returned to the bedroom.

My husband was asleep. I crawled into bed and curled up against his back. He didn't stir.

I lay awake, wondering if the dark spirit had left, abandoning whatever purpose had brought him here, and then felt the slightest touch upon my head, as if soft fingers ran though my loosened hair.

I lay still, the touch gentle, that which a woman receives from a man who cherishes her.

I quieted my thoughts, waiting, drawn to this mysterious male presence who would not reveal himself.

But only silence greeted my curious vigil, all sensation ceased, and I nodded off, sleeping undisturbed till morning.

*   *   *

The next day Richard went out to the Department of Public Welfare, and the dark spirit returned.

I could sense a bit more of his appearance, envisioning black hair, a long, angular face, and his tall and trim figure clothed in a black, tailored business suit. I distinctly felt that he was allowing me to see this, revealing himself a little at a time. I wondered if he chose this pacing because he was unsure of himself, afraid I would reject him, or simply due to his owning a recalcitrant nature.

I was in the kitchen, once more, when he reappeared. My hands were greasy from stuffing the roasting chicken. Daniel lay in his baby carrier, which I'd placed on the table beside me, watching me work and playing with plastic rattle-keys. The radio on top of the refrigerator broadcast pop tunes.

I reinforced the psychic auras around myself and the baby and tried to ignore the dark presence.

—*Leigh Ann,*— he murmured, seeming quite at home with my name.

I gave no response.

—*Leigh Ann . . .*— More insistently.

On rare occasions, when I was alone—Daniel too young to understand my words—I spoke aloud to spirits. Now I did so deliberately, to emphasize that this spirit had violated my mortal territory and had broken my standards of psychic courtesy, but in doing so had merely gained my anger and disdain, never my fear. "You know my name," I said softly, "but you're impolite. You haven't told me who *you* are." I waited a minute for this to sink in, then said, "Go away."

He, too, paused. —*I cannot.*—

This ambiguous answer puzzled me. "Cannot go away, or cannot tell me who you are?"

—*Cannot tell you who I am.*—

"Then leave, please."

I finished stuffing the bird, rinsed off and dried my hands, and began selecting my poultry seasonings, unscrewing their caps. Daniel watched me, lifting his pudgy little hand to make his keys rattle.

—*I have something of importance to tell you.*—

"Then tell me and leave."

—*You must not make love with your husband anymore.*—

I said nothing.

—*He will hurt you. He will bring you pain and illness. Do not let him lie with you!*—

Jealousy edged his words. My face reddened, and my anger flared. "You've delivered your message! Now, leave!"

A tense, responding anger chilled me, prickling my skin.

—*Remember,*— he said curtly, and then the sensation of psychic cold dissipated, with his presence so strikingly removed, the kitchen seemed brighter by comparison.

When Richard came back early that evening, I presented him with a decent dinner—roasted chicken, stuffing and peas, the last of our vegetables. I had even baked cookies, and we munched them over coffee for dessert.

I considered telling him about the spirit, but decided it would only add more conflict to the marriage. Richard had been somewhat successful at the welfare office. We were to be issued food stamps next week. It didn't relieve my long-term worries. I intended to launch my idea, my plan, that weekend. That, too, I kept from Richard.

Our evening passed pleasantly, without argument. Daniel nodded off to sleep at 9:00 PM, and when Richard later reached out to me, I didn't turn away.

I let Richard make up that night for the previous night's *coitus interruptus*. His renewed interest toward me gave me hope that our marriage might repair itself.

I would normally explore a spirit's warning for potential substance and validity. But I gave no credence to the crass blathering of the dark presence. I ignored his warning.

-2-

We drove up to Philadelphia in the little Volkswagen Richard purchased in the last year. It was used and had twice needed repairs. I remember worrying if it would break down on the way, but it didn't. It rode us smoothly into Northeast Philadelphia, where my parents, sister and brother lived in a tall, single home shaped like a dutch windmill, on a sunny tree-lined street.

The whole area had once been farmland, but after World War I, developers had come in. They laid streets where dirt roads had connected the remaining older houses and stores and created a large residential and commercial section which flourished further after World War II. GIs brought their brides to newly purchased row homes there, and couples raised their children in an atmosphere both countrified and citified.

My father, Bill Elfman, had been among the lucky ones, able to purchase one of the fine old homes built around the beginning of the 20th century for less than $15,000. His GI benefits helped finance it and also helped him pay for vocational school, learning air-conditioning, heating and plumbing. He later concentrated on the latter, becoming a master plumber, and now served customers throughout Philadelphia and southern New Jersey.

My mother, Miriam Elfman, gave birth to me in 1948, two years into their marriage. She didn't work, as was the fashion then, although raising children, house-cleaning, cooking and laundry could hardly be considered leisure time activities.

Heaven and Earth may have been spinning their celestial plans, but life went on quite mundanely in the mortal world.

Five years later, my sister Ginger was born, named not only for her curly red hair, but because Mother, an incurable movie fan, adored Ginger Rogers. My brother Fred was born five years after Ginnie. My own name was a curious combination of Vivian Leigh and Ann Miller, the former having mesmerized Mother in *Gone With The Wind,* the latter having thrilled her with her saucy dancing techniques. "Vivian Ann" would not have done, but Mother felt Leigh Ann sounded sophisticated.

Father picked out Ginger's and Fred's middle names (Melissa and Allen, respectively), but I was the only one who seemed destined to be called by both names, at least most of the time.

Ginnie, at least, was pleased with her name. Fred, now thirteen, had declared we were to call him Rick, from this point forward. All of his friends called him Rick now, frustrating Mother, who pointed out that Rick was short for Richard, not Frederick. My brother, she said, shrugged and told her that rules were meant to be changed. As we pulled up to the house, I thought of how funny it would seem to call my brother by a name I'd never used for him.

He was to be Bar Mitzvahed this year, and was feeling quite the young man. He had pointed out to Mother that, according to Jewish custom, children should be named after long-lived deceased relatives and not movie stars. But Mother, whose parents had died in the Holocaust, had no stomach for tradition. She herself had only survived the war because she had been a strong healthy teenager, capable of handling the rigors of slave labor in Auschwitz. After the war, she had immigrated to America, sponsored and welcomed by her Aunt Ida in south Philadelphia. She and Dad had met in 1946. Her defiant, inquisitive blue eyes, her fiery short hair curling impishly over her ears, and sturdy hourglass figure had captivated him. She in turn found his deepset brown eyes, dark brown hair, and strong trim build, hardened by his stint with the Marines, equally attractive. They had a whirlwind romance ending in marriage six months later.

Fred knew this, and so did the synagogue to which we belonged. He had already talked with the Rabbi with whom he studied Hebrew and Torah, who okayed the mention of his chosen nickname when he was called to the Torah during the ancient adulthood ceremony.

Father was more inured to tradition and deliberately had given Fred and Ginnie middle names in memory of his uncle and his aunt, who had also been murdered in the Holocaust. The rest of Father's family had immigrated to America long before the war, escaping such a fate.

I had little idea what Richard, a lapsed Catholic, thought of all this. He commented little when we spoke of our family backgrounds, during the early days of our courtship, except to say that wars based on religion were a mark against a society, showing its spiritual ignorance.

We were both naive in those days.

Fred was coming out the front door as we got out of the car.

"Hey, Leigh!"

"Hi, Fred . . . I mean, Rick. Darn, I'm going to have to get used to this!"

He laughed. "It's okay. Doesn't matter. Let's see the kid . . . will you look at that? He's got my hair and eyes." Fred winked at Richard, then bent down to smile at the baby in my arms. "Hey, Daniel! Hey!

It's your Uncle Rick."

Daniel looked at him blankly, then at me, his expression almost asking for explanation. "That's *Rick,* Danny. *Rick."* The baby's face dimpled, mouth widening to a grin, and he gave a little burst of laughter.

Fred made a face, and Daniel laughed again. "Listen, Sis, I've got to go. Basketball practice. See you tonight." He kissed me on the cheek, then turned to Richard. "Good seeing you, Richard." They shook hands briefly. "I'll catch you all later."

He smiled as he left, and I thought how similar his smile was to Daniel's, a wistful upturning of the lips.

I knocked on the unlocked door as we went in, shouting, "Hello!"

A pause and then, "Leigh Ann?," as Ginnie's voice travelled loudly from the kitchen. She came bounding into the living room, a grin of welcome on her face, Mother following her, with her own pleased look. Her eldest had come home, and that look communicated that she knew I had a problem and needed her.

"Baby," she said, her arms circling both me and Daniel, and kissed me on my cheek. "Oh, look at him!" She reached out and took Daniel's right hand. He obligingly wrapped his small fingers around her forefinger and held tight.

"Oh, he's beautiful!" Ginnie said, and to Richard, "You must be really proud."

Richard nodded. "Of course."

"Well," Mother addressed him, "you must be tired and hungry from your drive. Let's go into the kitchen and relax. I'll fix us a snack."

"Sounds good," he answered.

"Just leave the suitcases by the chair. You can take them up later. I've got the girls' old room fixed up for the three of you, even made a little cradle of sorts for Danny. I used an old large laundry basket, with soft blankets wrapped in a sheet. Of course, you'll have to share the room with Ginnie, but she doesn't mind. You and Leigh Ann can bunk in her old bed." Mother chattered on as she led us to the kitchen. "Oh, I'm so glad you came. I've missed Leigh Ann terribly, and we haven't seen you or Danny since our short visit to your apartment in Queens when he was, what? Two weeks old?"

"That was five weeks ago, Mother," I said.

"I know. But my baby has a baby, and I missed you both!"

"Oh, Mother!"

"You, too, Richard."

"Glad to be included," he said, and let out a short jabbing laugh.

"Now let's see what we have." Mother opened the refrigerator.

"I've got some chicken cutlets, and some fresh tossed salad, and some cola to drink, unless you'd like some apple juice. Your father should be back soon, Leigh Ann. I sent him to the supermarket to pick up extra groceries. I'm going to make a roast beef dinner for everyone. How does that sound?"

She bustled around, putting the cold platter lunch, beverages, and paper plates and cups on the table, masking an anxiety which she knew I felt emanating from her. Underlying her hidden stress was a strong antipathy seemingly directed at Richard, though I wondered if the true target was the dark spirit who had harassed me the past few days.

"So how have you been treating my little girl?" she asked.

"Oh, she's been okay." Richard leaned back in his chair, turning slightly to face me, a touch of a smile on his lips. "I don't see any marks on her from the beating. Must have all cleared up."

"Oh, Richard!" Ginnie exclaimed, rolling those blue eyes I'd been so envious of as a child.

"He's joking," I said with my own small smile.

"I hope so," my sister said. "You'd probably beat him back up, and probably win. She's a real meanie, Richard. Don't mess with her."

"I won't," he said, and helped himself to lunch.

My father came home an hour later, and the greetings and small talk were repeated. It wasn't until later that night that Mother and I could talk privately. After dinner, Fred went out, and my father went upstairs for his customary nap for an hour or two. Richard had called his parents in the nearby Burholme section of northeast Philadelphia, to arrange our stopping by there on Sunday on our way back to New York. He didn't know I had no intention of returning to Queens. He also called two high school buddies and asked me if I'd mind his going off to see them for awhile. I didn't mind.

Daniel fell asleep in his makeshift crib; Ginnie had a Saturday night date with her current beau, but promised to get back before midnight for late night sisterly talk.

Mother and I were finally alone. She washed the dinner dishes and I dried them. And the first words from her mouth were: "How bad is it?"

I hesitated, my feelings so repressed I hardly knew where to begin.

"Well?"

"It's bad, Mom. He hasn't found work, the rent's due, and we barely have food. He doesn't know I packed the last cans of baby formula we had."

"You're coming home?"

"I'd like to."

"What about Richard?"

I sighed. "He can go back to Queens, settle our accounts and bring the remainder of our clothing and stuff back here. Thank God, it's a furnished apartment, and we don't have to haul large stuff."

"And after he carts your belongings here? Do you want him to stay with you and Daniel?"

"He's my husband, Mom. Unless you feel it would be too crowded. Then maybe he can stay with his parents until he gets a job, and we find a new home for us here. I want to be home, Mom, here in Philadelphia. Just in case of emergency."

She handed me the last dish. Her blue eyes were hard with worry. "You think you can save your marriage."

"I . . . I don't know. He's just going through a bad slump."

"He hasn't really laid hands on you?"

"No. We've just had some problems communicating."

"Seems rather big ones, I'll bet."

I said nothing.

"Well, you're welcome to come home, and Richard's welcome, too. You can tell him it's all right. You can bunk in your old room until he's back on his feet. Ginnie might prefer him to sleep in Fred's room, under these circumstances; you'll have to work that out with her and Fred."

"Uh, Mom? Richard doesn't know yet."

She stared at me incredulously.

"I haven't told him yet. I only made up my mind to do this last Thursday."

"Last Thursday? And what happened then that made you plot this escape behind Richard's back?"

"Problems just piled up, and I knew we weren't going to solve them in Queens. Or alone. Thursday, I just . . . finally got the courage to make a decision on it all."

"But not enough courage to discuss it with Richard."

"I just . . . just didn't want to create more conflict."

"Are you afraid of him?"

Again, I hesitated, considering exactly how I was reacting to Richard. "Not physically. Emotionally, though . . . emotionally, he shuts me out. Almost as if he has a do not disturb sign on with smaller writing under it that says proceed at your own risk."

She was silent for a moment, wiping dry the sink area. Then,

"Have you tried to probe him psychically?"

"Yes. It's very disturbing. There's a lot of anger. And that very definite warning to keep out."

She turned, leaning against the kitchen counter. "Leigh Ann. Are you sure there isn't another source, besides the two of you, causing his reaction?"

"Well . . . yes. The baby. Richard made it plain he wasn't ready for fatherhood. And now, even though he seems to love Danny, he seems to resent me."

"Leigh Ann." She spoke quietly, as if to an idiot child. "You have a tendency to overlook the obvious—a tendency I wish you'd lose."

"What do you mean?"

I suddenly felt a protective aura build around me, beyond the one I normally bathe myself in each morning upon awakening. It felt strong and heavy, an auric safety net over a lighter safety net over the normal psychic aura that surrounds each living thing, whether seen and understood by humanity or not. "Mom . . ?"

"Leigh Ann," she repeated, saying my name three times, and an old folktale came to mind: that if someone said your name three times, the angels would reveal your heart's most deeply hidden secret. And her tone dropped a notch or two as she said, "There's a spirit standing directly behind you. He's tall . . . with black hair and eyes and a ruddy complexion."

I gaped and whirled around. Of course, I saw no one mortal, but I caught a fleeting glimpse of him, handsome and sensual, as he backed away from my sudden and unexpected turn. "He's followed me from Queens. I've been calling him the dark presence. He's pestered me since Thursday afternoon."

In my mind's eye, I saw him raise his hand and bring it toward my face. I froze, nearly flinching, thinking he would strike me, forgetting that Mom had reinforced my aura. I caught a clear impression of his face; he grinned, a perfect double line of teeth like a Cheshire Cat. Then his hand stroked my cheek, gently and deliberately, the touch in itself a message, a reminder: *I would never hurt you nor your child.* "He's obviously attracted to me, though I don't know why. He believes he knew me before."

"And did he?"

"I haven't searched. It's been too hectic." I noticed that *he* stood slightly off from us, listening to Mother and me, no longer blocking me from visually appraising him. "He's very possessive and demanding, and has an aversion for some reason towards Richard. He wouldn't identify himself when I asked him to repeatedly."

"Well, where attraction exists, mortal spouses become rivals to them." Mother moved a few steps toward where she sensed he stood, and looked toward him. It amazed me how closely she gauged his whereabouts to where I saw him. "Who are you?" she asked. "We mean you no harm, but you cannot interfere with Leigh Ann's mortal life. If you need to communicate, to express some past life conflict and lay it to rest, we will be able to hear your spiritual voice through telepathy. But we need you to identify yourself, before we explore your presence and your relationship with Leigh Ann further. Do you understand?"

He had been standing there quietly, listening to us, a small closed smile on his lips. Now the smile widened again into that Cheshire grin and opened up into spasms of laughter.

We waited, wondering what in Mother's words had proven such a source of amusement. His spasms subsided into chuckles, and he studied us with a glint in his eyes, sizing up both us and his answer.

—*My name is Bael,*— he said with a cryptic glance at me. He pronounced the name as if it conjoined the words "bay" and "eel."

Mother tried a different tack. "Ba-hel. That's Hebrew for Barry. Are you Jewish?"

The slightest touch of irritation crossed his thin face. —*With all due respect to your mortal mother, Leigh Ann, she should leave detective work to Mr. Holmes. I pose no mystery; I give my name simply and truly. Bael.*—

I said nothing, allowing Mother to continue her own probe. I saw her glance toward the clock, knowing my father might awaken and come downstairs, abruptly ending our search for answers, and Mother blocking the spirit from further interference with the proper mentally-spoken prayer or two.

"Where are you from?" Mother asked.

—*A place where Leigh Ann and I were to be, and a place where I could not let her follow me.*—

"A riddle. He's evading our questions. What year did you and Leigh Ann know each other?"

No answer. That question seemed to upset him, bristling his cool, composed demeanor.

"What year do you *claim* to have known Leigh Ann?" Mother repeated, emphasizing her distrust of his veracity.

—*No year known to mortalkind, and every year since, when angels were forced to live among mortals to save those pale imitations. And every year thereafter, she was kept well-hidden from me, but now I mean to win her back!*—

The violent force of his words was like a potent spell paralyzing us. We reeled; I felt Mother's dizziness along with my own, nearly fainting. And then I felt his hand. It reached out and steadied me. In that instant, the powerful emanation broke, but I could feel his anger, coiled and contained.

Mother seized the moment, holding onto the counter to brace herself, her own fiery maternal anger lashing out to him. "I command you in the name of God and all that's Holy, to reveal your true self and true purpose here!"

I saw him suck in breath, his teeth clamping, and then he was gone.

Mother and I stood there, breathing heavily, regaining our composure. "The name of God disturbed him," she said finally. "He could be demonic in origin. Not good."

I wanted to dispute her, shaken as I was. "He said he would never hurt me or Daniel."

"Be careful how you define *hurt*," she said. "You know the expression about the road to Hell. I would be less concerned about his intentions and more concerned with how in God's name you're connected to him. I'll reinforce protection around the entire household to try to keep him out. If he hasn't the good sense to stay away, we'll mentally recite the 23rd psalm." She turned her head toward the arch leading to the dining and living rooms. "Hush now. I hear your father coming."

I nodded.

"In the meantime, we have enough to handle with your financial and marital problems. Oh, hello, dear."

My father came into the kitchen and stopped, staring from my mother to me. "I know that look on your faces. All right." He wearily pulled out a kitchen chair. "So tell me what's wrong."

Mother sat opposite him. "Bill, Leigh Ann feels they're on the brink of disaster in Queens. She hasn't told Richard yet, but she wants to stay here, for us to put them up until they get resituated. I told her they could."

Father sat quietly, contemplating it. I could tell he didn't like it. "There goes my peace and quiet." He sighed. "Well, first, I think we ought to tell Richard this great plan of yours, Leigh Ann. It'll be crowded, but if you think it's that bad, and your mother wants you to stay, okay. But you'll have to tell him and hope he takes it well."

Mother got up from her chair. "I'm going upstairs to use the bathroom and check on the baby. I'll be back."

I slid into the chair. "I'm sorry, Dad. I didn't mean to impose on you and Mom."

"We're your parents," he said. "We're not going to turn you down. But men have their pride, and he may not take this well at all." He lowered his gaze to avoid looking at me, and said, "I told you not to marry him. But you wouldn't listen," then shook his head at the stubbornness of children. "Why don't you make yourself useful and get me a cup of instant coffee?" I got up and began searching for it. "Bottom right-hand drawer. And by the way, Leigh Ann—don't tell your mother this—but if that bum of a husband of yours doesn't get a job and earn his keep within a reasonable amount of time, I'm kicking him out. You and the baby can stay, but I'll kick him the hell out!"

When Richard came back that night, Dad led the conversation, telling him I didn't want to return to Queens, and that he would drive his truck back to the apartment on Sunday, following Richard in the Volkswagen, to collect our belongings and bring them back to Philadelphia.

Richard reacted oddly, chiding me with more than a hint of disgruntlement for not discussing this with him beforehand, but he also seemed relieved. He agreed that this would give us a chance to start anew, and he returned to Queens with Dad that Sunday, packing and loading our personal belongings in the truck, then insisted on staying in Queens to settle affairs and say goodbye to friends, since we had one week of paid rent left on the apartment. I later discovered, rather rudely, that one affair he stayed to settle had been with a woman I'd never met, and only found out about due to a dangerous legacy she had passed on to Richard, who had then passed it on to me.

If Richard had played his adulterous games in the 1990s, the news he brought back the following Sunday might have been my death sentence. But the AIDS virus had not begun to spread rampantly among heterosexuals in the early 1970s, and at least Richard had the common sense to tell me he had syphilis. Early diagnosis allowed him to cure it with penicillin. He strongly advised me—his departmental words exactly—to see a doctor and get some penicillin for myself.

I immediately called a Planned Parenthood clinic, let them take a blood test, and was also put on penicillin. The doctor said he would call if there were further complications, but I had apparently escaped Richard's foolhardiness, as no further problems surfaced medically.

Emotionally, I had to confront the truth, two truths to be exact: that Richard had been unfaithful to me, and that the dark spirit calling himself Bael had good cause to ask me to refuse Richard's sexual advances.

I needn't have worried about Richard making further moves on me. He knew how deeply upset I had been about his cheating and the syphilis. He told me he'd be staying with his own folks until we resolved our marital problems. I won't deny that I was vastly relieved to hear this. But I never believed he was simply being considerate of my feelings and my family's comfort. It seemed to me he really wanted his freedom. He even told my father that he'd done a foolish thing and felt I'd need time away from him before I could forgive him. My father didn't respond to that, already furious with him, for Father was a man who held steadfast grudges. But he did tell Richard to find a job and act like a good husband to me, and then perhaps his wife might forgive, if not forget, the bad marital beginning.

I neither forgave him nor forgot, and from that moment on, I no longer loved Richard.

-3-

No one in my family blamed me. They seemed to accept my separation from Richard as the lesser of two evils, as if they thought the future would be far more horrid if I stayed with him. I agreed.

I finally told Mother, on a quiet Monday afternoon two weeks after moving back to Philadelphia, of the warning the dark spirit calling himself Bael had given me, and my initially pegging it as possessive jealous intrusion. Mother listened carefully as I related the psychic conversations I had had with him, those last two days in Queens.

"Are you sure you haven't sensed him in the slightest way since your first night home?" she asked.

"Not at all. It's almost as if his only purpose was to prevent me from catching VD."

"That doesn't jive with his story about returning to claim you, obviously as a lover, which *would* be an intrusion into a mortal woman's life." She cupped her chin in her hand, her eyes taking on the distant look she always wore while thinking. "It could have been symbolic," she said finally. "He loved you then, and he *returned* to keep you from potential harm, and departed to his own proper plane of existence, the job finished. A fine theory, except that he seemed to flee at the mention of God."

I spooned sugar into my coffee and stirred it slowly. "I'd like to know the answers to the riddles he gave when you questioned him: He's from a place where he and I were meant to be, but he couldn't let me 'follow' him there . . . and he seems to claim he knew me before historic times, but he's been watching me ever since. Watching over me?"

Mother pursed her lips. "I'm not sure. His last response mentioned angels living among mortals . . . no. *Forced* to live among mortals. And he called us 'pale imitations.' Of what? Angels?"

"There's one fluke in your theory. He specifically said—the last thing he said—he means to win me back." I hesitated, then decided to spill my gut feeling. If I needed my mother's help with this, I couldn't hold anything back. "I get the feeling this is unfinished business, Mom, at least as far as this Bael spirit is concerned. But I can't pick up on having known him before. I've probed and probed, and I'm coming up blank. And yet . . . ."

There are moments when a strong current seems to enter a conversation, and you know someone has something very important to add, a fact or a response which holds a key, a breakthrough, to its comprehension. Mother must have sensed this, for her head, which had been lowered introspectively, snapped upward, her posture, her expression, and her voice sharp with attention. "And yet *what?*"

I wet my lips, afraid to admit it, fearing her ridicule, her horror, or both. I had no idea why I thought she would respond that way. What I felt could take on a hundred different meanings, spurred by a hundred different causes, and even be a misinterpretation on my part, near the mark, but not correctly on it.

"Well, Leigh Ann? You may as well talk it out. We're not going to solve this by running away from it. You know as well as I do that in psychic disturbances, fear and ignorance—especially ignorance masquerading as innocence—can be deadly."

"I feel as if I love him." I said it simply, with no flourishes or emotion.

"Love him? Or *loved* him?"

"Love him. Deeply and unconditionally. But I can't recollect any lifetime, not a single memory from what I can recollect, in which we were together."

Mother sat stock-still, not looking at me, having gone from pursing her lips to gnawing on her lower lip.

"I know that sounds ridiculous. I know you probably think I'm succumbing to some silly romantic notion."

"Or to a sexual entrapment spell."

"It doesn't feel like that. I'm completely capable of refusing or ignoring him if he acts untrustworthy or dangerous. And I wouldn't accept him as a spiritual guide or contact anyway. Not unless I solved the question of who he is and why he's here, and he proved worthy of my attention."

Mother stood up abruptly.

"What?" I asked.

"Nothing," she said. "I thought I heard Daniel crying. He's about due to wake up from his nap, isn't he?"

I glanced at the kitchen clock. "Probably. He's been asleep for two hours now." She was studying me somberly. "Funny. I didn't hear anything."

Not answering, she moved through the dining room and living room, then stood at the base of the staircase, looking up.

"He will wake up if we talk here," I said.

She nodded and motioned us back to the kitchen. "Must have imagined it." She dumped our coffee cups into the sink and began selecting food from the fridge to prepare for dinner.

"At any rate," I told her, "my attraction to this spirit, whatever's causing it, is a moot point. He's apparently gone. I just may be a silly romantic goose, simply because he was right about Richard and acted so protectively toward me. It's obvious *I* never knew him before, or I'd have remembered him, pushy behavior and all. All I can come up with is the possibility that we never really met, but he somehow *knew of* me, and built it into some intense and unrequited fantasy about me."

Mother stopped chopping the lettuce and leaned, wearily, I thought, on the counter. "We've completely overlooked something else he said, which *I* just remembered. Leigh Ann, he said you had been kept hidden from him."

"That may just be his interpretation, if he only knew about me, but couldn't meet me, simply an expression of his frustration." Mother's quick glance clearly didn't buy that. "I know, I know. Yes, I'm making up my own interpretation. But keeping me hidden from him isn't the same as giving me the world's longest case of amnesia!"

"What makes you think you've remembered all your past lives? Amnesia is exactly what the higher planes instill in most people to keep them centered on their current lifetime. Do you think we're exempt from such need, simply because our psychic talents enhance our ability to see beyond the mundane this go-around?"

She shook her head briskly. "I've told you a thousand times, but you don't listen. Psychic ability and knowledge is a gift, not a privilege, and the gift does not come with a lifetime guaranty, no pun intended, my dear daughter. The talent won't work, the knowledge won't come, if somehow your using it or knowing it would prove harmful to you or others, no matter how innocent or beneficial your intentions are . . . or if you were unscrupulous, God forbid, no matter how deserving the targets of your evil intentions might be. Our free will is tempered under the ever-watchful eye of the High Council and *their* involvement tempered by the tapestry of our souls, all woven together throughout time. The Creator's game plan, ongoing and immortal.

"But our mortal lives are in themselves important, together making up the sum total of our learning experience in this plane of existence and the value we've achieved and can take with us to use when we graduate from it and go permanently beyond."

Her lecturing had riled me, as it had through my childhood and teenage years. Neither Ginnie nor Fred got these lectures, but, of course, they hadn't inherited Mother's psychic abilities. And when I got riled, I generally took Ginnie's advice. Ginnie had as little tolerance for lectures as she did for psychic subjects. She ignored both, being ultra-independent and set on making her own decisions and choices. "I appreciate your telling me all this, Mom, and I know about the mysteries. No one knows everything. But I can't believe they would have blanked my memory of him if he were that important to my spiritual development. *Some* memory would have surfaced, as deeply as I've probed."

"It did. Your love for him. The question is: is that slight opening something deliberately left unhidden, or is it a glitch in the system designed to protect you? And more importantly, is his so-called returning to you—giving you the benefit of doubt with your unrequited love theory—beneficial or detrimental? Are we dealing with good or evil here?"

I bristled at the thought of Bael's being evil. He had already proven himself beneficial and protective, not destructive. "I think the best thing to do is take it slow and if he returns, reinforce our auric protection and examine his behavior very carefully. I also feel I should get on with my real life, Mom. I'm separated from my husband, probably heading for divorce, and have no source of income. What I need to concentrate on is getting daycare and a job, not this Bael. There's really no time to waste on him."

"Is that how you really feel?" She said it quietly, as if she would accept whatever answer I gave and work through it with me.

"It's not how I feel. It's what I have to do. I have no time for obsessions in my Earthly life, not if I'm to get on with it."

"Then you won't become obsessed. Intent is half the battle."

I nodded, glad she believed in me, at least on that point. "I'm going to get Daniel up. He's been asleep for nearly three hours now. If he sleeps anymore, he'll be up half the night."

"Mmn. Go ahead. I'd better get this dinner started. And Leigh Ann— " I turned back to her. "—don't be afraid to tell me anything, if you think I can help."

"I'm not afraid, Mom."

"I know you aren't. I guess 'embarrassed' was the word I meant."

A small smile crept onto the corners of my lips, and I guess I blushed. Mom was never shy or subtle. I didn't answer—my reddening was answer enough—and headed upstairs to wake Daniel.

As I walked down the hall to the old bedroom, which Ginnie and I both shared growing up and now shared with Daniel, Mom's earlier disquiet resurfaced in my mind. I opened the door and walked over to the crib which Dad had brought back from Queens.

Daniel wasn't in it. Horror constricted my throat, but I forced myself to stay calm, my eyes scanning the floor around the crib— nothing—and then moved around the crib and spotted Daniel asleep on my bed a few feet away. The bed pillows had been removed and flung on the floor between the bed and the closet; the covers had been pulled down, and only the top sheet covered my son to his waist.

No one had been in the house that afternoon except my mother and me.

I checked Daniel's breathing; it seemed rhythmic and normal. Then I flew down the stairs and into the kitchen. "Mom. I need you upstairs. Right now."

I spent no further time in explanation, tearing back up the stairs and into the bedroom where Daniel still slept snugly on the bed. Mother had followed me in. I gestured toward the baby and whispered, "I didn't move him."

We both knew Fred and Ginnie were at school, and Dad was at work. There was no way a nine-week-old infant could have gone from the crib to the bed, and pulled bedspread and blanket down or flung pillows onto the floor.

I reached out and slowly nudged Daniel. He awoke groggily, opening and shutting his eyes. "Mommy's got a little sleepyhead here," I cooed, and he slowly grinned at me.

"He doesn't seem hurt," Mother murmured. "Start to pick him up gently, using your arm and hand to brace his back, neck and head."

I did so, and lifted Daniel, holding him against my chest. He squirmed and tried to reach my shoulder. "He's all right. Thank God."

Mother and I stayed silent for several minutes, both of us, I knew, wondering how this could have happened and why. She walked to the crib and bent to check out the wooden floor under it, then searched under my bed. I heard something shake in her hand. "Here's his key rattle." She straightened up, her hand grasping the side post of the crib to steady herself.

At first, we heard a tearing creak. Mother watched as the post loosened and leaned toward her. She grasped it quickly in both hands, trying to hold it up and push it back in place, but the bars on her side sagged down and fell with a thud to the floor. As we jumped back to avoid being hit, the thin boxspring also came loose. It tilted at a forty-five degree angle to the floor, the crib mattress sliding off of it and slipping to the floor.

We both stood there, shaking, while Daniel stared at the broken crib curiously.

Then Mother checked the crib post that had started it all as I watched. A large screw hung from its hole at the top, ready to fall, a large crack running down the post from the screw hole. She removed the screw and studied it. "This has been stripped, its grooves worn smooth. It's possible that the wood in the post was bad, too."

"My God, Mom. Just think! If Daniel had been in that crib . . . ."

"Somebody took him from it. Somebody who *knew*."

I hugged the baby to me. "And who knew it was as dangerous to lay an infant down on a pillow." I looked at her, helplessly upset. "And took great care to keep the heavy bedclothes off of him, when placing him on the bed."

Mother nodded. "Somebody obviously protecting him, on all counts."

"Who?"

"I don't know, but I'd say it was a good guess that your Bael is back. The front door is locked. No one else came in and foresaw this happening."

"Then this proves Bael is protecting us, that he means us no harm."

"Maybe. I'd just like to know how this crib became so dangerously defective. It certainly makes your dark spirit a shining hero in your eyes, doesn't it?"

I clutched Daniel more firmly; he had come fully awake and squirmed in my arms. "All I know is the baby's safe. He could have been badly hurt. Whatever miracle caused him to be removed from that danger, I'm grateful."

She put her hand on my shoulder. "I thank whatever agency's responsible for his safety, too. Perhaps this Bael is a protective spirit watching over you and Daniel. Perhaps he's one of many. It's just that I've never seen a manifestation like this—Daniel moved halfway across the room and asleep to boot—and I'm shook up. But he looks healthy and happy, so it obviously *was* a gesture of love. Come on, let's go downstairs. Maybe Dad can fix the crib after dinner. If not, we'll have to get a new one."

She led the way through the cheerful hallway, late afternoon sun streaming in the window at the top of the stairs, and then down to the living room. "By the way, honey, who put Daniel's crib back together when Dad brought it back from Queens?"

"Richard," I said.

It had been a used crib to begin with. When Richard came over that weekend to visit Daniel and me, to *talk,* Mother and I showed him the dismantled crib, now stored in the garage.

We left the supernatural out while telling him our story, as we had when telling Dad and Fred. In our modified version, Daniel had been awake and safely with me in the kitchen when the crib collapsed, that Mom had grasped the crib post while tidying the room, when the whole thing came tumbling down. The three men agreed we had been damned lucky the baby hadn't been in it. Some might think we deceived the men, but they wouldn't have believed us, had we told them the entire truth.

Only Ginnie had been told the whole of it, while we dismantled the old crib and once again set up the old laundry basket as a temporary overnight crib for Daniel. Ginnie listened without her usual skepticism, knowing that even if someone had broken in and moved Daniel, knowing about the crib would have in itself been a psychic act. But Ginnie conveniently detached herself from our unorthodox brand of the supernatural by ascribing Daniel's mysterious relocation to God. "Miracles are God's province," she said firmly, "alone. I really don't have any other explanation, unless one of you moved him earlier and have developed temporary amnesia about it."

"Amnesia has been under discussion lately," Mother said wryly. "But we only told you, dear, so you could be on the lookout if anything of an unusual nature occurs." She was well aware of Ginnie's blithe disdain of what she called our hocus pocus. "Will you help us out?"

"I'll be your Sherlock Holmes in all things mundane when it comes to the out-of-the-ordinary. But I doubt if I'll ever see a ghost or spirit, and if I did, I'd be looking for the projector, thank you very much. And don't expect me to be picking up on any telepathic conversations either. But, yes, I will keep this weird occurrence that you've told me about a secret, a desire I can plainly read on your faces and know from long experience."

"That's two for Sherlock Holmes," I murmured.

"What?" Ginnie asked, holding Daniel and shifting him to her other shoulder.

"Nothing," I said. "I'd really appreciate your detection work, if anything else happens, especially because you measure things so logically."

"Appreciate my finer talents, huh?" She laughed. "I think this kid of yours has gone to sleep. You sure he won't crawl out of this basket bed?"

"Gin, he's only nine weeks old. And after what happened this afternoon, I definitely think someone's watching over him."

"God."

Mom took the baby from her. He yawned as she lowered him into the basket bed. "And sometimes God's agents."

Ginnie shrugged. "I'd rather cut out the middlemen. But can we talk about something else? The baby's all right, and all this business about dark spirits and protective auras is giving me the willies. I've had to listen to that stuff since I was old enough to understand English, and I've never experienced one whit of it. Why don't we talk about clothes? My sister's back and I haven't even had time to go shopping with her . . . and Leigh Ann, they've got some divine numbers at the mall on Cottman Avenue. Maybe we can go tomorrow night when I come home from school."

"Maybe Leigh Ann and I will be shopping for a new crib tomorrow," Mother cut in. "Hopefully one with an instant delivery schedule. In the meantime, it's nearly midnight. Time for bed." She lightly kissed Ginnie and me on the cheek. "Try to keep quiet," she said. "Your father's already conked out, and you know what a devil he is if his sleep is disturbed."

She headed down the hall to her and Dad's bedroom.

Ginnie shrugged and began undressing. "Then let's go mall shopping this weekend," she said.

"I haven't any money, Gin. And with you in nursing school, I wonder that you do, unless Dad's being less stingy with allowance this year."

She pulled a nightgown over her head and tugged it down. "Dad stingy? I've told you. You just have to butter him up. I just hug him and talk sweetly and, presto chango!, he's as generous as can be."

"That's one magical act I haven't managed yet." I took my old night shift from the other closet, undressed quickly, and put it on. I picked up our day clothes—Ginnie's lay on the floor as usual—and chucked them in our hamper. Just like old times.

"You know, that's your problem," she said, sprawling on her bed. "You're too damned honest. Even with your and Mom's, uh, refraining from discussing your psychic stuff, you're so direct, it irritates him and then Dad gets all grumpy with you. You have to learn how to coddle. I mean, he's the one who told us you get more flies with honey than with vinegar. It's one of his favorite sayings."

33

"Too late." I lay back on my own bed. "We're both set in a pattern, Dad and I. If I started to kiss up to him now, he'd know it. Besides, I've never been able to fake anything very well."

Ginnie yawned. "Never too late to learn. If not with Dad, maybe with other men. It's possible to be *too* honest, Leigh Ann. I mean, you're not doing too well in the love department, heading for divorce, with a young baby and all."

"I really don't know where I'm heading with Richard. Maybe I can forgive him. He seems to want me to."

"You'll have to make up your own mind about that." She yawned again. "Turn off the light, will you? You're closest to it."

I checked on Daniel in his temporary bed, satisfied that the sturdy plastic basket prongs were high enough to keep him inside, then switched off the overhead light. "Goodnight, Gin."

"Night, Leigh Ann." Another yawn, silence, then, "I can't see what you see in Richard. You can do a whole lot better than him."

"I'll put up a sign," I murmured. "Only slightly used woman with child. Looking for an improved version of Prince Charming. Willing to barter."

"Oh, Leigh Ann," she whispered back. "Good night."

"Good night," I answered, and lay awake for a short while, trying *not* to think, until sleep claimed me and I dreamed.

It seemed so real—my first inkling that mortal reality did not consist only of wakefulness, sleep, and the dream state. Both Mother and I knew that dreams could include past as well as present life memories, subconscious symbols skewered together with surprisingly strong and recognizable images. But neither of us knew that we could *relive* a memory, as clearly as if we were experiencing it for the first time.

Since then, neurologic science has found that an area of the brain, when externally stimulated in surgery, will cause this virtual memory to be relived mentally, as if it were happening physically.

But that night, I knew nothing of this potential to go back in time and feel things as if my mortal life was the dream, and I, the dreamer, fully awake. It was not a cognizant dream; I was not aware that I was dreaming. Later on, I trained myself to dream cognizantly, for there came, into my dream world, times of danger when the ability to wake myself became imperative.

But that night I dreamed I was in Eliom, and knew it was a different dimension from Earth, and that Earth was a youthful planet that we, my people and I, were still forbidden from visiting and exploring.

34

We looked human, but we were not human. If you were to gauge time as we did, and the manner in which we grew and changed, you would call us immortals. We were also the beings Earthly religions would one day call angels, although the correct name, if translated from our language, would be "angelfolk" or "people of the light."

Bael was one of the angelfolk, and I watched him approach my *thachka,* our word for the cottage-like dwellings we lived in, from a small window near my pallet in the loft. His father walked beside him, and I became excited, knowing Bael would keep his promise, made after a hasty stolen kiss last evening on our way back from working in the Garden.

I say *stolen* because we were not supposed to embrace before Bael formally declared for me and my father Michael formally received and approved my acceptance. A kiss or two was generally tolerated before betrothal during the courtship ritual of initial mating, but not more than that. When you came of age in Eliom, you were watched over by your elders, even more so than when you were a child. Whether male or female, you were taught that sexuality was one of the Creator's greatest gifts, to be treated as sacred.

I watched until Bael and his father passed beneath the door lintel, out of my range of sight. They were wearing the traditional short, white, sleeveless robes of summer, but adorned them with soft purple sashes worn loosely around their waists. The sashes ended in a tassel of gold.

I moved away from the window and sat down in my curtained alcove. The curtains enclosing the three alcoves could be swept back and away to make a dayroom filled with sunlight. But this morning I wanted privacy, nervous, knowing my father would soon call me downstairs.

The curtains hid a painful reminder that love could be destroyed by acts of rashness. My father now slept upon a single pallet. He had long ago detached the twin pallet once belonging to my mother.

I was five when she and her brother had disobeyed our Creator's edict. She and Adam had trespassed on Earth, leaving the protective dimensional winds on a mutual dare.

Like willful children bent on peeking at a forbidden object, they had planned to look and leave and, believing they had done no harm, expected to be forgiven, should the Creator spy them.

It was folly. The Creator knew and saw all. Eve and Adam knew this. They truly believed the Creator, out of love, would absolve them, but the first great tragedy they brought upon themselves.

The unstable atomic structure composing the mortal dimension of Earth—unstable to the molecular structure of the angelfolk—instantly altered Mother and Uncle Adam into a hybrid of angel and human, with the angelic DNA dominant. They became half-mortal, their bodies metamorphosing within seconds into temporal flesh . . . trapped on Earth, unable to leave that world, except through a process foreign and incomprehensible to us until the Creator described it.

Death.

We were told all this, and still my father believed my mother would be returned to Eliom and him.

Celestial time, we were told, differed from mortal time; a span of minutes, hours, years on Earth lasted three times longer in Eliom. It was also carefully explained to us that life in the mortal world was challenging and cyclic, a learning ground for its natives. The transition called death, which ended one cycle and began another, was triggered by both environmental and biological factors. For mortals, it was followed by rebirth. Mother and Adam, however, would be released from mortality's cycle, once they underwent this death. The Creator would then correct the imbalance in Earth's atomic structure to prevent such hybridization from recurring.

My father waited fervently for five of our years. Then one day, without explanation to me, he went up to the sleeping loft and dismantled Mother's half of their pallet. I asked him why he did this. "They are lost to us," he said. "They may be lost to us forever." All of my later questions brought two consistent replies: "Only time and the Creator can answer that," or "You're far too young to understand."

From that day forward, he no longer believed, and I knew with a child's instinct that Mother and Adam had in some way further angered the Creator.

Father would not explain. He became loving but quiet, seldom smiling. When he did, a wistfulness played at the corners of his mouth, as if he could not be happy without also acknowledging his sadness, and his light melodic laughter seemed gone forever.

I became my father's helpmate, keeping house for him as I grew older, protecting his need for peace and silence, and loving him dearly despite his grief and reticence.

The rest of the angelfolk in Eliom were solicitous and watched over us, none more so than the family of Lucifer. His wife Affaeteres often had me visit their thachka, slightly larger than ours, for it sheltered them and their three boys: Ashtoreth, Bael, and Azmodeus. Ashtoreth, three years my senior, was gentle and kind to me. Bael treated me warily, as if a girl one year younger than him acting so sedately and modestly proved an unfathomable mystery. Azmodeus, a year younger than I was, paid me little attention until we grew older, and then attempted to shock me with teasing and mischief. His older brothers pounced on him for that; it only fueled his rebellion further. He found me too quiet, too ladylike, and labeled me "Miss Perfect."

Notwithstanding Az's behavior, I was always welcomed in their house, and Affaeteres often visited my father and me with food and other gifts, mothering me in a fussing affectionate way.

It seemed natural now to me, as I listened to the men below, that Bael and I, despite our initial shyness toward one another, should fall in love.

The careful mutual wariness had been put to rest last summer. The sun had shone pleasantly hot as we completed our tasks in the Garden, and a group of us, teenagers and younger children, had rushed off to the lake to cool down with a swim. As we splashed about, Bael's thick black hair became wet and stuck to his head. His tall, elven-shaped ears, usually covered, were exposed. Some of the children began snickering, laughing and calling out. "Pointy ears! Pointy ears!" they cried, and their own fingers mimicked the object of their mirth.

Bael's face flamed as hotly as the sun. His hands rose to cover his pointed ears—an uncommon genetic trait among the angelfolk, but by no means rare—then abruptly lowered as he stared defiantly at the chittering youngsters.

His lower lip trembled, and the ache of oncoming tears glistened in his eyes as they swept over the faces of his tormenters.

I lashed out vehemently at the name-callers. "Stop it! Leave him alone. There's nothing wrong with his ears. It's yours that are short and stunted!"

The children, startled at seeing this quiet, demure, little mouse suddenly roar at them, fury in her gaze, stance and clenched fists, stopped their shrieking and jeering. I was well-liked among them and had never chastised them before.

"Apologize to him!" My tone had dropped, my anger cooling. "You've been rude and cruel, to someone your elder, no less. You know this behavior is not proper in the Eyes of the Creator."

The small band of harassers sloshed uncomfortably in the lake waters. One of the smallest, Avram, waded forward, looked at Bael, and murmured, "I'm sorry." Golden-haired Elisha moved beside him and echoed his apology.

Bael had kept his lips firmly set, his posture stiff and expectant. Now he slowly relaxed as the other children mumbled their retraction, glancing at me. I nodded approval, and they went back to their water play.

Bael had maneuvered closer to me. I returned his stare, but not without a hint of my old uncertainty, his gaze so unflinching and direct.

"Why did you do that?" he asked.

My words rushed out in one breath. "I couldn't bear to see them hurting you."

"You didn't have to do that," he said. He splashed off and joined his friends, his younger brother Azmodeus among them.

"Leianna's in love!" the willow-thin fourteen-year-old with his mop of unruly blond hair shouted, mocking me.

Bael cuffed him lightly. He protested, not at all injured, then swam off with his brother, who left him behind with swift arm strokes.

I waded back to the shore and sat watching them frolic in the water. My friend Chloe came over, sitting beside me, her short robe dripping. "Are you?" she asked, her fingers untangling her long brown hair.

"Am I what?"

"In love with Bael."

I murmured, "How would I know what love is?"

"You don't *know* love," she said. "You *feel* love." She laughed, noting my blush. "It's getting late. We should be going."

"You go on," I told her. "I want to sit here a bit longer. It's cool and restful."

Chloe's grin challenged me. I lifted my eyebrows, my eyes widening, denying her the insinuation that grin plainly expressed.

"Fine," she said, and stood up. "You're so proper, you'll probably make him swim the lake back and forth for you." She started off, then turned back. "Why don't you just tell him?"

"If I do things improperly," I said, "I'll have both my father and the High Council come down on him and me."

"Oh, pooh on propriety!" she said and walked up the bank toward the path leading back to our village.

The sun was setting as the boys meandered out of the lake. Bael said something to his friends and left them, walking swiftly toward me.

I sat motionless, watching his approach, looking up when he stopped a few feet away.

"Come on, Leianna. I'll walk you back."

He held out his hand. I grasped it, and he pulled me to my feet.

We let go of one another's hands, walking back to the village, not speaking, our silence easy and unstrained.

We reached my father's house. Bael smiled softly, secretly, and headed off to his own home.

That afternoon proved our true beginning. Our friendship blossomed, the shyness we had once felt replaced with the pure enjoyment of being together, a growing respect, and, yes, an intense attraction and need also grew between us.

I was fifteen; Bael, sixteen. We were children no longer. And just yesterday, as we worked side by side, tending new shoots in the Garden, Bael had asked in a low whisper: would I accept if he declared for me?

My breath seemed stoppered. I could only smile giddily at him.

"Will you?" he repeated, his tone an urgent throaty growl.

"Yes," I finally whispered back. "Yes."

"Tomorrow, then. Tomorrow I will come and declare our betrothal."

On the way back to the village, we found a less-used trail, and under its canopied arch of tree foliage, alone together for a moment, Bael leaned over and kissed me. I returned his embrace, all traces of resistance shattered. The kiss lasted only five seconds, but lingered on my lips as Bael led me from the shaded side-path. We heard a rustle of footsteps not far behind us. No doubt, an adult, watching at a distance. We grinned conspiratorially as we joined the others, traveling home from their day's work in the Garden.

We reached my thachka and Bael, with a knowing glance and smile, saw me in before hurrying off to speak, I knew, with his father.

That night sleep was elusive, and I awoke barely rested. My father raised his brows at my sudden smiles and the pinking of my cheeks when he caught me in languid reverie, but never complained when I burnt the flower cakes at breakfast and steeped the tea too strongly, actions so unlike his perfect daughter.

Unable to hide my feelings from him—for the man must make the Declaration of Betrothal and the woman not discuss it with her family beforehand—I climbed up to my sleeping alcove to do my mending.

Father had smiled at me then, not wistfully, but as if he *knew*.

An hour later, Bael and his father had greeted my father and been welcomed inside. I could hear their voices below.

I concentrated on the robe I was repairing, trying to compose myself.

It didn't help. When Father called my name, I jumped.

"Please come down here," he called. "We have visitors."

I watched my footing as I climbed down the ladder and turned to see my father, Lucifer and Bael smiling expectantly at me.

"Leianna," Father said, "Bael has declared himself as your betrothed, in the presence of Lucifer, his father. You may accept or deny him as your intended husband. What say you?"

-5-

That was the scene that remained hazily in my mind, as I awoke from the dream. My eyes opened groggily, scanning Ginnie's alarm clock. 7:45 a.m. Ginnie still slept, and Daniel lay quiet in his makeshift crib. A peacefulness pervaded the bedroom as I lay back on my pillow.

Leigh Ann. Leianna. How strange. I remembered Bael's intensity, his eagerness to claim me as his own.

Angels. The angelfolk. Michael, Lucifer . . . and Bael. The names of his brothers, Azmodeus and Ashtoreth, were unknown to me, but not so the names of Eve and Adam, the missing mother and uncle of my dream self.

Adam and Eve, the first humans in the bible, the parents of mankind. Were they two and the same? Or were the names a coincidence or a symbol from my own subconscious? In my dream, they were brother and sister, exiled on Earth from some place called Eliom in an immortal dimension.

The name of Lucifer was also all too familiar: the fallen archangel who founded the mythic Hell. Bael, who seemed to exist outside my dreams, had been his son.

Eliom seemed to be both the name of the village we lived in and the name of the land itself. It seemed to be an agrarian culture with huge plots of cultivation people tended as farmers—no, gardeners. I saw no equipment, no mass production. The people worked with small tools and their hands. They even called the rolling expanses of fields and groves the Garden, verbally capitalizing the name, almost reverently.

But it surely was unlike any mortal garden ever known. Bael and I had worked on a section of small pepper-like plants. The peppers grew plumply, but were a soft periwinkle blue. I remembered thinking how good they would taste when harvested.

Weedlike plants, with triangular leaves and small yellow flowers crowded the peppers, but we made no move to pull them. Instead, they received the same reverence we offered to the pepper plants.

We cupped our hands around the base of each plant, concentrating until a shimmering white mist appeared within them. The mist seeped upward to bathe the entire plant in a sparkling cloud. Energy the angelfolk generated daily to the flora of the habitat known as the Garden.

I saw no fauna in the dream, but heard the chatter of birds and insect sounds in the canopied forest glade where Bael kissed me.

"Good morning." Ginnie studied me with half-shut eyes and yawned, stretching in bed. "You looked like you were a million miles away."

I lay there, quietly regarding her, then asked, "Ginnie, do you believe in the stories about Heaven?"

"I, um, just woke up, and you want me to discuss religious philosophy."

"The best time. Just pluck your answer from your fading subconscious."

Gin gave me a small crooked smile. "Before rationality returns, you mean. Okay. Yes, I believe in Heaven. Most humans have, since history began. And even today, with all our scientific breakthroughs, people still believe, both educated and uneducated and from different cultures, in some sort of Heaven."

"And Hell? What about Hell?"

She cast me a doleful but forgiving look. "Oh, God, Leigh. You're getting *too* heavy now."

"Well?"

"From what I've read, it's a dumping ground for old deities which people used to worship hundreds of years ago. The newer religions turned them into devils and demons and stuck them in Hell. Made it taboo to worship them."

"Gin, the concept of Hell existed long before modern theology."

"Yes, but it wasn't *evil*. Everyone went to Hades or whatever name each culture called their afterlife world. Honestly, Leigh Ann, I think I've studied more mythology than you have. I don't want to get into a heavy debate, but listening to you and Mother chatter on endlessly about ghosts and ghoulies, I got curious. And while I don't seriously believe in this stuff, but I do enjoy reading it."

"You do?"

"Sure," she grinned. "I've always liked fantasy."

I threw my pillow at her. She caught it deftly.

"So you don't," I said, "believe in Hell and the concept of eternal damnation. Lucifer, Satan, and all that."

"No. It's not a Jewish belief. Other religions arbitrarily condemn people to Hell simply because they don't subscribe to their particular religious doctrine. How could anyone believe that a good soul who loves God in his or her own way could be condemned for that for all eternity?"

"But what about really evil people?"

"I didn't say God wouldn't condemn people who commit acts of evil, just not for all eternity. If there is such a place as Hell, maybe they condemn themselves to it, knowing that their actions make them unclean in the presence of God until they change and repent. But Lucifer's Satanic hierarchy lists quite a few gods and goddesses who predate Christianity and competed with Judaism's monotheism, rival deities who were turned into Lucifer's fallen minions. Ashtoreth, a Canaanite and Phoenician fertility goddess also known as Ishtar in Babylon, changed into a handsome, blond, blue-eyed, male devil with great wisdom of the sciences, especially the medical arts. He also knew all events throughout all of time."

"Was Ashtoreth a fallen angel?" My mouth felt dry. "I mean in the Christian myths, about Hell."

"Yes. He became a demon prince."

"And who was Azmodeus?"

"How did you know about him?"

"I . . ." What could I tell her? "Oh, never mind. You're right. This is getting too heavy." The alarm clock buzzed. I leaned over the bed to check on Daniel. He was awake, quietly resting in the converted laundry basket. "The baby's up." I got out of bed and took him in my arms.

Gin got up and turned off the buzzer, looking at me strangely. "Azmodeus was a demon prince of lust and lechery. Old legends say he was the get of Adam and Lilith, Adam's first wife."

"I thought Eve was his first."

"The sources are murky, but Genesis 5.3 says Adam was 130 years old when he had his first child with Eve, a son. Apparently Azmodeus and a host of other little devils came earlier, through Adam's union with Lilith."

"Mother and I never dealt with demonology. What really made you read up on all of this?"

"Are you kidding? All of that constant white light protection stuff? You never gave the bad guys a name, but it scared the hell out of me when I was younger. So, instead of looking for bogeymen in the dark, I decided to study up on it. And found it was all a bunch of rewritten religious hogwash. To the victor goes the edit job. Come on, let's go down and get breakfast. I've got a class at eleven, and I can't be late."

"Just let me check Daniel's diaper . . . wet. You go ahead. I'll change him and be down in a minute."

"Okay. Morning, Danny." She tickled his chin lightly, making him smile. "You want coffee and toast?"

"That's fine." I laid Daniel on his bassinet, unsnapped the bottom

43

of his sleeper and drew his feet and legs from it. I removed his rubber diaper — disposable diapers hadn't yet flooded the market and conversely the landfills — and unpinned his soiled cloth diaper. Only urine stained it. I chucked it into the plastic diaper hamper beside the bassinet.

Ginnie's answers plagued me as I rediapered the baby. Aside from the typically irritating behavior of the pre-adolescent Azmodeus, none of it jived with my dream. Of course, there was the myth of Lucifer's fall from grace, from Heaven. Was Eliom symbolic of Heaven and Lucifer portrayed in the dream before his infamous exile?

I pulled Danny's rubber diaper and sleeper bottoms back on, picked him up, and went downstairs to join Ginnie. Mother and I hadn't mentioned Bael's name to her, perhaps because of Mother's penchant for exactness when dealing with Ginnie's skepticism.

I wanted to ask Ginnie the etymology of that name. I was also afraid to.

Coffee was waiting on the table, and Gin was putting bread into the four-slice toaster. I put Daniel into his highchair, took a sip of coffee, then mixed the baby's powdered formula with water for his bottle.

The coffee had been made earlier by Dad, who had left for work at eight. Fred was already on his way to school, and Mother was still asleep, a privilege she insisted on three days a week—Tuesdays, Wednesdays, and Saturdays—now that her children were older. Today was Tuesday. Later on, she and I would shop for that new crib for Daniel.

Gin had warmed the coffee. Our toast popped, and Daniel's bottle was ready. I sat at the table opposite Gin and fed Daniel while we ate.

Gin resumed the conversation for me. "You never did answer my earlier question."

"What was it?" I couldn't remember, my head filled with all the names and histories she'd mentioned.

"I asked you where you'd heard the name Azmodeus. I mean, it's not your normal top-of-the-morning conversation, and you didn't sound as if you knew the biblical history on him."

I thought of citing a book or even a movie, but decided the truth served me better. "I dreamt about someone named Azmodeus. It was a very strange dream. I lived in a land called Eliom where I and others worked in this huge garden. I lived with my father—my mother had left us when I was small—and we were friends with another family. The family consisted of Lucifer, his wife, and their three sons. The sons were Ashtoreth, Bael, and Azmodeus."

Ginnie silently sipped her coffee, not answering at first. Finally,

44

she set her cup down. "Eliom sounds suspiciously like *Olam*. You know, *Baruch Atoy Adonai, Elohenu Melech Olam*. Blessed art Thou, King of the Universe. I think *Olam* means Universe. It sounds to me as if your subconscious was working overtime. There are other word-sound connections I picked up right away. Eliom and a vast garden. The Garden of Eden. And I'm sure even you remember the serpent was in the Garden—Lucifer. As far as the other demonic names, you must have picked them up from some source, and buried them until they appeared in your dream. You do have one heck of an imagination."

I froze at the implication in her tone.

"What? Oh, I didn't mean it that way. Maybe some of this psychic stuff is real. I'm just reminding you not to forget there are other explanations."

"Maybe." I relaxed again. "So the name Bael is among the Satanic Hierarchy?" I asked her casually, so casually that I wondered at my calmness.

Gin considered her answer carefully. "Yes, but it's another case where the name appears in different forms, each with separate legends attached to it. Bael is supposedly a great king in Hell and looks rather strange with three heads, only one of which is a man's. Then there's Baal, which in ancient Hebrew meant 'little god,' and who also doubled as a fertility god in Canaan. Not a nice guy. His cult sacrificed children by burning them . . . Leigh Ann, you're blanching. Look, the book you ought to read is *The Black Arts*. I have a copy of it hidden in my closet. Mother doesn't know, and I don't want her to. Keep it that way."

"Where is it?"

"In a box on the top shelf."

"Gin, how come you're not shocked? That I even dreamed these names?"

She gave me that challenging look that often changed conversations on the paranormal into heated arguments. "How come you're not shocked that I know of them and their histories? That I'm hiding that book from Mom?"

"You've already explained that."

"Yeh, well, that wasn't the whole explanation."

"What was?

"That I want to be prepared."

"Prepared for what, Gin?"

"In case these entities are real. Knowledge can be a powerful weapon, Leigh Ann. It can dispel the darkness and change something potentially fearful to laughable or absurd. You and Mother believe so strongly in the unseen good. I want to be prepared for the opposition, if you accidently tamper with it or unleash it."

"Unleash what?"

"Evil." She leaned back in her chair, grimly satisfied. "I strongly suggest you read that book. Maybe it'll cure you of such dreams. If not, next time you dream of this Bael or Baal, you can tell him to take a hike back to Canaan!"

Her face flushed and her blue eyes flashed molten daggers at me. "Gin. Ginnie . . . ."

Her breath came heavily and with a sick shock, I recognized the expression on her face. It was one and the same with that worn by the smirking Azmodeus in my dream.

"No one wanted you to come back into our lives," she drawled sarcastically. "Why don't you drop all this talk about Bael and save *your-self*, before you're in too deep?"

Her features had altered, her pale blue eyes flecked with green and her fiery hair emanating a light yellow mist. Even her cheekbones sharpened tautly, suddenly thinner.

Daniel began crying. He pushed his bottle away. Gin's eyes slid caustically to him. She raised her hand slowly, edging toward his throat.

"GIN!"

Her hand dropped as if it belonged to a puppet. She glared at me, her eyes confused, but they were her eyes, pale blue, and her hair and features only. The strange manifestation had fled.

She picked up her coffee cup, sipped, and put it down. "You really do need to read that book. If only to know how absurd some of this mysticism can be. It could even be dangerous if you mixed with the wrong nuts. Why's Danny crying and looking at me that way?"

"You got a little . . . emotional there. It scared him."

She didn't answer, confused.

"Gin, are you angry that I've come back home?"

"Angry? With what you were going through back in Queens? No. I'm glad. I want to see you and Danny have a better life, and you need a safe haven to start over. What better place than with your family?" She glanced at the clock. "Oh, my God. Look at the time. I've got to get dressed, or I'll be late." She stood up, looking at Daniel. He had quieted. "I'm sorry, Danny. Aunt Ginnie didn't mean to upset you." She took his small hand in her fingers. He seemed to forgive her.

"Ginnie, wait." I moved around the table and clasped her in a hug. "Thank you for caring about me, Gin."

She hugged me back. "You're welcome. I love you, too, but I've *got* to get dressed." She broke away and laughed as she walked away. "What did you just do, Leigh Ann? My skin's tingling, and my stomach has butterflies."

"I hugged you. That's all."

"Hmn. Must be static electricity."

I watched her closely as she reached the living room and headed to the stairs.

The aura I had enveloped her in radiated a strong blue and gold. Blue, representing Heaven's protection, gold, the highest degree of intelligence. Gin's own natural aura, a soft orange, shimmered close to her body, followed by the blue and then the gold emanations. I had psychically sealed the outer gold so that no other psychic force could penetrate it to harm her or attach itself to her psyche again.

I was less concerned about Bael. Wary as I was, my gut feeling insisted he would never hurt me or mine. But his brothers—at least my dream portrayed them as his brothers—concerned me greatly, especially the cocky snide Azmodeus. Someone, if only for scant minutes, had invaded Gin's psyche, using her sudden anger as an entrance point. The entity had shown a sharp resemblance to the 14-year-old in my dream, but his words, his tone on delivering them through Ginnie, had been menacingly adult.

My sharp shout to her had brought Ginnie back to herself. She had no memory of the intrusion.

I knew Ginnie well enough. She wouldn't believe any of this, if only in defense against what she obviously feared. She had always been psychologically resilient and resourceful. Had her own mind shaken off the psychic intruder, or had something or someone else . . . possibly Bael . . . forced it from her? Or had it left on its own, using her as a temporary conduit to deliver its nasty message?

I didn't know. I only knew Ginnie's sanity, strong and healthy now, might not survive another attack.

I picked up the baby and mentally sent a prayer that the forces of good protect my family beyond my own efforts. I felt my skin prickle and my own aura grow, blazing golden around me. The baby giggled. He, too, was bathed in gold, and I knew instantly that the rest of my family had been similarly armored. —*Bael,*— I thought.

—*No. My name is Quatama. Come to me when you sleep tonight.* —

— *Qua*-ta-*ma?*— I repeated, putting the accent on the second syllable, trying to pronounce it as he had. —*Who are you?*— I received no answer, only a feeling of well-being, of being guarded by Quatama beyond the simple definition of good and evil. A shiver ran through me, not of fear but of awe, knowing somehow that his was an intellect that understood both good and evil and sought to balance these opposing forces of the universe for the stability of the universe.

All fear left me, replaced by curiosity, a desire to remedy my own lack of understanding. I picked up the baby, heading upstairs as Ginnie, hastily dressed, her schoolbooks in hand, waved on her way out the door.

I eased Daniel onto my bed and took down the small box from the top of Ginnie's closet. The box contained a dozen or so books on mythology and religion. The Old Testament crowned it.

The Black Arts was wedged face down at the bottom. I removed it, put the box back, sat down beside Daniel, and began to read.

I had about an hour before Mother got up. If Daniel cooperated, I could possibly come up with some leads on the unsettling occurrences my family and I had experienced over the last three weeks.

If Mother rose sooner, I'd stash Ginnie's books back in her closet. It felt strange hiding this from her, beyond honoring Ginnie's request. But Mother, in all my training by her, had never accepted the existence of a dark side, of Hell. She bluntly refused to consider a netherworld of lost souls governed by fallen angels demoted to devils and demons. Her saying that Bael could be demonic confused me. She believed existence was composed of layered dimensions, our own physical universe only one of the layers. And each soul itself, according to Mother, created its own Heaven or Hell, depending on the lessons learned and the work done or shirked upon completion of its sojourn on Earth.

I still preferred Mother's views, but wondered if some of those dimensions could be in ideological conflict with each other. The concept of demonology baffled me. My being involved in it, even marginally, startled me even more. I wondered about the role of the mysterious Quatama in all of this, but had instinctively trusted him during our brief moment of telepathic contact.

I paged through the book, glancing at random paragraphs in each chapter, until I came to the one entitled *Lucifer's Minions*. It compared the histories of pre-Christian gods and goddesses with biblical histories describing demons and devils listed as members of the Satanic Hierarchy. The names were often the same or very similar, but their descriptions varied.

The name *Bael* had another variation beyond the three-headed king of Hell and the monstrous Canaanite Baal. Baalzebub was a Philistine god, the last two syllables of that name meaning "of the flies." King Ahaziah implored their Baal to rid Ekron of an infestation of flies. When the flies flew away, the Philistines rewarded Baal, making him their supreme deity: Baalzebub. Lord of the Flies. Jewish tribes later drove his worshippers from their lands, corrupting him into Beelzebub, the Prince of Demons.

The chapter never indicated whether the Phoenician Baal and the Canaanite Baal were one and the same. It did say that the name Baal had meant Lord or God in Syria and Palestine.

In the British Isles, the Celtic sun god Belenus, his name

latinized from the original Bel, was worshipped during Beltane with crackling bonfires and ribald abandon.

What relation did these early gods have, if any, to the handsome young man in my dream, the protective spirit, Bael?

Skimming through a chapter on Satan, I found that *satan* in early Hebrew had once meant the adversary or judge in legal disputes. Later, Lucifer became the supreme Satan: God's adversary, sternly judging God's own creation: mankind.

Again I wondered how this fit the quiet pleasant Lucifer of my dream. And Azmodeus had been his son, not the offspring of Adam and his first wife, Lilith.

I rummaged through the remaining books and pulled out a hardcover called *Man, Myth, and Satanism*. One section showed crude drawings of Bael and Ashtoreth. Ashtoreth, looking like a handicapped angel, his rubbery limbs bent over under the weight of enormous batlike wings, sat astride a dragon of Hell that more resembled a deformed dog. The sketch of Bael did have three heads: the center head was a swarthy, thin-faced man wearing a crown, his left head, a frog's, and his right head, a cat's. A spider's body squatted beneath the heads.

I couldn't recall Ashtoreth in my dream, although my dream self apparently knew him well. In the sketch of Bael, the human head did have pointed ears, but as I read the text, I found that these drawings had been created by Louis Breton, a French engraver in 1863. Mr. Breton had admittedly used his ample imagination in interpreting the royalty of Hell.

The sound of movement down the hall, the creak of a bed, alerted me to Mother's awakening. I stashed the two books back into the box and returned it to the top shelf of Ginnie's closet.

Daniel still lay on the bed, watching me with a quiet fascination. "You're such a good boy, Danny," I told him. He smiled back broadly.

"Leigh Ann?"

"In the bedroom, Mother." I picked Daniel up and met her in the hallway. "Morning."

"Good morning." She tied the belt around her pink terrycloth house-coat. "Have you eaten yet?"

"Yes, but we'll keep you company."

"Fine," she said, "and afterwards, we'll get dressed and go out to find that new crib."

"Sounds good."

While she ate, I told her part of my dream, not admitting to knowing the names of Bael's family members, and leaving out the story of Adam and Eve and their self-imposed exile on Earth. I did describe Eliom and the other events leading up to Bael's formally declaring us betrothed.

She swallowed her mouthful of cereal. "Betrothed. He came to ask permission to marry you."

"Yes, in what appeared to be a very formal ceremony."

"Pity they don't always have such niceties today."

"Richard asked Dad for permission to marry me."

"After about a year of your father telling you he disapproved. You and Richard were both stubborn. Your father decided there was no stopping the two of you."

"I wish he had refused us."

"What would you have done if he had?"

I paused, then smiled sheepishly. "Gotten married anyway, I suppose."

"You see? We decided to let you find out on your own. You were too starry-eyed to see past your nose, let alone understand our concerns. So in this dream of yours, did your dream-father approve or disapprove of Bael's proposal?"

"He didn't say. He asked *me* whether I would accept the betrothal. He seemed to be delighted with it though. I got the feeling he and Bael's father were close friends."

She gave me a crooked smile. "So what was your answer?"

"I don't know. I woke up, exactly at that moment in the dream."

She drank her tea slowly, then asked. "A past life, do you think?"

I shrugged. "It felt like a memory. Very detailed. Mom, is it possible to have a past life in another dimension?"

She raised her eyebrows at that. "Anything's possible. Why do you ask?"

"It didn't feel like Earth," I said.

"I think there's more to this dream than you're telling me."

"Yes, but I think there's something else you ought to know, something more important. Ginnie's afraid of all this stuff."

"Afraid of what stuff?"

"Of things that go bump in the night."

Mother leaned back, toying with her cup on the table. "You mean afraid of the stories in those books in her closet?" Her eyes met mine, weary but patient.

"You knew."

"Of course, I knew. If you want to hide something, don't put in closets where mothers hang finished ironing. Either that, or do your own laundry. The shelf came loose one day. I had to remove what was on top to fix it."

"You never told her."

"No, I didn't see any reason to. I knew she didn't believe in demonology any more than I did. I'm sure you noticed the bible was also in the box. If she wanted to discuss it, she'd tell me. If not, I respected her right to privacy and her need to work through her fears and curiosity herself."

We sized each other up across the table. Daniel squirmed in my arms. "Wait a minute," I said and got his baby swing from the living room and put him in it. He bounced happily inside it, playing with his rattle keys. "You're right about the dream. There is more. And I have to tell you about my strange conversation with Ginnie this morning."

She heard me out as I filled in all the gaps, but as I related Ginnie's sudden personality change, complete with words she had no memory of uttering and her near attack on Daniel, Mother's patient expression hardened in anger and alarm. I quickly informed her of the prayer I'd sent out for greater spiritual protection, the instant and intense granting of it, and the brief contact with the entity called Quatama.

Mother lifted her cup to her lips, drained the remaining tea, and put it down. "That was what I felt this morning."

"What?"

"A feeling of immense well-being, of love. I was lying in bed, half-dozing, and thinking, well, worrying about you. Then suddenly I knew you would be all right, that everything would be all right. But everything isn't all right. Ginnie was psychically attacked, used, to issue you a warning."

"That was before Quatama appeared. Ginnie's protected now. I *know* it."

"I'm not so convinced." She shook her head.

"Mom, you told me you don't believe in demons."

"I *don't*." She spoke in a firm voice that underscored her words. "But there are entities who, through their own negative natures, act like demons. They may create complete personas to fuel their egotism. They take the names of characters out of legends, to fool the unwary and frighten or impress the gullible. It's all a bunch of warped fairy tales, but it doesn't mean these entities aren't potentially dangerous."

"Do you think Bael could be dangerous?" I nearly whispered it.

"I don't know. Thus far, he hasn't been."

"You told me he might be demonic."

"When?"

"The night he revealed his name, and you asked him, in the name of God, to state his purpose in seeking me. He disappeared at the mention of God, and you said he might be demonic."

She sighed. "I'm sorry, dear. A semantic slip of the tongue. I was speaking psychologically. That he might *believe* he was demonic, a negative entity."

"Mother, what exactly *is* a negative entity?"

She deadpanned me. "A spirit on an ego-trip. Same as a living person with a bad emotional disorder, only in spirit. Leigh Ann, I want you to cut off all contact with this Bael. Even if he's not directly to blame, he's creating a psychic situation, possibly attracting other elementals, that might badly disrupt our mortal lives. Ginnie was right. You have unleashed something—now, don't look at me that way. I know it's not your fault. I know you didn't start it—this Bael did. But you did respond to it, to him, and formed an attachment to him. You have to break it now, for all our sakes."

"But Quatama is protecting us."

"I don't know this Quatama," Mother said. "It's possible he is protecting us, possibly also telling me to tell you to end this. You're making a second mistake in your life, this time with a noncorporeal man who has no place in it. For once, listen to the experience of your elders, Leigh Ann, if not for your own sake, then for ours. Think of Ginnie, your brother, your father, me . . . ."

Her eyes shining, on the brink of tears, she sat stiffly, nervously, needing my unquestioning obedience.

She was also afraid. Of what?

The thought of breaking off all contact with Bael felt immeasurably painful, no, impossible. I sensed his presence, his mind touching mine, listening, assessing this new conflict.

"All right, Mother. I'll correct the situation. There'll be no further disruption of our lives. I won't permit it." A reservoir of strength poured into me, and the slightest breath of a whisper spoke silently and privately close to my ear.

—Well-said. There shall be no more disruptions. I will not permit it.—

"Promise me," Mother said, her voice softer, her tense posture loosening. She appeared unaware of Bael's interjection.

"I promise. I'll straighten it all out. No more admittance to spirits who act unwholesome." I tried for light humor, hoping to relax her, to assure her.

—I am whole again. I have found you and you, me.— His intimate murmur acknowledged my determination and control, carte blanche, an equality between us that, nonetheless, championed me, allowing

me to take the wheel firmly as we steered ahead into uncharted waters.

Mother stood up. "Good. I know you'll keep your promise. Honesty is one of your better traits. Now I'm going upstairs to take a hot shower and calm down. Then we'll all get dressed and go find Danny a crib."

"Go ahead, Mom. I'll wash up the dishes."

"Thank you, dear." She leaned over and pecked a soft kiss on my cheek.

"And Mother? Please stop worrying?"

She offered me a wan hint of a smile, nodded, and went upstairs.

As I soaped, rinsed, and dried the breakfast dishes, I thought about how hard it had been to answer her without lying. Lying horrified me. As a young girl I had been unjustly accused of lying and punished for it. That experience had molded me—my honesty both a blessing and a curse. I knew I could not break off all contact with Bael, but I could direct the inevitable journey of exploration, shape it to my will. Perhaps Quatama had given me my newfound strength and self-assurance. His brief message—to come to him as I slept—suddenly resurfaced in my mind. But how? Another dream?

I put away the dishes, glancing at Daniel, who had been remarkably well behaved all morning. "I guess I'll figure it out when the time comes," I told him.

He waved his hands and bobbed up and down in his swing.

I bent to pick him up and felt an invisible touch upon my shoulder. A shiver went through me, travelling down my arm and back.

—*Tell Quatama I still love you. Tell him he must allow us to seek an answer, to heal the rift that once tore the angelfolk apart.*—

A different kiss brushed my cheek, full of longing, an aching sorrow barely checked.

My breath caught in a tight band between the pit of my stomach and my throat. Then the sensation, the emotional connection, ceased. My chest heaved, releasing, relieving, the constricted air in my lungs.

I hefted Daniel up out of his swing and into my arms, carried the swing back to the living room with my free hand, then took him upstairs to dress us warmly.

-7-

March, although nearly over, kicked up strong cold gusts at us as we locked up the car in the mall parking lot. I looked forward to the winter ending, to Spring's new beginning. But the trees and shrubs on the streets of the Northeast still sported bare budless branches, and patches of remaining snow mounds still dotted sections of the mall.

Carrying Daniel, I followed Mother into Lit Brothers and rode the escalator up to the second floor. The children's department contained an infants' section which included furniture. We looked at the two cribs displayed, Mother sighing at the prices. "Thank God for charge cards," she said as a burly balding salesman lumbered over to us. "Can I help you, ladies?"

"Yes, we'd like to purchase this crib." Mother pointed to the less expensive of the two. "We'd also like it delivered today, if possible."

"I'd have to check the delivery schedule, Madam. It normally takes at least two days to schedule a delivery. If we *can* accommodate you, there'll be an extra charge."

"Fine. Please see if you can do so."

The salesman bristled at Mother's clipped response. He wrote down the model number and price on his sales pad. "If you'll come this way, please."

We followed him to the sales counter. "Let's see. Without delivery, that comes to $195.63. I'll call downstairs to see if any of our truck drivers are available today."

A rack of infant clothing caught my interest. I walked over, Daniel on my hip, to rummage through it.

"Excuse me, Mr. Thompson. How much are you selling that crib for?"

The new voice, eerily familiar, brought my head up sharply. I glanced toward the counter. Mother and the pompous Mr. Thompson stood on either side. A younger man, behind the salesman, now peered over his shoulder at the figures on the sales pad. "That crib has been reduced," he said. "We're discontinuing that model to make room for new inventory. It's $99.95. We have two more left in the storeroom."

"Nobody told me, sir."

The new man's back was turned to me, but my mouth hung open at his tall thin frame, his thick and luxuriant black hair. He moved sideways, affording me a better view of his face as he wrote a new slip with the sale price. I nearly choked at his uncanny resemblance to my dark spirit, to Bael.

"Will you need delivery, Madam, or be taking the crib now?"

Mother smiled prettily at him, not seeming to mark his appearance as a strange coincidence. Perhaps she hadn't telepathically seen Bael as clearly as I'd thought that first night. "Actually," she told his look-a-like brightly, "we need this crib *today*. My grandson's original crib collapsed rather dangerously a day ago, and the poor child is sleeping in a makeshift cradle. I understand there'll be an extra charge for same day delivery, but we're willing to pay for it."

"Nonsense. There'll be no extra charge." He picked up the phone with a sharp glance at Mr. Thompson. "Hello, Walt? This is Bill. Who do you have down there running deliveries today?"

Within minutes, delivery was set for four p.m. that afternoon—a last, previously unscheduled stop for their driver. Mother handed him her credit card.

Bill, our mysterious champion, assured her as he completed the paperwork. "This crib will be sturdy and safe. As you heard, I told our man to put it together for you, to make sure it's properly assembled. I take it your grandson wasn't hurt when the old crib collapsed?"

"No, thankfully. He wasn't in it. This is so *kind* of you."

"Think nothing of it."

"Well, thank you anyway. Leigh Ann," she called. I turned and walked slowly toward them, afraid of facing this man, in voice and appearance so much like Bael. "This very nice gentleman has taken care of everything. Daniel will have his crib today."

"Thank you, " I said and looked him fully in the face. Up close, the similarity faded. The man had full cheeks and a rather round nose.

"You're welcome, young lady," he said. "If you have any problems, or if we can be of further service to you, please ask for me, Bill Withers. I'm the store manager."

"My daughter," Mother gestured, "and grandson."

"So I gathered."

"Well, thank you again. We'll see your man at four." She headed toward the down escalator, and I followed.

I glanced briefly back at the manager. His eyes were on me as I turned, and from a distance, once more, he resembled Bael. Then, realizing I had caught his look, in fact returned it, he lifted his hand in a friendly wave.

The crib arrived precisely at four, but when the delivery man carefully assembled it, it turned out to be the expensive one, not the half-price crib we'd purchased. We pointed this out to the man, but both the model number on the crib and our sales slip matched. Everything was in order. No mistake.

We signed his packing slip, accepting the crib.

Everything seemed normal again by dinner time. Mother waxed poetic about the luck we'd had buying the new crib. Fred talked about the science project he was working on; Ginnie complained about the chemistry exam she'd suffered through at nursing school that morning. Dad was interrupted during the meal by a customer's emergency call and went off to fix a hot water heater with a broken valve later that evening. And Daniel fell asleep soundly and snugly in the new crib that night.

Ginnie still had no inkling of the brief possession she'd undergone that morning. We undressed quietly for bed, speaking in low tones, the bedroom rearranged and somewhat cramped. My bed still paralleled the larger crib, sandwiched between the crib and our dresser and closets.

Ginnie had always been a touch claustrophobic. Now she knelt on her bed on the other, less cluttered side of the room and opened the side window a smidgen, insisting on some fresh air.

"It was pretty brisk this afternoon at the mall," I told her. "We might get cold."

"It's only open a crack." She sat cross-legged on the bed. "Did you get a chance to look at those books?"

I walked over and sat beside her. "I went through them this morning."

"Did you see how stupid it all is? It's just legends and myths, all twisted up by ignorance and overworked imaginations."

I answered her slowly. "Well, it's hardly scientific. And psychologically, I wonder about the followers of some of those early religions. But I can understand the symbology, the reasons behind their belief in those gods and demigods."

"Fear," Ginnie whispered emphatically. "Fear of the unknown, of death, of the future. Nothing more than mystical talismans to get them through the days and weeks. I'm glad we live in a more rational century."

"So am I. But I think there may have been some real-life events that triggered those legends and myths."

Ginnie smiled uncertainly. "If that's true, they became pretty distorted afterwards."

I smiled back, then glanced at Daniel, who slept on, undisturbed by our quiet conversation. "Gin, do you remember playing 'Whispering Down the Lane' when we were kids?"

"Sure. Silly game."

"It was. But that's what this reminds me of. Someone or something starts a legend that satisfies an intense and universal human need. The more it spreads, the more it's interpreted differently down the line. Some of the changes are subtle. Some have a large, distorting impact. Some changes are based on reverence, some on a population's barbarism, some on a competing religion's disdain. I find this a quite believable premise. When we played that whispering game as kids, the first person would start off with a completely uncomplicated message. But no matter how simple it was, it was always ridiculously distorted by the time the last child repeated it aloud."

"That was the whole point of the game. It was funny, we laughed, and found out how important it was to communicate accurately, all while having a good time."

"So . . . maybe poor communication is the culprit behind some of the strange things we've . . . I've been experiencing. Maybe I'm not seeing the whole picture—or clearly."

"Maybe you're viewing these things *irrationally?*"

I thought about it. "Possibly. Maybe there's an explanation that's not the one I'm pinning on it. Maybe some facts whispered down the lane so much, the original truth was lost."

"Now you're talking sense." She yawned. "Now all you have to do is look for the truth."

"Ginnie? Uh, this morning? You seemed awfully afraid of . . . well, you called it *evil*. Are you still upset?"

She hesitated a heartbeat or two, seemed to hold her breath, then sighed heavily. "I was afraid . . . for you. I was worried about you." I waited, needing more assurance, not knowing how she might assure me. She stared briefly at me, then cast her glance downward. "I was afraid you were heading off the deep end with all this psychic stuff, that it would spread like a contagion, until there was no peace at home. Okay, I was afraid for myself, too, and angry. I wanted you and Mom to leave this stuff alone and let us lead a normal life. I can't separate myself from it the way Dad and Fred do. I was so upset I couldn't remember what I'd done to upset Daniel. That bothered me the most. I could barely keep my mind together when I drove to school. And then . . . well . . . I stopped at this light, and it turned green, and the weirdest thing happened."

"What?"

"I . . . wasn't worried anymore. All of those fears left me in an instant." She lifted her head, our eyes meeting. "I knew we would be all right. *You* would be all right."

"How could you know all that in an instant?"

She flushed, her smile almost beatific. "I know that this may sound as self-indulgent as some of your and Mom's beliefs, but I know God is watching over you. Call it faith. I knew it the moment the fear left. I know God's protecting you."

I shivered at her intensity, the strength and conviction she conveyed.

"You're protected, too, little sister," I whispered, hugging her. "I won't let anyone or anything ever hurt you, Gin. Not ever."

"It's all right."

"It is," I said. "Now let's get to sleep."

She nodded. I bunked down in the bed beside Daniel, still dreaming in the land of Nod in his fancy crib.

Gin turned off the light. I heard the rustle of her covers as she pulled them up. "Good night, Leigh Ann."

"Good night, Gin. Sweet dreams."

"For both of us," she murmured, and then silence filled the room.

I didn't sleep immediately, dozing lightly, snatches of thoughts and images drifting before my mind's eye . . . one image in particular. A face had come sharply into focus, eyes alight with gentle humor, mouth a lopsided grin. Chloe. The girl from my dream of Eliom, who had teased me about love and Bael. Her curly brown hair cascaded down and wisps of it framed her forehead and cheeks. I gazed at her soft blue eyes and awoke with a jolt.

Her eyes, so clearly before me, had been Ginnie's eyes.

Curiouser and curiouser, I thought.

My own eyes wanted closing, wanted the oblivion of sleep. I wanted no more shocks, no more dreams to puzzle out in the morning.

I began to drift off again, my body heavy and numb, but pleasantly so, sinking away from consciousness.

My bed creaked softly; I felt the mattress sway with an additional weight. A gentle sensation of touch caressed my left breast, hardening its nipple, my flesh responding to the feather-light exploration. A second simultaneous caress brushed my inner thighs, then moved like a soft breeze over my pubic hair. It swept over my vaginal lips to my clitoris. I arched sharply in response and sat up.

The room remained silent, no one but myself on the bed.

—*Bael,*— I thought and felt his lips press, barely tangible, on mine.

—*Lie back.*—

—*How did you? . . I'm clothed—covered with a blanket!*—

—*My hands slide through them. Have I pleased you?*—

I could psychically visualize his dark eyes, shining, mesmerizing, the curve of his lips, his lean taut body leaning over my own. My physical eyes were blind to his presence. —*I can't see you.*—

—*Of course not. In your plane, I am spirit-fleshed. Close your eyes. I can cross the gap between our dimensions through touch.*—

—*No.*—

His anger rose palpably at my refusal, then ebbed, as if he struggled to suppress it. —*I have waited over four thousand years, Leianna. Do you deny me this long-awaited fulfillment? And your own?*—

—*My son. My sister.*— I gestured toward Daniel and Ginnie.

—*They sleep. They need not know.*—

—*I can't. Go now, Bael. I have to sleep. I have to find Quatama.*—

—*Quatama will not run away.*— His tone became petulant, then coaxing. —*I have sought you for so long. I must join with you. Let me rock you to sleep.*—

—*No.*— I turned on my side, facing him. —*Not until I know more. You promised me control.*—

He bristled, the current sweeping over me physically. —*We will finish what we once* began,— he snarled, furious.

I lay curled in a fetal position, waiting, unafraid, but determined to defy him, to hold him to his psychic word.

A standoff silence, electric and hot, ran between us.

And then, like a capricious wind suddenly shifting direction, he vanished from the room.

-8-

The Snow Queen. It reminds me of Hans Christian Anderson's famous story, everything white and crystal. The crystalized plain, smooth and shining, seems to travel to an endless horizon, only small white huts with frozen gardens and shrubbery dotting the flat landscape. In the distance beyond the village, the plain rises to the right, a forest flowing outward, and dips to the left, continuing the line of flatland.

The spirit masters live in these huts. Quatama calls himself my spirit master.

We walk along the crystal ice to his dwelling. I remark upon the wintery, fragile, fairy tale appearance of this place.

"It is winter here, just as it is in your world. The spirit planes of Eliom and of Earth are very close and share the same seasonal rotation. But the seasons are enhanced in our world, made pure in a way that cannot be matched in your dimension."

I notice I'm barefoot, in my nightgown, yet only feel a pleasant coolness beneath me and around me. Quatama is clothed in a brown longsleeved robe that seems much too roomy for his short, almost scrawny frame. His thin black hair curls over his neck. Tendrils cling to his forehead. His face is neither old nor young and difficult to focus on, as if it were a flickering hologram. From what I can see of it, he has small, opaque, black eyes, a pointed but small nose, thin cheeks, and thin, relaxed lips. His skin is sallow and pale.

We reach Quatama's hut. There is no door, just an entrance way we pass through. The inside is sparsely furnished: a low table, no chairs, rugs on the floor. Shelves and hooks hold belongings, but I cannot focus on them.

Quatama sits on the rug in the front room. There is a smaller room beyond it, which also seems bare, empty, but I cannot see fully into it. Quatama gestures beside himself, and I sit down next to him.

"I don't know how I got here," I tell him.

"You are out of body. Your mortal, Earthly body. Your spirit is now encased in your astral body, a more permanent vehicle of expression."

"I don't understand."

"Think of stacking dolls, one fitting within the other. The outer body is the physical body, within it, the mental or emotional self attached to the physical. Within that, the astral body which is a viable thought form created by the spirit which rests within it, which cradles the spark of life fueling each individual."

I blink at him, understanding, experiencing my multiplicity as he explains it. The feeling is uncomfortable. I struggle and return to a sense of just one self.

He laughs, three fluted notes of perfect tone and duration.

"No," I say, "I don't understand *how* I got here. The transition from the mortal world to this one."

"Oh," Quatama says. His speaking voice, a soft, gravelly rumble, differs from his laughter, not a musical note to be heard. "It is similar to dreaming. As your physical body slept, your spirit, or mind, if you prefer, responded to my summons, locked onto my location and, within seconds of your mortal time, journeyed here by activating your astral or spirit body for dimensional travel."

"Does the astral or spirit body grow and eventually die, like the physical one?"

"The spirit body is of a more permanent nature. We judge time here differently, in fact, control it to our needs. Time is a concept. Through it, we interact through space with matter, and by it, we gauge our experience and growth. But, yes, the spirit body can be changed, altered, to reflect stages of growth, and is eventually discarded by most in what you would call the far distant future, though sooner by some."

"Discarded?"

"Even death on Earth is a need to discard the body when the life experience goal—the growth it was fashioned to express—is finished."

"And what if the growth wasn't properly . . . expressed?"

A faint hint of a smile crosses his lips. "Then the lesson must be relearned."

"Take the class all over again."

"Live another Earthly life with that lesson as part of it once more."

"We have no free will?"

He looks surprised, then laughs again, but this time the notes hold a sad timbre. "All is free. Nothing is forced. Everyone of us is responsible for our own decisions."

"But . . . what if you don't want to learn the lesson over again?"

"Then you will not grow," he says somberly, "and stagnation will set in until, in time, you realize the need and accept the responsibility for correcting your faults."

I squirm on the rug. It appears to be a simple rug, a light olive green, cool and comfortable. My restlessness is due to my uncertainty. Why has Quatama brought me here? What has he to do with Bael and my dream of Eliom? What did he say—as we walked to his hut—about Eliom?

"Quatama? Where *is* Eliom?"

"You are in Eliom."

I furrow my brows, confused. "This doesn't look like Eliom in my dream."

"Ah, yes. Your dream. Reliving a memory 35,000 Earthly years old."

"35,000?! Bael said he had waited four thousand years."

"He has found you before, despite our vigilance." Quatama gestures at the low table before us. A glazed earthenware pot of steaming liquid and two small cups appear upon it. Quatama pours what smells like a fragrant cinnamon tea into the cups.

"Do we need to eat and drink on this plane?"

"We may not need it. We may desire it."

I sip from my cup, the taste pleasant, slightly sweet. "Bael gave me a message for you, Quatama."

"Then you must deliver it, for he is not permitted to travel to this place, and I have no desire to seek him in the depths."

The depths!? "He said you must allow us to seek a new beginning." In my astral state, I find it hard to clearly recall Bael's words. "He said you must allow us to try to heal the rift . . . although I don't remember exactly what the rift was. Did Bael and I fight? End our previous relationship in Eliom? Quatama, I don't understand any of this. I don't remember what happened to Bael and myself all those centuries ago in Eliom."

Quatama rises from the floor, literally, his legs still tucked beneath him, robe flowing over them. He straightens them in one fluid motion, standing now, and reaches out a hand to help me up. "He refers to the rift in the heavens."

"I still don't understand."

He leads me outside. "Shut your eyes, Leianna."

I do so, and feel him briefly touch my hand again.

"You may open your eyes now."

We stand on one side of a city street. A sculpted stone balustrade, wide clear walkways, and corner gardens surround a large stone building, designed like a Roman temple, its stairs leading to thick scrollworked columns at its entrance. Across the street is a park; down the street, in what appears to be a shopping avenue, colorful stores gaily display their items and wares. People pass by us, unconcerned by my nightgowned figure. It appears to be a normal day, the people intent on their own business. I notice they are also clothed, pretty much, for winter. But although the few trees lining the thoroughfare are still leafless, neither snow nor ice can be seen.

"The climate here is more controlled," Quatama answers my unspoken question. "The population has unanimously decided on an early Spring. Soon the trees will bud."

He walks up the stairs to the Romanesque building. "This is the Hall of Seraphic Records," he explains. "We are still in Eliom, which has grown and changed with the passing centuries. This city is known as the City of God. It exists here on the eighth physical astral plane, along with other cities resurrected humanity has built."

"Resurrected humanity?"

"Those who have finished all of their Earthly lessons and no longer incarnate."

"Are *unfinished* humans allowed up here?" I wonder if the question is moot, being *I* am up here.

"They normally inhabit the sixth physical astral plane . . . the sixth heaven . . . between incarnations. Those still mortal can visit their deceased loved ones on that plane as well, although few remember such visits."

Huge engraved doors open as we approach them. We enter the Hall of Seraphic Records. Inside, a long corridor stretches into the distance, seeming much too extended, impossibly so, for a building of this size. Quatama doesn't remark on my amazement, simply leads me down the corridor about thirty yards and turns right down another corridor. We continue on another twenty yards or so, passing doors with frosted glass and lettering I can't quite read. The entire interior reminds me of a school, the walls green and yellow, the doors dark brown with golden handles.

We pause at a door on the left. The lettering, large and black against the glass reads: *Auricular-Visual Recall.* Quatama pushes against the door. It swings open. I follow him inside. A pert blonde with a hairstyle and face reminiscent of Sandra Dee or Doris Day from the early sixties sits behind a brown wooden desk, off-white filing cabinets behind her, and another door to the left of the cabinets. The woman wears a flowery, gauzy blouse that nonetheless is discreet.

"Hello, Master," she greets Quatama, with a curious but pleasant nod to me.

"Hello, Rosemary. We would like to review this young lady's first lifetime in segments, starting with her infancy."

"First Earthly lifetime?"

"No. First immortal lifetime in cognizant form. It took place in old Eliom."

"Oh." She glances at me, impressed, and gets up to open one file drawer. Unconcealed by the desk, I realize she is clothed in an Indian sari. "Her spiritual name?"

"Leianna, daughter of Michael and Eve."

The woman's hand freezes, motionless, as she reaches into what appears to be an empty drawer. She looks at me, her expression both surprised and subdued, then at Quatama, her brows lifting sharply. I wonder what caused her double-take, but she doesn't explain it.

Quatama glances over it, saying with gentle patience, "I wish her to review certain significant events, but it cannot be done in one mortal night. I wish her to have total conscious mortal recollection of that lifetime, sharply detailed, with full comprehension when she awakens on Earth. It cannot interfere with her mortal duties and activities, and we must guard against sensory overload. I would like her gauged as to her limit and a buffer transmitted into both her astral and physical brains, to stop the transmission the moment her emotional and intellectual levels reach capacity. The memory regenerator should also be set to mark the stopping point, to gauge where to begin the next segment."

"Yes, sir," Rosemary says. She pulls a red accordion file from the previously empty drawer and places it on the desk. I peer into it. There appears to be a plain manila folder, lettersized, a shiny hard black rectangle approximately five inches by seven inches, and what looks like a diamond prism. "Everything in order?" she asks me.

"I wouldn't know," I tell her.

"You wouldn't?" This clearly confuses her, which in turn confuses me. Why does she think I would understand any of this? This is the craziest dream I've ever had.

"It is *not* a dream," Quatama says, and upon hearing that, I start to hyperventilate.

Quatama reaches out and touches my inner elbow. A cloud of silver sparkles seems to rotate around me, in front of my eyes, and I suddenly feel calmer.

"She doesn't *know*," Rosemary says, her voice hushed again.

"No. She doesn't know," Quatama agrees. "Is the viewing room ready?"

"I prepared it a second ago, sir. And the report on her intake limitations is in the small folder. The buffer crystal is also set and ready for transmittal."

Quatama lifts out the onyx rectangle. "The record is detailed?"

"Nothing pertinent left out, master."

"I will probably realign it for virtual reenactment later on. For now, we'll let her start her past life recall from a spectator's viewpoint."

"The record is set to that option, sir."

Quatama offers her a pleased smile, returning the black stone to the accordion file. "You're a very efficient aide, Rosemary."

She beams. "Thank you, Quatama. So many people find this service so helpful. I get excited just knowing I'm helping them to help themselves." She says this so sincerely, I think I am back in the sixties. *Peace, love, and brotherhood.*

Rosemary's eyes dart over, locking sharply with my own. "I *did* mean that."

"Oh!"

Quatama is grinning, closed mouth. He appears to be holding in a gale of laughter. Picking up the file, he moves to the inner door, opening it outwardly. I see another corridor beyond. "Leianna?"

I head through the door, then turn back to Rosemary. "I'm sorry. I didn't mean to be rude. I think it's wonderful that you love your job."

I get an amused smile in return.

She regards me, then Quatama. "You really did keep a tight veil over her, didn't you?"

"Yes." His smile remains ever patient. "But now we are lifting it." Rosemary parts her lips, about to speak. "Please, no questions," he tells her. "I do not have answers yet."

Beyond the door are smaller enclosed rooms. Some are apparently occupied, a small triangle glowing white on the center of their closed entrance doors. We reach one whose triangle appears to be clear glass.

Quatama touches the triangle; it begins glowing beneath his hand and the door opens, as if welcoming us. We enter what looks like a small projection booth: a white screen about three yards square fills the bulk of the wall beyond us, in front of it, two cushioned, quite comfortable-looking chairs. Quatama gestures me into the right-hand one, and places the accordion file on the wide seat of the other chair.

Lifting out the small manila folder, he scans the data inside, puts it back, and removes the tiny diamond prism. "It is skane, not diamond," he says.

"Skane?"

"Pure energy, compressed and solidified. Very precious."

He brings the sparkling prism over to me. "This will not cause you any discomfort."

Still, I back perceptibly into the chair as he aims the prism toward my diaphragm. He stops, holds the prism flat in his hand and offers it to me. "Here. You can insert it yourself. Touch the edge to your solar plexus. It will disappear, its energy transferring into you. The energy is predirected. It will guard you against overstimulation of your neurological synapses."

I take the prism from him gingerly and, with some trepidation, rest the edge against my stomach.

"A bit higher," Quatama says.

I move it slightly upward and watch dumbfounded as its radiance begins to build rapidly until I hold nothing in my hand, now open and empty, my mouth gaping in wonder, as what appears to be sparkling atoms rotate slowly and seep into my astral body.

I feel a tickling in my stomach and a lightheadedness, and then these sensations stop. I feel normal again . . . as normal as possible under these circumstances.

"Good," Quatama says. "Now we can begin."

He removes the black stone from the accordion file, holds it before the viewing screen and gently pushes it into the clear white space. The screen gives way, as if it were wet sculptor's clay, absorbing the opaque rectangle completely.

Quatama places the file on the floor between our chairs and sits down. "There is no need to show you your immortal birth. Many are embarrassed viewing that. My goal is to show you the people who shaped your first entry into eternal life, their influence upon you and yours upon them. You must understand the interaction between souls, for in the future, you may have to make decisions based upon the goals, needs and desires of those you interacted with in this particular lifetime . . . as well as your own needs, goals and desires and those of your loved ones in your current life."

The screen begins to flicker, to take on shape and sound. Images congeal and sharpen, and I stare at Eliom, the Eliom I'd dreamt of, living with my father Michael.

The clay cottage with its thatched roof is outwardly similar to the other homes dotting the undulating rises and dips of the land, the hillscape of Eliom, more widely inhabited than the current landscape where Quatama and the other spirit masters reside.

The screen image alters, showing the interior of my and Michael's cottage, much more gaily decorated, evidencing a woman's touch other than my own. Refreshments—fruits, vegetables, and nuts, both whole and prepared in tempting-looking recipes, spicy breads and sweet cakes, and jugs and pitchers of what looks like honeyed wines or fruit nectars—are laid out on a broad wooden table. Wooden cutlery and plates and clay goblets also rest on the table.

All appears untouched, as if awaiting guests at a feast.

Thick cushions rest in corners of the front room; some cover a long wooden bench paralleling the laden table.

A young man descends from the sleeping loft above, turns and moves forward on the screen. He smiles gently down at something. The picture adjusts to show the object of his interest. He peers paternally into a small, ornately carved, wooden cradle, a tiny infant asleep within it.

The man seems vaguely familiar with his curly brown hair and soft brown eyes. I have no inkling of who the baby might be.

I hear Quatama's light musical laughter again. "The child in the cradle is your own infant self, Leianna. The man is your father, Michael, before sorrow lined his face."

A woman enters the room, from the backroom, the storeroom. She carries a bowl of bright orange leaves, placing them on the feast table. Her soft auburn hair falls in lush ringlets to the small of her back. She is short, small-boned, an aura of fragility about her. She turns to Michael, and I study her face, vaguely familiar, but somehow disturbing, as if those alarming green eyes, diminutive nose and softly curved lips have somehow caused me great pain.

"Your mother, Eve," Quatama says. The light in the viewing room dims until we sit in near darkness, as if in a theater.

"Yes," Quatama remarks. "Very much so. The darkness allows concentration, filters out distractions. I have chosen the second important event of your childhood in Eliom to begin your memory recall. Although you were only newborn, the people and events around you were quite pertinent. On this day, you were named, your soul offered in service to our Creator, and received in return a sacred blessing, but in a manner which no child before had ever experienced."

Michael, wearing a fresh white robe, sat on one end of the bench and watched the food being set out. On this day, his infant daughter would be named, and her family and their friends among the folk who lived in Eliom would witness her dedication to the Creator. Eve's mother followed her tensely into the front room. Deianna's long dark hair, pinned up in a great mound of tendrils and curls, bounced and quivered as she paced, her nervousness marring her tall and shapely figure and elegant face.

She rearranged a fruit compote more centrally on the long table. "Where is your brother, Eve? Why hasn't he arrived yet? He must be present when Michael lifts the babe to the Creator."

"Adam will arrive," Eve assured her.

"How sad that Michael's own parents won't witness the ceremony."

Michael got up, placing an affectionate arm around Deianna, hugging her. "Zoras and Heira are already deep within somnambulation somewhere along the first pathbeam. They came last night to see the baby and say their goodbyes. Leianna is already at home in their gift."

Deianna studied the intricately carved wooden cradle holding her tiny granddaughter. "It's beautifully crafted. Does it play music?"

"No, Mother." Eve carried another wooden bowl, filled with slivered almonds and figs to the table. "And you still haven't presented your own gift to Leianna, your first grandchild, whose name honors your own."

Deianna smiled haughtily and reached for her *scarpa,* her cloth pouch, on the edge of the table. She took out a tiny wooden box, opening it. A gold ring crowned by a brilliant blue stone lay within. "My love is within the gem. It imparts wisdom and direction." She handed it to Eve. "Give it to Leianna on the day she's to be married." She ignored the startled glances Eve and Michael gave her. "The others will arrive soon. Where is Adam?"

"Here I am, Mother."

Adam appeared in the doorway, wearing a shortened and sleeveless blue summer robe. Handsome despite a pale complexion, his sandy hair tousled and hazel eyes laughing, his voice rang out, so silken and rounded, it irked rather than warmed the ear. "May I enter, in peace and friendship, the home of my beloved sister and her family?"

"Enter, Adam ben Mercurius," Michael responded properly, "and share with us the spark of life."

Adam avoided his mother's glare, moving to the cradle and studying his newborn niece. "She's beautiful. We'll have to keep the boys at a distance when she grows up."

"Only at arm's length," Michael answered, his words clipped and concise.

Adam picked the child up in his strong hands. She whimpered at first, then quieted as he rocked her.

His sister hovered beside him until Deianna, her finger softly brushing Leianna's cheek, noticed her daughter was level with her own height. "Eve, you're lifting again."

"I'm happy," Eve said simply.

"Even so, lifting is only for far-journeying. Talents are not to be wasted, and you know it. You have feet . . . plant them please."

"May the House of Lucifer enter?" A new, much softer voice drew their eyes to the doorway as Eve lowered to the floor. An attractive young man with a mane of golden hair and startling blue eyes smiled warmly at Michael, receiving in return a grin borne of their longtime friendship.

Lucifer's wife, dark golden hair piled high and fetchingly, her deep green eyes meeting Michael's and Eve's in greeting, stood beside him. The statuesque woman held Bael, their youngest son, firmly in her arms. The child's small elven ears were nearly covered by his rich black hair; his piercing eyes cast curious darting glances about.

Ashtoreth, their three-year-old, his gaze shyly averted, clutched Lucifer's hand. His hair, the same thick waves of sunlit blond as his father's, was unruly.

"Enter," Michael said. "Enter and share with us—always—our blessed new spark of life and the friendship which burns brightly and eternally between us."

The family crossed the open threshold. Lucifer nodded toward his one-year-old, who yawned and burrowed his head into the crook between his mother's upper arm and chest. "Bael's just waking up. He slept most of the way, lulled by the sun and Affaeteres's gentle gait." He smoothed his elder son's wild locks quickly into place. "Ashtoreth. Go and sit some place quietly until the others arrive."

The boy scampered to a cushion near the kitchen entrance, hair falling in his face again. Aside from his renegade curls, his white shortrobe was spotless, as perfectly smooth as his father's.

"Here, Ash." Eve found a skane playball and handed it to him.

He lifted his bright aquamarine eyes up to her, the precocious patrician cast of his cheeks, nose and mouth somber, at first, then blossoming into an appropriately childish smile of gratitude. He fingered the soft clear globe. Three inches in diameter, it came to life in his hands, pulsating with glowing colors and patterns as quickly as Ashtoreth imagined them. Lavender, yellow and orange rays swirled and leaped within the tiny sphere, bouncing colorful shadows around the room. One danced across his little brother's face. Bael reached out, trying to grasp the elusive streak. Ashtoreth laughed.

Bael's eyes, midnight black flecked with gold, focused on Ashtoreth and the bright ball. He strained forward in his mother's arms. "Meh!"

"No," Affaeteres said, holding him tightly. She leaned over to lightly embrace Eve and Deianna, then nodded to Adam, smiling warmly at the newborn in his arms. "So this is our godchild."

"Yes." Eve took the baby from Adam, tucking her back into her cradle. "This is Zoras and Heira's gift to her."

"It's lovely."

Lucifer joined them. "The child outshines it." His lips curved upward in amused approval. "Have your parents left?" he asked Michael.

"Yes. Early this morning. Eve's father, Mercurius, is keeping the tally of those leaving on the transgalactic journey. I almost envy Zoras and Heira and the other elders chosen. To be helping our Creator establish a new world of sentient beings at a distant point in the universe . . ." He grinned pensively. ". . . almost worth the loss of separation from Eliom for 35 millennia."

"Perhaps. Well, *we* will have to tend both the Garden and the Council in their absence, although I'm sure our remaining elders will be quick to advise us, solicited or not. But with good advice, no doubt, and many of us may rise more quickly to elder status now. Has Mercurius had a chance to see Leianna?"

"He's been unable to visit. He sent a congratulatory message, along with a tiny skane pendant for Leianna."

Lucifer clasped his shoulder, nodding understanding, both he and Michael watching Ashtoreth toddle over, the globe toy, now unhandled and returned to a milky white, abandoned on the floor cushion. The boy stared into the cradle, nose wrinkling. The baby, in turn, smiled up at him, her infant eyes alight with curiosity.

"What's her name?" Ashtoreth asked, cheeks reddening slightly.

"Leianna," Michael said.

"Ley-ahn-nah," he imitated the formal name.

Affaeteres, one arm holding Bael, reached down to smooth her firstborn's hair. "You see, Ashtoreth, the name 'Leianna' has an 'ah' on the end to give it the third sound. 'Leiann,' her little name, only uses the first and second sounds. A special name just for friends."

"Ley-ahn," he repeated. "Do I have a little name?"

"Yes. You have two. Ash or Ashtor."

"I like Ash," he decided and continued to study Leianna with an air of concentration normally reserved for frogs and bugs.

"He's too young to take an interest in such things," Lucifer said.

"That's not true." Affaeteres regarded the boy with more than a hint of maternal pride. "I've begun teaching him phonics and lettering while you're away sharing *your* own brilliance with the Council. He enjoys learning."

Lucifer's pale brows rose, his lips played at the idea of a smile. "My industrious wife. But then you've always been fruitful with time and talent." His smile ripened; she smirked meaningfully back at him. Michael and Eve watched their repartee, sensing a hidden layer of meaning behind Lucifer's jest.

Eve raised her own inquiring brows to Affaeteres, who laughed goodnaturedly and said, "I suppose we should tell them."

"Aff is with child again," said Lucifer. He moved to kiss his wife's cheek. Bael, in her arms, leaned forcibly outward, his parents quickly grasping him.

Bael's chubby arm continued reaching downward, wriggling toward the cradle, the newborn within it. "Uh," he gibbered, fingers pointing toward Leianna.

Affaeteres tightened her grip on him. "Whatever Ashtoreth finds interest in, he wants it, too. That's Leianna, Bael. Lei-an-na."

"Lehn!" Bael mimicked, his small hand stretching insistently toward the infant.

"Perhaps he's in love," Lucifer grinned.

Michael tickled the soft flesh under Bael's dimpled bantam chin. "Perhaps." A soft gurgling laugh erupted from the child, and a new voice sounded from the doorway.

"May we enter, Michael ben Zoras, in peace and friendship?"

Quatama, short and slight of build, wearing the unadorned brown robe of a master, waited before the threshold of the thachka, his dark eyes reflecting his illimitable patience. By his side stood a man identical in face and figure to Michael.

Michael greeted them both. "Enter, Quatama, my revered mentor. Enter, my worthy brother Gabriel. Enter and share with us the sacred gift of life."

He held both hands out to Quatama.

Quatama clasped them in his own in a dignified but warm manner, then broke the hold. "The Creator has blessed this child," he said, walking past him to the cradle.

"Every child is blessed."

"No, this child is special. But I do not know the purpose of this blessing or how it may manifest itself in her life."

Gabriel moved stiffly over to view the infant. "This child has goodness within her."

"As do all children," Michael repeated, more gently than he might have, had Gabriel not been his brother.

"Not all," Gabriel replied. "Not all with goodness centering from the core of her soul, undimmable." He, too, wore the brown robe of a master; his bearing and tone defied argument.

"I thank you for your praise in my daughter's name," Michael deferred, "being she cannot do so herself. May we all benefit from that goodness."

"It is time for this very good child to be presented to her maker," Quatama murmured with wry amusement.

Leianna, in her infant's robe of gossamer, looked up as he wrapped her light blanket of lambs' wool around her and lifted her from the cradle. He held her gently, her small head resting against his chest. Her tiny mouth opened in a yawn, then closed.

The spirit master led them in ceremonial procession, Eve and Michael following side by side, and Gabriel and Adam, Leianna's blood uncles, behind them. Deianna walked regally behind them, unperturbed by the absence of Mercurius, her one-time consort and father to her children. Behind her walked Lucifer and Affaeteres, Bael wide awake and squirming once more on his mother's hip, her arms locked tightly about his bottom and back. Lucifer carried Ashtoreth, his head resting sleepily on his father's shoulder, his legs dangling down.

The celestial sun, descending, filled the sky with soft hues of blue, rose, and lavender against lingering filaments of gold.

Along the cobbled road, other friends and neighbors stepped out of clay thachkas to join the procession with nods of greeting to the principal celebrants. The assemblage became a pious parade, for Michael and Eve's cottage was the farthest from the fields and forest they now headed into, stepping onto a pathway of flat multihued stones of orange, brown, yellow and red.

The Garden's beauty, rich with maturing summer, accompanied them as they strode, men, women and children, along the ceremonial pathway. Its stones glinted with sunset, and one lone singer, the *canehya,* began the evocation, her voice swelling out, her tones as dulcet as a wooden flute.

"Adenoy Dominey,
Tu laleh a bin ay,
see bashtay e nah dinay
n see dahnay e ta leh
been tah n cuwh."
[Translation from the Eliomese:
"Oh, Creator Supreme,
the Light that guides our way,
we greet You on this day,
and we pray for Your Blessings
of praise and love."]

Other voices threaded around the *canehya's,* blending magnificently. The musical prayer travelled with them on their long trek through the Garden, its fields, meadows and forests.

They sang of using their creative powers to honor the One who gifted them with those powers. They sang of their work in the Garden, of its fruits and fibers and grains, of the life force within the sacred soil. They sang of the harvest and the energy the bounty of the harvest brought, and of their dispensing of that energy in work, in meditation, in craft, in dance and song, in love and in marriage. They sang of the most sacred act of creation: the quickening and birth of offspring, the vessel through which the spark of life grew and expressed itself.

They sang of the soul's sojourn, maturing from childhood to adulthood, walking its own creative path, guided by the One and the teachings of parents and Elders in Eliom, the difficult journey of learning, growing wiser and applying knowledge and wisdom.

They reached Garden's End. The *canehya* chanted the ending verses of the Song of Creation, speaking solemnly of the newborn asleep in Quatama's arms, of Eve and Michael, their family and friends among the angelfolk, of the Creator blessing their child and acknowledging her eternal name.

Behind them lay the stone pathway and the cultivated lands it ran through, from which they drew their sustenance; before them stretched a large prairie, its ecology unaltered, pristine. In the far distance, a forest outlined itself against the sky.

Quatama bent down, the child nestled fast against his robe. The others silently followed his example, going down on one knee, eyes lowered reverently.

"Adenoy Dominey. See nee ha," the spirit master intoned. His voice projected clearly in the sudden hush. "Oh, Supreme Creator. We bow to You. Having passed through the Garden, we now enter the Virginal Sanctuary on our path to the Shore of the Seraphim and the Well of Being. Guide our steps, that we do not disturb the life which Your Sanctuary protects. If any creatures within its boundaries wish to share our joy and our journey, we welcome their presence. Know of our love for You, Creator, and our joy in Your Presence and Your guidance on this Day of Naming."

Quatama rose and led them through the bright summer prairie, a riot of wildflowers rivalling the thick swatches of tall grass. The sun's rim caressed the horizon ahead, where flatland gave way to trees thick with foliage and dappled with equal accents of light and shadow.

The celebrants walked in silence now, journeying through the grassland and into the forest beyond. Tall and regal branches of oaks offered parallel salutes as the procession trod beneath their overhang. Shadows of true dusk deepened moss-flecked trunks and the angular faces of the elvenfolk appeared in the gloom, as they crept from their recessed nooks hidden beneath tangled tree roots.

A young hare scampered over, hopping excitedly alongside Eve, a recognized friend, no doubt, who had helped her or kept her company when she tended a row of lettuce, giving it its leafy share to take back to its burrow and feed its family. It stood up to greet her. Eve stroked its soft head, and it kept pace with her in scuttling spurts on the mossy woodland path. A small raccoon ran beside Michael as he walked. Michael smiled at it, and extended his arm. The raccoon followed uncertainly, then sped up and jumped, scampering along Michael's sleeve to sit on his shoulder, enjoying the ride for a bit before jumping to the ground and scurrying off.

Woodland birds, sparrows and thrushes, chittered a soft song on the tree branches above. An occasional flutter of wings beat a soft patter.

The solemn eyes of a young elf met Michael's. The elf raised a wine gourd, and his eyes and his mouth indicated its rich contents. Michael nodded, his own lips curling upward in appreciation as he passed. The elf followed him, joining the procession.

The forest gave way to more open prairie with a slight rise visible in the distance.

On the plains, an eclectic mix of animals appeared, flanking the celebrants. Mares, stallions and their colts trotted along, kicking up small swirls of dust. A pack of wolves padded silently after them. Snakes, scales rippling hotly in the last vestiges of sunset, slithered by. Two prides, of leopards and of lions, moved majestically to the left;

two herds, one of slow-moving elephants, the other, fleet gazelles, followed the lions. On the right, a clan of bears lumbered past a flock of ambling pheasants and peacocks, tails dragging. Above the whole procession flew bright formations of birds, a graceful *V* of geese high up, flocks of blue jays, sparrows and seagulls swooping and soaring further below against the colorful sky, a profusion of wings.

Angelfolk, elvenfolk, and animals now climbed the rise, surmounted it, and began their descent to the Shore of the Seraphim.

The midnight blue waters rushed against the scalloped edges of the shoreline, a soft golden foam flickering and coating the sand as each spent wave receded into the sea. The gold and blue waters also circled around the Well of Being, further up the beach, its weathered stones glistening not only from the spray that leaped upon it, but from the glimmering substance of the foam.

Neither its height nor its width were impressive, roughly three to four feet high and five feet from center to rim. But it was not a well of water. Swirling vapors emanated from its shaft, wisping in trails above its rim. Its nebulous mist drifted beyond the shoreline, creating a haze of fog.

The celebrants traveled down the slope to the beach and the Well of Being. Quatama, Leianna in his arms, stood on the seaward side of the well at its centerpoint, facing it. Michael stood to his right, Eve, to his left.

On Michael's right stood Gabriel, then Adam, then Lucifer, holding his son Ashtoreth, staring wide-eyed at the well and the throng around him. To Eve's left stood Deianna and Affaeteres. Bael, still held fast against her, for once remained quiet, staring at the vapors rising from the well shaft.

Across from them, four other Elders, the young male elf holding the wine gourd, and an older female elf filled in the opposite side of the well. Tendrils of mist floated and swirled in the air.

A space still existed between the parallel half-circles of celebrants around the well. Fair-sized gaps remained, the circle unclosed.

From the packs, herds and flocks of animals that had joined the procession came a rustle of movement. A tawny lion emerged, strode over to Affaeteres's left, and sat quietly on the sand. A small sparrow flew gracefully upward against the vaporous currents of the Well and fluttered down, lighting between the lion and a portly bald Elder.

To Lucifer's right, a strong grey wolf padded softly over, his tongue lolling in a wide lupine grin, and stood proudly and attentively. A gazelle bounded down the slope, slowed to a canter, and took her place to the wolf's right.

No spaces remained around the well.

Quatama lifted the infant in his hands, holding her over the well shaft. The mist increased, obscuring the child within the thickening cloud.

"We present this child to You, our Creator. She is named Leianna, first born of Michael and Eve, niece to Adam and Gabriel, godchild to Lucifer and Affaeteres. We offer her to You, that she may know You, that You may recognize her, the special spark within her born of the eternal Flame that lit Your universe. Commune with her, Creator, that she may know her place within it."

Quatama released the child, slowly spread his arms, and empty-handed, stepped back. None seemed alarmed for the child's safety. They waited serenely, unmoving, with an obvious certainty that she would soon be returned to them.

-10-

I watch the screen, which seems to have frozen in place, nothing happening in this movie-like reenactment of my immortal beginning. The people and animals circling the Well of Being stand as rigidly and noiselessly as ancient statues. The thickening vapors from the well begin to billow out, blocking my view of the celebrants. It finally hides them completely, the screen a wall of coarse grey. I wonder if the technical difficulties are due to a glitch in the viewing station or in my own mind. Quatama turns briefly toward me. "You are seeing the journey you took to God, through the Well of Being." He returns his gaze to the viewing screen. I do likewise and wonders why a journey to God should seemingly pass through grey fuzz.

A kaleidoscope of shimmering, blindingly colorful light abruptly replaces the grey, stunning me, pushing me back against the chair, my hands lifting to shield my eyes against its scintillation. A baby chuckles, obviously delighted with the lightshow—the child I had been, thousands of centuries ago.

I slowly lower my hands to my sides. "I . . . I remember," I murmur, amazed that I can. "It was . . ." I search for adult words, find that they fail me, accept instead the infant's response. " . . . so pretty."

Quatama nods reverently. "The light of creation always is."

—WELCOME, CHILD.— In a voice that seems to radiate from everywhere at once, a voice I hear not with my ears or mind, but with the very core of my being, an all-powerful essence greets me. The voice is rich, resonant, its tone clear, yet neither loud nor soft, high nor low.

Then I no longer sit in the chair, in the viewing station, on the eighth physical astral plane, but am once more an immortal babe, seven celestial days old, floating in an undulating spectrum of light.

I reach out and touch the essence, which is both contained and all-encompassing, a shifting focus of energy and all energy, bridled and unbridled, within the cosmos, and I see, for a microsecond, all of creation. The vision is so vast, *so intricately whole,* it seems, for that instant, a toy of immeasurable design, which *I* can explore for all eternity, walking through its rooms, noting every texture, sound and sight, playing happily with and studying its minds, all connected to my own, bright baubles glistening throughout, with *the capacity for expansion.*

My baby self gurgles, cooing appreciatively.

—YES. BEAUTIFUL, ISN'T IT?— The great essence chuckles,

hearing my baby self's nonverbal agreement.

—LITTLE LEIANNA. I GIVE YOU THIS UNIVERSE. YOU MUST TREAT IT KINDLY. YOU WILL SHARE ITS WORTH ALWAYS WITH OTHERS. FOR I MAKE YOU A KEEPER AND CHARGE YOU WITH ITS WELL-BEING, YOU WHO ARE WORTHY. AND IF THE DAY SHOULD COME, WHEN YOU FEEL UNWORTHY OR UNCERTAIN OF YOUR TALENT OR YOUR STRENGTH TO CONTINUE, YOU MUST SEEK OUT OTHER KEEPERS, HOWEVER YOU MAY FIND THEM, AND THEY WILL AID YOU UNQUESTIONINGLY. AND SHOULD YOUR STRENGTH STILL FALTER, AND WEAKNESS ENTER YOUR VERY CORE, YOU MUST SEEK ME AND I WILL ANSWER AND REPLENISH YOU.

—FOR THIS COMMISSION SHALL BE ONGOING, WITH MANY HANDS, GREATER AND LESSER, UPON IT, TO HOLD IT INVALUABLE AND INVIOLATE.

—AND REMEMBER THAT THE VALUE OF THE UNIVERSE, OF ITS WHOLE, IMMEASURABLE THOUGH IT BE, IS NO GREATER OR LESSER THAN THE VALUE OF ITS PARTS, WHICH MAY BE MEASURED, THOUGH BY LESSER CRITERIA, OFTEN INADEQUATE CRITERIA.

—REMEMBER THESE WORDS, LEIANNA. REMEMBER THE COMMISSION I PLACE UPON YOU, FOR I SEE YOU ALREADY LOVE IT AND WILL TREAT IT KINDLY.

—AND, BY THE WAY, LEIGH ANN ELFMAN, WHO IS LEIANNA, THE GREY FUZZ IS THE PROVERBIAL "DARKNESS BEFORE THE LIGHT." YOUR POETS ALWAYS TRY TO FORCE REALITY TO SUCH EXACTNESS IN THE SHORT-CHANGED NAME OF CLARITY. THE TRUE PROVERB IS "THE GREY AREAS OF FUZZY THINKING BEFORE BLINDING CLARITY OF ALL ASPECTS." DO YOU UNDERSTAND?—

God laughs. It is a measured thoughtful laugh, with much love behind it, but nonetheless a laugh and . . . .

It woke me abruptly. I sat bolt upright in my bed.

Ginnie slept blithely on, Daniel slept, the bedroom dark, the night-silence thick. And now the familiar tingle of an unseen hand slid up my arm, resting on my shoulder. Bael's hand.

—Did you tell him, Leianna? Did you tell him he must let us heal the rift?—

—What? I think so. I don't know! I've got to get back! I was talking to God.—

79

—What? What did Quatama tell you?—

—Not Quatama. God. I've got to get back. Did you wake me?—

—No, I awaited your return. I would not disturb your sleep. What did Quatama tell you?—

—He showed me. I was a babe, newborn. You were a baby, too.—

A different throaty laugh tickled my inner ear. *—Your Naming Day. He showed your journey through the Well of Being.—*

—Yes.—

—And. . . ?— There was slight hesitancy, a fear.

—You don't know?—

—Know? I don't know my own Naming Day journey and its results. These are things hidden deep within our cores, a master program motivating our outward selves. Do you think you could function as an individual, having consciously carried back the memory of the Universal Mind?—

A nebulous twinge of distrust toward Bael drifted through me. *—You thought I would know.—* I had felt that expectancy, distinctly. *—And I thought . . . well, I thought I had remembered the journey and had told you of it in our other life, in Eliom.—*

—You are special,— he answered me slowly. *—I, too, thought you might remember, just a glimmer, having reenacted the journey.—*

—Reenactment . . . —

"No," I murmured aloud, then caught myself, glancing at Ginnie and Daniel.

—No,— I continued telepathically, *—God spoke to me by my mortal name. First He addressed me as the immortal infant I once was. He commissioned me to do something. I can't recall what. Something to do with keeping something, I can't recall what. Then He answered a question I'd had before, when I was watching the reenactment as if it were a movie. Something to do with the grey mist. And God told me what it was. He said it was "the darkness before the light."—*

I sensed the amused tolerant smile on his face.

—Well,— I insisted, *—that was what He said. If God wants to use a cliche, who's going to judge Him?—*

—It's not the cliche that gives me pause. It's the masculine pronoun.—

I stared into the darkness, puzzled.

—God is neither male nor female, Leianna.—

—Oh? You've caught God bathing in the buff, I suppose.—

He chortled. *—No, but the angelfolk never described the Creator in sexually preferential terms.—*

I shut my eyes, the need for sleep returning. *—Well, people on*

Earth generally describe God as male.—

—Sheer ignorance. The Creator, our original Creator, has both male and female traits. The One understands both as part of Its Whole.—

I remained silent at first, the early dawn and my broken rest lulling me back to sleep. "It's all right," I whispered. "It's a habit. God won't mind."

—What's in a name?— Bael paraphrased. *—That which we call God would sound as bittersweet . . .—*

"'Sall right," I sighed, barely hearing him, slipping back into unconsciousness.

The viewing room screen is off. Quatama sits, relaxed, in his chair, as if patiently awaiting my return.

"God addressed me as I am . . . today," I say. "How can He address me as an immortal babe, all those centuries ago, and also instantaneously address me as I am now?"

"The Universal Mind need not view time as you do, Leianna. Sometimes it is more important to understand the message, rather than when it was sent. Our Creator can be everywhen at once."

"Did you stop the projection . . . the recall?"

"You and God stopped the recall, by means of the buffer." He stands up, displaying the buffer, the skane prism in his hand, and places it in the red accordion file. He lays his hand flat on the viewing screen. The shiny black rectangle slowly emerges. That, too, is carefully returned to the file. "Do you recall the message?"

"Yes, but I don't understand it? What is a keeper?"

"Ah, but what were Adenoy Dominey's final words to you?"

"Something about fuzzy grey becoming blinding clarity. I don't recall it exactly." I try to smile and fail. "Have I done something wrong?"

Quatama reaches out, his hand lifting my chin, turning my averted face to his. "No. You do recall it, deep inside, in a place where sacred knowledge sleeps until understood and *used.* For now, I will remind you of the definition the Creator gave to you, as Leigh Ann Elfman: the grey areas of fuzzy thinking before blinding clarity of all aspects. But the final words asked of you were: Do you understand? That question only you can answer."

Another smaller, almost insignificant question nags me. "Quatama, I know this is going to sound trivial, but the names of the angelfolk—Lucifer, Affaeteres, Michael, Eve, Ashtoreth and so on, they seem to originate from different Earth cultures much more historically recent than these ancient events in Eliom. How is it that the angelfolk had these names beforehand?"

Again, Quatama smiles patiently. "The Eliomese language was rich and varied. It contained many nuances that later translated into different Earth languages as the angelfolk incarnated. As mankind developed writing and other cultural tools, the linguistic trace memories of the Eliomese became homogenized within human languages, religions and myths, as did many other Eliomese traits."

I nod. His explanation makes sense, although I haven't the foggiest idea as to how trace memories continue between incarnations, despite my own doing exactly that.

"Time to return to Earth and sleep now, Leianna, for your mind, as much as your mortal body, now requires rest. I will prevent Bael from disturbing it."

"He . . . he's asked that we be allowed to heal the rift."

Quatama studies me intensely. His eyes seem to bore into my heart, to painlessly dissect it and restore it to wholeness again. "Such healing lies not in your and Bael's hands alone. You and he were victims of the rift, not its authors. But you, Leianna, may provide a light to guide him in his darkness. Tell him he will be monitored. Now you must return to Earth. The mortal dawn in your hemisphere is not far away."

I hesitate, a final question on my lips too embarrassing to ask a spirit master.

Quatama's own thin lips slowly stretch into a tolerant grin. "If he proves himself sincere, we will relax our vigilance . . . at times."

I am about to explain, to tell him that my love for Bael has survived the centuries. But Quatama's fluted laughter fills my ears, and I float on each note, homeward bound.

Descending, descending, until my mind floats in a peaceful void, and I am whole again, all of me stacked neatly within my mortal flesh, sprawled in slumber upon my Earthly bed.

-11-

An image of Terence, anxiously staring at me, awoke me.

—*You're back,*— I thought. His disappearance had markedly paralleled Bael's arrival in my life.

—*You've got the devil himself shadowing your steps.*—

—*Bael?*—

—*Baelzebub.* —

—*No, not the same,*— I shot back. —*A fantasy god created hundreds of years ago by uneducated mortals. By human ignorance.*—

Daniel whimpered. I stretched, loosening my muscles.

Ginnie's alarm clock buzzed. My sister moaned, tightened the covers about her, and tried to ignore the clock's whine.

I got out of bed, bracing myself against the chill in the room. I walked over to Ginnie's dresser and pushed in the alarm switch. "You'd better get up, Gin. School day."

Daniel was also awake. I picked him up and carried him back to my bed, slipping my legs back under the covers and pulling the edge of the blanket around him.

"What time is it?" Ginnie mumbled.

"Seven."

"Mmn." In one continuous motion, Ginnie flung off her blankets and scurried to the bathroom down the hall, making chilly noises on the way. Daniel had begun to nod off again, lulled by the extra warmth of my blanket and my body heat.

I didn't disturb him. I savored the quiet, the renewed warmth.

Terence approached me again. In my mind's eye, I could see him clearly: moderate height, shoulder-length dark blond hair, watery blue eyes, stolid proletarian curves in his Anglo-Saxon face. A solid Englishman . . . yet not quite as proper a Brit as he'd wish to appear.

I had "met" him in New York's Central Park in January, 1969, about two months after his death. He had played a trick on me when we met, but I caught him at it. He hadn't expected me to, as he bent down to softly kiss my lips and lightly brush his hand across my shoulder and breast. He was new to the afterlife and, up till then, no other mortal had paid the slightest attention to his ethereal presence. He hadn't known I was psychic. His curiosity made him follow me home to my Manhattan apartment where I lived in 1968 and 1969, enjoying my first taste of adult freedom, working as a typist and dating Richard. Terence promptly made himself at home in my apartment and kept humming a haunting strain of classical music, piquing my own curiosity when he claimed the musical passage was from his own composition. I finally tracked down the debut album of Terence's work, which also became his only recorded work. His music had been beautiful, produced by a major label. The album blurb praised him as an emerging talent. But he, as a classical composer, while he welcomed the money, felt his success was a fluke. The critics had been scathing, and opportunities to perform his work live, the proper venue for classical music, evaporated. His compositions had contained descriptive fantasy elements, a sort of program music made popular in the 19th Century. He later found out that the record company had classified his compositions as instrumental pop music, which horrified him. He knew his work was not well-regarded by the classical community.

The scant articles I found on him agreed. Terence Dearborn's brilliance, properly nurtured, might have developed into genius. But due to "a romantic temperament," Terence had floundered on his first steps to success, insisting that the style of the 19th Century romantic composers was equally valid as a modern compositional form, but turning down other modern opportunities to prove it. A film company approached him with an offer to compose the background music for an upcoming fantasy movie. He refused the offer, again believing that the world trivialized his musical vision. He soon wore out the help and compassion of colleagues and friends trying to save him from himself.

One blustery night, late in the Autumn of 1968, having wandered away from a friend's party and drunk on booze, pills and self-indulgence, he drowned in the sea off Blackpool. The authorities ruled his death a suicide. Terence said that it wasn't.

He didn't seem to regret dying at the tender age of twenty-nine. The afterlife suited him, no more worries over material sustenance and shelter. He continued composing on the upper planes and shared his love of music with me by helping me when I played my guitar, developing my talent.

But lately his constant advice on my personal life had become irksome. He was, after all, only my *secondary* guide, and inexperienced. My major guide was an older man named Emmett, tall and thin, always clothed in a brown robe.

Brown robe! The reenactment of my immortal Naming Day flooded back into my mind. A brown robe! Both Quatama and Gabriel had worn such robes. Michael—the man I now knew to be my immortal father—had been dressed in simple white. His face now came strongly to mind. Although identical to his brother Gabriel, both with cropped brown hair and quiet brown eyes, both with thin but strong jawed faces, I *knew* that Michael was also the major spirit guide who called himself Emmett. Like Michael, Emmett was quiet, shy, and wise enough to point me, not push me, as a guide.

But why the deception? Why the false name?

—*Because you weren't ready,*— Terence broke into my thoughts. —*To remember, love. And I know Quatama, too. He's also my spirit master. He's also Patrick's. You remember Patrick, love, my poet friend.*— Patrick was an older man with a mane of silver white hair, craggy features, and a barrel chest in an otherwise slim physique. He wrote lovely poems but apparently had never published them on Earth. He said he had been a doctor, but I hadn't been able to verify his mortal identity. Now, however, he appeared to be a poet and only a poet. Heaven's reward.

—*Quatama is* your *spirit master?!*— Terence and Quatama seemed an incredulous combination.

—*Oh, ho! You thought he was exclusively your own, did you? He's spirit master to many people. Don't you know who he is? You're a bit ignorant of other religions, love. I'll have to* guide you *to a certain book, just to lay a clue before you,* inexperienced *as I am . . . or maybe I'll just tell you, blow your mind a bit, though it may. He's . . .*—

Ginnie came back into the room, grabbing her school clothes from the closet. "Hey, Leigh Ann. How about going downstairs and starting some breakfast for us, so I can get out on time."

I yawned, wondering what Terence had been pompously driving at. —*Later,*— I mentally told him, but received no response. "Sure, Gin." Daniel stirred at the sound of my voice, let out his own tiny yawn, and opened his eyes. "Good morning again, pumpkin," I greeted him. The baby giggled as I checked his diaper: dry and clean. "Come on, Danny boy. Let's get some grub started." I hefted him against my shoulder and got up. "See you downstairs," I called as Ginnie slapped on her student nurse's uniform, racing against the cold.

"Mom really ought to raise the thermometer," she said.

I put Daniel in his baby swing as I heated his bottle and perked the coffee. The kitchen thermometer read 69 degrees, but the air in the house still carried a nip. "Hard to believe it's nearly Spring," I told Daniel as I tested his bottle. The trickle of milk ran warmly down my wrist. I filled the toaster for Ginnie, lifted Daniel from the swing and cradled him in my arms, feeding him.

—*I've been* told *not to tell you Quatama's true ID,*— Terence suddenly intruded.

—*Back again?*— I still resented his calling Bael a devil. I almost

85

suspected Terence of jealousy.

—*Well, I'm not, and he is,*— he caught my train of thought. —*Now, at any rate. It's all well and good to say human ignorance created the job title, but you might remember you're human as well, quite mortal, and in possession of a soul that might be a premium purchase.*—

Resentment slowly metamorphosed into a deep desire to slug him. —*I didn't take you for the fanatical religious type.*—

—*I'm not. But I know the scent of eau de brimstone when it wafts under my nostrils.*—

—*These are beliefs created by a humanity terrified by the unknown. Heaven and Hell aren't places of reward and punishment. They don't exist that way except in the minds of the fearful. The only thing that really exists are levels, based on the soul's advancement.*—

—*Or downfall into indescribable depths,*— he persisted. —*Look, I admit I didn't believe in these things when I died. But there are demarcations, love. I can't believe Quatama is allowing that bloody downsider within a five foot radius of you. Quatama must mean to pull you out of it, and ship him back to the pit.*—

— He *has* a name!—

—*I'd rather not say it aloud. Might attract bad karma, you know.*—

—*His name is Bael, and he doesn't rule flies.*—

—*No, he rules the damned. Take care you don't fall within that boundary.*—

—*Bastard!*—

I felt him redden, a slow anger pulsating from him.

—*What did you call me, Leigh Ann?*—

I took a deep breath. —*I'm sorry. Just please don't prejudge Bael.*—

—*He's already* been judged, *love. That's what I can't get through your thick head.*— Disgust ringed his words.

—*Then I may just open up the case. Now be quiet. Ginnie's here!*— "Toast is ready, Gin. So's the coffee."

"Thanks, Leigh Ann. Want me to pour you a cup?"

"Please. Danny's taking forever to drink his bottle."

Ginnie brought butter, milk and the sugar bowl over to the table. She poured two cups of coffee and carried them over, then placed her toast on a plate and got cutlery from the drawer. She plunked herself down opposite me, sliding a spoon to me. "So when are we going mall shopping?"

I propped Daniel's bottle under my chin to hold it and added sugar and milk to my coffee, pulling a napkin from its holder on the table. "When I get a job and some money."

"Oh, come on, Leigh. You don't have to buy anything. Just come along. I need a new pair of dress jeans, and we can check out the spring clothes together. We can go this Saturday."

"Oh, all right. Danny will probably like an outing."

Our mother came into the kitchen, followed by Dad and Fred, the kitchen suddenly crowded.

"Good morning, moppets," Dad said, unfolding the morning paper. "Did one of you make the coffee?"

"Leigh Ann did."

"Good. Saves your mother time. Now you can get to work on an order of eggs and toast, Miriam."

Mom had already taken the frying pan out. She held it menacingly. "Do you want anything else?"

"I'll take a glass of juice, fresh squeezed, of course." His eyes twinkled; he winked at me.

Mom put the pan down and grabbed a stack of small plastic tumblers from the upper cabinet. She pulled a pitcher of orange juice from the fridge and plopped tumblers and beverage on the table. "Processed. You want fresh squeezed, get up early and squeeze them yourself, Bill."

"Hey, but that's what I have a wife for." He grabbed the prepared juice and poured himself a glassful.

"Mmn. What do you want for breakfast, Fred?"

"Just some cereal, juice and toast. I'll make the toast for Dad and me."

The family ate hectically, Ginnie and Fred finishing and rushing off to their respective schools. Dad lingered over coffee. Mom finally sat down with her own cereal and coffee.

"So, Leigh Ann," my father said, "have you made any decisions since the weekend?"

"Find a good day care for Danny. Find a job for me."

He glanced at his grandchild. "I hope he doesn't turn out like his father."

"Dad . . ."

"I mean it. I'm almost tempted to tell you not to work, to stay here and raise him properly. But we really can't afford to keep you both. You'll have to make your own way. If you're going to live here, you have to contribute your share of the household expense. Ginnie's going to discover that, too, after she graduates nursing school."

"I intend to. But first Danny needs day care."

"I agree. Miriam?"

My mother held her cup thoughtfully, quietly. "Your father and I have decided to let Danny stay here when you find a job. I'll babysit him until he's old enough for preschool, or unless you and Richard patch up your marriage and he finds decent employment to support his family. Considering how shaky that prospect is, it can't hurt for you to learn self-sufficiency. You may need to rely on yourself alone, Leigh Ann, in the long run."

I sat very still for a minute. "I don't expect the marriage to work out. Not after everything that's happened."

"Your father and I figured as much. We just wanted to be certain. Well, a divorce in your case will be cheap enough. No property or other finances to fight over."

"I just want my freedom."

"Freedom," my father mused. "Nothing in life is free, Leigh Ann. Just make sure you don't barter away the things you value and the things that make life valuable on another useless, self-centered mistake." He rose from his chair. "I've got to get going. Pete and Jerry are picking up the new water heater we're installing at Smokey's Bar on Walnut Street. They're meeting me downtown." He tapped his newspaper. "Start looking for a job, kiddo. Don't wait for Richard to magically transform. You'll be lucky to get child support from that guy. Depend on yourself." He kissed Mom and gave me a quick pat on my shoulder. "See you girls tonight." He headed out the side door.

Daniel finished his bottle, making air bubble sounds through the nipple. I pulled it from his mouth. "My, you're hungry today."

He let out a huge burp and some of his formula with it.

"Ugh."

"It's all over your nightgown, Leigh Ann." Mom went to the sink to wet a dish rag.

As she handed it to me, I caught a mental burst of laughter and a glimpse of Bael's amused expression. I carefully wiped the spit-up off the bodice of my gown, taking equal care not to acknowledge his presence and wondering if Terence was also still there.

—*No. He appears to be afraid of me. Ran like a spooked puppy. What do you see in him? His music? Well, I suppose one could forgive him his faults for that. Though he screwed it up far worse this time than his last stint as a classical composer.*—

I didn't answer, using a clean section of the rag to wipe Daniel's mouth and chin.

—*You might as well not regret his loss to the world. That singular recording, talented though it be, will soon be forgotten as new stars mount the horizon. His other work will never be recovered. His last girlfriend was particularly spiteful, when she found he left no will and his family snubbed her at the funeral.—*

I knew Bael was deliberately intriguing me. Terence never spoke of having unpublished, unperformed music, nor of any other lifetime as a composer.

I also wondered why Bael was chancing my mother's notice, blabbing on this way.

I heard another stabbing laugh from him as I put Daniel back into his swing. Mom squeezed the rerinsed dish rag out and draped it over the faucet to dry. "Now, I don't want you to feel pressured," she said, sitting down again. "Find a job you think you'll like, possibly one with extra benefit perks like tuition reimbursement if the course relates to the job."

I picked the paper up gingerly, turning to the help wanted pages. "A job, huh? Let's see. I'm a high school grad, no college, but I type well, was always good at English and have about two years of experience as a typist. I suppose I'd qualify for a secretarial job. Here's one. High school grad, typing, filing and receptionist duties. Willing to train. Girl Friday."

Mom smirked. "I've never liked that title. Is it full-time?"

"Doesn't say. I'll have to ask them. Mom?" I decided to test her awareness of Bael's presence. "Do you sense anything?"

She seemed confused, then smiled. "Oh, you mean about this job. No, not at all. You'll have to check it out yourself, starting with a phone call. And remember, you don't have to rush. Your father and I want you to make a good start at a job with a future. Take your time and don't rush into things blindly, dear. I'm going upstairs to shower and dress. Talk to you later." She hesitated, then impulsively bussed my cheek. "Good luck."

"Thanks, Mom."

I stared pensively at my empty coffee cup and at Daniel, who stared back in an almost unsettling way. The baby's key ring rested on the table. I gave it to him. He jiggled it happily as I called the phone number listed for the Girl Friday job.

Daniel began whimpering as soon as the receptionist put me through to the personnel supervisor, the baby's crabbing slowly rising in volume every time I tried to ask a question or hear its answer. His bawling, randomly interspersed with high-pitched shrieks, made it impossible to hear or think. I finally shouted an apology, promised to call back and hung up the phone. "Danny! What *is* the matter with you?!" I glared at him.

He sniffled, hiccupped, and leaned to the side as far as his swing chair would allow. His small hand stretched toward his key rattle, which had fallen onto the linoleum. I returned it to him and took up the phone again, determined to redial the call.

Daniel studied the phone and started his fussing whine again. I hung up again, picked up Daniel, and checked him all over. He giggled at my scrutiny, apparently abandoning his renewed crying jag with no other visible problems.

I put him back into his swing. He watched me intensely, as if gauging my next move.

"Are you afraid of the phone, Danny? Look." I picked up the receiver again. "It won't hurt you or me."

I started to dial the number a third time, and saw Daniel suck his mouth into a pout, his small brows furrowing. I hung up, and his face smoothed back into the picture of a patient infant. "You are really weird today," I told him and wrinkled my own brows into a pout. "Like mother, like son." Daniel broke into a toothless grin at the face I made, forcing me to laugh along with him.

"Oh, all right. I'm beginning to think that you've been put up to this, that someone doesn't want me to try for that Girl Friday job. Is that it?" Daniel just looked at me, unnaturally still. "I guess I'd better check out those ads again for jobs that meet your approval!"

An hour later, I had marked off three other jobs to call about: two for clerk-typist, and one for junior medical secretary. The latter especially interested me. I was a good speller and felt sure I could learn the terminology on my own, using Ginnie's medical dictionary.

I spent half an hour playing with Daniel in the living room, singing silly children's songs and dancing him around in my arms. Mom came downstairs in the midst of *I've Been Working On The Railroad,* smiling as her daughter and grandson swirled around the room to the old folksong.

"Don't forget to teach him *Playmates,"* she said, getting her coat from the dining room closet. "I'm going out to get a few groceries. See you when I get back. Did you make any calls?"

"Danny got cranky. I'm going to try again in a few minutes."

"Good. Just keep your voice cheerful, and tell them how much you'd love to interview for the job. Answer their questions briefly, but *don't* tell them your life story."

I grinned. "You know me pretty well, don't you? I won't. I promise."

"I should know you. I raised you all these years. Bye."

"Bye."

I carried Daniel back into the kitchen and mixed some baby cereal with strained pears. Daniel ate about half the bowl, then pushed the spoon away.

"Full? Okay, sonny boy, I'm going to put you in your swing again. Let's see if you can stay quiet while Mommy makes some calls."

He didn't protest, content and full. I dialed the three new numbers. One job was already filled, but the others were still open, and I arranged interviews for both. One was for a clerk typist position at a manufacturer in the far northeast. The other was the junior medical secretary job at Hahnemann Hospital off Broad Street in the heart of downtown Philadelphia. Their personnel officer said they would train me, if I proved a good candidate in their other test requirements. I liked the idea of working in the health field.

On impulse, I decided to also call back the number for the Girl Friday position. It couldn't hurt to have a third interview, in case the first two fell through. I snuck a wary glance at Daniel as I dialed. He was engrossed in his key rattle, ignoring me.

I intended to explain the earlier interruption to the woman supervisor I'd spoken to, or tried to speak with, before. But now the receptionist cut short my request to be transferred to the woman, explaining that they'd had too many responses to the ad, had booked enough interviews, and weren't scheduling any more at present.

As I hung up the phone, I noticed my son's absolute disinterest in my job search, as opposed to his early morning caterwauling. I offered him the leftover fruit and cereal mix. He gobbled it up and yawned.

"Tired, sweetie? So am I. Come on. Let's go upstairs."

I left my mother a note: "Got two interviews. One on Friday at Hahnemann Hospital! The other on Monday at a paper manufacturer on Bustleton Avenue. I'm upstairs, getting Daniel ready for his nap. Leigh Ann."

Daniel gibbered and cooed on the way up, and let out infant sighs as he lay in his crib, preoccupied with a thorough study of his fingers and sleeper-clad feet.

I rested on my bed beside his crib, watching him, the house quiet, the ticking of Ginnie's clock audible in the stillness.

I fell asleep before the baby did.

-12-

Mists swirl around me, white against a moderate blue background that waivers in hue, slightly lighter, slightly darker. The clouds, if clouds they are, drift by me. Yet my feet stand firmly on something soft but solid.

In the distance I spy Terence, his blond hair, white poet's shirt, brown pants and boots cutting a sharp contrasting figure against the blue and white ether. His back is to me. He turns and looks at me, as if just noticing my arrival. Then he turns away, as if denying my presence, walking on.

"Terence!"

I want to run, to catch up, and suddenly I am there, right behind him. I reach out and grab his shoulder. "Wait!"

He faces me silently, sullenly.

"Why were you running away?"

He doesn't answer for a minute. When he finally does, his words spew out in a pettish miserable torrent. "You and that bloody downsider! Prying into other people's lives. Now he's trying to destroy my soul as well as yours. Well, you can play in his bloody pit all you like. I'm climbing out, fast as I can. Leave you behind, I swear it. Let Quatama figure out how to rescue your bloody arse if you fall too low. I'm not your fucking Prince Charming. Smear your own face with the ashes from the fire. I won't have it. None of it. I'm off the job. Ta!"

He turns to leave. I try to push in front of him. The atmosphere in this void feels thick, as if I'm under water when I deliberately try to move, yet when I think about, desire a movement or action, it occurs so fluidly, it seems to happen almost simultaneously. I give up trying to physically catch his retreating figure, and simply concentrate, imagining appearing in front of him, bringing him up short.

"Leigh Ann, please stop that! I want to go." He glares at me; I *have* jolted him, materializing so close to him, we nearly collide. "You have plenty of other spirit guides. I've no doubt of that, having learned about *you,* my girl. You'll do fine without me. Now please let me pass."

"You're angry. It's about your music, isn't it? Why didn't you tell me you had other compositions?"

"Other composi . . . !" He sputters, unable to even complete the word. "You are talking about my life blood, my magnum opus, the gems I seduced from the Muse after I recovered from the depression caused by my critics trashing any pleasure I'd had in the debut of my first record. None of my peers thought my work had merit. But that record was like glass compared to the diamonds of my final compositions. And I hoarded them, like a child with a wondrous secret, holding back to dazzle my mates with three new musical triumphs in one fell swoop!" He lapses back to silence, sucks in a breath, and shivers as if chilled. "No one knew they existed but Cecily. Bloody beautiful Cecily. I told her not to tell another soul. I planned to tape them after our return to London from Blackpool. Just shut myself in with the piano and the recorder, put in all the orchestral parts of the symphony, finish it, then record the sonata's interweaving movements, and finally, get my nocturne, short but excruciatingly seductive, down on tape! I'd only dreamt of creating music like this before, Leigh Ann. That recording you think so highly of equalled my metaphorical toddler steps, learning to walk as a composer before discovering I could run! And that bastard, that absolute *bastard,* saying the bloody bitch destroyed it all!" He lifts his hands helplessly to me. "I only had one set of it all, written in musical script. My symphony, my sonata and my poor little nocturne. I tucked them all in a large envelope and stuck it inside the piano bench before we left for seaside. So she destroyed them. Cecily destroyed them." He heaves a sigh. "Not that I couldn't recreate the music, upside in the afterlife, you know. But you want to leave your greatest work . . . " He huffs out another sigh. ". . . in the plane of life you created it on. I was waiting. I thought perhaps Cecily would have shown them to my publisher after I died. It's been three years, hasn't it? On Earth?"

I can read the resignation in his eyes, his posture. "Three new compositions? Lost?"

"Three long leaps in my musical virtuosity. Gone forever, it appears. Not to be part of my scant legacy on Earth."

I lift my hand and rest it on his shoulder. He glances at it, unsure of my intentions, but allows it to remain there. "You were eavesdropping on Bael's taunts this morning. I thought you had left. Bael said you had, but you were listening in."

Now he does move, dislodging my hand as he paces to the left. "I went off into the living room. But the words of that wondrous fallen angel of yours were meant as much for my ears as for yours. He means to crush my soul, to ship me to the spiritual boondocks. Away from you, no doubt. And he said my final works were lost, didn't he? Said they would never be recovered. That Cecily had been particularly spiteful."

"Was she?"

"I . . . umm . . . didn't attend my funeral nor look in on friends and relatives after I drowned. I really don't know. I met Patrick shortly after I went through the death process, the transition. He'd been on the upper planes some twenty to thirty years, and they'd assigned him to act as a sort of welcoming committee and messenger to me. The message was that I had unfinished business on Earth and would have to return to take care of it."

"Well, the method of return obviously wasn't reincarnation."

He smiles halfheartedly, his melancholy and aching vulnerability visible. "No. Actually they didn't tell me what the unfinished business was. They said I would know after I'd completed it. I expect it has something to do with my music." He looks at me expectantly. "I wonder if I could dictate those lost works to you? Can you read musical script, Leigh Ann? I've never seen you do it, but . . ." I shake my head. "Well, there goes that idea. Probably wouldn't work anyway, trying to convey musical notation through telepathy, remembering the exact compositions."

"Even if I could, I'd probably mess it up in more than one place. Not to mention the problem of trying to convince others that it's *your* music, Terence."

Another flicker of hope lights his face. "Perhaps it hasn't been destroyed."

"Maybe we can try to contact this Cecily," I offer, then correct myself, "Maybe I can try to contact her, in the physical world. Do you remember the address, where you lived with her?"

His pale brows furrow. "It's been so long. It's hard to remember details like that as well when you're dead. What? Oh, come now, I am dead, you know. In your world, at any rate."

I sigh. The word really gives me the willies. I find it difficult accepting the mortal description of death. In the mortal world, one is indeed gone, never to regain one's physical form in that particular lifetime, when one dies. But I still view Earthly life as the fantasy, the dream from which one awakens. "Perhaps," I agree. "But death is a transition, not a permanent condition. It's not my fault that most mortals treat Earth as the only dimension succoring life and the physical body as its only vehicle."

"Tell it to the coroner. Look, Leigh Ann. Even if I could remember where I lived with Cecily, what surety do we have that we'll translate the address correctly? Psychics can miss by a kilometer. It's one thing to mix up a simple conversation a bit. It's another to give specific information that needs proving out. I don't even know if Cecily still lives there. Maybe we should forget this."

"No. We're not giving up that easily. We have to try to recover your lost works. But one thing does bother me. Why didn't Cecily take them to your publisher or to someone else in authority in the classical music field? No matter how badly upset she was after your death, it would benefit her. She'd become a celebrity. The media would eat it up. The grieving heroine who saved her sweetheart's music from oblivion."

Terence considers that. "You don't think she did, and the publisher turned it down, do you?"

"Highly unlikely. Your earlier works had been popular despite the critics. Dead composers with newly discovered works can get more attention than living ones that are still composing. So why didn't she open the piano seat, scoop it out, and wave it in front of the music world's face?"

Terence furrows his brows again, as much at a loss as I am, then his mouth opens, his expression stricken. "Oh, my God. Oh, my God, Leigh Ann!"

"What?"

"Dear Lord, I didn't tell her."

"Tell her what? You said you did tell her about the new music."

"No, no, no! I mean I didn't tell her where they were. I lifted the piano seat, placed them in the compartment inside, and locked it, while she was packing the car for seaside."

"Well, wouldn't she have looked for them? I mean, afterwards?"

"I don't know. She wasn't musical, you know." He sighs again, heavily. "Wherever that piano seat is, my music may still be."

"Well, we've got to try to contact her. Think! Try to remember the address where the two of you lived."

"Umm . . . Doughty Street! In London. I can't remember the number. Was it 42 or 44? Damn! We lived right up the street from the Dickens House."

"The Dickens House?"

"One of the houses Charles Dickens once lived in. They converted it into a museum."

"The street number, Terence," I remind him. The sound of faint crying begins to distract me.

"The number . . . yes, yes! It was No. 44. 44 Doughty Street. We rented the second floor. Yes, that's it. The second floor flat at 44 Doughty Street in London," he repeats, then peers at me. "Are you all right, love?"

I can't answer. For one instant longer, I stand facing Terence in the blue and white ether . . .

. . . half a second later, my eyes opened to afternoon sunlight brightening the bedroom as Daniel's loud bawling filled my ears. I got up and picked him up, checking his diaper. "Oh, boy. It's all right, Danny. Mommy will get you cleaned up."

I removed the soiled diaper, wiped him around with a wet wash cloth, then dried, powdered and freshly diapered him. Even his outer rubber diaper had leaked through to the butt and legs of his sleeper. "What a mess." At least, the crib sheet had stayed dry. I retrieved a new rubber diaper and sleeper from below the bathinet. I redressed Daniel and laid him in his crib. "Stay put for a moment, sweetie. Mommy has to wash your dirty diaper out."

I went to the bathroom to rinse off and flush away the feces. As I wrung the cloth out tightly, Terence made a sudden reappearance, asking in an agitated rush, —Do you remember?—

—What.—

—The address! Lord, I hope you've gotten it right.—

—44 Dougherty Street, second floor, in London.—

—Not Dougherty. It's Doughty. Like the dough you bake bread and biscuits with.—

—Doughty. Okay? Now, I've got things to do, so cool it.—

I took the rinsed diaper back into the bedroom, dumping it in the pail, then threw the wet baby clothes into the hamper.

Daniel reached out his hands to me. I lifted him into my arms and headed downstairs.

Terence trailed after me. —When are you going to write the letter?—

—Later.—

—Can't you do it now? You can walk it to the post. It's a lovely day. Take Daniel for a ride in his pram.—

I walked into the kitchen. My mother wasn't there, but the door to the basement was opened. "Mom?"

"I'm in the laundry room, ironing," she called up.

—I've remembered Cecily's last name,— Terence cut in. —It's Saraband. Cecily Saraband. 44 Doughty Street, second floor, in London. Please, Leigh Ann. For the possible sake of posterity?—

I gave in. "Mom? Do we have any stationery and envelopes? I want to write a letter to someone in England."

"In England? Who do you know in England?"

"I'll explain later."

"Look in the hutch in the dining room. Top left drawer. Is Daniel up?"

"Yes. I've got him with me." I found a matching set decorated with a border in the drawer. Putting Daniel in his swing, I sat down to write, wondering how to best put what had to be said—in mundane terms that wouldn't alarm the woman.

I started,

"Dear Cecily,

"You don't know me, but I am an admirer of the music of Terence Dearborn. Having researched his life, I found that you and he were sharing this address before he . . ." (I hesitated, wondering how to put it delicately, and decided prettifying it would sound pretentious) ". . . died. I hope you don't find me presumptuous, but being a musician myself, and having found and loved Mr. Dearborn's one album, I wonder if he left other musical compositions, as yet undiscovered. It seems strange that he hasn't, as someone as talented as Mr. Dearborn surely would have been working on new compositions after his successful debut.

"Is it possible that unpublished music was misplaced and forgotten following his demise? Pianists often store music in the compartments beneath their piano benches, although I imagine you and his family have already checked this possibility. Consider me a concerned fan who feels some exploration ought to be made.

"If you do turn up any recovered work by Mr. Dearborn, I would greatly appreciate hearing of it. Hoping this letter reaches you and will hopefully bring fruitful results, I remain,

Sincerely yours,

Leigh Ann Elfman"

I addressed the envelope and held it and the letter up for Terence's inspection.

—*I can't read it. It's hard to read physical writing through spirit eyes. Some can. I'm not particularly adept at it.*—

—*Would you like me to read it silently?*—

—*No need. I caught your thoughts as you wrote it. I'm quite satisfied.*—

I slipped the letter into the envelope, sealing it up. I had some money from a small allowance my father had given me. "I hope this doesn't cost too much to mail overseas," I muttered, then called down to the basement. "Mom. Danny and I are taking a walk to the post office. Do you need anything while we're out?"

"No, dear. I got groceries this morning." She appeared at the base of the stairs. "You can help me make dinner after you get back. Do you need money?"

"No. I'm fine."

I dressed the baby and myself snugly and, Daniel held firmly in one arm, pulled his carriage outside with my other hand. I put him gently inside, drew the carriage blanket around him and wheeled the carriage down the pathway to the sidewalk.

The weather had warmed, cotton clouds drifting through a pastel blue sky.

It would be a triumph, both psychically and culturally, if Cecily Saraband found the missing music. —*So much for Bael's prediction,*— I telepathed to Terence. —*With any luck, we may yet resurrect your lost symphony, sonata and nocturne.*—

Terence remained silent, walking beside us for two or three blocks, then, so softly I almost didn't catch it, said, —*Thank you.*—

We continued to saunter along, the pleasant day lulling us. Then a faint unarticulated question played in the corners of my mind. It concerned Terence's death.

—*Why do you have to know how it was for me?*— he asked me.

—*Well, you're the first person I've met psychically who, well, has died. Just curious to know what it's like.*—

—*I'll tell tonight, while you're out-of-body. I'll try to wake you up afterwards. It might help you to remember. That is, if your precious Bael doesn't come around to interfere. Although we seem to be spared his presence for now.*—

I let that last terse remark rest. Terence still smarted, no doubt, from Bael's crass denouncement on the fate of the lost compositions.

We reached the Castor Avenue post office. I parked the carriage outside and carried Daniel into the building. A man coming out held the door for us.

The line wasn't long, the letter to Cecily Saraband quickly weighed, stamped, and deposited in the overseas mail bin. I took Daniel back outside, snuggled him into the carriage and headed home.

I wondered if the letter would ever reach the woman and, if so, if Terence's missing music would really be recovered. I knew the difficulties involved in trying to work from psychic clues. Failure was more of a potential than success.

I wondered if I should have done more mortal sleuthing, written a letter to the recording company producing Terence's album, asked them for his publisher's address. But the authorities might find it strange at best or an intrusion at worst if I asked for the current mailing address of Cecily Saraband and Terence's parents. I could imagine the polite response letter, if I received a response at all: "We are not at liberty to give out personal information of this nature." That left me back at square one, mailing the letter to Cecily at the address Terence remembered, our only option, short of Terence haunting his ex-girlfriend and parents, and trying to lead them to his music.

—*It's not the same for everyone,*— Terence said. His words seemed unrelated to my current thoughts.

"What's not the same?" I asked aloud, then brought myself up short for it. Someone not near enough to hear me clearly might assume I spoke to my baby, but it was definitely a bad habit to get into.

—*No one heard you.*—

—*I still shouldn't answer verbally. People sock you away in mental institutions for things like that.*—

—*Oh, you'd give them a lovely run, I've no doubt, if they stuck you in one. Probably give them a nutshell lecture on the universe's dimensional nature.*—

—*Then they would throw away the key.*—

—*My guess is they'd throw you out to save their own sanity.*—

—*I'll definitely take caution over being committed. It's a rational thing. I prefer not having to stage escapes from loony bins.*— We had turned the corner to my street. —*So what is it, that's not the same for everyone?*—

—*The death experience.*—

—*Well, then,*— I told him, steering the carriage up the walk to my family's house, —*I couldn't tell anyone the whole truth.*—

—*Not at all,*— he conceded. —*It appears to be all relative to one's state of mind.*—

—*When you die, you mean.*—

—*How you die and, apparently, how you live, before and after.*—

I unlocked the door and pulled the carriage with Daniel in it up the front steps and into the porch. Carrying Daniel into the living room, I rested him on the sofa, unsnapping his jacket. My mother walked into the room, carrying a finished basket of ironing. She glanced about the room with an expectant air, as if sniffing a scent. "There's a male presence in the room, Leigh Ann."

I hesitated then said, "His name is Terence Dearborn, a classical musician who passed away about three years ago. I have the first and only album he recorded. The letter I mailed was an inquiry concerning his work. Not that there's any guaranty that the person we wrote to will get the letter."

She put the basket down and sat opposite us on the sofa. "Leigh Ann, there's a difference between having psychic ability and immersing yourself in it."

"I'm a medium, Mom. I can't help it anymore than you can."

"But you can control it."

"I do, Mother. But Terence has unfinished business on Earth,

99

probably to do with some missing classical compositions he wrote. I've done my best to help him find them, and I worded the letter carefully. Not a hint of anything psychic in it. If the letter fails and his lost music doesn't surface, maybe he'll be able to let it go. But at least he'll know I tried."

"But it's not your job to find his music. It's one thing to deliver a message from a spirit to surviving relatives or friends who request that communication. It's also acceptable to help spiritfolk let go of the mortal concerns that hold them Earthbound. But *they* have to do the work, not you. You can't cohabit with them as if they were still physical." She leaned toward me, both her tone and blue eyes intense. "Trying to balance two dimensions is a precarious tightrope act. You know the psychic's first rule for emotional stability. Our primary allegiance is always to the living, Leigh Ann."

I shifted my own gaze away from that sharp maternal glare. I knew I was being advised to set limits, uncompromising limits, on my interaction with spiritual entities. "You want me to impose strict rules on myself. We share similar talents, and you've taught me well to measure my experiences carefully and protect myself. But I'm an individual, and our experiences may not be the same or call for the same limitations. Mine may even require an openness in areas yours don't. You're going to have to trust me to judge those experiences on my own terms if you want me to learn and grow from them. I'm not a child anymore."

She slowly shook her head. "Sometimes I wish . . ."

". . . that I had never inherited your gift," I finished for her. "Mother, has it ever occurred to you that the gift isn't inherited, that it comes from a different source? And the reason you also have the talent is to help me over the initial development of my own talent? There is a point where the mother bird has to let its young leave the nest."

She smirked with all the insouciance a redhead could muster. "But, darling, you have returned to the nest. And helping you to develop does include passing on the wisdom of my own 25 years of hobnobbing with the dead."

"You need to trust me, Mother."

"I need you to be *trustworthy,*" she countered firmly.

"Then give me a chance."

My mother sighed, then gave me a hard glance that seemed to war between foreboding and faith, before rising and picking up her basket of freshly ironed clothes. "Will you let me have a final say?"

I nodded. "I'm listening."

"Then a short piece of advice. Keep your psychic encounters

firmly separate from your everyday mortal life. Mortal needs weren't meant to be fulfilled in the nonmortal realm. It can be dangerous, can lure you away from our world. Safeguard yourself. Draw a line. Let no one force you across it."

"That's intelligent advice, Mom, and I do intend to follow it. But there may be exceptions to that rule . . . and I may have to extend that line to explore them, for reasons that may go beyond any normal mortal life you and I may want me to have. But I promise you I'll respect my responsibilities and my needs and not let anything interfere with their fulfillment or their stability."

She hugged the basket closer to herself, as if its weight might symbolically anchor her to the solid and real. Then she nodded, and I knew I had gained a measure, at least, of her trust. "I hold you to that promise, Leigh Ann. Confide in me or don't, as you see fit. But remember that this mortal world will always demand at least the illusion of your acceptance of its laws of nature and of the limitations those laws seem to impose. Don't hurt yourself. Don't try to make the whole world conform to your visions."

"I'm not stupid, mother." I gazed down at Daniel, busily studying the taste and shape of his fingers. "I know how to keep my visions to myself."

"Then God watch over you, Leigh Ann and guide you to make the right decisions. And I'll trust you to balance your own life and seek your own wisdom as you live it."

It took a moment to sink in, to understand the full impact of her concession. My mother had relinquished control, bestowing on me the mantle of maturity, the privilege of my own choices, the responsibility for their outcome. "Thank you," I murmured. A rite of passage, however subtle its ceremony.

"Now I'm going to unload the ironing before my arms give out." She headed upstairs. "We'll prepare dinner when I come down. In the meantime, you might compose your resume for those job interviews. I wouldn't count on a reward for that music. I don't know who you wrote to, but unless you luck out, it'll probably end up in some dead letter box in England."

I sensed Terence standing by the foot of the stairs, looking up at Mother's retreating figure. —*Was that a joke?*— he called after her.

She either didn't hear or ignored him. I hoisted Daniel up, taking him to the kitchen and setting him in his high chair, while I warmed up his four o'clock bottle and found some paper and a pen.

I held Daniel's bottle up for him with my left hand, drafting my resume with my right.

For one sardonic minute, I considered putting down gardener and musical detective as past employment, then laughed at my silliness and got down to serious work. I listed the few jobs I had temporarily held; I had last worked as a typist at the certified public accounting firm in New York City until the last three months of my pregnancy. Detailing my minimal job experience as impressively as possible, I added a statement of my employment goals and finished the resume with a one-line listing of my hobbies. I didn't include psychic phenomena on the list, although I sorely wished I lived in a world in which I could, without fearing its mockery and rejection.

I set the resume aside for later typing, burped Daniel and held him, musing over the nearly irreconcilable difference between my mother's and my own approach to psychic exploration. Mother treated her own unique talent with an ironclad caution, prepared to protect herself, whether against spiritual evil or the disdain of a mortal world with limited vision. I knew, with a deep gut knowledge, that I would explore beyond the sensible boundaries my mother had erected. I would be the one to extend the barriers rigid science and timid religions laid, refusing to acknowledge the versatility dimensional reality might possess. I would be the one to burst through the mold of mortal denial, to overcome the fear and embrace the universe with a child's sense of wonder, unafraid of the challenges ahead, welcoming the risks.

I would be the one to chance opening a communication between two worlds—possibly three—since time immemorial closed off to one another.

I had no foreknowledge of how I would work this miracle. I only knew, felt, the pull of a path being laid before me. I would follow it where it led, only certain that the Creator guided me and would help me along the way.

As Leigh Ann Elfman, I would live my mortal life as honorably and as honestly as I could without denying my own uniqueness and vision.

As Leianna, I would seek to repair, and once again hold dear, bonds between loved ones long ago torn apart. I could see the fabric rewoven, a tapestry of souls throughout time, made whole again, its sundered sections rejoined, the dimensional universe restored to a glory and coherence hitherto unimagined.

Living both lives, existing in both worlds, I would nevertheless be whole, be unified, be one person, my duality necessary aspects of one eternal soul.

It had to be that way. My duality was the key.

Somehow, together, I would unlock forgotten doors and ultimately heal the rift between Heaven, Earth, and Hell.

-13-

I curl up against the crushed velour of a comfortable forest green sofa in the small but pleasant living room of Terence's apartment. He prefers living on the sixth physical astral plane. It feels more like Earth, due to its proximity to the existential dimensions comprising mortal life . . . the first physical astral plane being structured through elemental matter, the second being the catalyst of the mental and emotional conscious minds, and the third being the impetus of the creative symbolic subconscious mind. In the fourth physical astral plane, the nature of time changes. It ceases to exist chronologically, becomes a gateway to all time and therefore timeless. On the fifth physical astral plane, the nature of space becomes pliable with the touch of a thought. The sixth physical astral plane expands as its inhabitants, collectively and individually, will it to, having all of the characteristics of the first five planes in enhanced degrees.

I could, if I wished to, create the English tea Terence is preparing in his kitchen, or more likely an Americanized version of it, directly in front of me, and while I'm at it, also create a tea trolley to serve it on. But my ability to visualize and create is limited by my lacking a clear knowledge of tea trolley designs. There are people on the sixth plane who excel in designing furniture. Mine would likely be rickety, possibly evaporate. Objects don't break at this dimensional level, unless you want them to. They simply disintegrate back into their original energy atoms.

Terence has a nice tea trolley, ornately carved, paid for with exchanged skane points he's earned through guide work, encouraging young mortal musicians. Skane points are not true skane, like the diamond-shaped buffer I've used during recall; points are symbolic skane, the measure of the energy expended doing good works, easily earned by spiritfolk and even by mortals whose work enhances the lives of others. The energy is immediately detected and recorded by means of a network, which is, I am told, older than human history. How this network is run, by what method it records its data, is also not within my scientific grasp. It functions, they say, on simple mathematical codes duplicating themselves ad infinitum.

I could, if I wished to, create a meal I specifically know the ingredients of, create clothing, the fabric and design of which I am familiar with. I will not create Terence's tea or tea trolley. Terence likes to create his teas himself, bringing it all out with a flourish, the steaming pot, the tempting mix of tiny sandwiches, the sweet scones, and assorted cookies, which he calls biscuits. He wheels the trolley now from his kitchen to the low walnut table fronting the sofa, pours tea for us, and selects sandwich wedges, a raisin scone and biscuits for me. He knows I dislike the clotted cream, only spooning dollops of strawberry jam and lemon curd on the side of my plate, handing it to me. He fills his own plate, including the cream, placing it and fragrant cups of tea on the table, and sits down beside me.

I sip the hot beverage. "Mmn. Darjeeling. Must be four o'clock."

"It's always tea time, if you wish it."

"It seems so strange to be discussing your death in the midst of this charming repast."

"We can hold off if you'd like."

"No. Now's as good a time as any." When he hesitates, I urge him on. "It's something I have to deal with sooner or later. Getting over my subconscious fear of dying, I mean. Might as well be sooner. Go on."

Terence inhales a long steadying breath and lets it out slowly. "All right, then. I will."

I suppose I should start at the beginning (Terence says) or rather at the beginning of the end. The end as in death, as in kaput, as in deceased and done for. *Finis coronat opus.*

Which I found, of course, it was not.

It does seem strange, that I once believed in the Dickensian image of the ghostly afterlife. I found out belatedly, quite literally, (he laughs), that ghosts on the average don't wander about in shrouds, dragging chains composed of sins, or float mindlessly in a vacuum through the winds of time, unless the poor spirit is deranged. We think and feel emotions as strongly as you, perhaps more strongly. You might say we have more time for mental pursuits.

But we're not all that different from you. Oh, yes, we walk through walls and all that rubbish; our bodies, created by thought waves, vibrate at a much higher frequency than mortal science can yet record. And so most psychics . . . mediums . . . (he gestures towards me) expect us to perform those boring parlor tricks. Imagine someone finally achieving a state of existence in which we can learn to fully control our creative powers. And then being expected to prove that existence by moving a tea cup, or rapping on a table, or flickering the light in an electric bulb. We hate performing parlor tricks and often won't roll over and play dead, unless someone at a seance desperately needs reassurance that their deceased loved one is all right. We all have the need to love and be loved and worry over those we love. That doesn't stop because you're dead. It's being treated like mental incompetents that gnaws at our otherwise kindly intentions, and the fact that your world blames us for your own lack of communication tools. When we can't produce physical effects, which are difficult to effect, to say the least, many psychics with less scruples than you either fake it or cover it up with a lot of meaningless psychobabble with no resemblance to anything we've actually said!

(He huffs. Terence is very good at huffing when exasperated.)

Well, then, I promised to tell you how it was for me. Aside from having our work performed, we classical composers generally support ourselves as members of orchestras and by teaching music. After I graduated with an advanced degree in music composition, I lived with my parents and worked as an assistant professor at the local university. The few concerts of my music were politely received but, as I said, deemed too fantastically romantic for critical praise.

Then I landed the recording contract. The album earned me a bit more income and a small measure of fame outside of the strictly classical world. When I met Cecily, she became quite smitten with me and offered to move me into her flat. Cecily supported me, believing I was meant for greatness, and I came to love her for it. But genius needs patience and development in order to surface properly. My worst trait was a total lack of patience. Very little self-control.

I let the Muse control me. I should have controlled it.

She was a pretty bird, my Cecily, and I basked in the warm glow of her praise and fattened up a bit off her care and cooking. I wanted to please her, you see; she had such faith in me. It took the edge off of the pain caused by the straight-laced criticism by some reviewers of my work. Well, drink helped, too, but I finally regained my own faith in myself. I plunged back into a compositional frenzy, forcing inspiration to come, so oblivious to anything but my work, it began to frighten her. Too many mornings she awoke to find me unshaven and sleepless, still notating away at . . . the lost pieces we're hoping to recover.

When I announced their completion, she was vastly relieved. I did play the nocturne for her. She loved it. Some final work still had to be done, but Cecily rang up some friends of ours who were throwing a bash at their beach house in Blackpool that weekend and told them we'd be attending. She made me shower and shave, insisting that we were going on holiday, and I could finish up my musical projects when we returned.

So I cleaned myself up while she packed up our luggage. I stuck the symphony, the sonata, and the nocturne into a sturdy manila envelope, locking it securely inside the piano bench while she hauled our weekend bags out to the car.

As we drove out to Blackpool on that Friday morning in late Autumn, I cautioned her not to tell anyone of the new music. There are always kinks and glitches that have to be worked out when you actually play, record and listen back to a freshly created composition. We laughed about what a lovely surprise it would be to all our friends when the new works were professionally recorded.

We were very excited, but agreed to ban all shoptalk from the weekend; if our friends found that mysterious, we'd say I was unwinding from overwork. And Friday evening and Saturday morning and afternoon went by swimmingly, if you'll excuse the pun. It was on Saturday night, when our hosts threw their big party, when things soured.

The booze was flowing in a steady stream, and I was getting more than a bit plastered. They were also popping pills, and someone was passing around joints and a pipe of hash. I took a few tokes off a few joints, just to appear sociable, but I stayed away from the heavier stuff. Booze and an occasional smoke, that was for me.

Either I was more geared up in a drunken creative rush than I realized, or someone slipped something, an upper, speed maybe, into my scotch. Suddenly I felt this overwhelming pull, creative juices flowing, guiding me out of Beth and Robert's house. I found myself on their back veranda, its steps leading down to the sand and the whispering sea. Cecily came out to join me, and we watched the waves rising and falling, coming nearer, and turning to white muted foam as they broke along the shoreline.

"It's rough tonight," she said.

"No, it's lovely," I told her.

We stood there for a long while, my arm around her. We didn't kiss. I wish now we had kissed. She complained of being cold and said she was going in.

I told her I was staying out there. I was mesmerized by the motion of the waves.

"Don't stay out too long," she said. "You'll catch your death."

I nodded to her. The pounding of the breakers and the susurration of the frothing sea had turned into music inside my head. I heard the violins and the clarinets and flutes, and the drums . . . booming, crashing, a wild majestic dance.

Cecily squeezed my arm and walked across the veranda, sliding open the glass door, returning to the warmth. She hadn't known I wasn't in my right mind. And I was too keyed up, perhaps an aftereffect of working too hard, to know that sirens lured me with a madness too sweet to resist.

The sea quieted for a few minutes, its thunder diluted to a murmur, beckoning. I walked down the steps to the sand, kicked off my shoes and took off my socks. The sand felt cold beneath me, but invigoratingly so, not uncomfortable. I rolled up the legs of my slacks to my knees and walked unsteadily on the lumpy beach to its shoreline. The music continued inside my head, softening, gentle now, a flow of violins and flutes interweaving with piano.

And I began to dance, dance on the beach to the music the sea poured into me. When I reached the dampened shoreline, I drew back instinctively as icy waves rolled over my bare feet. I could have, at that moment, awakened from my dream, torn myself from the sea's enticing melody. A sober man would have.

But I was drunk, God knows what else. A new wave reached me, breaking about my feet, receding in a way that seemed to murmur, "Follow me." Other words came into my head. The sea became my lover, pleading for my human empathy, a symbiosis in things best left to metaphor and nature. "Yes, I am cold and cruel," she murmured, "but also beautiful and bold. Let me bathe you with my love, magnificent and dangerous. Let me play you my own music in its fullest grandeur, that you may carry it back with you, in your soul, and transmute it, that mortals might hear me and know me in all my splendor."

A feeling akin to sexual desire overwhelmed me. It may be hard for you to understand, but it warmed me. I wanted to embrace the sea in its entirety, as if it were a woman, to make love to it and bring back the essence of its secret beauty and, yes, to transmute it into a conjoined and sublime music.

I began to wade beyond the shoreline. The small waves broke against my thighs, my pants below the watermark wet sheets of icy cloth, but the sea's frigid kiss only excited me further. My hands cupped the cold seawater, and I drew them to my lips, my tongue sampling the salty broth. And the music swelled in me, crashing loudly with the waves as I pushed about in the ocean, a slow-motion ballet dancer, riding them.

I finally realized my predicament when a huge wall of water smashed down on me. My arms flailed insanely, my feet searched for bottom, but couldn't gain purchase. The undertow had caught me unaware; the distance to shore had more than doubled. And then clouds obscured the moon, dropping what little visibility there was into darkness. I tried to swim back to where I thought the beach lay, to safety. It seemed to be impossibly far off, an indistinct smudge, my sighting of it cut off again and again by rough, buffeting waves.

My lover, the sea, lunged at me, grasping me in icy jealous fingers. I felt my limbs growing numb from her cold assault.

As a dying man will do, I shouted for help, yet knew with a slow resignation that no one would hear me. A miracle, I thought desperately, let there be a miracle, a powerful wave to throw me back onto the shore, half-dead from hypothermia perhaps, but saved, rescued, to recover from this near-fatal folly.

And a second later, I knew there would be no miracle. I could not feel my body, no sensation at all, save a great tiredness, an irresistible weariness that lulled me into sleep.

I do briefly remember the sea entering my nose and mouth as I sank into it, that I tried instinctively to exhale it, to spit it out. Then I fell unconscious . . .

I may have spent minutes or possibly hours in that state of nonbeing. I haven't the foggiest. I only know that I came to as someone waking into twilight sleep might . . . mind groggy, body unresponsive, heavy. With a start, I realized I was floating haphazardly, limbs akimbo, in the sea, and was further shocked to see monstrous walls of water cascading over and onto me . . . and neither reacting to them nor feeling their impact.

I was dead. I knew this now and knew that somehow my consciousness had survived and was trapped within the bloating useless flesh. I wanted to run, to rush away from my physically deceased form, which now horrified me.

And suddenly I felt myself turn abruptly, as if fleeing from an enemy, and my consciousness seemed to stretch like a rubber band, its tail end snapping as if released by an unseen hand, forward momentum slinging me away, plunging me into the froth at a distance from my floating corpse.

I flailed once again, this time under water and, with a second shock, could feel the movement of my arms and legs. Forcing myself to calmness, I inspected myself.

I was butt-naked, but now felt no more than a light tingle in the frigid water. I appeared to have regained a bodily form, but it was wavery and indistinct, perhaps an effect from being underwater, or perhaps my new eyes weren't focused properly. I knew this body wasn't physical. It glowed, you see, all around, a variety of colors, mostly light—I remember yellow and orange—some darker ones, a deep purple flared off and on, dark moody sunspots against the brighter hues.

I tried to manipulate my new limbs to push upward, but the turbulent ocean impeded each movement. I wondered why I couldn't simply swim up to the surface, and suddenly found myself rising upward and breaking through the foam.

The clouds had blown away, the moon full and reflecting its glinting light on the waves. I spied my abandoned mortal form half a meter away to my right. It drifted toward the shore, now distinctly visible in the moonlight. I mentally bid my old self goodbye with a natural, I suppose, sadness, and wondered why I still bobbed between the waves. Wasn't there supposed to be a light, or some sort of pathway, to guide me to Heaven? A horrid thought hit me, that perhaps I was not bound for Heaven, and an even worse thought followed it: what if there were no Heaven or Hell, only an endless disembodiment, cut off from mortal needs and pleasures, death a dimensional trap door with no way out?

I continued to bob, riding the waves, wondering if I should head for shore and explore my options on dry land, when a bulky shape appeared far off, out at sea, its dark sleek lines punctuated with lights. One of those lights cast itself over the ocean, seemed to search the multitudinous waves as they crested and ebbed. The vessel drew closer. A large transport ship. Its search light passed over me, drew away, then returned to rest directly on me.

The ship advanced toward me. Some deck hands leaning over the rail heaved a long rope ladder over the side. I caught it firmly and wondered how a ghost could do that, let alone board a mortal vessel. Yet there wasn't any doubt. They not only saw me, they were there to rescue me.

"Hey, buddy? You gonna use that ladder, or you want to swim some more?" a curly-haired, burly man called down to me. His mates laughed. They were all dressed in seamen's white.

I hastily stuck my feet in the rope-rungs and hauled myself up. They helped me over the railing and onto the dry deck.

"How you doin', sailor?" the heavy-set fellow asked me.

"Much better," I answered, "now that I'm out of the sea."

A younger, blond-haired man grinned at me. "Abandoned ship for the last time?"

I was at a loss at first on how to answer him. "If you mean, am I dead, I suppose I am. The next question is: are you?"

"Of course," he answered.

"Then my next question *should be* what port this ship is heading for?"

The man laughed, and the others echoed him. "Not 'where can I get some clothes?'"

"I suppose that's on my mind," I said.

"If it is, then why don't you make them?"

Now I was totally confused.

"He doesn't know how," the burly man told the blond-haired man, then explained. "You're in the astral dimensions now, sailor. Thought is our creative medium. Just think the clothes you want to be wearing, and they'll appear. That's it. Just think of them, of yourself wearing them right now."

I looked down at my body. I had on my "comfortable" outfit: white turtleneck sweater, blue jeans, socks and brown loafers. "Thanks. Now can you answer my second question?" I said. "Where are we heading for?"

"Where do you want to head to?" the burly man replied, running quick fingers through his unruly curls. I was beginning to think he didn't know his own destination.

"Not Hell," I told him.

The man let out an amused chortle. "We don't pick up people heading downstream. Different company, arranges its own transport for that cargo."

"Well, then," I asked, "where *are* you heading? Heaven?"

He shrugged. "Heaven's got levels. You'll find out. And you gotta do intake. We usually ship you newcomers over to personnel, unless a relative or guide shows up to escort you there personally."

"What *is* this ship?" I asked him.

"Ocean patrol," he said quietly. "We pick up drowning victims. Help them get dry and warm, psychologically speaking, and through the transition."

"The death transition," I emphasized.

He nodded. A clipboard materialized in his hand.

"Well, I've got to go back," I told him. "I've left Cecily there on her own."

"Cecily will be fine," he assured me. "They've already discovered your body and have given her a sedative. She'll get over it. Besides, you can't go back." He wrote on the clipboard. "Terence Dearborn. Died November 30, 1968."

"Dear God!" was all I could respond.

"Yeh, the Big Boss is plenty special," he answered. "Come on, let's go below. Maybe someone's waiting there for you already."

I hesitated. "Below?"

He grinned again. "Below deck. Come on. It's all right."

I followed him to a stairwell, and we descended into the ship's belly. He led me to a large cabin, well-appointed with a shiny wooden desk and a plush sofa. A younger, dark-haired man in a blue dress uniform sat behind the desk. An older man with silver hair and sky-blue eyes lounged on the sofa, dressed in casual attire.

My rescuer ushered me in, announcing, "New arrival, Captain," and backed out, closing the cabin door behind him.

The Captain gestured to the sofa, which could easily fit two, possibly three. "Have a seat, Terence. I'm Captain Ellsworth of the SS Jordan. This gentleman is Dr. Patrick Callowhill. He's been assigned as your guide."

The good doctor—Patrick—turned to me as I seated myself. "How do you feel?" he asked.

"Confused," I said.

"There's a terrible sense of ultimate reality when you pass over from the mortal world," he agreed. "It's a shocker, and you have to adjust, more so than the loved ones left behind do. Of course, you will be reunited if you want to be. But by that time, you'll be helping *them* to adjust to crossing over."

"Let's just deal with helping *me* adjust right now," I suggested, nonplussed.

"Certainly," Patrick said. "Captain, we'll let you get back to business. Now, Terence, we're going to travel dimensionally. It'll be best if you simply take my hand, hold it and shut your eyes. I'll tell you when we get to where we're going. Then you can open your eyes."

"Rather like a surprise," I said, not quite trusting him, despite his pleasant and paternal demeanor.

"Not really," he explained. "It's just that newcomers tend to get vertigo if they keep their eyes opened. It's a vast dimensional universe with portals leading every which way and in all directions, and we haven't even left the ethereal levels paralleling mortal Earth." When I hesitated, he assured me further. "We travel by thought, willing ourselves from one place to another. There's nothing to it. Think of it as traveling in hyperspace without a ship. Pardon the expression, Captain."

The Captain leaned back in his chair, smiling softly. "No offense taken. We use the illusion that works."

Patrick held out his hand. I extended mine cautiously and felt his fingers and palm close around it firmly. "Now shut your eyes."

I did so and, an instant later, he said, "Open them now."

We were in a gentleman's study with bookcases lining one wall, a sturdy brown desk and chair, and a small typing table and typewriter on it. I studied the volumes of books: literature, predominantly on poetry and poets. "My library and office," he said proudly. "We're in my brownstone in the Back Bay section of New Boston."

"Aren't you a doctor?" I asked him. "Where are your medical

books, your equipment?"

"Oh, I let that go when I came here," he told me. "Some doctors do continue to practice after passing over, helping mortal doctors and their patients, and helping the astral folk up here to stay in balance. Medical knowledge is much more advanced up here, and we try to filter down as many breakthroughs as we can to Earth, as much as political traffic will allow. Mortals get all muddled up with cost effectiveness and controlled management. But I hung up my stethoscope when I crossed over. After fifty years of practice, I needed time for pleasures I couldn't indulge in fully as a mortal physician. I decided to fulfill a long-denied dream. I write and study poetry now. I've had three volumes published, plus a critique on the works of Wordsworth. Poetry, you know, has its own healing properties."

"Perhaps," I said. "That folder there, on your desk. Is that your poetry?"

His blue eyes regarded me softly, sympathetically. "No, that's your folder, Terence."

"Doesn't look quite full."

He sat down at his desk, waved his hand in front of it, and another chair appeared. I touched it experimentally. It felt solid. I sat down, bracing myself for the interview.

"It's not quite full because it's merely an agenda for this initial review, plus the standard documentary attachments. You'll review your Earthly life more fully when we go to the Library of God. The Seraphic records are housed there. The Library itself has a complete record of all human knowledge, quite fascinating. But, no, our task here and now is to decide the best means of balancing you in your current persona. For example, you've lived far too short a mortal life, and although some mortal souls learn all there is to know from a given lifetime, regardless of its span, you're not one of them. For example, you missed experiencing the one thing that makes all human lifetimes complete. Without it, all other things are fleeting and temporal. It's also one of the prerequisites before you can finish mortal lifetimes and exist eternally in the higher dimensions."

"What is it?"

"An ongoing and balanced love relationship. Some people learn it early in their lifetimes. Some take centuries to develop the ability to love without a lopsided selfish agenda. You were heading in the right direction with Cecily. Then your creative ego overcame your common sense and killed you. That's another failure."

"I didn't intend to kill myself."

"No, but in your musically metaphoric way, you wanted to couple with the sea. Genius and drink do not mix, Terence. It tends to release your subconscious desires into physical expression. Genius is a gift, not a privilege. It has to be controlled, or it can destroy you, overtly or covertly. You should have denied that sublime music the moment it began to lead you into danger. The sad thing is that you could have pulled those magical notes from Euterpe later on, safely in your flat. It might have taken a while to surface and perhaps been slightly flawed, not as perfect as the music you composed in your head while drunk and dallying in a fatal rendezvous with the sea, but both you and the music would have survived. Now no one in the mortal world will hear it, not as your composition. But that leads me to the second reason you have to go back. You've left unfinished business, loose ends that you'll have to find some way to tie up, complete."

"Go back?" I asked. "You mean, be reborn?"

He pursed his lips and shook his head slowly. "No. You're going back exactly as you are, in spirit form."

"A ghost," I said.

"A term they've created to explain or dismiss something they don't have the scientific advancements to understand comprehensively," he said, adding with a smirk, "Many learned men, now up here with us, once didn't believe they could exist beyond mortality, or that interactions between the mortal and astral planes were possible. Now they interact all the time, although their charges often aren't consciously aware of their presence. Of course, there are always some who feel it's for the best, that most mortals can't sense our presence. I personally disagree. I've always believed that a dose of eternity can never hurt."

"Must I go?" I asked.

"Yes, but don't look so glum. Once you've tied up those loose ends, you'll be free to direct your eternal life in any direction you find beneficial to yourself and others. And if you feel you need help or advice, just think of this room and me, and I'll connect with you and either guide you here or come to wherever you're at. Remember, thought is the key. To think it is to do it. And now I've got to run. I'm giving a lecture at one of our universities on the romantic poets."

"How are Lord Byron and Percy Shelley?" I asked him rather flippantly.

He pointed with his finger. "Down there. Geniuses! Always forget the ordinary stuff counts, too."

"They're in Hell?"

"No, no. They've reincarnated. Byron is a film director. He considered a career in the music industry, specifically the rock and roll field, but rejected it as too crude and obvious. Didn't want to lead a second-rate musical copy of his former lifetime. Figured critics would make unkind comparisons with no inkling of their accuracy. Figured the film industry would lend him greater diversity. Shelley's now a psychologist leaning heavily on Jungian theory, which he found suited his own philosophy to a T. Well, good luck, Terence, and I'm sure we'll talk again soon."

"Wait! What *is* this unfinished business I'm supposed to take care of?"

"I can't tell you everything, Terence," he said, gathering another folder from a drawer, possibly his notes for his lecture. "Some things have to be figured out by yourself. That way you'll straighten it out without gumming up the process with expectations."

"But how am I to know what it is, if you don't tell me?"

"Oh, you'll know. You'll know when you complete it. You'll *feel* complete. See you later." And with a smile befitting a doctor reassuring his patient, Patrick disappeared completely, off traveling to some astral university to lecture on two great English poets now living mortal lives as a director and a psychologist. Learning the ordinary things that count.

Life didn't seem fair.

I had, however, other concerns at that moment. Let Byron and Shelley work out their own eternal paths. Mine was still stalled in Patrick's study. There were no windows, and I could not get the knob of the one door in it to turn, notwithstanding feeling strange about wandering about Patrick's house without him, if I could.

"All right," I told myself. "Think yourself out of here." But where was I to go, where was I to begin my quest in search of those mysterious loose ends? It could be anywhere on Earth, and not necessarily somewhere obvious, such as London.

I decided to try Dorothy's philosophy from "The Wizard Of Oz," revising the script a bit, aiming for the general and letting fate take care of the specific.

I did leave out the heel clicking. Loafers didn't seem as magical as ruby slippers.

I stood up, clasped my hands behind my back, shut my eyes, and chanted fervently, concentrating with every ounce of mental energy I could muster.

"There's no place like Earth.

"There's no place like Earth!

"There's NO PLACE LIKE EARTH!"

Upon opening my eyes, I found there was indeed a place like

Earth, and I had landed at the intersection of Broadway and 42nd Street in New York City.

Somewhat unsteadily, I started across 42nd Street and suddenly saw a cab careening around the block, heading straight for me. I froze. There wasn't time to avoid impact. I threw my arms up in front of me and prepared for the worst.

The cab hit—I felt it only as a slight bump upon my stomach and my legs—then continued on as if no impact had occurred. But it hadn't gone straight through me. Some sort of interaction had taken place, for the contact flung me, somersaulting like a punched helium balloon, seven or so feet up in the air, where I remained for several minutes, drifting like some ghostly float above the traffic and pedestrians, who took no notice of my acrobatic rise in status.

That was when the awareness of death hit me, far more virulently than the cab had. I floated down to street level and peered at the clock high above Times Square. Noon.

I walked on, being ignored by the mortal humans about me. It seemed a fair guess that the first person to recognize my presence would also be a ghost. I couldn't be the only spirit sent back to Earth. There had to be a fair amount of the Earthbound hanging about, attending to their own unfinished business, especially in the "crossroads of the world." Manhattan seemed as likely a place to start my search as any.

With a bit of concentration, I transported myself to Central Park, needing some solitude, time to think. And time had somehow passed, speeded up a bit, on Earth. It was wintertime there now, the falling snow producing a curious sensation as it lit on me. No wetness nor chill was felt, but rather a sense of merging when it hit my body. It tickled, actually, in an inoffensive way. But my mind still held Earthly mannerisms not yet discarded, and I instinctively thought I should be covered up. Immediately, the cozy shelter of an overcoat appeared on me, a perfect fit, and the tickling sensation stopped. Pleasantly amazed, I further created high boots, gloves and a bright green scarf and, properly attired for the season, wandered about in the park, hoping to make contact with *someone* who might set me on the right course to tie up the mysterious loose ends of my former mortal life. And it was a mystery to me, how one could do such a thing as a ghost, an Earthbound spirit.

The snow had finally abated as I walked, the park grounds becoming slushy, but my footsteps left no impression in the snow nor splattered the slush. My feet and boots were now composed completely of mental substance and created no imprint nor affected the material world. The loss of such carefree interaction with physical life was sadly missed, even more so because I'd taken such simple pleasure utterly for granted when I was alive. It seemed a spirit could create new clothes with a single thought, but could not make the snow fly underfoot.

Of course, I met you in the park that day, having decided to play a trick on a pretty bird sitting on a park bench, enjoying the wintery beauty of nature and waiting for her boyfriend to show.

I was rather glad Richard was late that day, or you might not have been there when I tested your response to my ghostly touch.

All right, stop laughing. So it was a bit sensual. It was as much of a shock to me, that you reacted to it. And even more so when your mind connected with and locked onto mine, and you demanded to know who I was.

So I naturally followed you and your bloke around when he arrived. Didn't like him from the start, but you were the one I was intrigued by.

I've met other Earthbound spirits since then, trying to tidy up their own unfinished business. But I truly believe I was meant to meet up with you while you were living in New York City that year, trying to break into the music business and heading for an unsound marriage to Richard Warren, having his own New York adventure. He really should have stayed at sea. Some people are born with wanderlust, you know. Sorry, love, but you can't say I didn't warn you.

Anyway, now you know the entire story, my ending days on Earth, how I died, and the events that took place following my death until we met.

The only thing I never quite told you was how much of a greenhorn I was to the spirit world upon our initial meeting. It bothered me that you questioned my identity. That's why I kept humming strains of my music. You finally did find my record album, proving my existence, playing the measures I'd hummed to you. At that point, I began to believe that you might help me, that we could find the key to unlock the door to what I've left undone. Hopefully, we will. More tea?

I woke abruptly in the darkened bedroom, got up quietly and checked out the clock on the dresser. 3:00 AM.

—*Well, you've been told,*— Terence murmured telepathically. —*Do you remember it?*—

—*Yes,*— I answered sleepily, getting back into bed. —*Not only that. I could picture it as you described it. One thing puzzles me. Did you ever get your full review? In the Library of God?*—

—No,— he muttered, a tinge of unhappiness also coming through. —*Apparently I have to solve the mystery of my unfinished business first. I do hope that letter reaches Cecily. I've a strong feeling she's a key player . . . and I do miss her. But every time I try to contact her or think myself to her, something always blocks my passage. Perhaps that's another mystery we'll clear up.*—

-14-

Life on Earth. Ordinary to the unsuspecting mortal eye.

I successfully interviewed for the junior medical secretary position, and traveled downtown each weekday to my new job, Daniel left in my mother's care. My father's plumbing business absorbed the bulk of his waking attention, both days and evenings. When it didn't, he watched TV, read, or Mom and he escaped their newly crowded family life by strolling out to the neighborhood movie theater or, less frequently, the local night spot for dinner and dancing.

Ginnie continued nursing school, firmly entrenched in its arduous studies, and Fred muddled through junior high school, wishing he could major in basketball.

Life on Earth. No psychic events altering or upsetting the daily challenges it already presented. All talk of ghosts, unwise demonic lovers and angelic guides stopped, as if by some subliminal consensus. From time to time, my mother cast sidelong glances at me, eyebrows slightly raised to catch the slightest offscale nuance in my behavior. But I always remained rooted in the here-and-now.

It was what my mother needed and, to mortal appearances, was granted.

It was only in the secret caverns of the mind that echo out and beckon us through their portals, from midnight chime to morning's rude alarm, that I led another life.

I walk down the hall with Quatama and turn to enter the door marked *Auricular-Visual Recall.*

"No," Quatama says. "I have decided to use virtual reenactment."

I pause. "Virtual Reenactment?"

He nods once. "You will reenact your past, as if you were living it again—and—as if you were the other angelfolk who lived it with you. Access to your own as well as others' memories. Much faster.

"You have much spiritual ground to cover. Remembering your first immortal existence is important, but not the major crux of your karmic tapestry. It and other key lives were the foundation and building blocks of your eternal journey. But the journey is ongoing, and the crux of its value rests not in your memory of its past, but in your understanding of choices once made, and their impact upon the choices and decisions you must face now. Come."

He leads me to a small pleasant lounge and seats me on a comfortable sofa. His empty hand reaches out, and a small halo-like hoop is suddenly clasped within his fingers. "Thank you, Rosemary," he says, but no one else is there.

He places the glowing hoop upon my head. It encircles the crown snugly, from forehead and temples to the back of my skull. I feel a tingling sensation. My brain seems to vibrate, and I, as Leigh Ann, shut my eyes involuntarily, a mere second or two, and emerge thousands of years in the past, living my lifetime as Leianna once again.

The celestial sun rose high over Eliom on the day of my and Bael's betrothal. My father Michael was alternately swelled up with pride and beset by poignancy. He had said it only once, when we first awoke and broke our fast. His voice had been soft but audible, tinged with sorrow: "How I wish your mother could be here to see you betrothed." Then there was no more talk of Eve, lost to both of us.

We both knew where she was. All of Eliom knew. She and her brother Adam were trapped upon the Earth, metamorphosized by that dimension's inherent atomic nature, living as mortals. All of Eliom knew now of mortality and its cyclic structure of birth and death, of the tenuous souls of the Earthly environment, constantly renewed, constantly reborn.

Mortals were not angelic, but Eve and Adam, snared by the heavy molecular catalyst of Earth, were. They would revert back to their true selves. So the Creator had promised.

When mortal death released them, my mother and uncle would reclaim their angelic forms and return to the gentler bosom of Eliom.

I, too, wished my mother could be here. I felt very badly, knowing Eve would go through the painful release from mortal flesh, her internal organs ceasing their functions, her very breath—incredibly—snuffed out. Only then would her immortal soul drift free of the heavy spent flesh, reconstitute itself, and regain enough consciousness to travel the dimensional corridor back to Eliom.

But my worry over this, the ache it brought, was a long-suffered familiar pang. I put it aside now. It couldn't compete with the joy of becoming betrothed to Bael. The very thought of him brought an altogether different ache, a happier one, soon to be soothed.

Although the folk treated sexual desire as an adult privilege, they never confused it with the fuller union of marriage. The betrothal ceremony, in Eliom, was a prenuptial ceremony. The elders, in their wisdom, knew that love in its first bloom could also be in error. They also knew that love could not be denied. The betrothal marked the intention of the lovers, their choice to commit to one another. Full privileges were awarded to the betrothed couple following the ceremony. Sexual desire might blossom and be fulfilled between them. Their union was recognized and respected by the adult community. It was, in fact, one of the initiations into young adulthood.

After a year of betrothal, if no serious dissension or conflict had marred the union, the couple committed permanently in the marriage ceremony. But if, conversely, the betrothal was broken, the lovers, while now required by law to return to a chaste life, were still adults in the eyes of the community, reaping both the privileges and responsibilities of their coming of age.

-15-

There was one who, try as he might, could not throw off his nagging unhappiness at the thought of Leianna's betrothal to his brother. Their father's gentle jibe, as his sons clothed themselves for the ceremony, unintentionally pierced a wound Ashtoreth had hid for more than two years.

"Isn't it time," Lucifer had asked, "for my eldest to consider betrothal as well?"

His father had smiled, blond brows raised, blue eyes waiting for an answer. Seeing none forthcoming, save for Ashtoreth's obvious discomfort, Lucifer had thumped his eldest son's back with paternal understanding. "Never mind. Time will heal it."

Ashtoreth knotted his woven belt with an unnatural clumsiness. He felt Lucifer gaze at his fumbling fingers and hands. He drew attention away from himself, turning to Bael, busy tying the straps of his sandals. "How does it feel, getting betrothed?"

Bael, thinner and taller than Ashtoreth, but as firmly muscled as his older brother, looked up from his task. "Why, right now, it feels quite pleasant. And after the ceremony shall come much more pleasure indeed, which I look forward to."

His father and his younger brother Azmodeus laughed richly at his sexual innuendo, Az somewhat more raucously, but that was to be expected from a 15-year-old whose lack of experience was dictated by community law. Still, the youngest of Lucifer's sons had an extraordinary interest in the mysteries of love and questioned his elder brothers on it incessantly when their father was out of audible range.

He only received hearsay and speculation from them, as neither Bael nor Ashtoreth had any experience, also being constrained by law.

"And I'm looking forward to hearing about it," Azmodeus said, sitting next to Bael on the cot, his expression candid to the point of lasciviousness.

He did not see the lightning stroke of Lucifer's hand, landing a cuff to his ear. "You'll hear no more than you should," his father told him sharply, then lifted his gaze to his eldest son. "Ashtoreth. Explain the rule of privacy to him, for I fear he may act waywardly. He is too impetuous at best and has disgraced us before."

"Perhaps that is Bael's right, as it concerns him most," Ashtoreth suggested lamely, forcibly repressing the thought of Bael and

Leianna making love following their betrothal.

"You," Lucifer said, a touch of fire in his eyes, an implicit warning. None of his sons had ever questioned his orders in the presence of their brothers before. That was *his* rule, and Ashtoreth knew it.

Their father turned and drew aside the curtain of the large sleeping loft his sons shared. "Your mother is waiting for us below. Educate your brother quickly and join us, lest Leianna fault Bael for tardiness on their Betrothal Day."

The curtains fell softly into place behind him.

"Yes, Ashtoreth," Az said with a cynicism beyond his years, "educate me." His expression—heated stare, pursed sardonic smile—seemed to taunt, as if he knew Ashtoreth guarded his own secret, honorable if kept contained, shameful if exposed.

Ashtoreth glared at him, anger quickening in him, fists clenched. "Yes, that I will do, although I shouldn't have to. You know the rule of privacy, Az, although you've dared to break it once before."

"Thwarted in my innocent quest for knowledge," Az said, batting his eyelashes impishly.

"Stopped in your prying invasion," Ashtoreth corrected him. "It is forbidden to deliberately spy on the intimacy of those betrothed or married. That is why they shield themselves, joining their auras during union, that by the blurring and obscuring of their forms within the white light, an accidental onlooker is warned away and removes himself or herself without disturbing them."

"The fluffy white cloud that cloaks bliss." Azmodeus chuckled. His tongue flicked out and licked his upper lip, as if tasting the pleasures that hid within such a cloud. "The ones I saw forgot to cloak themselves in time."

"Until your presence alerted them," Bael cut in harshly. "Ashtoreth has explained the rule of privacy. It matters not whether lovers shield themselves quickly or tardily. It only serves as a protective measure, for *your* soul as well as for theirs. Curiosity is no excuse; if fueled by a deliberate desire to spy on lovers for your own pleasure, it becomes a grievous fault, punishable by law if the offense is repeated. I will not have you shamed in the village center, because of your youthful willfulness. Cease this dangerous path. The law affects all youth. You will have your day, as will Ashtoreth."

"Oh, no," Az disputed him airily. "Ashtoreth will never declare. She whom he would choose is already chosen."

Ashtoreth stiffened. Unheard by his brothers, a silent scream welled up in his throat. With a massive effort, he controlled himself and spoke clearly, forcing his words to come out sonorously and steadily. "Your youth allows me to forgive you, Azmodeus. You judge too swiftly and tell tales that are at best the mangled issue of your own imagination."

"I have eyes."

"Then your sight is faulty." He even managed a convincingly condescending smile, the humoring by the oldest brother of the youngest brother, all of four years his junior. "You don't know my intentions. You pretend to a knowledge you impatiently lack and think in causing contention to catch some missing gem we've hidden from you. A wiser course lies in admitting your ignorance and asking directly and respectfully for the answers you seek. You know nothing of my choices concerning marriage, not now nor those I might make in the future. And as far as the situation you so blithely ascribe to me, there is redress for it. Can you tell me what it is?"

Azmodeus offered him a sullen glance before studying the floor.

"Ah. You aren't taught law and its finer points for another year yet. It does allow for group marriage where there is conflict, when more than one person loves the same man or woman. But the remedy brings with it a larger, more serious commitment. It must be entered into bindingly by all involved. A serious decision and a serious choice."

Azmodeus listened dubiously, but the cocksure defiance had left his face. "Still, I have eyes," he said. "I have seen no group marriages in Eliom."

"There have been none for four generations. Our great-grandfather on mother's side and Chloe's great grandfather both loved the same woman. As I said, it is a difficult choice to remedy a difficult situation. But it is prescribed by law, if all parties consent."

"So? Are you? Going to have a group marriage?"

Ashtoreth noted the softly spoken boyish curiosity in the question, the caustic precocious edge gone from Az's voice.

"I have already made my choice," Ash answered as softly.

"Who . . ," Bael began and was cut off by Lucifer's sudden drawing aside the curtained barrier.

"Have you *finished* the lesson?" he asked Ashtoreth heatedly.

"Yes, father."

"And have *you* learned that which *he* taught?"

"Yes, father," Azmodeus said.

"And have *you* remembered that your betrothal takes place at sunset?"

"Yes, father," Bael responded dryly, "but it was you who requested that the lesson be taught and learned."

"I asked that the rule of privacy be explained. I did not ask the three of you to hold an extended forum on the subject. Your mother feared you'd taken root up here and couldn't move. Come."

Lucifer led the way down the broad wooden stairs descending from the sleeping lofts.

Ashtoreth caught Bael eyeing him, his face openly questioning the long-hidden secret Az's sharp observation had nearly brought to light.

At least the girl's identity—hopefully—still remained hidden. Az seemed less sure of it now. Perhaps he now believed he had missed the mark entirely, that another girl had caused Ashtoreth to nobly sacrifice his own needs.

He met Bael's probing glance and stared firmly back, his expression unmistakably answering Bael and demanding that the subject not be broached again. A silent communion passed between them, an understanding and an agreement.

This was Leianna's Betrothal Day as well. Neither he nor Bael would do anything to hurt her.

Ashtoreth had made his choice.

Bael would not question it again.

The village center had once been a large stretch of virgin meadow around which the dwellings of Eliom originally grew. It still retained its soft grassy carpet, although the blades were short and stunted, trod upon daily by the angelfolk.

The expansive circle served several needs each week: on the first two afternoons, it served both Junior and Senior Council members as a law forum; at midweek tables dotted its circumference as the Eliomese set up market, bartering and trading their foodstuffs and craftwork; during the final two weekdays, their youth learned a plethora of lessons, seated in smaller groups around different elders who instructed them in various subjects, according to the age level of each group.

At week's end, the village center became the site of festivities, of social and of spiritual gathering, the folk sometimes celebrating an unique occasion, more often simply unwinding with talk, entertainment, and community prayer.

The betrothal of Leianna and Bael would be conducted and celebrated this evening, as the village streamed into the clearing, carrying blankets for resting upon, and food and drink for the feast, their communal gift. The long, wooden plank tables had been set up to receive the tasty offerings the angelfolk placed upon them. Spreading their blankets, the folk sat down, relaxing, murmuring and awaiting the betrotheds.

The spirit master Yeshua arrived, and the murmuring increased. He cut a deceptively youthful figure as he strode along the wide path the angelfolk had left unclustered, his soft brown hair dappled with the last rays of sunlight, curling luxuriantly at the nape of his neck, his light blue eyes contemplative, the beardless contours of his cheeks and chin sharply defined and firm, yet hinting at the promise of a smile. The hem of his long brown robe rustled in the gentle summer breeze as he reached the middle of the meadow ground and waved his hand in an arc. The angelfolk cooed and aahed appreciatively as a flower-twined bower composed of two living, rooted trees materialized before him, their branches bending toward each other, interweaving together. Cherry blossoms grew thickly upon the branches, covering the bower and sweeping down the tree trunks in bright streamers.

The breeze picked up, playfully swirling the blossoms from the trees and depositing them erratically onto the pathway to the bower, laying a dotted carpet of pink and white against the green and yellow tufts of grass.

Four elders walked up the path: Ezekial, Elijah, Quatama, and his wife Mirisham. They stood behind Yeshua in a half-circle, Council witnesses to the ceremony and advisers chosen by the newly be-trothed couple.

An expectant hum rose among the spectators, heads turning toward the outlying rim of the village center. The betrotheds and their families mingled at the opening to the grassy, petal-strewn aisle leading to the flowering bower. Yeshua and the four other elders stood patiently, awaiting them.

In my white gossamer and silk betrothal robe, festooned over bodice and waist with an interwoven chain of morning glory, I stepped softly down the path of cherry blossom petals. In my left hand, I clutched two golden wrist bands, baked and sun-hardened out of the luminous sand of the Shore of the Seraphim. I felt the tiny ridges and minute bumps in each circlet, each band as thick as my thumb, yet polished to a sleekness my fingers ran smoothly over. The circlets were wide and would slip easily over my and Bael's hands, after Yeshua disconnected the bands, for the two had been crafted one within the other, linked with no visible break. Only a master could separate them intact, altering the skane, the energy, to permit one band to pass through the other band, and yet emerge intact.

I shivered, despite the mild evening, as my steps neared the bower. How symbolic, the separating of the bands. Recognizing the unity of the betrotheds, and yet their need to grow uniquely, as individuals. Bael and I would, following the ceremony, come together as one, intermingle with each other, fuse, and yet still come apart, changed but separate once more, carrying the memory and the commitment of that unity.

I reached the bower and knelt before it, head held high, smiling up at Yeshua, who solemnly but pleasantly returned my smile with one of his own. I barely saw my father, my Uncle Gabriel and my Grandmother Deianna, whose steps had followed my own, moving to my right, taking their places in front of Ezekial and Elijah, but I felt my father's eyes on me, and I blushed. A twinge of sorrow over my mother's absence rose briefly in my throat, more for my father's sake than my own, for I knew he felt her loss on this day of all days. But then I felt Bael approach and saw him from the corner of my eye, kneeling down to my left.

Moving past him came Affaeteres, Lucifer, Ashtoreth and Azmodeus, my young tormentor, for once not indulging himself in salacious remarks and improper behavior. They took their places quietly before the solemn figures of Quatama and Mirisham.

Yeshua offered his right hand to Bael's left, his left hand to my right. We grasped Yeshua's hands. He began the ceremony.

"And so we are come here to witness the betrothal of Bael and Leianna who have chosen this day to profess their love and their decision to commit their lives to each other. And whosoever the Creator has touched with love, let none deny them the right to walk their life paths together." Yeshua gazed at me softly. "Will you, Leianna, abide by your decision to cleave to Bael for a year?"

"Yes."

Yeshua turned his gentle azure eyes to Bael. "And will you, Bael, abide by your decision to honor Leianna with your faithful troth?"

"I will," he answered softly, and I felt the heated pull of his nearness.

Yeshua took our two hands, Bael's left and my right, and drew them inward, causing us to turn towards each other, then released Bael's hand. "Leianna, place one circlet over Bael's left hand and wrist." I did so, the connecting bracelet hanging loosely down. Yeshua released my hand. "Bael, place the remaining circlet over Leianna's right hand and wrist." With his free hand, my intended slipped the remaining circlet on, our hands drawn inward and upward, nearly touching, by the interlocking bands.

Yeshua grasped our banded hands within both of his. "So you are bound, entwined, one within the other, of your own desire and choice, and declare your love and trust for each other before the knowing Eye of our Creator, and of the angelfolk assembled. Yet separately you are whole, created uniquely, and you must never lose that spark of creation that is you, nor submerge that special spark you each are, not even in the name of love, or in the union it brings. For love can only survive if its glow enhances, never if it reduces.

"And so, though you are linked, you are also separate, and, in joining, give of each other, each making the other greater, but never reduce the other nor take away from each other. And so, as separate entities, so shall you be stronger for your declaration to each other, for you shall now carry each other as you live and learn and grow together.

"In this way do your souls mingle, share and enhance each other from this day forward until the end of the betrothal year. At which time you shall return the circlets upon better judgment, or keep them and declare your love in eternal marriage."

Still grasping our hands, Yeshua slowly drew them apart. The tension in the entwined bands held for a few brief seconds. Then a soft yellow glow enveloped the point where the bands joined. Its light spread upward, around, down and under, following the circumference of the bands, meeting its own radiance once more at the joining.

Yeshua gently widened the distance between my and Bael's hands. The golden bands slid free of one another. Yeshua drew our hands together again, until Bael and I clasped them, right and left, the freed betrothal bands resting separately on our wrists.

"Go forth, from this moment on," Yeshua said, his arms outspread in supplication, "with joy for each other in your hearts, with respect for each other in your minds, and with love for each other in your souls. Your betrothal is recognized in Eliom by the angelfolk and by the Creator as is the maturity which it signifies and which we celebrate." Yeshua smiled at us, his chest rising slightly in a barely perceptible sigh. "You may rise and embrace each other, and then we shall embrace you as your kin and celebrate your coming of age in the name of love."

Bael rose first, reaching out to clasp my other hand and help me to my feet. I was grateful. The excitement of the betrothal ceremony and his nearness made me giddy.

His left hand reached down, the betrothal band dangling from it, and stroked my cheek. I looked up, my heartbeat rapid, my breath nearly stilled, at the shining intensity in his dark eyes. He bent, his lips taking what little breath remained away and then returning it. Passion bloomed briefly in our kiss, and then he pulled away, as if aware of the eyes of the angelfolk upon us. Grasping my hands, he turned to Yeshua. "Thank you."

Yeshua returned his smile. His eyes held a knowing glint. "May you return to renew your vows."

Bael nodded, and placing his arm around my shoulder, led me to his family, pausing before Lucifer, Affaeteres, Ashtoreth and Azmodeus. Each in turn clasped his free hand and kissed my cheek. Ashtoreth's kiss was gentle but firm, and I felt the warmth of our long friendship within it. I couldn't avoid stiffening as Azmodeus, not much taller than myself, leaned toward the side of my face, and was relieved when he merely pressed his lips quickly to my skin and backed away. I cast a quick unavoidable glance at him and caught those lips curling upward disdainfully.

The promenade continued: accepting the glad hands and soft busses of my father, uncle and grandmother, of Quatama and Mirisham, of Ezekial and Elijah.

Bael then led me through the living bower, beneath its blossoming intertwined branches to the great huzzah of applause and congratulations from the assembled angelfolk. His arm still possessively around me, we veered off the petal-strewn path, interweaving through the smiling boisterous crowd as our well-wishers moved toward the long plank tables laden with sweet cakes, with tangy vegetables, fruit and nut dishes, and with ciders and wines.

Bael and I, along with our families, Yeshua and the four spirit masters who were our betrothal guides partook of none of it yet. We continued greeting every well-wisher, receiving their effusive praise, their smiling nods.

The sun had long set when our betrothal party finally made its way to the refreshments. A crowd formed around us as Cornelius, a round, apple-cheeked spirit master, handed Bael a pitcher of honeyed cider and slid two wooden bowls across the table to him. Grinning, Bael poured the rich liquid into the bowls, handing one to me. I accepted it gratefully. He picked up the second bowl, and we raised them to our lips simultaneously, drinking down the sweet fluid. The crowd shouted and laughed, showing their approval.

Bael took my hand, strolling by the plates and bowls still holding generous portions of food, selecting this morsel here, a spoonful or two from there, filling both of our bowls. He held a tasty piece in front of my mouth, which I opened to receive his offering, laughing inwardly at the innuendo in the gesture and his eyes. Then the onlookers laughed aloud when he licked his fingers with pointed slow exaggeration, and even I could not help joining in. The cause of this spicy but good-natured humor was even less immune to his own jest. He nearly upset the bowls of food he held, shaking with laughter as well. I took one bowl from him, my fingers sliding gently across his to calm him and restore some dignity to the evening. Although the festivities permitted such jesting, I appreciated the growing dusk. It shadowed the blush heating my cheeks.

"Are you uncomfortable, my beloved?" he asked me suddenly.

"No," I murmured. "It's just the headiness of the day—and the newness of our finally becoming betrothed."

He bent close to my ear. "And perhaps the ribaldry?"

I pursed my lips in a dismissive smile. "No. I know it's all in fun. Well, perhaps the thought of . . . will it be all right . . ." I stopped in confusion, unable to express my worries about our impending union, having no experience, neither in the act, nor in the knowledge of what might go awry.

"You might have to wait for the morning to concern yourself over such things. The festivities may go on for quite a while yet. When they end, you may be too weary to offer me more than a lingering kiss at your father's door. Or if we do walk out to the darkened Garden, you may fall asleep and leave me with only faint moon and starlight as companions in my loneliness." Then, in a rush of breath, "I wish we were married already, not only betrothed, and a bed awaited us in a thachka of our own."

"One cannot come before the other," I said. "If need be, we can wait until tomorrow." Silently, I welcomed the delay, time to compose myself and face the new and wondrous privilege of lovemaking with calm, believing all would go well and I would please him. I wondered if Bael harbored such concerns. For all of his apparent self-assurance, he, too, was virginal.

"Tomorrow then," he said, and foraged a bit nervously, I thought, in his bowl with a soft pink stalk of tangari. Hollowed at the tip, he spooned some greens into its depression and ate them slowly. I used my own stalk to attack the tasty fare in my own bowl, my hunger finally surfacing.

"Mmn," I murmured between mouthfuls.

"Will you say that to me when we join?" he whispered.

I chewed the apple and nut pastry, savoring it before swallowing and answering him. "If my feelings for you now are any evidence, that and more. I love you, Bael." The intensity I felt upon speaking those words made me wish the festivities over and done with, to be free to do as we wished, as was traditional following the betrothal ceremony.

We ate and drank and wandered among the folk, conversing amiably. The night deepened. Bael's nearness and my knowledge that restrictions no longer hindered our desire for each other made me restless. As we sauntered toward my father, speaking quietly to Cornelius near one perimeter of the village center, Bael suddenly grasped my arm, leading me to Michael and the cheerful rotund spirit master. "Father Michael," he greeted him formally and nodded to his companion. "Cornelius."

"Bael," Michael acknowledged him. "You must be the happiest young man in Eliom this night." He smiled fondly at me. I felt another blush warming my cheeks from his praise as I smiled back at him.

"I am, sir. We came to tell you Leianna is feeling a bit lightheaded from all the festivity. We thought a leisurely walk in the Garden would refresh her, especially in the quiet of the night."

Michael studied us critically. I could not help grinning back, knowing Bael's excuse was merely a ruse. My true complaint, which he shared, was obvious. The corner of my father's mouth lifted, half-smile, half-smirk. He turned back to Bael. "Then I would say: 'seek the remedy.' I'm sure you can find your way back to my thachka when the night and its quiet has worked its wonder. I notice the celebration in your honor is waning here. The village center has regained more clearing."

"Yes. Many have taken their leave of us. My hand is worn from its grasping of others' in farewelling and well-dones."

Michael laid his own hand on Bael's shoulder. "Then go. No need to shake mine in parting. It's late, and this grassy expanse will soon bear no more than the moonlight upon it. Those still around will understand, I'm sure." He leaned over and kissed me on my cheek, then straightened with a quick quiet glance to Bael. The glance was telling, even to me. *This is my daughter. Treat her well.* Bael's own eyes softened and turned to gaze at me, answering him.

"Come." My betrothed offered his hand. I took it and, with a final smile to my father, we left the village center, walking through night-hued Eliom, two soft midnight shadows, my heart hammering in anticipation, my desire heightening as we left the village and trod the pathway together to the dark Garden.

-16-

Azmodeus had watched them walking away from the village center.

What would they do, aside from the basics, which he knew about?

But how would it feel? Was the excitement he felt in his groin and chest at the sight of a pretty, well-developed girl and the thought of committing the act as pleasant as it got? Did it burn like a fire and then, fulfillment reached in the final tearing thrust, sizzle out and die down into cold dampened ash, like cooking stones his mother doused with water after the meal was heated and consumed?

Az had no experience, that was true, but the promise of being touched, of flesh upon laboring flesh, lent realms to his imagination.

If he spied on anyone else again and was caught, the auric reconstruction, enforced upon him publicly in the village center, would only be the beginning of the price he'd pay. But would his own brother haul him up for judgment? No, Bael would not allow that to happen to him. Possibly knock him silly and do some considerable damage. But not publicly. That Azmodeus was certain of.

His eyes traced the steps Bael had taken, leaving the village center with his shapely betrothed. Az wondered if Bael had escorted her to her father's thachka. But, no, something in the way the lovers moved, as if in unison, even in the few minutes before their figures dwindled, disappearing into the village, was an unintended signal to Az's sharp eyes and instincts. He knew where they were heading.

He was standing near his father as Lucifer quietly conversed with Mirisham.

Az interrupted their talk of the betrothal, of Lucifer's satisfaction with Leianna. "Father, I'm going to start home now."

Lucifer paused in mid-sentence, staring at his youngest, nonplussed. "We'll be leaving shortly. Why don't you find your mother and Ashtoreth, and we'll go together?"

Az stared back, thwarted. Lucifer's distrust showed plainly on his face. "Yes, father." Disgruntled, Az started off in the deepening dusk. He spied Yeshua and his mother nearby, engaged in an animated discussion, and ambled sullenly over to them. Had he the gift of Yeshua's good looks, he wouldn't waste them in a stupid vow of celibacy. There were plenty of other ways to please the Creator as well as oneself.

He enjoyed breaking up their conversation, sneaking up behind them in the gathering gloom. He wondered if his mother, resplendent in an embroidered lavender silk robe, found Yeshua attractive. "Mother. Father says we should find Ashtoreth and go."

Yeshua stopped speaking. Both Affaeteres and the handsome elder turned around. "Greetings to you as well, Azmodeus," Yeshua said, "although you haven't said two words to me during the evening's festivity."

"No, I haven't. But now I've said . . . eight."

"I'm doubly rich, twice," the spirit master answered him, one eyebrow cocking, making him appear critical despite his gentle tone.

Azmodeus didn't like the look in those bright azure eyes. Lucifer would hear of any insubordination to Yeshua, if insubordination it was pegged. "It's hardly every day one's brother gets betrothed. A strange feeling and one that didn't lend itself to words for me. Not many. No offense intended, elder."

"None taken," Yeshua replied. "You must accept those feelings, for we cannot hold the universe in stasis. It isn't static, and those we love must be allowed to undergo necessary change." He turned back to Affaeteres. "It's difficult for some to accept change. There is always the risk of losing status and facing new challenges."

His words struck Az like a fist. "I'm not afraid," he blurted out, causing both his mother and Yeshua to stare down at him wide-eyed.

"I did not say you were," Yeshua said. "Merely that you may find it difficult, sharing your brother's affection and love with a new person. With Leianna. It may help you to accept Leianna in her new status . . . as your potential sister. You may then realize you not only retain Bael's love, but gain her affection as well."

Az felt a momentary loss for words, but Yeshua's logic had not produced the altruistic response Az felt sure the spirit master had hoped for. Anger and dismay crawled in Az's gut again. He struggled to control them. "I've got another brother," he answered flippantly. "Kept one more around just in case."

"I'm sure both brothers love you," Yeshua said soothingly. He glanced momentarily at Affaeteres.

Her face and bearing remained gracious and unruffled. "It is quite late," she said and clasped Yeshua's hand lightly and briefly. "Thank you for conducting the betrothal ceremony, Yeshua."

"I wished to. I will pray to the Creator to guide Leianna and Bael."

Affaeteres nodded and put her arm around Azmodeus, leading him away with her. "I'm sure we'll be dancing at their wedding in the new year. A restful night to you."

Smiling, Yeshua turned and headed to his own small thachka near the pathway to the Garden.

Azmodeus wiggled away from her light hold. "Mother, I'm *not* a child."

Irritation finally showed in Affaeteres, a tightening of the muscles around her pursed mouth, her relaxed posture suddenly stiffening as she walked, a slight hunching of her shoulders and neck. "I should hope you are not one anymore. Although you have suns and moons to go until you consistently act as if you are not."

Twice belittled, first by Yeshua, now by his mother. He clumped angrily along, keeping pace with her, although he felt like hanging back, like slipping into the nearly full night to attend to his true interest. The village center, now nearly emptied of guests, played host to gentle night winds. One capered around Az, ruffling his blond locks, billowing the hem of his robe and then releasing it, nearly tripping him as he plodded on blindly in his single-minded slump.

They spied Ashtoreth, standing beside Lucifer and Mirisham, joining into their conversation. Quatama, Mirisham's husband, also stood nearby, listening.

Az hated them all . . . well, maybe not Ashtoreth. Ash was all right, even if he was a bit of a rooted stalk, so dependent upon pleasing everybody and following their dumb rules, always willing to bend if the wind didn't blow in the direction of his own desires. Azmodeus even felt a little protective toward him, despite Ashtoreth's being *his* oldest brother.

And maybe he didn't hate Bael. Az couldn't blame him for taking that pretty slip of a thing for his betrothed. Perhaps that shy and submissive nature of hers wasn't such a bad thing after all. It would certainly help Bael to train her and make her compliant to his will. It was just so irksome when seen out of that context. There wasn't much to her from what he'd seen so far, outside of her looks. Accept her as a sister? Pah!

And Quatama? There was one he had to be careful around . . . looked right into you and saw things you didn't want him to see. Az carefully blanked his mind as he approached his father and brother and the two spirit masters.

"Ah," Lucifer said, "I see you've found your mother. I believe we'll wish you a good night, Quatama and Mirisham."

"And we, you," Mirisham said and took her husband's hand.

They exchanged parting smiles, even Azmodeus, who kept his fixed upon his lips until his family crossed the perimeter of the village center and headed along the pathways to their thachka. Az kicked up dust and stones as he walked. "I suppose Bael will be home by now," he said to no one in particular.

"Possibly," his father answered him. "Possibly not. A newly betrothed couple has much to talk about."

Az nearly snickered, repressing the urge quickly.

"Or simply needs time to be together," Ashtoreth put it more honestly.

"Are you angry," Affaeteres asked suddenly, and when no answer was forthcoming: "Azmodeus?"

"I'm sorry, Mother. I did not realize your question was directed to me."

"Well, now you do know. Are you? Angry?"

"About what?"

"Your brother's betrothal."

"No. Confused perhaps. It *is* a change."

The soft aura of the night lamp, glowing out the energy within, illuminated the pebbled path leading to their doorway. Lucifer opened the door, holding it for Affaeteres and Ashtoreth. Azmodeus followed them, but his father's quick touch on his arm halted him. Az looked up hesitantly. While his father's eyes were not unkind, they held him as firmly as the roots hold the tree. "Yes, father?"

"It *is* a change," Lucifer agreed in a low voice that suggested his words were privately meant for Azmodeus alone, "but one you will get acclimated to." He gestured with his free hand for Az to go inside, entering after him and shutting the wooden door.

Within the thachka, smaller night lamps had lit automatically as the family entered their home. Az climbed the stairs to the sleeping loft and found Ashtoreth had already disrobed and was lying on his cot, waiting for him.

Bael's cot was empty.

"Do you want to talk about it?" Ashtoreth asked.

"No."

Ash lay down, accepting his refusal.

Az shed his own robe and sandals and stretched himself out on the cot. As his head came to rest against the soft linen, the night lamp sitting on their window ledge flickered out. Were he to rise again, the glow of its energy would brighten again. And what if, at that moment, Ashtoreth awoke?

There was no safe way to sneak out to Bael and his intended.

Azmodeus shut his eyes, swallowing his frustration. And then opened them, the bud of a new thought unfurling in his mind.

At worst, he would tell his eldest brother he was restless and un-

able to sleep. And have to accept the fact of his curiosity going unsatisfied.

At best, however, Ash would remain asleep.

Az waited until the household seemed quietly at rest, then rose
from his cot and put his robe and sandals back on. Ashtoreth shifted
but didn't awaken, their night light flickering out as Az left their curtained alcove. He crept down the stairs. The first floor night lights
shone briefly and then went out like stars in the wake of the sun, one
after the other, as Az crossed the room and went out the door, slipping
into the night.

-17-

Hands held, their bodies otherwise separate but straining as if with an internal sensual fire in their need to join completely, Bael led Leianna through the Garden toward Sky Lake. A wry smile creased his lips, remembering how, at that lake, one annum ago, Leianna had finally revealed her feelings for him. The incident had initially embarrassed both of them, but it had been her signal, and he had answered her with both alacrity and relief.

Both had been afraid to voice their feelings. Both had feared rejection, but more so Bael, who believed Leianna's shy nature would impede his courtship. And one other fear: her cheerful animated friendship with Ashtoreth. But Ash had made no move to declare for her, and Bael had waited nervously for some small gesture showing Leianna reciprocated his own feelings, that might allow him to press his own suit and claim the prize Ashtoreth had forfeited.

Her defense of him at Sky Lake, the summer before, had freed them both of their fears of unrequited love, but not from constraint. The elders had declared they must wait a bit longer for betrothal, until Leianna's sixteenth year and Bael's seventeenth. Her father had requested this.

The folk in Eliom discovered, during the long—or so it felt to Bael—waiting year, the richness and intensity of his affection for Leianna. He appeared at her thachka whenever he could to escort her wherever she need go. He plucked ripe flowers from the Garden, making intricate bright gifts of them for her, sometimes simply bunching them and tying the blooms with a thread of fiber, on occasion constructing loose lattice holders out of short flexible branches woven together, placing the flowers in intricate patterns through the lattice holes and tying their stems together.

There was a possessiveness to his newly gained freedom to lavish her with attention, but she seemed to thrive on it. He had fielded many a compliment from the folk, on how Leianna had broken through her earlier shyness, dazzling almost everyone with her seemingly perpetual smile and newly acquired poise. She had always shown a caring attentiveness to those around her, but now a gracefulness pervaded her thoughtful concern for others.

He had always known she would be a wife a man would place great value on. And although that was another year off, their commitment had been publicly declared and freedom to express it had been granted.

He wanted to make love to her with an intensity superseding anything he'd ever desired before. His hand clasped hers more tightly, somewhat nervously, he admitted to himself. His father had advised him, one week before the ceremony, on the finer points of love-making, not only on the specifics of sexual union, but also on the niceties, the touches, gestures and words that might wash away their awkwardness and fears. Bael hoped to make his and Leianna's first union a memorable treasure they would share, both as betrotheds and again as husband and wife in the future.

At the far side of Sky Lake, the dunes gave way to brush and then an enclave of trees. Small clusters of azalea and honeysuckle bushes fronted a wide pool of water, small sister to the lake. It formed a pocket of privacy where lovers might shield themselves.

Bael sat Leianna and himself down on the soft expanse of soil and sand beside the pool, well behind the flowering greenery. The night sky was just beginning to lighten, the Eliomese moon lower in the star-flecked sky. Leianna looked up at it. "A different moon from Earth's," she said, "or so I'm told."

"What makes you think of Earth? Do you think our happiness will reach down there?"

Her lips held the smallest sliver of a smile. Her face was bathed in silver moonlight, her brown eyes gleaming, the soft tumbled curls of her auburn hair, fiery highlights muted, on her shoulders. "I was thinking of my mother, of how she might have felt the first time following her betrothal. And I wondered if she might be looking up right now, seeing the Earthly moon, and if she thinks of me and how I fare. If we perhaps are thinking of each other at the same time."

At first Bael remained silent, wondering if her thoughts of her mother indicated her uncertainty at her own inexperience. He felt the unseen presence of Eve in Leianna's tone, saw it like a vaguely remembered reflection in his beloved's placid face. He reached over and touched her cheek, drawing his fingers down to her chin, gently lifting it, causing her to look up at him. "Perhaps she is. But she would know that you are well-loved and provided for. And when she returns, she will know I am the one who will love and provide for you for all eternity."

Her mouth opened at that moment, not, he knew, to speak, but as an offering. He met it with his own, and they drank of each other, tongues exploring as their arms encircled one another.

He drew away from her, holding her by her shoulders. "Sit still," he said, and she smiled at him, unmoving, as he began to untwine the sturdy garland of morning glory from her bosom and waist, releasing her soft robe. It loosened in folds around her shoulders and waist, and he reached out and drew the cloth down her arms, exposing the plump curves of her breasts, tinted with white and charcoal in the growing encroachment of the dawn.

He ignored their temptation for a moment or two, as his father had instructed him. Instead, he bent again to press his lips to hers, then sat back, seeing how her nipples rose, hardening in expectation. Now his fingers lightly explored them and the soft mounds radiating out from their circumference. He cupped their weight, his fingers and palms lifting them upward, and he bent his head to taste their sweetness and texture. He resisted the urge to flit from one to the other, and concentrated fully on one breast before releasing it from his hungering mouth to discover the pleasures of the other. He varied the pressure of his lips and tongue, his hands grasping then caressing Leianna's arms and shoulders with the lightest of touches as he suckled.

Finally he lifted his head to hers. She nearly bruised him with the force of her returning kiss, then lay down on the soft ground, tugging gently at his arm, wanting him to lie beside her.

"No," he said, nearly breathless. "We must cloak ourselves, first."

"Why?" She smiled dreamily up at him as he leaned beside her. "There is no one about at this hour. No one will see us."

"It is prescribed," he said softly. "A certain remedy against the unexpected."

"If you say we must. Only hurry. My limbs and belly are exploding with wanting you, and it is time for me to become a woman, my love."

"You already are, my love."

"Not yet. Put the light of privacy around us and return to your gentle ministration." She giggled, the sound as light and melodic as a rain shower.

He smiled down at her, amused. "I can only create my own, Leianna. You must build your own light, and then together we must join them."

"Build my own light?"

Her confusion shocked him. "Surely your father . . . you weren't instructed?"

"No. Is it done differently by a woman?" He saw the anxiety in her face.

"No, no. It must be the same. Let me teach you. It's similar to drawing out our energy to nurture the plants of the Garden. We build an energy field around ourselves and then join our auras within it."

He instructed her to concentrate on transferring her bodily energy, drawing it out through the pores of her skin. After two failed attempts, a white cloud finally began forming separately around each of them.

"But, Bael—now I can't see you."

"Nor I, you. As it should be. Now reach out your hands, and I will clasp them within the cloud."

She appeared to be shaped of sparkling hazy light, extending two smaller clouds of light toward him. His own arm and hands, even as they moved to meet hers, seemed just floating mist. Yet within the wisping camouflage, their hands met solidly, flesh touching, muscle and bone beneath.

"Now," he said, "you know how you expand your aura when we build upon the plants' energy in the Garden to help them grow. Instead of placing your auric energy around the plants, you must now send your auric energy *into* me, and I will send mine into you."

"Into you?"

"Yes. Send it through the center of my palms. That is the conduit."

"Will it hurt?"

"No. We will simply be able to see one another within the energy cloud we've hidden ourselves inside. Ready?"

He couldn't see her face nor did she answer him verbally, but he felt a small hesitant flow of energy enter his palms. The flow became clearer, stronger, and he began to direct his own auric essence into Leianna's hands. The feeling it created nearly overwhelmed him, but he steadied himself and her, wrapping his fingers around hers, palms tightly pressed, arms extended between their seated bodies.

Slowly, the white mist seemed to recede, slowly exposing them to each others' eyes, the cloud settling around their bodies, surrounding them and covering them as if they were one entity within it, but no longer separating them visually.

"I can see you again," she giggled again. "I can even see somewhat beyond the mist that covers us."

"Yes, but none can see within it to us. They will only see the cloud of privacy."

"How long will it last?"

"Until the energy we expended dissipates, both in the cloud and inside ourselves when we joined our auras. Enough time. Long enough." He closed the gap between them and drew her firmly against him, his lips finding hers.

She pulled him down on top of her, legs spreading in anticipation, her fingers trying to undo his robe.

"No, wait," he gasped, sliding off to lie beside her. "First, I must make you ready."

"I *am* ready, Bael," she said, sounding impatient and needful.

"You think you are, but you are *not.*" He raised himself on one elbow. "There is more to love than the final joining. Lay still. Let me show you."

"How do you know these things?" she teased him.

He was thankful that she couldn't see the warm blush he felt spreading across his cheeks and nose. "A man knows these things," he answered, "is taught them before betrothal."

"So much to learn," she murmured dreamily. "Instruct *me* then."

She looked so enticing, waiting supinely for him, her breasts little hills for his tongue and fingers to climb and descend, and her seat of mystery, tufted with golden hairs hiding the entrance to her pleasure, awaiting him, awaiting his mastery.

His own control was slipping; he wanted nothing more than to plunge himself into her and reap the ecstasy of that contact alone. His betrothal robe, still covering him, felt cumbersome, but if he removed it, his own needs might overwhelm him, destroy this delicate dance of sensual heightening he hoped to perform on Leianna. His own pleasure was only as valuable as her pleasure. His happiness without her own was tainted, would forever be found wanting.

Crouching between her legs, he slowly drew his hands caressingly up each of them, stopping before his fingers reached the edges of her labia and then repeated this a second time, then a third time. She moaned, her back arching, and he allowed his fingers access to the labia, gently massaging the inner folds, pressing closer and closer to the vaginal entrance, noting with satisfaction the moistness accumulating there. His fingers then slid upward, along the folds, to press gently on the vulva, and then claim her clitoris, squeezing softly on either side of it, until it hardened, becoming erect, awaiting his final act of preparation.

He now knelt, as if in supplication, for he found her seat of mystery a beautiful extension of the Creator, a mystery now opened, displayed in all its wonder before him. Lowering his head, he carefully surrounded her small clitoris with his lips, pursing them, suckling it, pulling backwards on it and releasing it, and then reclaiming it to begin his obeisance to her womanhood again. He heard her sharp intake of breath, felt her fingers fluttering in his hair. More vaginal moisture touched his chin, and he pressed it gently against her aroused flesh.

She arched her lower back and hips again, a sigh escaping her and then a small whimper as he flicked his tongue against her clitoris, a final salute, and brought his mouth fully against her vagina. His tongue darted in, tasting her wet sweetness, and her squirming became frantic.

His mouth relinquished her then, for his erect penis, engorged with desire, throbbed almost painfully. With equally frantic fingers, he pulled at his knotted belt, finally untying it and drawing his betrothal robe off. Naked, he leaned over her, seeing her intense need of him in her eyes, her pupils enlarged, shining as he hovered above her.

"I'll go slowly," he whispered. "Tell me if I cause you discomfort."

"Enter me, please!" she murmured back. "Let us be one!"

He guided the head of his penis into her vagina, the feel of it against his manhood sending shocked thrills through his groin that continued to course like a fierce wind throughout the rest of his body. He groaned as he pressed himself farther into her; slowly, slowly, he told himself, forcing himself to maintain control against his own need. She sucked in her breath, but otherwise lay still beneath him.

He arched his back in a final push, his penis fully sheathed within her, their groins pressed together. She was fully moistened, despite the tightness of her vaginal muscles against his embedded offering. Bael stroked her cheek, feeling her rapid heartbeat against his own. "Are you . . . ?"

"I'm fine," she murmured softly. "It felt uncomfortable at first, but now it feels quite wonderful, having you inside of me." Her chest rose and fell rapidly against him, and she shut her eyes, but her lips curved into a smile, telling him she reacted to pleasure, not pain. He pulled himself slightly back and then pushed forward into her, beginning his thrusting. From that point, he abandoned self-control, moving rhythmically to the tune of his own pleasure, and then harder and more erratically, his penis driving within her vaginal walls to glean every touch of ecstasy their wet grasp upon it could offer.

A quickening heat exploded from his groin. He felt as if it would burn the very inner walls of her welcoming flesh, and he was glad, for he felt, in an instant, its fiery emanation could only bring them greater pleasure. And then the heat erupted, hot semen flooding into her vagina and over his own penis, spent and victorious, within it. And satisfaction flooded through the whole of him, that she was his, and this ecstasy they shared was no other man's right, but his alone.

The fragrant but cool air of early dawn within the Garden began to chill their unclothed flesh. They lay huddled together, clutching one another, arms and legs entwined. Bael awoke with a start and caressed her shoulder tenderly. "Leianna."

She awoke, her eyes still tinged with sleep, then she closed them again, smiling contentedly.

"Leianna."

"Mmn?"

"We need to dress. I've no true idea how long the cloud of privacy will last, and I do not wish any of the angelfolk coming upon us, in all our revealed glory."

She grinned, then stretched and sat up on the smooth sand. Pulling her rumpled robe out from beneath her, she put it on. The morning glory garland lay nearby. She leaned over and grasped one end, pulling it to her and fixing it clumsily around her waist and over her bodice. "Look. The flowers haven't wilted, and the vine they bloom upon still holds tight. Help me fix this. I cannot seem to tie it firmly."

He took the remaining vine, wrapping it once more around her waist to her back and firmly tied it in a double knot. "Leianna . . . there was one thing I forgot," he said, putting his own robe back on, knotting its belt. "When we were consummating our betrothal."

"What?" she asked, toying with her sandals, but not putting them on.

"To say that I love you."

She studied him silently with the smallest touch of perplexity. "But I already know that."

"Ah, well, yes . . . Still, I should have told you."

She reached out and traced his lips with her fingers, causing a flush that sparked the embers of his earlier desire. "But you have," she said. "Bael, the morning hasn't fully arrived, and I don't wish to leave you and go to my lonely bed. Let's sleep a while, together, by this pool."

He drew her down then, cradling her head and neck in the crook of his arm, her arm draped across his chest. He stroked her hair until his hand stilled, and they both slept.

-18-

Ashtoreth's hand clamped as hard as stone around the upper arm of his reluctant youngest brother. Azmodeus snarled at him as he headed back to their village. The snarl did not inspire Ashtoreth toward leniency as he dragged the recalcitrant youth along.

"You're hurting me!" Az cried out as they passed the first quiet thachka.

"Hush up, you precocious fool. Or do you want all of Eliom to awaken and ask why two of Lucifer's sons are abroad in the early morning and arguing? And worse, it being the morning following his middle son's betrothal. And all of Eliom knowing how you shamed us once before. Still your tongue, and Father might convince the elders to mete out your punishment privately."

"They will not know if you stay silent."

"Are you asking me to hide your transgression?"

Az jerked his arm away.

Ashtoreth noted with grim satisfaction the red indentation he had caused. "How can you ask such a thing of me? You've twice broken the rule of privacy. It has to be done. You must be punished . . . much to our shame."

"What transgression? I saw nothing."

"You were crouched behind the honeysuckle bushes, watching. We both know what couple lay within the concealing cloud."

"And, alas, I was too late again. I saw nothing." His thin lips stretched, a slashing grimace. "Nothing, but the folds of their robes and Leianna's discarded garland of morning glories being pulled into the cloud. They were obviously done and dressing."

His tone infuriated Ashtoreth. It was not merely disappointed curiosity, but cold disgruntled lewdness. "And asleep when I found you watching them, judging from their stillness."

"They might have awakened, started again. The cloud might have dissipated by then."

"You have absolutely no remorse, do you?"

"No. Nor guilt. What harm would I bring to such lovers in watching them? I see no reason to force all of us into a committed union, simply because we wish to pleasure ourselves. Why can't we simply explore it without connecting it to matters of the heart? Are we committed to a vegetable or fruit when we try it for taste? Preferences are based on appetite, food or sex. Why can't we dally and be done with a woman when we no longer crave her sweetness or tire of her and wish fresher fare?"

Ashtoreth studied him silently, then replied: "Because women are not empty vessels to be callously played with. Nor do you realize—and I shudder at your ignorance—the degradation it would bring upon yourself."

"Pah! What you call degradation, I call honesty without the hypocrisy of making a simple bodily need into some ceremony blessed by the Creator. What you call ignorance, I call the intelligence to see through a false ritual designed to trap us by our own natural needs into a restricted life, without freedom, without choices."

"No one is forced into betrothal or marriage," Ashtoreth said quietly. "If you desire neither, you are free to remain celibate. There are no other choices now permitted under the laws of Eliom. Even a broken betrothal does not permit the unbanded couple the right to seek other partners sexually without a newly declared betrothal. The body is sacred, the source of life. Its procreative functions are not a trifling gift to amuse yourself with. They are a privilege, to be treated with respect."

"What of Deianna and Mercurius, Leianna's grandmother and grandfather? They never married, yet they mated. Eve and her brother are proof of that. Why was such sacrilegious behavior accepted then and not now?"

"Because it displeased our Creator to see the gift of procreation treated so shallowly. The Creator permitted the betrothal year but forbade further sexual union without marriage. Those who later disobeyed brought judgment down on us. You know what befell Eliom in the next generation. How can you even question the law? Our parents were among the few who conceived, even after the Eliomese bowed completely to the Creator's will. Were it not for the blessing on our house, we would not be here, Azmodeus. And many of our people still suffer, barren, childless. Would you chance destroying our future for the sake of your selfish whim?"

Az glared at him, hissing something inaudible, his breath ragged with barely restrained anger.

Ashtoreth stared back at him, dumbfounded by his continued defiance. "You are ill, little brother. Your mind and soul need healing."

They were a few steps from the pebbled path leading to their thachka's door. Az lowered his voice. "The only illness I claim is a bodily need left unsatisfied."

"Then be patient." Ashtoreth also dropped his voice to a whisper. "You have but two years to be of age for betrothal. If you mend your ways and mind your tongue, you might find that the adoring attention of some attractive girl alters your entire outlook on betrothal and marriage. You may fall in love and want her to bear your child. We are trying to recover our honor now, and the laws of Eliom protect us, especially from those among us who act rashly."

Az stood by the door to their home, his eyes serious as he answered his brother. "I do not wish to sire children. To be straddled with my progeny well into their adulthood for countless years does not appeal to me."

"There are many angelfolk who don't share that view. Children are precious to us now. Father and Mother were blessed three times, but they have not conceived since your birth."

"Thankfully, eldest brother," Az said coldly. "They might have had a girl."

Ashtoreth studied him quizzically, trying to understand his brother's strange disruptive behavior, then shook his head, unable to comprehend it. He pushed open the thachka's door.

"Keep quiet," Az advised him as they entered the cottage, "or I'll say you accompanied me for your own visual delight."

A voice spoke out roughly from some shadowed recess near the cooking alcove. "Little good that will do you."

Az pivoted around, as if to bolt out the door again, but Ashtoreth held him back. "If you believe so firmly in your need to alter Eliom's mores, then stand firm when you face your opposition."

Lucifer rose up from the bench in the dusky corner, coming into the light, anger tightening the muscles in his neck and jaw. "Or do your rebellious convictions fail you in the presence of your father?"

Azmodeus said nothing, holding himself rigidly still.

"So you are afraid," Lucifer said, almost kindly. "I can't blame you." He addressed Ashtoreth. "Where did you find him, and what transpired there?"

Azmodeus turned his head to lock eyes as cold and hard as wintry icicles with Ashtoreth's own.

Ash ignored him, still exhausted from being groggily awakened hours ago by the sudden brightening of the lamp in the night. Ash had lain on his cot, his back to Azmodeus, tired and longing only to return to the comfort of sleep. And he had done so, never thinking his youngest brother's wakefulness was more than restlessness. The night lamp had flickered out, momentarily awakening him once more. Ashtoreth had stretched, assuming Az had returned to bed. Shutting his eyes again, Ash began to regain his own needed rest. But soft footfalls descended the ladder stairs to the family rooms below. Ashtoreth lay still, hearing the door open and close, and then silence.

Minutes later, Ashtoreth sat up, activating the small lamp. He stared at the two empty cots across from his own. Then the curtain to the brothers' sleeping loft had been slowly drawn aside. Lucifer had entered the room, his sleep robe drawn loosely around his body, chest bare, rising and falling, controlling his temper. "Follow him," Lucifer ordered Ashtoreth. "Follow him and find him and bring him back here. And observe his behavior. You must tell me if he is dimwitted enough to try to disregard our laws a second time. If he's lucky, you'll find him before he displays such ignorance."

Ashtoreth obeyed his father. He searched for and found Azmodeus and brought him home to his fate.

Now, despite the acrid seething fury Az directed at him, Ashtoreth remained calm, not at all sympathetic towards his youngest sibling, relating simply and without embellishment what he had seen upon catching up with Azmodeus. "I found him crouching on his belly behind a copse of honeysuckle and azaleas. Through an opening between the flowering branches, he watched a well-cloaked couple. They were obviously asleep. I crept up to him and, by gestures and facial expression, insisted that he leave with me. He did so, and we returned home."

"What?" Lucifer scowled at his youngest. "No reluctance? No attempt to persuade you to watch?"

Ashtoreth ignored his father's sarcasm, knowing it wasn't directed at him. "No. He crept away quietly with me. We didn't disturb the couple."

"Do you know who this couple was?" Lucifer asked Azmodeus.

"We both knew," he answered. "What other couple was abroad making love? In need of a quiet spot to be alone in and concealed?"

Ashtoreth cut in. "He has no shame. Nor regret."

"I see that," Lucifer slowly said, his eyes sweeping over Azmodeus as if he were some new species of insect he'd discovered in the Garden. "It's without precedent to my knowledge. All of the others who've brought this degradation upon themselves had enough sense to admit they were wrong, to be abashed.

"So, Az," he continued, his voice taking on a false camaraderie, "how do you know it was Bael and Leianna? There are other betrotheds in Eliom who might have been in need of a private glade or nook."

Az seemed to hesitate, not trusting his father's easy conversational tone. "I . . . I do not know. I did not actually see them. It may *not* have been them."

Ashtoreth pursed his lips in consternation. A clever response. By his own admission, Az had only seen their clothing being pulled into the opaque energy cloud surrounding the lovers. But he had bragged about recognizing those robes, the garland which had decorated Leianna's. Ash thought it unlikely that another woman wore a garland of morning glory at that hour. He broke the thick silence now building in the room, borne of Lucifer's need to decide his youngest son's fate, of Azmodeus's fearful anticipation of that judgment. Ash knew it would go harder on Az, once Lucifer knew that he nearly disgraced his own family. But Leianna had been compromised. "He knew it was Bael and Leianna. He admitted seeing the flowered garland of her betrothal robe."

"Another woman may have worn the same," Az broke in, but Ashtoreth cut him off.

"He named them, voicing with cold and lascivious words his disappointment at having missed their union." His own anger caught him, his next words stammered through clenched teeth, his fists balled. "I find it hard to believe he is my kin!"

"And I, to believe that you are mine!" Azmodeus shouted.

"Enough!" Lucifer commanded, and to Az, "Go upstairs and remain there until I call for you. I would have had you punished privately, had you shown some remorse. Now I will have you publicly corrected."

"I will leave!" Az said hotly.

"You will not leave," Lucifer said. "Where would you go? This is Eliom, our world, our home. Would you wander on the other ethereal planes between our world and Earth? There is nothing there but undeveloped dimensions. The sixth and seventh planes are uninhabited. You could lose yourself there or wander the endless empty space of the fifth plane. Or perhaps you'll choose to wait forever on the timeless fourth plane. If so, I promise you loneliness and boredom in that eternal present, and guarantee you'll soon want our abhorrent society with all of its laws.

"Or would you disobey the Creator, as Eve and Adam have done? Perhaps the Supreme One will not retrieve your damaged psyche, forcing you to suffer, over and over again, the pangs of mortal death and of mortal birth, caught in a neverending dance of futility and repetition.

"So tell me, my wayward son, where will you go? Name it and I will hold the door for you in farewell."

Ashtoreth watched the contained anger on Azmodeus's face and wondered if the furious youth was considering Earth. Their father never spoke falsely. Lucifer would hold the door and close it on his youngest, if Az chose to leave Eliom.

The tension again thickened in the close quarters of the room. Azmodeus still hadn't moved. And breaking the smothering silence, soft footsteps pattered down the broad wooden ladder-stair.

Affaeteres stopped on the bottom plank, surveying the tableau before her. She uttered a single word that seemed, to Ash, to voice her worry and her hope. "No . . ."

Lucifer responded wearily, confirming her concern, denying her the slightest shred of comfort. "Yes."

She descended the last step and edged slowly to Azmodeus. "You didn't. You didn't breach your own brother's right to privacy? Tell me you didn't."

At the sight of their mother's stricken face, Az raised one eyebrow, his eyes searching hers. He spoke slowly. "I didn't see anything, Mother. I admit to curiosity, but I reaped no prize in my quest to satisfy it."

"Then he's *done no wrong,*" Affaeteres murmured, turning to Lucifer, arms extended, hands reaching out to him.

Lucifer took her hands in his. "That is *not* true. That he saw nothing is the Creator's blessing on our house, lessening our shame. But he sought to break our law a second time after being warned. He doesn't understand my need to inform the elders, that we must cleanse his soul. His sickness runs so deeply within him, he cannot perceive the crooked from the straight."

Affaeteres snatched her hands away. She clutched the front of her night robe, her hair loose and tangled about her shoulders. "He's young. Young and full of impatient curiosity. A fault, yes, but not a sin. He has committed no sin. Please, Lucifer. They must not correct him publicly. If they must rebalance him, let it be done privately."

Lucifer lightly stroked her cheek, then silently turned around, his back to her, to their sons.

Ashtoreth placed his hand sympathetically on her shoulder. "Azmodeus," he called, "can you say to our mother what you said to me as we journeyed back to our home?"

Az eyed him wrathfully. "I do not wish to marry," he said.

His mother laughed nervously. "But you are young. We don't expect you to— "

"I wish the freedom to sexually please myself without the hypocrisy of an abominable commitment."

Affaeteres stared at him, stunned. "But who would you—what woman would allow such a thing? You speak foolishly."

"How would I know?" Azmodeus lashed back at her. "Would any

girl or woman admit to feeling as I do in the face of your confining laws?" He leered and scowled, twisting his adolescent features, aging them. "Perhaps the laws are too constricting and do not suit all who live in Eliom."

Affaeteres's mouth hung slightly opened, her green eyes expressing her shock. Her chest heaved with a sudden intake of breath. She expelled it raggedly.

Ash put his arm around her, steadying her. "Mother . . . we have no choice. Father and the elders must uphold the laws of Eliom. If it's any comfort, I agree with you. Az is only guilty of an intended breach of the rule of privacy and of a rebellious attitude. Perhaps his cleansing will be quick, repairing his psyche swiftly, causing him little pain."

Lucifer, his back to them still, spoke out hoarsely. "Azmodeus, I gave you a choice. To leave Eliom or to stay and face the laws of Eliom. Have you decided?"

Azmodeus answered insolently. "I have. I will face my accusers. There is no sin. Only desire and its fulfillment. All else are restrictions your foolish laws place on that fulfillment."

Lucifer slowly turned around, his stony countenance aimed at Azmodeus. "Restrictions? No, my son, all else is *containment* of the fulfillment. Now go upstairs and remain there until I call for you. Our laws are just, for the good of all. No . . . what you will face is your rebalancing. And it will heal you."

Azmodeus began to reply, thought the better of it, and stopped. He trudged up the wide stairs, his steps heavy and stiff despite his slight frame, flung the curtain to the brothers' sleeping alcove brusquely aside, and disappeared behind it.

Michael had carried a small bench outside after awakening early the following morning and finding Leianna hadn't returned home.

He sat down in the warm pleasant dawn, studying the small bed of flowers lining the walk, marigolds, pansies and asters, carefully tended by his daughter and himself. To the right of the walk as it faced their thachka, a bed of vegetables grew: carrots, peppers, cabbages and tomatoes. Eve had kept—and now Leianna maintained—the herbal garden in the cooking alcove, below the one wide window allowing light into the thachka's first level.

He waited for her, knowing she was not his alone any longer. This was as it should be. As her father, he had raised her into a well-liked modest girl. That Bael, son to his good friends Lucifer and Affaeteres, had declared for her and been accepted by Leianna, had been a double blessing. Michael had no doubt of the betrotheds' future. At year's end, the couple would declare their intentions to marry. They and the village would plan and build their thachka a week before that final ceremony. And soon enough, if the Creator willed it, a grandchild would be born one day, playing, laughing and learning from its grandfather . . . and its grandmother. Eve would surely return to them by then. There might even be two grandchildren by then. A rare occurrence, but still possible. Lucifer and Aff had been the last couple blessed with three siblings.

And so he was content this day, knowing all would be well in the end if he just remained patient and trusted the Creator to right it all. Eve would be restored to him, humbled by the mortal hardships she and Adam had brought upon themselves, but learning from the price they had paid. Bael would wed sweet Leianna and protect her within his enveloping care and love. And perhaps they might not be the only ones who might bring forth new life.

Perhaps when Eve returned to him . . . Ah, well.

The thought played itself delightfully out in his imagination, spinning, growing, creating a more joyful future for himself and his wife as well.

Perhaps it would be a boy, this time.

Michael noticed he was hovering, while still in a seated position, floating inches above the wooden stool.

He lowered his auric vibrations, a sheepish grin on his face, and pulled himself back onto the wood.

Light pealing laughter sounded nearby. He saw Leianna and Bael in the distance, her arm linked in Bael's, Leianna murmuring something to him, which caused him to grin wildly, to cover her arm with his free hand and give it a squeeze.

As they came closer and shouted their high-spirited greetings to him, he wisely refrained from inquiring about their jest.

Bael entered his family's thachka quietly, expecting his parents and brothers to still be asleep, expecting to return to his own rest. He was pleasantly tired, looking forward to stretching out on his own cot before escorting Leianna to the afternoon gathering of praise and songs to the Creator.

Instead, Lucifer, Affaeteres and Ashtoreth sat morosely at the oaken table, leaning forward on the long benches that flanked each side. Bowls of fragrant jasmine tea sat on the table, the only sign of cheer in the room.

His mother's face, upon his entrance, had taken on that peculiar puckering of eyes, cheeks and mouth that always signaled a crying spell. Affaeteres was in many ways like Leianna: sensitive and easily caught up in other people's moods, although Leianna didn't have his mother's curious habit of crying over happiness. The last time, however, she had wept from sorrow was when Azmodeus had been caught watching lovers.

Bael noticed his youngest brother wasn't with them.

"What ails Mother? Is she nearly crying because her son's a man and will marry within a year? We'll be close by, Mama," he said, thinking that the childish endearment would turn her pucker to a smile. Instead, her dam of self-control broke, a flood erupting from her eyes.

"Mother?"

Affaeteres turned her head away from him.

As unaccustomed as Bael was to the misery now being shown by his father, mother and older brother, he wondered if a tragedy unique to the angelfolk had struck their home.

Dissipation, the closest thing to mortal death experienced by his people, rarely occurred. An afflicted person became weak, the cohesive network of bodily cells breaking down, winking out like bubbles frothing off a shore, until the body disappeared completely.

The elders said it was choice, that the dissipated person chose to leave them, called by the Creator to another dimensional plane far removed from Eliom, to further the Creator's work in some other guise, some other life. The angelfolk believed those who dissipated went to a higher existence, were elevated by and brought closer to the Seraphim and the Creator. "Has Az . . ." The words stuck in his throat. Those who dissipated were usually old, some by many centuries. But every century or so, a younger person succumbed to the mystery of dissipation.

"Yes!" His mother answered with such anger, and that anger reflected so harshly on the faces of his father and Ashtoreth, that Bael drew back, away from them, confused. "But if it is the Creator's will," he began and stopped, a welling up of his own sorrow choking off his words.

He saw surprised confusion on their faces as well.

"If *what* is the Creator's will?" Affaeteres asked, plainly amazed, and Bael knew he had misinterpreted their unhappiness.

"Where is Azmodeus?" he asked.

"Upstairs in your sleeping alcove," Lucifer said, his eyes and the cast of his mouth showing distress and a forced resolve.

"Is he well?"

"Yes, he is well, although he'll no doubt not feel well in the near future."

"Is he dissipating?" Bael asked, simply to settle the question.

Affaeteres let out a small horrified exclamation. "Creator forbid!"

The rigid solemnity on Lucifer's face broke into a pained smile and then into a wild grin. He broke out into raucous laughter. Even Ashtoreth began to smile, coughing to overcome his own urge to laugh. Only Affaeteres retained her frown, casting injured disapproving glances at them.

"Creator forgive me." Lucifer controlled himself, breathing in deeply. "But that sorrow would not taint us. That would be a sorrow that *was* our Creator's will. One that would abate into acceptance in time. Not one that reflected my failure, that will follow me like a shadow until Az is cured of his rebellion."

Bael folded his arms across his chest, waiting. Lucifer simply stared at him, and suddenly Bael knew. He glanced at Ashtoreth, who nodded back at him. "My own consummation?" he asked incredulously. "With Leianna?" And then plainly answering himself: "He broke the law a second time, disgracing his own family."

Ashtoreth nodded again.

Bael leaped for the stairs and had gained the second plank, when Ashtoreth, streaking from his seat, intercepted him. "Stop! He saw nothing."

Bael stared down at his brother's grip upon his lower arm. "You do not know that. Unless you watched him the entire time he watched us."

Ashtoreth let go. "I came upon him as he hid behind some foliage. You and Leianna both slept."

"And how much time had elapsed between his first stealing away from you—for I'm sure he didn't depart your presence openly— and your finding him?"

"An hour perhaps. He returned home last night with us and apparently pretended to sleep. He left the thachka in the early dawn hours, unaware that he'd awakened Father and me. Father bid me follow him, suspecting what proved true. But you and your betrothed . . . you both slept . . . the cloud still visible, your bodies within it well-hidden."

Bael felt the tension in his jaw, neck and shoulders lessen. He unclenched his fists. "When exactly did you come upon us and him?"

"Night had left the sky. Morning was just shedding light over the Garden."

Bael studied Ashtoreth quietly. "Yes, we were asleep, Leianna and I." Ashtoreth nodded a third time, and Bael detected a sudden relief in his eyes. He smirked coldly. "How fortunate for Azmodeus. Otherwise, I might have been tempted to add to our family's distress. Inflicting bodily harm is also prohibited, but my fingers ached to blot out his vision and hope that the elders could never restore it."

A small gasping cry escaped their mother's lips. Placing a comforting hand on her shoulder, Lucifer spoke. "No one will harm anyone. Az will be corrected. Because he shows neither regret nor shame, I will ask that his punishment be conducted publicly, that he might see his community's reaction to his lawlessness."

"All well and good," Bael answered, "and while I promise not to damage him, I invoke my right—and Leianna's as well—to confront the one who has transgressed against me." He started grimly up the stairs again.

"The law only permits that in the presence of a witness." His father slowly climbed the stairs and stood beside him.

"Very well, then. You may act as witness." His anger still tightened inside of him like a coiled snake ready to strike. They gained the landing, drew back the curtain, then pulled it closed behind them for privacy. Azmodeus, sitting crosslegged on his cot, looked up, his eyes reddened and puffy.

Bael cocked a suspicious brow at him. "What? Tears, Azmodeus?"

"Do you think I am incapable of producing them?" Az muttered.

"A rare occurrence at best. I believe the last time I saw you weep, you were eight."

"And Ashtoreth had knocked me about for disrespect. I was glad that Father punished him. Yes, that was the last time I cried, before this morning. I try not to waste precious bodily fluids."

Bael controlled a keen urge to upbraid the tartly tongued youth. He asked, "And what compelled you to shed such excess now?"

"Hindsight."

Lucifer glanced at Bael and then at Azmodeus. "A bit late for that."

"But Father, please," Az faltered. "I've thought it over. My argument with the laws of our society may be justified, but my manner of disputing them was wrong. I had thought that Bael, who at least now understands the need for pleasure, would understand my own lack of it and be less disturbed if he caught me sharing his vicariously."

Bael felt an entirely different desire now: to punish Azmodeus, coldly, slowly and with a decidedly *perverse* pleasure, in ways as equally forbidden as Az's transgressions. He cast the foreign thought from his mind, appalled that he could envision tormenting another so horribly, regardless of his anger. "And what of Leianna? Would she have been less disturbed, had she seen you? Knowing you only wished to share the pleasure of her initiation into womanhood?" His voice remained soft, but his eyes held a brutal sarcasm, his nostrils flaring as if smelling something foul.

"What of her?" Azmodeus asked. "She is yours now and would have to abide by your response and decision about it."

Lucifer sighed and sat down with deliberate calmness on the cot beside Azmodeus. Az stiffened, but Lucifer merely turned to him with a weary patience. "Leianna is not your brother's possession, Azmodeus, to do with as he pleases. Had you listened to Yeshua's description of betrothal during the ceremony, you would have learned this. I've no doubt of what you were thinking of, and so you learned nothing. You must be corrected, your thought processes and behavior rebalanced and restored to harmony with the rest of Eliom and its folk. I will leave it to Bael to decide if the punishment will be private or public. But it restores my heart somewhat to know that you were even the smallest bit regretful of your actions." He reached up with his forefinger and smoothed the reddened skin under Azmodeus's eye. Az flinched backwards.

Lucifer stared at his youngest, his confusion plainly showing, and Bael wondered if Az had feared a sudden injury to his eye. But Lucifer stared at his finger, rubbing it with his thumb, the skin of each tinged bright red. "What game is this?" he asked his youngest. "To play at regret, smearing clay dust around your eyes? Where did you get it?"

Azmodeus stared blankly ahead, saying nothing.

"I *asked* you: where did you get it?"

Az slowly reached under his cot, pulling out a small pot of the red earth. He handed it to Lucifer. "It often works with Mother," he said. "It nearly succeeded with you." His lips twisted into a defeated smirk.

Lucifer stood up and turned to Bael. His hurt over the deceitful ploy, the lack of respect it implied, was evident. "Have you decided?"

"I have. Publicly correct him."

"So be it," Lucifer said. He handed Bael the pot of clay. "Take this from my sight, never to be seen again."

Bael took it, drew apart the curtain and went briskly down the stairs. He spoke to neither Ashtoreth nor his mother, who stared at him, questions in their eyes, instead walking quickly out of the thachka and through the village and away from it. He reached a small wood near the Garden and in a secluded grove of willows he emptied the red dust between gnarled tree roots. Then taking a stout stick, he dug a deep hole and placed the empty pot within it, refilling the hole and tamping the soil firmly down until it showed no trace of his work. The overhanging branches of the willows rustled about him in the midmorning breeze as he made his way back to the village.

-19-

The hot noon sun shed its rays mercilessly. A light sweat glistened on her swollen stomach and limbs. Eve bent down on her knees, digging up the edible tuber roots with the rest of the wives. Cwuh, her mate, had little sympathy for a pregnant woman, nor had the rest of his clan. Eve had watched Dhar cramp with birth pangs last week as she stripped berries from the thorny stalks, her hands bleeding from pricks, her concentration muddled. Dhar had finally signalled the other women that the child in her womb had dropped into the birth canal.

They had gotten Dhar back to her husband's hut in time. She had screamed three times, and a girl child had slid out, healthy and unblemished, the skin smooth and brown. Dhar had recovered and the next day was out with the other wives and daughters, her baby girl strapped with cloth to her stomach and breasts, the infant's mouth in easy reach of her mother's nipple.

Eve's memories stretched back two years ago, when Choly, Adam's second wife, had gone into labor with their third child. The women had all been foraging in the savannah, seeking out fruit that had survived the summer heat. Choly had lagged slowly behind the other women, her eyes dull and distant, her skin discolored and drenched with a heavier sweat that seemed extreme in the mild warmth of the day.

Choly had begun to bleed, then fainted as she reached for a branch. The clan carried her home, and her cries later broke the evening's peace. The old crone could do nothing for her. The child within her was positioned wrong. All attempts to turn the unborn infant failed. Choly and her baby died before the moon reached full height.

Eve now took her sack of roots, holding it against her wide girth. Time had passed quickly while she and the women foraged and dug. The sun had sunk westward: time for the wives to head back to the village, to relieve the elders watching the younger children, to begin preparing the communal evening meal. And then finally, Creator be blessed, Eve could rest.

She had cursed the day she and Adam had drifted away from the dimensional wind, thinking to quickly explore Earth like playful larks. She had never known how fortunate her life in Eliom had been until this heavy planet had transformed and claimed her. She had adjusted but, unlike Adam, had never reconciled herself to this world, to her fate.

Adam, truth be known, had found his niche. He was now the headman of his own clan, formed from the outgrowth of Cwuh's over a ten year period. Adam had taken his wives, children and followers a day's walk to the west along the river, establishing his own village, but remaining allied with Cwuh's clan. Eve thought it completely within her brother's character that he had left her to fend for herself, calling her fortunate and well-protected as second wife to Cwuh, the head of this village, and the mother of five of his children.

Adam had no faith left in their rescue from this world. He believed they would be trapped here to suffer or overcome by their own wits whatever fate mortality might hand them. He believed the Creator had cast them out of Eliom forever as punishment for their willful disobedience. They were doubly guilty. The Creator had forbidden any angel to descend to Earth's surface. And thought-travel, the instantaneous transport she and Adam used, thinking they would never be missed in so short a time, was only allowed during spiritual ceremonies. Adam blamed her: her laughing suggestion that they sneak a fuller glimpse of the new planet resulted in their exile upon it.

She trudged back to the village now, the weight of her belly bearing her down, the other wives chattering amiably as they hauled back their sacks of roots for soaking and boiling. Eve walked silently beside them, recalling how she and Adam had first wandered naked and frightened over this savannah. Their garments had disintegrated when their bodies underwent that strange and painful metamorphosis in Earth's atmosphere, becoming half-angel, half-mortal.

They had draped pliable leafy branches from a truncated tree around themselves, tying them tightly together with stalks of rushes discovered near the banks of a lake. Thus covered, they had encountered Cwuh and his hunters returning home across the savannah with their kill.

The hunters had reacted with surprise and fear. They had never before encountered such pale-skinned people with hair the color of the sun and fire, a woman with eyes the color of the leaves, a man whose eyes matched the sky. The leafy garments Eve and Adam wore caused Cwuh and his men to cringe, believing them to be nature spirits.

Eve inadvertently settled that suspicion, reaching out her hand, speaking softly in Eliomese, asking if they had food to share. Then she caught sight of the dead antelope lashed and swinging slightly from the poles upon the hunters' shoulders, the animal's bloodied side wound gaping. She screamed, and one hunter, thinking it an ululation of evil magic, instinctively hurled his spear at her. But his aim was nervously haphazard. The sharp point struck a glancing blow on her lower arm as she turned to flee, breaking the skin, but doing no serious damage. Eve kept running, her own blood flowing from her lacerated arm.

The hunters, recovering quickly from their initial superstition, had grabbed Adam, restraining him. Cwuh himself ran swiftly after Eve, catching her roughly and carrying her back to the band. There he set her down and barked at her gutturally. She knew from his inflection and pointing gesture that he commanded her to stay.

Her leafy garment had come undone in her flight. She stood naked before him. His eyes appraised her as hers took him in. He appeared to find her desirable, saying something in his thick-tongued language to his hunters that caused laughter.

The hunters bound Eve's and Adam's hands tightly together and took them to their village.

Eve kept glancing in horror at the dead antelope. She wondered why they had killed it. In Eliom, although animals hunted and ate their natural prey, it was strictly forbidden for the angelfolk to eat animal flesh, only the produce of the fields and orchards. Even the silk worms' cocoons were only harvested after they had broken free.

The villagers had stared at Eve and her brother with blunt curiosity, bright strangers in the midst of a uniformly swarthy people. Their bodies had been poked, their hair stroked and pulled, their eyes peered at closely to the point of rudeness.

They had been treated as children, told what to do and when to do it. She and Adam had been separated. A man named Mgwa herded Adam to his hut, his long spear convincing her defenseless brother to comply. Cwuh had taken her to his own hut and to his bed after the evening meal that night. She had fought, and he had subdued her and taken her anyway. She had thought to call out to Adam, but the fear that they would harm him had silenced her.

Afterwards, Cwuh had washed her injured arm and placed pungent leaves upon it, wrapping it in a strip of cloth. Eve later found out it was animal skin. She removed it, letting the air dry the small wound until it scabbed over.

Within six months she and Adam had learned enough of the language to communicate clearly with the clan. Cwuh's first wife, Tigah, made sure Eve understood, all the better to instruct her in duties.

At the anniversary of their capture, Adam was put through some private male ritual. He survived it, although it gained him wounds that turned to permanent scars. He refused to describe what he had undergone with Eve. But it marked his full acceptance as a member of

Cwuh's clan.

Eve had become pregnant with Cwuh's seed and, following the painful frightening birth, so unlike birthing a child in Eliom, had allowed herself to be wed with only a touch of guilt to Cwuh as his second mate. She had witnessed mortal death on this world, of a child, of an elder, and she imagined that her Eliomese husband, her beloved Michael, must believe her to be as equally lost to him as those whose spirits fled their bodies here on Earth. She had come to depend on Cwuh, this hulking brown-skinned man with his long torrent of curling sable hair and intense brown eyes. Their first child, a girl he named Tahmay, had reddish brown hair, brown eyes and golden-brown skin. Cwuh was well-pleased, calling Eve his gift from the gods, and even Tigah spoiled the infant Tahmay, for no child had ever been born with such coloring before.

In their second year on Earth, Adam took a first wife, and in their third, he married again. Both Zinah and Choly bore him children.

Now, ten years since becoming mortal, she was near term with her sixth babe, and Adam had married twice again. Through his three remaining mates, Adam had fathered nine children, four boys and five girls, all healthy.

A sudden burst of laughter erupted among the chattering women, interrupting Eve's reverie, bringing her forward to the present. The women headed across the savannah, their backs to the setting sun. The hunters would also be home soon, their bellies craving food. Their wives would have to cook the meal swiftly.

But as they reached the outskirts of the village, three children ran quickly to meet them, the youngest crying. Strange men had come, taking what they wished, beating one elder who had attempted to stop them. They had bound some of the oldest children to be taken as slaves.

Eve hushed the frightened children as they and the other women slipped back into the forest surrounding the village. Then Tigah and two other wives returned to the savannah to find and alert Cwuh and his men.

Time passed too slowly as Eve huddled silently with the remaining women and the three youngsters, knowing blood might soon be shed. Then came a rustle of movement nearby, the crackle of three branches, the snapping of twigs underfoot. An unknown man drew apart overhanging branches to discover their hiding place. He grinned smugly at them, calling out in an unknown language. More strangers broke into the glade where she and the others crouched.

The men advanced on them, grabbing them, squeezing and

pinching, dragging them back to the village. Eve tried to run and was caught. She fought her tall captor, sinking her teeth into his arm. The man yelped and threw her to the ground. His foot lashed out and kicked her viciously in the buttocks. A fierce pain gripped her stomach as she struggled to rise. The man pulled her brusquely to her feet and shook her so roughly, she felt her neck would snap.

Both her strength and hope gave out. She offered him no resistance, limping with discomfort as he led her away. He herded her, along with the others, to the center of the village, where the elders and children were held. A wailing began when they saw their daughters and mothers. The raiders ignored their cries, examining their newest captives for potential chattel, keeping a wary ear open for their outlook's signal that the husbands were returning.

Instead, rising above the sobbing, a shattering cacophony of ululations sounded. A spear flashed through the air, stabbing deeply into the back of the tall raider Eve had bitten. He fell, twisted anger on his face. Cwuh and his hunters suddenly swarmed into the village center, filling it with violence. The wives, elders and children fled to safety, rushing through the battling men.

Another contraction ripped through Eve's belly. She panted, waiting for it to subside before she, too, could take flight. In the haze of her anguish, she saw Cwuh retrieve his spear from the back of the fallen raider. Tigah appeared behind him and rushed to Eve, hurrying her fearfully through the fighting and away from it. They passed the dead body of one of the strangers, possibly the lookout.

In the glade in the woods, the other villagers, too old, too young, or lacking enough skill and strength to help defend their men, had reassembled, awaiting the outcome. A few of their more agile youths had stayed in the village, watching cautiously behind cover, ready to bring information to the hiding ones or to bring them back if their men defeated the strangers.

Eve now felt as if knives tore at her girth, the birth pangs sharp and frequent. Tigah and the other wives placed her on a hard bed of leaves and surrounded her, shielding her. Eve felt her legs being raised, knees bent. She saw Tigah lean over her, her hands squeezing Eve's belly, checking if the child was ready to emerge. She seemed to grunt approval, then sighed, turning her head worriedly toward the village.

Another contraction rippled through her. Eve groaned, feeling warm fluid rush out between her legs.

Tigah shook her head. "There is too much blood, Eve. But your water has burst." She turned her head again impatiently toward the fighting. "Hurry up, Cwuh. Kill the cursed outsiders. This is no place to birth your child."

An immense pain struck Eve, like none she had ever experienced in mortal childbirth. She screamed in fear and anguish and felt Tigah clamp a hand over her mouth to muffle the sound. She felt pressure build in the birth canal and the sliding of a bulky weight between her legs, and she knew the child had pushed itself free.

"A boy," Tigah said, and Eve laughed in relief as the pain subsided, smiling weakly at the infant's first squeal as Tigah held him up. She quickly cleared his nose and mouth and gave him to Dhar, who handed her own baby girl to another woman and began to nurse Eve's newborn to quiet him.

And then the pain began again. "Tigah," Eve gasped, "the cramping . . . it's begun again."

"The afterbirth. No different from any other difficult birth."

"Different," Eve panted, the lower half of her body tearing apart again. She shrieked, clutching Tigah's leathery brown hand. "Too much pain. Too much pain!"

Tigah examined her belly. Eve could feel the ripple behind the first wife's probing hand. More contractions traveled down her back, burning her innards as they coursed through her pelvic muscles, making her moan again and again. Her body felt punished, a final judgment against her.

"Release me, Creator," she whimpered and heard Tigah say, "Twins. The second child has not yet descended. Eve, you must try to push. Help me get her into a crouch," she ordered the other wives.

Eve was lifted on her haunches, strong arms holding her up. It lessened some of the fierce cramping. She resumed panting, trying to push. Tigah kept one hand on Eve's stomach, the fingers of the other hand gently probing Eve within her. Finally both she and Tigah felt movement, within and without, and the second child slid into position. "Push," Tigah said. "Push hard."

Eve pushed, straining her abdominal and buttock muscles, bearing down. The second baby entered the world, held in Tigah's sure hands.

The women still held her gently. "The afterbirth," Tigah said softly. "Push out the afterbirth, Eve, and then you can rest."

Eve pushed again. She felt the refuse of the pregnancy expel itself from the womb and felt the blood that followed it, gushing out.

"Lay her down," Tigah commanded in a sharp voice. "Too much blood!" She had cleaned the second infant and showed him to Eve. "Also a boy. Eve, Cwuh is here. The fighting is done, the raiders dead.

May their souls wander tormented and never be born again."

Eve nodded wearily. She seemed drained of energy, and when Cwuh's face swam into view, she could barely lift her head. He cradled it in his huge hand, his other arm cradling one of his newborn sons. Tigah crouched beside him, placing the other infant in Eve's arms. "The younger," Tigah said.

Eve spoke faintly to Cwuh. "It is your right to name them."

He nodded and gazed down at the eldest twin in his arms. "He shall be Cahn. Strength." He looked over to the second baby, already seeking Eve's breast. "He shall be Ahbel. Wisdom."

Eve smiled tiredly and tried to free her breast from the folds of cured skins she wore. Cwuh helped her, kissed her forehead, and released her to the women's care.

While they carried her back to the village, the bleeding began again. But this time, there was no pain, only increasing weakness.

No milk flowed from her breasts, and the twins were given to Dhar to nurse. Runners were sent to Adam's village, to bring him back to say goodbye to his sister and be present at her death rites.

All these things Eve heard, but she couldn't speak to respond to them. *I'm still here,* she thought, *still here in this body. I'm not dead.*

But she couldn't see them, for night had descended, and the morning seemed never to come. They had put her in a darkened hut. But she could hear them, could hear Adam when he bent to her and whispered, "It's all right, Eve. Your time is done here. Let your spirit fly free. Fly home to Eliom."

They had told Cwuh and his people about Eliom and the Garden, but the concept of another dimensional world had confused the mortal folk. They believed she and Adam had been exiled from a fertile valley a great distance from the village.

Adam had leaned close to her cheek and ear, for she felt his breath as he murmured. "Cwuh has agreed to let me raise Cahn and Ahbel as my own, so that a part of you remains with me. They'll be well-cared for, Eve, and Cwuh will watch over your other daughters and sons."

And then faint light filled the hut. She heard the voices of her other children, saw their faces above hers: nine-year-old Tahmay, her red hair disheveled, tears in her eyes as she told Eve she loved her; eight-year-old Hahn, offering his solemn farewell; six-year-old Gita, her voice breaking as she prayed for Eve's soul; four-year-old Meih, calling out plaintively for her mother to heal; and three-year-old Tima, not understanding, following the instructions of his father and uncle, kissing her cheek and saying goodbye.

There were others who came to say their farewells, their voices fading and less familiar now, blending into a strange and sonorous monotony. It lulled her to sleep. She dreamed she was a wisping cloud, floating upward, white vapors ascending into the sky. The vast blueness about her was a relief from the thick darkness she had lain in. She reveled in the light, and suddenly she walked through a lush cultivated field, its neat, cared-for rows stretching out before her.

She vaguely knew she was naked. Her body felt lighter, her step seemed to float, and the very air seemed purer and filled with caressing energy. Her relief and exhaustion drew her to the soft soil with a sigh of gratitude.

She lay down on her stomach, her body curling slightly, and thought how strange that she should dream that she'd come home.

-20-

Disoriented, I return to the present, as if awakening from a dream of being someone else.

Quatama has removed the glowing hoop from my head. "Wait!" I protest. "I need to know what happened to my mother—to Eve! She suffered so much. I felt as if I was living her life—*was* her."

"Yes. That is the nature of virtual reenactment. Before the end of this century, mortals will develop a most basic version of this technique, creating a visual and audible virtual environment. Later, they will add the remaining physical senses of smell, touch and taste and, in the far future, also use it to relive memories."

"I want to go on," I insist. "Eve did return to Eliom, didn't she? She was reunited with my father and me, wasn't she? Did God forgive her, Quatama? And Adam, was he also forgiven, after he died on Earth?"

Quatama remains silent, his bright black eyes, the tightness of his lips, carrying a touch of sorrow. Finally he speaks. "There will be time enough to answer those questions. For now, we will take a respite from the past. You need to center on your mortal world for a while, to condense and file the memories of Eliom you now hold. We will resume the virtual reenactment a month from now, your time."

"And Azmodeus was never punished," I continue, ignoring Quatama's words, caught up in the memories and emotions I have been privy to. "That's why he became the devil of lust and debauchery, because he wasn't corrected."

Quatama's somber expression slowly breaks into a closed grin, puzzling me, and then his mouth opens, emitting a singular laugh. "So naive," he says. "Still so innocent. I will regret the day you lose those qualities. Go home, Leigh Ann. There is a letter waiting for you."

I truly awoke now, the alarm clock buzzing madly. Seven a.m. Ginnie's bed was empty; she was already up and in the bathroom, showering.

I got out of bed, yawning. My son still slept, which was fine. At nine months, Daniel now understood my comings and goings and would often throw a crying tantrum when I left the house to go to work. It made me feel guilty and often took me an hour or two to lose that feeling, even knowing he was well taken care of by my mother.

Later, at my desk in the Radiology Department of Hahnemann Hospital, I typed the medical reports, stopping and restarting my dictaphone during transcription to repeat difficult passages. I was careful and efficient, and the three doctors I worked for— two men, Dr. Anton and Dr. Cook, and one woman physician, Dr. Hasbell—all praised my conscientiousness and cheerful eagerness to better my medical terminology.

Two other women worked as secretaries for Radiology, their desks and equipment crowded near mine in the small room beyond the receptionist and the waiting room.

Willa was a petite black beauty with a quiet maturity. Her life centered around her two children, a girl twelve and a boy nine. The bulk of her salary went into their private schooling. Both were honor students and Willa's daughter was a musical prodigy, slated to attend the Juilliard to further her ability as a pianist.

Kate was also a black woman, but tall with a strong build and sharply planed facial features. More interested in sports than the arts, she had less in common with me, but Kate's plain-speaking, plain-living personality made her an enjoyable and uncomplicated co-worker.

The three of us now bent our heads to our jobs. I typed away, starting and stopping the foot pedal of my dictaphone, Dr. Hasbell's patient report droning through the ear piece. Then Willa's voice cut through the dictation. I looked up. "What?"

"I asked if you played an instrument."

Surprised, I nodded. "The guitar."

"I could tell by the way you typed. Very rhythmically, almost a four-four beat with paced rests between the tapping."

"Really?" The very idea that someone could hear my musical talent, what there was of it, in a typewriter, tickled me.

"I've played piano all my life," Willa explained. "Still do at church. I have a trained ear."

"Your daughter Stephanie must have gotten her musical talent from you."

"Oh, no." Willa smiled. "Her daddy's musical, too."

I returned the smile, enjoying the camaraderie we shared. "Have you ever heard of a composer named Terence Dearborn?"

Willa seemed startled. "Yes. I didn't think too many people knew of him. He's dead, you know."

"Yes," I said quietly, "I know."

"Some people said it was suicide. He drowned in the sea off Blackpool. More likely he was drunk and didn't understand how dangerous the undertow can be, that time of year."

I didn't remark on that, for I was psychically aware that Terence himself stood quietly beside my desk, physically invisible to me and the other women. Yet I could visualize him and subtly *feel* the vibrations of his energy form, although I couldn't physically *see* it. "I have an album of his music."

Again Willa seemed surprised. "So do I. He only cut that one, and they didn't reissue it. It's very rare now."

"It is? Why? I mean I really like his music, but he wasn't exactly praised by the classical music world, from what I've read, not like Mozart was or someone of that ilk."

Willa hesitated, then explained. "He was considered a romantic maverick, resurrecting musical themes popular in the 19th Century and discarded in the 20th Century by any respectable composer who wanted to be heard. When he disregarded the rules, he risked and nearly ruined his career. But because of his album's initial success with the public, those strict rules have become somewhat relaxed."

"You mean it's no longer against the rules for a serious composer to write romantic program music?"

"In some circles, it still is," Willa corrected me. "It all depends on how it's presented. But Terence Dearborn broke a taboo, and some say he became defiant in defending his position and his work."

"Did any other composers and musicians jump on his bandwagon, demanding a place for romantic fantasy in today's classical world?"

Willa nodded. "Sort of. His tragic death at the age of 29 gave his cause a mystique and platform it hadn't had in life. There may have been some guilt among his peers. It was rumored that he was deeply depressed by their derision."

Kate looked up from the report she'd been clacking out on her typewriter. "When the docs come in, we'd best be typing and not talking. You know Marietta."

Marietta, our office manager and supervisor, had a immaculate reputation, always on and at her job. Without saying a word, she conveyed the impression that those under her were expected to apply the same diligent standards when tackling the stacks in their in-boxes.

I readjusted my earphones to continue my transcription. Willa offered Kate a smirky grin. "Don't see why we have to be workaholics, too," she answered softly.

Kate shrugged. "Suit yourself. Just don't want her giving you grief for running your mouths instead of working."

Willa laughed. "Well, thanks for caring."

I started to push the play button on my dictaphone. "I guess we should get back to work." Then I paused. "Willa? Did Terence Dearborn leave any new music—you know—discovered after he died?"

Willa shook her head. "Nothing I've heard of. That album may be all that exists of his musical legacy."

"Mmn." I pressed the button and began to type to the tune of Dr. Hasbell's voice. I wondered about the letter I had mailed to Cecily Saraband, to the address Terence insisted was the flat he'd shared with her in London before his death. I had hinted in that letter that Terence's lost compositions might be tucked away and forgotten in the storage space beneath his old piano bench. Six months had passed since I posted the letter. Had Cecily even received it? Chances were she had moved from the flat. Nearly three years had passed since Terence died. If the carefully-worded letter did reach her, there was no guarantee she would search for his missing works, let alone answer me. The whole thing had probably been a wasted effort.

Intent on transcribing Dr. Hasbell's report, I slowly became aware of a white-coated figure standing by the desk. I looked up. Dr. Anton smiled patiently down at me. "I'm sorry," he said with his trace of an Italian accent I found so pleasant. "I hate to interrupt what you're working on, but I have a letter that must be done and mailed before the end of the day." He gave me a hand-written copy. "Can you finish the page you're working on and do this next?"

I took his letter. "Of course, doctor. Then it's not going into our mail pick-up?"

"No. I'll mail it myself. Thank you, Leigh Ann."

"You're welcome. It's only three p.m. I should have it done and copied by four. I'll bring it to your office."

"Fine." He smiled again and left the room, a tall lanky man with a thin face and receding hairline, who nonetheless always seemed the perfect picture of medical dignity.

I finished my current page, then put it with the other completed report pages. Drawing a sheet of Dr. Anton's stationery from my desk drawer, I began copy-typing his letter. Written to one of his patients who had relocated to Florida, it suggested an alternate treatment plan at another facility.

I handed the completed letter, photocopy and envelope to Dr. Anton. He had been on the phone, but he reached out for it with a nod. I nodded back, withdrew from his office, and headed down the hospital corridor to the secretarial pool. It was then that I remembered the last words Quatama had uttered before awakening me to face another mortal day. He'd said there was a letter waiting for me. Upon arising in my here-and-now world, I hadn't remembered it. The memories I now shared, of my eternal mother Eve's life and death as a mortal woman in a bygone prehistoric age, those belonging to others I had lived with and loved in old Eliom, usually dominated my mind as I rose in the morning. Quatama was pacing the virtual reenactment sessions on the eighth physical astral plane, not allowing me to become overwhelmed, maintaining the delicate balance between my nightly sojourns in my spirit body and the daily responsibilities of my Earthly life.

Now an excitement gripped me as I wondered exactly *what* letter awaited me. I finished typing Dr. Hasbell's report, checking it for correct spelling and punctuation, and silently praised my own ability to work diligently while my mind pondered a train of thought as alien and potentially disruptive to mortal life as the cancer Dr. Hasbell was fighting to arrest in her patient's lymph glands.

The balancing act between the astral and the Earthly *was* delicate; the line between had to be maintained with the iron control of a tightrope walker. Lean too far out, and you lost it.

And so I dampened my excitement, filed it in the back of my mind, knowing full well that the letter might have nothing to do with Terence and his missing music.

But, I thought, what other letter was I waiting for?

I sensed Terence's own eagerness, strong despite his silence, and his unspoken question: Was it Cecily who wrote?

I photocopied the medical report, placed the copy in a chronological file I maintained and put the original in the completed work bin Dr. Hasbell kept on her desk. It was five minutes to five. Kate and Willa said goodnight and went home.

I stopped by the ladies room, (Terence waited politely outside), and then began my own hour-long trek home on subway, elevated train and bus. I carried a book to read during travel —*Dear And Glorious Physician* by Taylor Caldwell—and although it transported me to a different time and place, my thoughts kept drifting from the book back to the letter Quatama had told me about.

And so I fairly jogged the three blocks from the bus stop at Knorr Street to my home, and my first words upon seeing my mother were: "Hi, Mom. Did I get any mail today?"

She raised an eyebrow. "Glad to see you, too. No, nothing came for you in the mail."

Disappointment washed over me. It wasn't just my own; I picked up on Terence's as well. "Where's Ginnie and Fred?"

"Ginnie's upstairs, studying for an exam. Fred's been invited to dinner at his friend David's house. Leigh Ann, you look crestfallen. Were you expecting something in the mail?"

"No, nothing. I just had, you know, a feeling."

"About what?"

I sighed and sat down next to Daniel, playing with his teething ring in his high chair. He grinned at me and said, "Ma," one of three words he now spoke: Ma, ba, and bye. I pulled him from the high chair, cuddling him. "Hello, pumpkin. Mommy missed you."

Mom handed me his bottle. "If you don't want to talk about it . . ."

"No. That's not it." I tested the bottle and tilted it toward Daniel. His mouth clamped its nipple; his pudgy hands clasped it. He drank heartily. "I don't mind telling you, although you'll tell me it's silly. I had a feeling I might hear from that woman I wrote to about Terence Dearborn's music."

"The one in England?"

"Yes."

"Yes, it's silly. Chances are she never got the letter. I take it your buddy spirit guide is still hanging around."

"Yes."

"How about the other one?" She began putting condiments and a large pitcher of fruited tea on the table. The dishes, silverware, napkins and glasses were already set.

"I haven't really sensed his presence." It was true, although I had tried again and again to psychically call him to me, after reliving our betrothal and love-making through the virtual reenactment. I had no idea if his absence was his own decision, or if Quatama blocked Bael's attempts to come to me.

"Neither have I." She checked the roast beef in the oven, pulled the rack out and spooned the beef gravy over the roast and potato chunks to baste them. "I think it was exactly what I predicted: a past life connection that ended as soon as he fulfilled his purpose here, alerting us to the dangerous condition of Danny's old crib."

I said nothing at first. I knew Bael had, towards the end of that brief time when he'd been coming around, successfully hidden his presence from my mother while coming on strong to me. And while I might not *contribute* any unsolicited information unnecessarily, I wouldn't lie to her, if pressed.

It seemed a good idea now to champion my right to privacy, while there was nothing to confess. I said, "Mmn. Dinner smells good. As far as Bael goes, whatever his purpose was, I'm glad he saved Danny from harm." I hugged my son and lifted him back into his high chair. He started to protest, to climb out. I gave him his teething ring which he grasped, forgetting his fuss.

"You don't . . ." Mom hesitated, then continued in a rush of words. "You don't still have feelings for him?"

Now I did hesitate, weighing my own need to judge and decide things for myself against Mom's honest concern. "What does it matter if I do?" I answered slowly. "Really, Mom, I thought we'd agreed I could live my own life. And be trusted to use my own common sense." I saw her anxiety and felt both love and guilt. "I'm not a little girl anymore."

She swallowed a lifetime of maternal worry. "I suppose it's personal."

I allowed the slightest trace of a smile. "Yes."

"I just hope you know it's *this* world you're going to need love and companionship in. Forgive me for butting in, but I mean a mortal man. I hope you know that."

I said softly, "I realize that. There are many types of love. Let me work it out myself, Mom."

"It's nearly 6:30. I have to pull that roast out and carve it up. Dad'll be here any minute. Would you go call Ginnie down for dinner?"

"Sure, Mom. Keep an eye on Danny. And give me some time to find this wonderful mythical man, huh? I'm not even legally separated from Richard yet. I have to get rid of one Prince Charming before I look for another."

She donned her oven mitts and removed the roast from the oven. "I know that, dear. I just want you to be more careful when you choose your next one. Make sure he's not covering up some warts."

I had to grin at the fairy tale metaphor; my come-back line sprang out instantly: "I'll examine each candidate from head to foot." Mom's mouth hung open, then she laughed at the spicy riposte.

"Not right away, I hope," she said, as I went to get Ginnie.

Two days later, a letter arrived, but not the one I'd expected. It contained a legal document: Richard was suing me for divorce. His lawyer's letter also outlined Richard's request for visitation rights with Daniel. I had already decided not to contest. As far as Richard's visiting our son, Danny had seen so little of him, since we moved back to Philadelphia, I was sure Richard's future involvement would be just as sporadic.

My family greeted this news with relief. None of them had particularly liked Richard. They treated the divorce as a necessary end to a bad marriage, the sooner over with, the better.

I experienced some guilt over the failed marriage, but my remorse quickly changed to irritation, when Richard came around the following week, demanding half the lawyer's fees from me. When my initial shock wore off, I refused to hand Richard a cent. I was already paying my parents room and board and took care of my own and Danny's other needs on my small salary.

My father, despite my protests, wrote a check to Richard for half the legal costs. There was no love to be lost between my soon-to-be ex-husband and my father, who wanted the divorce done and over with, something Richard didn't understand. He cemented Dad's disdain by asking to borrow twenty more dollars from him. A job was imminent, and he would pay my father back. Dad refused, trying to couch the rejection in kinder words than Richard deserved, telling him to ask his *own* family.

A month later, a second letter arrived from Richard's lawyer, telling me that the divorce proceedings had been halted, due to nonpayment of the required legal costs. I decided to save up the money and pay for the divorce myself. In the nearly eight months since we'd returned from Queens, Richard had only worked at temporary jobs, giving me either scant child support for Daniel or none at all for weeks at a time. Filing for support might also be necessary, but one, as the saying went, could not draw blood from stone.

September's Indian summer had given way to mild October days and crisp nights. Autumn had always been my favorite season. I enjoyed the cool breezes coming in the opened windows of the bedroom at night, the glory of snuggling underneath a light coverlet with fresh air circulating.

I took my mother's advice and gave up on expecting to hear from Cecily Saraband. Terence's renewed attempts to psychically contact his former love still failed. He couldn't seem to will himself to wherever she now lived, and his questioning Patrick about it only caused the elderly physician-turned-poet to shake his head and suggest Terence seek out another way to discover and complete his unfinished business. No further advice was forthcoming from Patrick. Terence decided that both Cecily and his missing music were equally lost to him. He began to wonder if the task he had to complete had nothing to do with his creative legacy.

I agreed that the answer to his dilemma might lie in another direction. I let him ponder that himself, for Quatama had informed me it was time to return to old Eliom, to the virtual reenactment of my memories and the memories of those who had shared my first immortal lifetime there.

-21-

I touch Quatama's arm lightly as we enter the quiet sitting room on the eighth physical astral plane. "I have a question before we begin. Quatama, where is Bael?"

Quatama gazes mutely at me. He seems loathe to answer.

"I mean, I *want* to see him, to talk about our life in old Eliom, but he hasn't come around, not even when I concentrated and called to him telepathically."

"Your telepathy may not be able to reach him," Quatama answers with a reluctant disapproval, which he makes clear through his tone and the sudden stiffness of his expression and posture. "In the depths of the Netherworld, your message could become distorted or dissolve completely. The nether regions hold different psychic elements from the higher regions, a difference that can be as sharp as that between a polluted swamp and a clear mountain spring."

His explanation and description upsets me. Could my Bael exist in a dimension with elements that foul? I sense only part of the truth is being told to me, and I won't accept less than the whole of it. "Even so, why hasn't he come around? Has he lost interest in me, after all his talk of love, of our healing that rift?"

"He has not lost interest in you. Do you have any memory of the actual events of that rift?"

"At first I thought it was a battle between Heaven and Hell," I admit. "And then you told me it was a rift in the heavens. But, no, I don't actually remember. Was I there?"

Quatama gestures toward the comfortable sofa. "Sit down and relax, Leigh Ann." The reenactment band appears in his hand, a glowing circlet of clear, blue light, nearly transparent. "We need to cover a total of four events which led to this rift. If possible, I would like to complete them tonight."

An angry petulance has built up in me. It outruns my patience. "Don't start until you tell me what I need to know."

"Tell you what?"

"Don't be obtuse, Quatama. Tell me where Bael is."

"Where you cannot yet follow."

"So he's told me. And why hasn't he come to me?"

"Because we have placed a protective aura around you," Quatama says, calmly ignoring my shock. "He cannot come near you on Earth, no more than he can breach the boundaries of Heaven. Let go of your anger, Leianna. You aren't ready to accept his return into your life or to welcome his promise of renewed love with your own. Your combined eagerness to heal a rift between vast dimensions without crucial understanding or preparation is akin to lovers leaping off a cliff, hoping they will learn to fly in midair."

I open up my mouth to speak, but he holds his hand up abruptly. "At least have the courtesy of letting me teach you to build a glider. Then if the currents prove tricky and you fly off course, you may at least land intact enough to learn from your mistakes."

I have never heard Quatama speak angrily before now. It worries and disappoints me. Bael would never harm me! "I just want to see him, Quatama."

He gestures once more to the couch. "You will. But let me build a foundation to guide you, Leigh Ann Elfman who was and is Leianna, and through you, to guide Bael. You mustn't rush blindly and ignorantly into a unique quest which could harm you both irreparably." He holds the reenactment hoop loosely in his hand. "Now that you have finally listened to me, you may tell me what you wish me to do. I will respect those wishes, even if I find them foolhardy."

"Would you remove the protective aura around me? Allow Bael to contact me?"

"If you ask it."

"You're allowing me free will, huh?"

"Your will is your own. We only guide you. Self-discovery is your path to wisdom, and no one but you walks it."

I sigh, sitting down, not looking at Quatama. "All right. I'll trust your guidance."

Quatama gently lifts my chin to face him. "Be patient. Your reunion with Bael was foretold. We simply wish the rest of the prophecy to unfold as auspiciously. We cannot build the future we wish to wisely without remembering the past and understanding its effect upon our present life. Even for immortals, this holds true. Thank you for your confidence and trust in me, Leianna. I will always stand by you as your guide and friend, whatever your decisions and experiences may be."

I know somehow that he will never break that vow.

He releases my chin and hands me the glowing hoop.

I fit it snugly onto my head, lower my hands to my lap and shut my eyes. The tingling begins, carrying me back into the days before the war in Eliom, into lives other than my own that, nonetheless, affected my own in the centuries that followed.

Out of all the angelfolk, only he and Yeshua were shown in advance the course of Eve's and Adam's forced Earthly sojourn. Quatama knew, though the blessing of foresight gifted to him and Yeshua by the Seraphim, that Adam would live on Earth for 300 mortal years. His angelic genes, despite the metamorphosis he and Eve had undergone, remained. Without injury, his body would age three times more slowly than true mortals. Because of the slowed aging, his resistance to disease increased. Only severe injury could fatally disrupt or destroy his body, as had the severe loss of blood killed Eve, freeing her to drift like a magnet through the dimensional corridors, back to Eliom.

Adam, shrewd, cautious and hardened by mortal strife, would avoid danger, becoming a patriarch and a legend. He would raise Cahn and Ahbel, the male twins Eve had birthed. They, too, were destined to become legends, the first tragedy among the hybrid offspring conceived by Adam and Eve and their mortal spouses.

Only Quatama and Yeshua knew that the mixing of mortal and angelic genes had irrevocably altered the planned evolution of Earth's indigenous life. Mankind would now rise supreme over the fauna and flora of Earth, and with the passage of time, upset its natural balance. The vitality of the planet might someday be endangered. Man had been slated for simple coexistence with the other species. Now he would rule.

The human brain would develop, evolving to shape and control its environment through ongoing, angelically-heightened awareness.

But the Earthly environment wasn't the ideal culture for the growth of that altered consciousness. Its inheritors would war among themselves over its power for good and evil, and some would divide against, conquer and subdue unaltered humanity. Eventually a mixture of humans with varying intelligence would populate Earth, some strong, some weak, some crafty, some simple. The diversions and contrasts in man's ability to learn and apply that learning to his world would increase, creating further imbalance with conflict and injustice following in its wake.

But man was still a babe, when viewed against the whole of his potential history. The ultimate danger to Earth and its inhabitants could be intercepted and thwarted, if its perpetrators, angelkind, accepted both the blame and the onus of the cure.

Perhaps the angelfolk would submit to their Creator's daunting entreaty that they devote themselves to the remedy. Perhaps they would refuse to shoulder the weight of a sin committed by only two of their kind. That remained to be seen, and both Quatama and Yeshua dreaded the potential chaos that might erupt.

For now, they set out across the quiet field where Eve slept exhausted and hugging the gentle Eliomese soil, her Earthly shell husked and abandoned, her immortal body regenerated. The air was cool with a hint of Autumn and the harvest fast approaching. Quatama carried a folded robe in his arms, a pair of small sandals atop it.

They would nurse her compassionately until her trauma lifted, allowing her to recover from the severe transition between mortal death and immortal resurrection.

Then she—and Adam *in absentia*—would be brought before the Seraphim to be judged and punished for their sin against mankind and disobedience to their Creator.

"There she is," said Yeshua.

Quatama followed his gaze and saw the crumpled, unconscious woman curled in the soil of the field. They moved silently over to her. She didn't stir nor sense their presence with so much as a flickering eyelash. She lay on her side, cheek pressed into the loam, her arm flung outward across it, shielding the front of her naked body.

Yeshua bent down and pressed his fore and middle fingers against Eve's forehead. Her breathing quickened. Seconds later, her eyelids fluttered up. She stared blankly at the feet of her rescuers.

"Eve," Yeshua whispered and stroked her cheek. "Awake now. We've come to take you home to Michael."

Eve rolled onto her back, plainly in a stupor. She looked up at Yeshua and Quatama, then suddenly became aware of her nudity, flinging her arms and hands across herself to cover it while rolling back onto her stomach. "Oh, God," she cried.

Quatama handed Yeshua the robe. The younger spirit master unfolded it, draping it across Eve's back and buttocks.

"Who is this 'god' she cries out to?" Quatama asked him.

"The mortal word for our Creator. The Seraphim have instructed me in the rudimentary tongue of the tribe she and Adam lived with. She may not recall the Eliomese language right away. She hasn't spoken it for ten mortal years."

Eve's shoulders hunched now; her body quivered under the robe, her head half buried beneath its cowl. Muffled sobs escaped.

Quatama slowly bent down and took Eve's arm, guiding it into one soft flannel sleeve. "Come, mithputhcha," he said, using the Eliomese word for the small, mischievous snowbird that had been Eve's tease-name as a child. "Put on the robe. You have enough strength. You cannot lie here in the field forever."

A strangled cry rose from her lips, followed by intense weeping. The spirit masters waited for her spasms to subside; Yeshua lightly stroked her tangled mass of auburn hair. She finally raised herself, placing her other arm in the robe, her back to the men, and pulled the warming cloth tightly around her. Then she turned, still sitting, to face them.

Quatama handed her the cloth belt and the sandals. "Welcome home, mithputhcha."

Eve said nothing, tears still streaking her cheeks, fastening the belt around her waist slowly with shaking hands. When Yeshua reached down to help her, she shot one hand outward, refusing his assistance. She finished securing it herself and slowly put on the sandals. Only then did she willingly extend her hands to each spirit master. Wetting her lips with her tongue, she murmured in halting Eliomese, "I don't know if I can stand."

"Try," Quatama said. He and Yeshua patiently helped her up and placed Eve's arms around their shoulders, their hands bracing and supporting her.

"We'll go slowly," Quatama assured her.

She nodded.

They walked haltingly over the field and onto the path leading to the village.

Michael waited nervously.

Quatama had entered the thachka briefly two hours ago to tell him and Leianna that Eve had returned to Eliom, the mortal energies binding her to Earth dissipated through death.

Michael had argued with the spirit master, wanting to run ahead to the field where Eve lay in shock from her abrupt and, to Michael, barbaric reintegration. To have one's very cells in flux, some fading into nothingness, others swirling to reform, seeking their original pattern, and the mind, the very soul, in flux as well until the process was completed! He wanted to fly to her—forget running—to cradle her in his arms and carry her home, whispering endearments and encouragement.

But Quatama had been adamant. He and Yeshua would bring Eve back. Michael should prepare Eve's section of the sleeping loft. She would need much rest.

Michael immediately climbed the stairs to the loft, Leianna following behind him.

So many years ago, he had removed the pole links joining his and Eve's cot, unable to bear its blatantly empty space beside him each night. Now he drew the two cots together again, the renewed joining symbolic of his renewed hope.

"May I help, father?" Leianna asked.

He turned at her soft-spoken question. "Yes. Help me slide the poles in the circled slots, then I'll tighten them." She did. "Your mother will need time to regain her full strength. A larger bed will provide more comfort."

Leianna nodded. Her eyes said she was glad for him.

My daughter is a woman now, he thought; *she knows my pain and my joy, the prayer answered and the price.* And then his mind dwelt only on the gladness, that if he could but hold Eve beside him through the nights to come, his loneliness would be no more. Contentment would grace his world again.

Leianna helped him arrange the bedding and smoothed the warm woolen blanket over it, murmuring, "Blessed are the beasts that offer us their warmth."

"Leianna . . ." Michael stood there, words failing him.

"Yes, father?"

"Your mother . . ."

She slowly shook her head. "I cannot remember her. Not fully. How old was I when she . . . left? Four? Five?"

"I . . . think you were five. The memory fades."

"Yes, it does. Even more so for me, I was so young. All I remember is Mother's red hair and her soft green eyes. I wouldn't know if she had changed beyond that."

A sudden fear welled in him, catching at his throat. Why had he never considered that his wife might well be changed, bearing marks both blatant and subtle inflicted by her ordeal?

"Father? Would you mind if I went and brought Bael back to wait with us? I am feeling very nervous. He would calm me."

"Quatama said we should wait, both of us. Your mother could arrive any minute now. If you left, she might miss you upon her homecoming. Your absence might cause her greater anxiety."

Leianna sighed, nodding, then caught his questioning look. She smiled to reassure him. He followed her downstairs, troubled by her reaction.

His daughter sat down primly on the long wooden bench, her back to the rectangular table. She had polished its surface to a gleam and placed a tall clay vase filled with late blooming flowers, still fresh from their morning cutting, upon it. It almost seemed as if she knew Eve would return on this day.

He studied her a moment longer, then asked, "Is this anger I see in you? Leianna, your mother did not deliberately abandon you."

"My mother has done our house and all of Eliom grievous harm," she murmured, surprising him.

"But it is done and over with, Leianna. She has come back, and she is still your mother."

She shook her head slowly, the contours of her cheeks and jaw tightening, her mouth pursing in an unaccustomed and unappealing pout. "It is not done with, father. What Mother and Uncle Adam have begun will not be finished for a very long time to come."

His own lips felt dry; he quickly ran his tongue along them to moisten them. "Leianna, while it's true that they've disobeyed the Creator, we don't know our Creator's will. It could be that their entrapment on Earth and the terror of mortal death was punishment enough."

"So I once thought myself," Leianna said, "but it is not done. Now I know. I fear for myself, and I fear for all of Eliom, and I fear for Earth."

He stared at her, puzzled, wondering if the shock of Eve's homecoming had unhinged her. He knew of only one remedy for a recalcitrant child, and so he spoke out firmly. "You will put these fears aside. When your mother arrives, you will treat her gently and show respect."

Leianna looked up at him pensively. "I would never act otherwise, father."

"I cannot walk, I tell you." Why couldn't Yeshua and Quatama understand that? She had tried to stand erect without their support as they travelled from the field back to the village. She fell twice, bruising her knees. Quatama, twice, had passed his hand over the discolored skin, stopping the sting and clearing it to health. Still, they insisted that she could walk on her own.

"Try, Eve." Quatama loosened his grip on her arm. "You are no longer mortal, this weakness of yours temporary. Our atmosphere is lighter, your body is lighter. You could have ridden the air currents with a simple lifting, instead of making us half-drag, half-carry you home. There, there is your thachka, your husband and daughter awaiting you. You can let go of your mortal persona now; you are angelic again, Eve."

"I can't! No, Yeshua, no, please don't let go. Don't let me fall down in front of them . . . oh!" She felt as if her world had suddenly frozen in tableau. Her eyes flitted from Michael, looking much as he had when she had left Eliom, to Leianna, no longer the small innocent child Eve had left behind. A mature girl stood framed within the doorway, standing beside her father, her hair a cascade of burnished red streaked with gold in the sunset. Her large brown eyes were solemn, her breasts rising and falling beneath her pale rose-tinted autumnal robe, her intense quietude suggesting both fear and expectation. Her daughter, grown now, and a stranger to Eve.

"Lei-lei?" Eve addressed Leianna by the toddler name she had not heard for well over ten years. The girl's eyes softened, but she gave no other sign of warmth or forgiveness.

It seemed an eternity, not seconds, as the girl worked her mouth and murmured in a barely audible acknowledgment: "Mother."

Eve cried then, a flood released, not only for her return to Michael and her daughter, but for the children her death on Earth had torn her from. At least she had not willed their abandonment.

She lifted her tear-streaked face to Michael and then her arms, which Quatama and Yeshua now released. She didn't fall, standing solidly before the doorway, but she feared walking on her own, even the few steps required to reach Michael and Leianna. Her outstretched arms, the turmoil and the plea on her face, no doubt made her look childish, but she could not move further, caught in a thrall of emotions too tangled to overcome. Yet Michael did not rush to her, scooping her into his own arms. He stood there stuporously, as if frozen by the very sight of her.

"Father, what is wrong with her?" Leianna asked coldly, with less empathy than he had seen her give a crippled beast. Michael hissed, *"Leianna!"* reprovingly, then swiftly covered the short space between himself and Eve, finally circling his arms around her, silently clasping his wife tightly against him.

I placed the bowl of lentil soup on the small, sturdy bed-tray Michael had woven for Eve.

Eve drew the bowl to her lips, tasting the seasoned broth. "Mmn. It's good. Your father told me you were a helpmate to him in my absence, taking fine care of him and the thachka. Even my herb garden has prospered, he says, you tended it so well."

"I did what was necessary, Mother." I hesitated, then admitted, "We missed you. There was not a day when you weren't thought of."

Eve scooped out some beans. She chewed them slowly, swallowed, then leaned back against the pillows serving as a backrest. "I'm sorry, Leianna. I'm sorry for the loneliness and worry I caused for you and your father. For the lost years, when I wasn't there for either of you."

"Mother, the important thing is that you're back now."

"Yes, and I hope the Creator will be gentle in meting out discipline. We trespassed, you know, on a world the angelfolk were clearly told was unfinished and unstable. We did other things while trapped there, your uncle and I. We . . . we ate the flesh of animals." Eve's shoulders slumped; she seemed to sink into herself, remembering. "The transgression was normal for Cwuh's tribe. He thought it strange that Adam and I refused at first to eat the meat. That's what they call the skinned flesh. Meat."

"How horrible."

"They did not leave the destroyed beast for the other animals to scavenge, for the remains to regenerate into the soil, as our beasts in the Garden do. They used everything. The skin and fur were made into garments, the bones and inner organs used for utensils."

"Did the beasts on Earth also do this as well as the people?"

"No. Their beasts acted much as our beasts here in Eliom. But the Earthly people feared some of their beasts. The mortals of Earth do not share their world with its animals."

"I don't understand."

"On Earth, Leianna, the lion might attack you, as surely as it hunts the gazelle on the savannah."

"People? Become prey?"

"Yes."

"How strange . . . and sad. How can the Creator allow such a thing?" I sat at the foot of the cot, as she finished her soup.

Eve drank the last of the broth and handed me the bowl. "Yes, the folk of Earth are strange, but most were good folk. Your uncle is still among them, headman of his own clan now."

I flinched at the mention of Adam, then calmed myself. I couldn't explain, although I had tried to express it to Bael, why I felt a great injury had been committed during my uncle's and mother's stay on Earth. I could not explain why I felt that the other angelfolk would be greatly affected and would suffer for it. When my father had asked how I could know such a thing, as we talked quietly while Eve slept above, that first day of her return, I had no answer. My foresight existed of its own accord, refusing to reveal more details when I attempted to probe it.

Eve was staring at me. "You're lost in thought, Leianna. Have I shocked you?"

"No. No, it's all right. I was wondering if you might attempt to dress and come downstairs this afternoon."

Eve looked at me dubiously, not answering.

"Mother, it's been three days. Quatama says the weakness in your legs is illusory, that you can walk."

Eve continued to gaze at me helplessly.

"Yeshua is downstairs, Mother. He wishes to give you healing, to build energy into your mind and clear it of the fears that are crippling you. Will you receive him?"

Eve opened her mouth, as if to speak, then sighed and merely nodded.

I nodded back. "I'll fetch him. There are also others waiting below to see you. Lucifer and Affaeteres, and also Bael."

"Your betrothed," Eve said softly.

"Yes. You'll like him." I smiled, feeling a tingle of heat flushing my cheeks, my heart lightening at the merest thought of him. "He's wonderful!" Clutching the empty soup bowl, I backed out through the curtains shielding the sleeping loft and turned, walking down the broad ladder stairs. The expectant gazes of my father and the others rose to meet my own. I told Yeshua: "She's agreed to the healing. You can go up."

*　　　*　　　*

Bael sat uncomfortably on the bench between Leianna and Lucifer. Affaeteres sat to Lucifer's left, on the end. Michael slowly paced before them. Lucifer stood up and placed his hand lightly on Michael's shoulder, stopping his harried movement, saying: "Yeshua will cure her. Sit down with us. Show patience."

Michael hesitated, then sat down beside Leianna. "I have shown a great deal of patience already, my friend. I hope Yeshua can cure this illusion of weakness in her legs. Whatever causes it? She refuses to talk of her enforced life on Earth. She calls it folly and says she prefers to forget it."

"That would probably not be wise," Lucifer offered. "It is probably the reason for her weakness."

Bael turned curiously to his father, who had reseated himself. "How so?"

Lucifer gestured, cupping his hand in the air, measuring the problem. "It's obvious something upsets her greatly concerning her mortal experience. Forgetfulness is not what is required. Would you cover a festering wound before it was healed?"

"No," Bael agreed, his own hand slowly clasping Leianna's for its soothing warmth, to quell his restlessness. Her fingers rested softly against his own, but he felt her own uneasiness coursing through them, wishing release from the silence and tension, the waiting. Finally, she spoke, her words muted, almost whispered. "I know what ails Mother, drawing the energy from her core, weakening her legs."

The others looked at her expectantly, but she had returned to silence, to introspection, her eyes lowered. Only Bael felt her hand tighten in his.

The silence cloaked them for a short while more, then the faintest sounds of weeping filtered down from the loft.

The images of her lost loved ones flashed through Eve's mind as her tears coursed down her cheeks. Yeshua stroked her hair, soothing her as she huddled face down on the cot. "Eve. Tell me of your children. Your Earthly children."

She lay still for a moment, face still turned from him, then fresh sobs welled up in her and cascaded out. "I've only told Leianna," she murmured, her mouth half-pressed into the sheeting. "Her Earthly brothers and sisters. All lost. Lost to me."

"Come. Turn around. Speak of them."

But Eve couldn't turn, the pain too large; she had to hide. She had to murmur, murmuring, murmuring the memories, out, out and away, freeing the crowded space within her where they now lived, suffocating her from within, making her own body heavy, to heavy to stand. "I've left my children in that horrible world, to face its dangers. My daughter Tahmay is nine, and her brother Hahn is eight, my first two babies, but they'll soon be grown, they grow so fast, the Earthly year goes so fast, they have no time at all. And no escape, sometimes no escape, from the dangers and the sickness that can come. But Tahmay and Hahn will be all right. Tahmay is a bright and careful girl, and Hahn has strength like his father. Strength—Cwuh named his first twin son with their word for strength—Cahn, and the other twin, Ahbel, their word for wisdom. But they are newborns. What strength and wisdom could they have? Who will nurse and raise them?! They will not survive, their mother's love taken from them."

"Another woman will nurse and comfort them." Yeshua stroked her head again as more tears and sobs erupted from her eyes and throat. "They will live."

"How can you know?"

"I know."

"Nothing is known in that horrid dimension. All is in flux. There is no promise of permanency or peace."

"At times there is. For some."

Eve finally turned, facing him. "But what of my other little ones? Gita and her little sister Meih? And Tima, he is only three mortal years! My babies! We fought off the enemy, this time. What if they return? They take children. Tell me it will not happen, Yeshua. Tell me it will not be so, that my children will be safe." She gazed directly up at him.

His eyes only echoed his concern and made no promises. "You will have to trust the Creator. Your children were not only born of you and of Cwuh's seed. The Earth is the Creator's, as well as Eliom, and all that dwell upon the mortal world are also the Creator's children. You have no choice but to trust and hope, if you would know peace again inside your soul and have your turmoil healed."

The dam within her burst and she let the pain rush out in a last heaving flood of tears. Yeshua's arms encircled her. She leaned against his shoulder and when she lifted her head from him, the weight of her fears had lessened, the stone in her stomach dissolved. "God watch over my children," she said.

"Come. Michael and Leianna are below, as are Lucifer, Affaeteres and Bael. They are joyous at your return and, as your return was destined, come and share their joy. Try to set aside your sorrow. Someday, if the Creator wills it, you shall be reunited with your mortal children. For now, return to us, your family, your friends, here in Eliom."

Eve hesitantly moved her legs, surprised that they responded with none of their sensation of crippling weight. She eased them over the side of the cot and stood up uncertainly.

"You *are* healed, Eve. You *can* walk."

She reached out her hand to him. "Will you help me? Just . . . just down the ladder stairs?"

He took her hand in his; with his other, he grasped her elbow. Together, they walked slowly from the cot. Yeshua released her elbow, drawing aside the curtain of the sleeping alcove, and led her to the top step. Slowly, like a toddler, Eve descended the stairs with him, planting two feet on each step. She concentrated on the movements of her legs, and only when she reached the bottom, the stairs behind her, did she turn her gaze from her feet to those sitting silently on the bench to her right.

Michael rose first, coming over to her, clasping her in an embrace. "Eve." And then Lucifer and Affaeteres rushed to her, their own arms encircling her. "Welcome home," said Lucifer, his voice booming out his pleasure. Affaeteres, her good friend Affaeteres—so long, so long ago!—said, "It's so good to have you back with us!"

She hugged them all in return, then walked teeteringly over to Leianna and Bael on the bench. They hadn't risen to greet her, and

Bael watched her with an expected respect and an obvious uncertainty. When Eve had last seen him, he'd been five celestial years old. Now a handsome young man sat uncomfortably before her, meeting the long-absent, now-rescued mother of his betrothed. "You have grown," she said, for he had, yet she could still see the moody child he had once been behind those dark eyes.

"Yes, I have," he answered her softly. "Welcome back."

Leianna looked at her with a strange pride, a woman's pride, and Eve knew this daughter had now lost forever the innocence of her childhood and belonged to Bael first and her mother second in matters of the heart. And Leianna said, as if she were impressing a familiar friend and not the mother who had birthed her, "We are to be married next summer. I too am glad you have returned, for I would have been sorry had you not been here to share our joy then." Leianna gently hugged Eve, then released her, leaning her body against Bael, whose arm wrapped protectively around her, as if they were extensions of each other and never meant to be apart for long.

Eve smiled softly at this, for she once had felt that unity with Michael. And foolishness had torn her away from him.

She hoped for Leianna's sake, that nothing would ever mar her future happiness.

Quatama removes the hoop from my head, and I am, once more, Leigh Ann Elfman, my former self, my shadow-immortal self relegated once more to memory with all of the other memories I've gleaned from these ancient families and friends.

"How do you feel?" he asks me.

"Fine." But I falter. Something about the last episode in the chronicle of lives I've been sharing bothers me.

Quatama waits, as if he knows this.

"I was a bit surprised by my attitude towards my mother—towards Eve—after she returned to Eliom."

"How so?"

"I should have been more sympathetic towards her, felt more love, some reaction to her being home after so long, to the hardships she went through."

"And? What did you feel?"

"Quatama," I tell him with a soft laugh, "you sound like a psychiatrist." Then I answer him, less light-hearted: "I felt resentment. I resented her return. And it felt like more than the abandoned child rejecting the suddenly resurrected mother. I seemed to forgive her for that."

"Then why? Why your resentment?"

"Something I knew—and yet didn't know. An intuition. It had to do with what you and Yeshua knew was coming—because of Adam's and Eve's trespass on Earth."

"The altering of the genetic evolution of humans."

"Yes." But I am still troubled. "How could I know that? I didn't have the gift of foresight that you and Yeshua had."

"Actually, you did. It was not gifted by the Seraphim, but by an even higher source—therefore more complicated, its insights much more nebulous."

I look at him skeptically.

"Remember your naming day," he reminds me, "and your journey to the One. You were named a Keeper, the fate of at least part of the universe partially entrusted to you, Leianna."

I pause. "Am I still Leianna now?"

"You are what you were, have become, and ever will be."

"A riddle?"

"No." He stares at me, not even blinking.

"I think my resentment was personal, nonetheless."

"Yes . . . on all levels."

I sigh closed-mouth, beginning to feel a weight upon me, never acknowledged before. "It would have been so much better . . . " My voice trails off, silenced by visions of what never came to be.

Quatama shakes his head. "The universe was not conceived in stagnation. Change came. Whether willful or innocent, we must make choices in response to it and hope that balance will be brought about."

"And so? Now? What are we seeking now? What is the purpose of all of this? What is my part in it?"

"We seek to heal the dimensional divisions that came about following the war in Heaven. This will mean unifying the separate dimensions of Heaven, Earth and Hell."

"And my part?"

"You are the Queen of Heaven and Hell."

I grin and stop myself just short of laughing out loud. "Me? Leigh Ann Elfman? Junior secretary at Hahnemann Hospital, soon-to-be the ex-Mrs. Warren and divorced working mother of a handful of a son just starting to toddle? Even if Bael's about to propose, I think that would make me a princess, not a queen, and one of dubious origins to boot."

Quatama smiles ever so slightly. "In sleep, a queen, but waking, no such matter," he murmurs, ignoring my raised eyebrow at what seems to be another riddle.

He waves his hand like a magician and the blue hoop within it disappears. He waves again and three more hoops appear. One is gold, one is red, and one is a murky purple. "Three more events to complete the life you knew in Eliom."

"Will we have time?" I ask, fearing oversleeping, neglecting my mortal duties.

"We have condensed them and can slow time, expanding the night in our little pocket of reality. I will see that you wake up refreshed and in time to start your mortal day."

I nod.

"First the gold. In it you will see the sacrifice of the angelfolk to save mankind from self-destruction and correct the damage done by Adam's and Eve's intrusion."

-22-

Michael would always remember Eve's smile, when she awoke beside him on that morning. They cuddled against each other, adding to the warmth of the light blanket, Eve's hair brushing his cheek as she kissed him. His heart quickened at this first show of intimacy since her return.

Eve had been doing so well, reacclimating herself to Eliom, to their family. She had even begun to strengthen the worn thread of her relationship with Leianna. Eve's winsome personality, serene and cheerful, lightened Leianna's heart, its foreboding. He could see it in his daughter's eyes: hope . . . that perhaps the Creator would forgive. That things might be righted without change in Eliom, with no harm done to the mortal Earth that the Creator could not easily correct.

Michael lightly returned the kiss.

"I love you," Eve murmured, pulling slightly back, gazing wondrously at him.

"That is my miracle, my sweet wife. That you still do."

Eve blushed, a slight tint highlighting her cheeks. "Time to greet the day." She slid from her side of their cots and got up, her night shift outlining her body, and drew back the alcove curtains. She called to their daughter's smaller alcove. "Time to wake, Leianna."

Movement sounded within it, and Leianna drew her own curtain aside. She had already changed into a day robe and grinned at Eve and at Michael, still in his bed. "My parents need to dress. I'll go downstairs to start our morning meal." She left them, descending to the family room and the cooking alcove.

Eve looked shyly at Michael, reclosed their curtain and, again for the first time since her return, drew her sleeping shift over her head, allowing him to see her nakedness, although she kept her back to him. She folded the shift neatly and placed it into her clothing chest beyond the cot. Still turned from him, she quickly performed the morning cleansing, standing still and concentrating, bringing forth the auric glow from within herself that washed over her body, cleansing it of all impurities. Then she reached into the chest and chose a winter robe, slipping into it and belting it securely.

She turned to Michael, smiling softly. "I'm going down to help Leianna." She pulled back the curtain and went out, letting it fall back into place, returning him to his privacy.

Michael lay back in bed for a moment or two more, treasuring an emotion which had been too long absent in his life. Contentment.

Then he rose, cleansed himself and dressed, and went down to join his wife and daughter.

They stood in the cooking alcove, their hands over the pit of rocks, conjoining their energies, heating the stones. The rocks began to glow red, and the heat also warmed and then boiled the water in the trenches that surrounded the pit, thin ones before and behind the pit for safety, and wide and square ones to the left and right of the pit, the left for washing and cleaning, the right for heated beverages and soups.

The breakfast cakes rested on a reed-woven tray suspended above the cooking pit, browning nicely. Eve ladled boiled water from the right-hand water trench, pouring it into small bowls of fresh mint leaves with honey. A larger bowl of fruit already graced the table in the other room. Eve removed the tray of cakes and carried it into the other room. Michael and Leianna followed with the hot tea. They sat down at the table to eat.

Knocks sounded against the closed thachka door. Michael rose and opened it. Quatama stood beyond the threshold. Behind him, Mercurius and Deianna waited, their faces sickly and pale, aged by a resignation that Michael instantly knew had to do with Eve. And beyond them, Michael's brother Gabriel stood.

Quatama gazed at Michael with eyes that seemed both saddened and hardened. "May we enter, Michael ben Zoras? There is a message I must convey to your wife, and your brother and her parents are here as witness and comfort."

Michael stood there dumbly, not bidding them welcome, fearing what he knew was to come. Yet not even Quatama spoke out to remind him of his duty. He and the others waited patiently.

"You may enter, Quatama, in peace and friendship, and also Mercurius and Deianna, beloved parents of my wife. And also my beloved brother, Gabriel," Michael finally said, the old bitter numbness returning. "Enter and share with us what you must."

They crossed silently within. Eve and Leianna looked up curiously from their morning meal, and then Eve left her tea and cakes, joining Michael where he stood, facing his mentor and brother and her parents. "What is wrong?" she asked. "Why must they act as witness and comfort?"

Quatama went over to her and quietly took her hand in his. "My little mithputhcha, I was called at dawn this morning to wait upon the Seraphim before the Well of Being. When they appeared, they enlightened me as to our Creator's wishes concerning your and Adam's trespass upon the Earth. In two days time, you must stand judgment along the Shore of the Seraphim, with Adam also judged *in absentia* for that trespass. At that time, you, your family, and the assembled angelfolk of Eliom will be told the truth and consequence of that trespass upon the Earth and the Creator's response and remedy. I, Gabriel, and your parents will return on that morning to escort you and act as your intermediaries."

Michael gazed briefly at his brother, but Gabriel's head was bowed, his eyes downcast, as if deliberately shielding his reaction to Eve's disgrace. Quatama released Eve's hand and moved between the brothers, addressing Michael. "I have also been told to bid you seek out the elves Eeztzu and Chamira in the forest. You are to travel there this morning, to ask that they represent their kind at Eve's judgment, for the Creator wishes them present as well."

Michael felt Eve leaning against him, nearly collapsing. His arms encircled her tightly. "Be strong, Eve. The Creator is not without mercy." He led her back to the table, sitting her down again beside Leianna, who put her arm around her mother's shoulders, steadying her. "Leianna," he said, "watch over her. Deianna and Mercurius also. Give her what comfort you can. I'll return from the forest as soon as I can."

Gabriel touched his arm. "I am sorry to bring you this news, Michael."

Michael stared at him, then nodded. "Will you and Quatama walk with me a bit to the edge of our village?"

Quatama answered. "We will. And Eve, know that our Creator will do what is best for all creation. You are a part of that, and you are still loved, by us and by the Creator."

Eve looked up at him. She did not seem at peace or convinced by his words. Michael went over and embraced her again. "I'll be back as quickly as possible," he said and kissed her cheek modestly. Then he moved to the door, glancing at Quatama and Gabriel.

Quatama walked over to Eve, sitting forlornly on the bench, her hands cradling her bowl of tea, her head lowered. His fingers gently raised her chin. "Be brave, mithputhcha." Then he walked to Michael and Gabriel beside the door. "Let us go," he said.

A crisp invigorating wind blew through Eliom and brought with it another dusting of frost to lie on the silent wintery fields. Michael walked across them, knowing that the healing warmth of Spring was not far behind.

He continued walking, leaving the fields, passing the Virginal

Sanctuary and the prairie and entering the forest beyond. A good portion of the morning was spent in reaching his goal, yet he never lifted to speed himself toward it. His worry weighted him down and he walked, wanting the firm soil under his sandaled feet, the movement loosening his tight muscles, freeing the emotional constriction in his heart.

The trees lining the forest path extended naked branches, but Michael noted the occasional bud. He continued walking until he came to the heart of the woods where the great trees stood, their gnarled twisted roots creating huge tunnels beneath the thick aged trunks, which led to the lairs of the elvenfolk. He approached one far to the right and untied the small gourd of wine from his belt, placing it beside him on the large root he seated himself on. Cupping his hand about his mouth, he trilled softly a particular cadence and song.

A different birdsong answered him. A flutter of pale wings circled his head, chattering noisily. The small mithputhcha landed on the root beside Michael, its silvery wing tips and tail feathers bright against the rest of its soft white plumage. It danced and strutted on the log, its beak pecking on the wine gourd. Michael stared at it.

A twig fell onto his head and bounced off. Michael looked up to see Eeztzu floating slowly down to the forest floor. "Creator forgive that poor imitation of the nightingale's call," said the tall elf, touching bottom. The mithputhcha glared at both of them, chirped defiantly, and flew off. "What brings you? You should be home with your new-found wife."

"Sorrow and a summons," Michael quietly answered.

Eeztzu sat silently beside him for a moment. During any season but winter, his grasswoven trousers and tunic and sandals of soft bark and reed nearly camouflaged him against the forest. Now he stood out, a swath of green amid brown and silver. "Then the murmuring in the forest, rustling through the fallen leaves, are true." He lapsed back into silence, his thin angular face, framed by lank brown hair, pensive. The late winter canopy of the wood seemed to enfold them soothingly. At length, Eeztzu broke its spell. "Which of my folk have been summoned?"

"You and Chamira."

"She is aged, the wisest of us. My mother will help you."

"Yes, but will she champion Eve?"

"She will champion the truth. She knows no other way. But her heart will be guided by her wish to heal your hurt."

"And you?"

Eeztzu hesitated. He twisted a strand of his long brown hair; his dark eyes studied the forest floor. "I will speak of hope."

"My heart is heavy. I feel I will sink into the ground, like a root past the golden days of harvest."

"You have undergone much, Michael. Hope is like a delicate flower. It can be crushed, its moisture squeezed out. I suggest replenishment." He took the wine gourd that sat between them and opened its stopper. He held it to Michael. "Here. Drink first."

Michael lifted the gourd, allowing the sweet wine to trickle down his throat, savoring its comfort. He handed it back to Eeztzu, who tilted it and gulped noisily. "Ah!"

"Yes, it's good wine."

"Hoarding it for a special time?"

"None better than this," said Michael.

Eeztzu thrust the gourd back at him. "Here! Drink more than a dainty sip."

"Would you have me return light-headed to Eve and Leianna?"

"Better than heavy-hearted."

Michael complied, wanting to wash away the helpless emptiness in his gut, to feel courage again, or else to feel nothing, if more pain lay ahead than he could bear. His ears caught a rustling sound, a foot treading upon the carpet of brown, decayed leaves. Bleary-eyed, he turned his head toward it. A silver-haired, silver-eyed elven woman, dressed in a pale flaxen robe, approached them.

She was sturdily built, handsomely aged, her hair braided, pulled back and wrapped into a tight bun. She paused before Michael, hands on hips, her expression bemused. "Why drink to avoid the future? You don't yet know what will be."

"It is easily predicted, Chamira."

"Nonsense. The future is much larger than you and I could predict. It goes on forever. At which point within forever are you so certain of its outcome?"

Michael answered her bluntly. "Two days hence at the Shore of the Seraphim."

"Ah! So you know the Creator's Will."

That subdued him, but didn't convince him. He answered more soberly. "I do not. But it is certain that Eve disobeyed our Creator, and Earth's future will be altered by her and Adam's disobedience. I know now; the hardships she suffered were not enough to absolve her. My daughter Leianna foresees this great turmoil springing from Eve and Adam's mortal handiwork." A small woodchuck had crept up to Michael as he spoke, its eyes questioning his sorrow. Michael gently smoothed its fur, reassuring it. "I do not know how my daughter knows these things."

"Ah!" Chamira slowly nodded, a touch of amusement in her smile. "The man trusts his daughter. What say you, Eeztzu? Shall Leianna be the finger we hold to the wind?"

Eeztzu smirked, not unkindly. "I say we wait until the gale is upon us and deal with it then. The wind can change."

Chamira nodded once more. "Is there more of that sweet fluid in the gourd?"

Michael lifted and shook it. "Perhaps two mouthfuls." He offered it. "My apologies, elder."

She put it to her lips, tilted it, and drank. "There." She handed him the empty gourd. "And now I am going to break with my people's ways and visit your house and family in the village of Eliom."

Eeztzu looked startled. "Mother?"

"And you will accompany me. I must speak to Eve and to Leianna. And then we will return to the forest, where our kind dwells separately." She stared directly at Michael and added dryly, "In peaceful simplicity."

He stood up. One did not argue with an elven elder. Eeztzu also rose in one graceful movement, looking uncertain. They both followed Chamira through forest and prairie, past the Sanctuary, and across the fields to Eliom.

It was dusk by the time they arrived in the village. Michael trudged alongside the more sprightly elves as they neared his thachka. Leianna opened the door at their approach, anxiety in her eyes. She stared at the two elves as if the unusual was to be expected, then led them within. "Mother has been weeping all day. My grandparents left at midday. When you hadn't returned by sunset, I fetched Bael. Lucifer volunteered to come as well. He's upstairs with her now, calming her."

Bael looked up somberly from the evening meal his betrothed had prepared for him, eyes widening at the sight of Chamira and Eeztzu. "Greetings, elvenfolk," he said, politeness masking his shock. "You break with tradition this evening."

"So we do," Chamira said. "For a short while only. Leianna, I must speak to your mother. You must also be present, for you share her destiny."

Michael saw his daughter's darting glance at Bael, the fear of losing him plain within it. Bael silently answered her with a look both possessive and determined. Michael shivered, a sudden premonition of chaos stiffening his muscles. "I thought you said we cannot predict the future, Chamira."

"I did and we can't. But there are certain things I can divine, as when someone's fate is intrinsically woven with another's, and the outcome of their decisions is important, reaching out to join with all the other strands in a tapestry."

"May I also be present?"

"No, you may not." Then, more gently, "It is the mother's influence on her daughter that I wish to guide."

He nodded once to the elven matriarch, accepting her judgment. But his sense of foreboding grew as Chamira and Leianna climbed the broad stairs to the sleeping loft above.

They heard Chamira's dry, cornhusk voice above them, and then Lucifer's. Their words were muffled, but Lucifer's surprise, followed by anger, filtered through. A moment later he emerged at the top of the stairs, then thumped heavily down them, glaring at everyone. At seeing Eeztzu, shock crossed his face again. His gaze swept back to Michael, their eyes locking in equal confusion, a dark fury building in Lucifer's.

"They are my guests," Michael warned him.

"Elvenfolk and angelfolk may tend the Garden together, but we live separately, keeping to our own ways and villages."

"And yet we have managed friendships." He glanced at Eeztzu, who kept a calm demeanor and distance from Lucifer. "And both our people are always represented when called to the Shore of the Seraphim. Eeztzu and Chamira will stand for their folk at Eve and Adam's judgment."

"Adam is not here," Lucifer snarled. "They throw the whole weight of the blame upon Eve, who has already undergone trial enough!"

Michael frowned, his brow furrowing. Lucifer's affection for Eve was well-known, but something far deeper now upset his normally balanced composure. *They* are the Seraphim, and they impart the Creator's words, law and judgment to us. Are you suggesting we question the will of our Maker?"

Lucifer remained silent, and Michael instantly regretted his question, for it implied that Lucifer challenged the Eternal One, Parent of them all. Only one answer was possible.

Lucifer finally, slowly, responded. "I have communed with the Creator, as have all the folk, elven or angel, during the high holy day of *Ch'llelen*. Our Maker's Presence is too great for eyes to conceive, for ears to hear, for touch to grasp. Only the heart can hold our Creator's greatness and commune with such vastness.

"Yet there is a thing none know but me. When my third son was born, I went alone to the Shore of the Seraphim and gave thanks. The Great One came to me—no spirit master nor any Seraphim acted as intermediary—and spoke through my heart, through my soul's essence, blessing my obeisance, and saying that throughout eternity my faith would light the morning, as burning as the sun that warms Eliom. For our Creator loved and cherished me above all others.

"I was amazed and fell to my knees, ever more love and thanks flowing from my mind.

"And then Eve and her brother Adam were taken from us, and the final son I had grown to love became a harsh stranger to me, ruthlessly denying the laws of Eliom and questioning the respect due his father and his community. These things the Creator should have corrected, if the Great One we have loved so long and unquestioningly was as perfect and flawless as we once believed."

Michael drew a sharp breath. "Don't!"

"Don't what? Don't blaspheme? Our *God,* as Eve now calls the Creator, is no more perfect than we are. What being can be perfect itself that allows imperfection in its offspring? How can there be Omnipotence if the smallest defect in the universe exists? Like father, like son, I say. Our Creator is no more perfect than I am, Michael."

"Lucifer . . . "

Even Bael now rose, to advance hesitantly, clearly horrified, toward his father.

Sorrow and rage mingled on Lucifer's face, twisting it, as he locked eyes once again with Michael's. "I do challenge this Creator of ours: to make sense of the tragedies that have marred Eliom. To explain the purpose and the pattern of the long sorrow you have endured, the persecution of your wife and my friend for a foolish act with consequences both unexpected and painful, and the metamorphosis of a child I cradled and reared into a monster with no conscience, perhaps no soul. Wrath now fills my heart, the heart of this sun of the morning!"

"You forget, Lucifer. There are laws to remedy such! The law of the One is sacred."

"And has been broken." Lucifer spoke harshly, sarcastically. "Explain how this can be, if this Creator, who hands them down to us, is perfect?"

"Lucifer," Michael whispered, his earlier weariness, escalated by shock, becoming exhaustion. He moved to the bench and sat down. "You are overwrought, my friend. Think upon your hasty words tonight, the anger that prompts them. Are these troubles brought about by our free will and therefore not foreseen by our Creator? Perhaps there is a pattern and a purpose, even in imperfection, which the Creator wills us to undergo. A lesson to be learned."

"Pah! I will hold my own judgment, since you request it, my friend. But I, too, will be present on the Shore of the Seraphim, when Eve is judged. We shall see then if our Creator satisfies my quest for logic and fairness."

"Father . . ." Bael touched Lucifer's arm, fear plainly showing in the youth's face. Michael knew it was fear for Leianna as well. "You state you will judge. Surely not against the Creator's Will?"

"As Michael so deftly pointed out, we have free will. Your younger brother has proven this can be used to dispute the law, and therefore, unless I am mistaken in my definition, the Creator's Will."

"It can be used," Bael answered haltingly, "and it can be punished into submission. There is community censure, Father. You yourself have said Azmodeus must be corrected. I believe you believe in the community's will. I have always been told that this is also the Creator's Will."

"Perhaps not," Lucifer replied curtly. "Perhaps we have too long accepted judgments we should be questioning."

"What of Azmodeus?" Michael asked him.

Lucifer simply stared at him, a long minute passing. Michael noted the suddenly tightened jaw muscles. Lucifer spoke hoarsely, a ragged whisper. "Enough. Let us save Eve from further cruelty. Azmodeus can wait."

"But what—"

Lucifer cut him off brusquely. "Look to your own house, Michael, and I will look to mine. And reflect upon what *I* have said, as you have asked me to reflect upon your words. I will meet with you again when the second sunrise finds us on the Shore of the Seraphim and prepare, in the interim, to face our Creator's Will. And pray that the Creator bless you and Eve with mercy and not cruel arrogance!"

Michael could only stand dumbly, mouth opened roundly, as Lucifer pivoted and strode furiously out the door without a backward glance. Michael, Bael and Eeztzu stared at one another.

Bael started hesitantly toward the door. "I will go speak with him."

But then Chamira's voice sounded. "Let him be." They turned to see her stern figure atop the ladder stairs. "I request your presence, Bael. There is something I would say to you and Leianna in Eve's presence."

Bael looked at Michael and Eeztzu and slowly climbed the stairs.

Chamira pulled aside the curtain for him and followed Bael through it.

Michael sighed. "It seems we are not needed," he told Eeztzu, "perhaps too ignorant to be given wisdom while the very ground beneath us pitches and shakes apart."

Eeztzu quietly studied the dirt floor of the thachka. "It seems quite solid to me. Perhaps such added wisdom is only for those who cannot separate fact from fancy."

-23-

The sight that greeted Bael in the sleeping alcove: Eve in her white winter robe, huddled on her cot, mussed blanket over her legs to her waist; Leianna beside her, arm about her mother, body stretched over the coverlet, comforting Eve, their foreheads touching; both crying.

Bael had little experience with grown women's tears. He had never taken his mother's brief crying bouts seriously; more than half the time she wept over something that brought her joy. Affaeteres was an emotional but resilient woman, rarely truly troubled, and never feeling the intense grief now exhibited by Eve and Leianna.

"What ails them both?" he asked. "Chamira, why do they cry?"

"An intuition," she said.

"An intu—" He walked over to the bed and grasped Leianna's shoulder. She turned from her mother, looking up at him, tears staining her cheeks and chin.

"Stop this. Stop this now," he ordered. "Whatever may come, we'll survive it."

"No." Leianna stood up, flinging her arms about his waist, leaning her head against his chest, seeking comfort. "The evil has already been unleashed. I can feel it. It's in Eliom. Eliom will be divided."

"Nonsense. You talk nonsense." But even as he chided her, a chill struck him, remembering his father's stormy blasphemy. "The Creator will be just. No harm will come to Eliom or the Garden. Or us," he insisted.

Leianna lifted her head, her gaze meeting his own, which tried so hard to be stern and in control. Her voice rose, equally insistent. "It will not be the Creator who brings us trouble. We will cause it. We cannot turn away from the Creator! The Creator knows what is just, what must be done to make things right, and we must obey!"

"You have heard my father speaking. His voice carried to this loft, upsetting you."

"No," said Chamira. "We heard nothing, this daughter—your betrothed—enmeshed in revealing her fears to this mother, both their lives entwined and indebted to a greater need than any of their own, separately or together."

"What need?" Bael asked, feeling a growing irritation with Chamira's obtuse elven explanation. "You said you had words to impart to Leianna and me in her mother's presence. With all due respect, elder, can you state them and give us leave to work through our own difficulties?"

Chamira seemed to bristle at his tone. Her chest rose and fell; he recognized the calming breath. But her eyes, level with his own, showed smoky silver glints of frustration. "You will not listen," she said. "You will not heed. It is merely the sense of the ending days of Eliom as we know it that I wish to impart. I sense the vision of destruction in this girl, your betrothed. All of Eliom has sensed the impending chaos, worlds invaded, change begun that cannot be undone, but only lived through until a new balance is achieved between them. The Creator knows and correction could come smoothly and without contention, if all would willingly bow before the Great One, ready to pay the cost. But such will not be the way of things. There will be war in Eliom, and you and Leianna will be forced apart by it."

He began to protest, but she slashed the air with her hand with a finality that unnerved him. "You must both do what you think is right, but this is the first thing I must tell you: do not lose faith in one another, although the very fabric of time and space splits, pulling you apart. The daughter of this mother will mend this torn tapestry, but not by her deeds alone. She holds the thread, but you, impatient young man, are the needle."

He and Leianna stared, stricken by Chamira's prophecy. Bael could feel Leianna's weakness, her shock, her posture slackening. He held her to him, supporting her.

Chamira calmed her anger, forcing her breathing, once more, to slow. "The second thing I must tell you is a message from my people. You three have been chosen to receive it. The elvenfolk are innocent of the trespass upon the Earth. If one of our number had committed such, all would work to repair the injustice. But none of us have, and we absolve ourselves of such responsibility. We will, however, offer to lend our wisdom, wherever useful, to those who must shoulder that responsibility. Otherwise, we will remain in our wood and live separately, as have we ever, although lives do touch in passing, when different folk have common need. And so shall my son Eeztzu and I return to our wood now, bidding you good night."

Leianna spoke faintly. "Dear Chamira—do not be angry with us!"

The elfwoman's eyes widened with surprise. "I am not angry with you, little one." And to Bael, also more gently, "Remember."

She slowly turned and left the room, drawing aside the curtain.

Leianna drew back from his embrace and sank wearily onto the edge of the cot. She lifted her head to catch his eyes and hold them with a pleading look.

He had no new answer for her.

Behind them, Eve slowly drew the covers down and stood up, tightening and smoothing down her robe. "No elven elder willingly breaks tradition. Chamira's requests seem simple, cut and dried. But nothing simple would have called her here from the elven wood. You must assume your faith in one another will be challenged, tested. As for me, my faith must be unwavering. I have caused all of this. Holding half the blame does not lessen the impact of what I have done. I will hold to the Creator's judgment and accept whatever retribution is meted out to me."

She moved to the curtain, pulling it along its rod and opening it fully. "I will brew some tea for your father and me. Would you also like some?"

Leianna shook her head, then addressed her mother fervently. "I want you to know I will do everything I can to help."

Eve nodded, then looked at Bael. He stared back at her, wondering if she expected a similar statement of support from him. His silence seemed to diminish her, making her look smaller than normal. She lowered her eyes, turned and started down the stairs, apparently seeing Michael in the common room, and calling out his name.

Bael reached out his hand to Leianna. She took it. "Come," he said, "let us find a quiet soft spot in the Garden where we can rest from all this chaos."

She allowed him to lead her downstairs where they took leave of her parents and headed off to find some seclusion. But she was too silent, unnaturally so, and he could not bring himself to ask her why, fearing she might extract a promise from him which he might be unable to keep.

*   *   *

Affaeteres cleared away the morning cups and bowls, bringing them to the clay basin and filling it with water. She scrubbed them thoroughly, then placed them upside down to dry in the tall oaken rack. Lucifer had built it and the storage nook for her in their third year of marriage, three months before Ashtoreth's birth. He had changed much since then and throughout it all, she had been steadfast in her love, supporting his needs, his demand for a comfortable organized home to live in and to raise their sons in. He insisted on her loyalty to him, his ways and beliefs, for he would not brook dissension in marriage or family.

Many times, in her own mind, she had disagreed with some argument or judgment he had championed in the Council. Lucifer's strictness, his zeal for the law, and his stubbornness against allowing all but the narrowest interpretations of its edicts had gained him a measure of fame. Few of the younger members of the Council challenged him in debate, he told her, and he had the Elders' highest regard. A star in the firmament of the law, her illustrious husband. Her own nature leaned toward empathy and tolerance, but she kept her silence and swallowed any words he might construe as disapproving.

The price for familial peace had been high. For while he praised her wifely ways, Lucifer treated her intelligence as negligible, totally oblivious to the hand he played in creating that image. Forgotten were the early years of their marriage when she had attempted to join discussions, offering her own opinion, and the sarcasm and ridicule Lucifer had lashed back at her with for daring to contradict him. Her meek retort that other couples allowed differences to spice their lives met with stony indifference and a cold shoulder and back turned to her in their bed at night. She soon learned; it was best not to contest anything with him. She kept their marriage congenial, both publicly and privately. In return, he privately lavished attention on her. In public, she often feared she had become his empty mirror, reflecting him to no further advantage. Her true feelings sank deeper within, her outward behavior a cocoon they hid behind.

That cocoon had once been kept tightly woven, the smallest crack in her resolve diligently repaired to keep peace in her household. Now it cracked and crumbled, her fears for her family's welfare more powerful than her fear of his disdain and anger.

She heard his muffled shuffle, the intense silence making the softest sound louder. He had entered the small nook beyond the family room, separated by a sturdy drywall, where she stored food and utensils and prepared their meals. Its opened doorway let the slanting sun of late afternoon in, but neither its warmth nor the cheerful sight of her garden behind their roomy thachka, awaiting the warmth of Spring and planting, eased the numbness and chill on her skin. Her husband's demands had uprooted her safe, ordered life, and she could not approve, not willingly, of a risk that might destroy her family's honor and respect among the angelfolk. Or worse. Lucifer proposed the unspeakable.

"I love you," she said to his silent presence behind her. "As dearly as when we first met and wed. I have kept my tongue stilled of any contention throughout the years. I have ever been mindful of my place, and yours as my husband, sire of our children. But I cannot stand by mutely now and watch you disgrace yourself before the Creator. Or allow our family to join you in such foolhardiness and share your shame, which will surely result from it." She turned angrily around.

His eyes met her emerald glare unflinchingly. For once she felt the extra inches of height she held over his height, in fact, was surprised that she had ever felt smaller and meek beside her indomitable husband. She had been a good wife. Now she must make him see the gravity of his behavior, the devastation that might await them all, if he continued to blaspheme. "It does you no good," she said testily. "In fact, I am shocked. The husband I know would not rebel against the Creator."

"The Creator knows all," he said softly, "and knows I will not accept an unfair judgment against Eve. We are the firstborn of the One, the slovenly creatures of Earth merely halfwits only blessed with our physical image and undeserving of even that. I cannot undo my decision or undo the course that following it will set me upon, not without denying myself before the Creator. It is against the law to lie, is it not?"

"Then do not deny yourself. Repent instead. Truly, in your heart, that you would never presume to judge our Creator's judgment, even if it seems unfathomable to you when first declared."

"Ah, Aff," he murmured, reaching out gracefully, his fingers gently brushing her right cheek. "I cannot repent for that which I am not guilty of, to One whom I no longer trust nor pledge unquestionable loyalty to."

She drew back involuntarily, recoiling from him.

The softness of his voice belied the horror of his choice, one she knew now was firm. He would not be deterred from this path, not by love, not by reason, not by fear. She asked, in a choked whisper, "What then of me—and our sons?"

He smiled, and his smile frightened her more, the smile of a rock so fortified with hardness and intent, none could crush it. "Whither I go, you all shall follow."

Her own face, she knew, reflected her defeat: defeat if she stood by him, defeat if she deserted him. She had already lost, and the battle had not yet begun. "Then we shall be alone? Your family outcast?"

His smile faded, his lips tightening, his head tilting and his eyes questioning, as if she had said something which surprised him. "Alone? Oh, no, my lady. We shall not be alone in our dissension. Your husband does not act rashly, and he intends to win this dispute."

Lucifer strode to Michael's house, his sandals kicking up tufting clouds of dust. Bael accompanied him, going—Lucifer knew—to see Leianna, his first concern. Bael had questioned him incessantly along the way, having been told the night before, amid shouting and arguments by Ashtoreth and Azmodeus, weeping from Affaeteres, and Bael's own stuttering protests, of Lucifer's decision to judge the Creator's judgment of Eve and Adam. Lucifer had known Eve since they were children playing together in the lush fields of Eliom. Their features were so similar, bright round eyes, strong chins and contoured oval faces, people had jokingly called them cousins, and they felt as if they could be. As they both grew to adulthood, their friendship matured. But the romance many expected to blossom never happened. They sought out other partners in life, but remained close friends, adding their families to that friendship.

The betrothal of Bael to Leianna strengthened the unity between their two houses. Lucifer had always like Michael as well, as forthright a man as Lucifer was himself. But now Lucifer wondered. How could Michael be prepared to accept Eve's castigation so blithely? Was he so nerveless that he refused to demand fairness and mercy for his own wife? Were they all sheep to be herded and sheared of any opinion that dared to disagree with their supposedly all-powerful Maker?

"Father," Bael interrupted his reverie. "I beg you to be patient and say nothing more to Michael until tomorrow morning. We don't yet know the Creator's Will. Lacking such knowledge, your rebellion is premature and, I fear, doing more harm to my betrothed and her family than good. Please, father!"

Lucifer scowled. "You bleat like a lamb."

"I'm well aware of the metaphor you've honored those of us who've counselled patience with. But the shepherd does protect the sheep from the wolf; therefore, few fall to feed the wolven cubs, the remaining sheep living long to rear more lambs and provide us with wool. Angels may also fall, upon occasion, from the Creator's good graces, despite our Shepherd's diligence, and the folk learn from their mistakes, growing wiser. We are protected by our obedience to the law and to the Creator who hands it down to us."

Lucifer studied his son's face. "I see by your expression that you doubt your own words. Obedience, by definition, is not a choice, but an obligation born out of fear, defining us as secondary to that which we obey. I tell you again, Bael: the Creator is not perfect. Therefore, that wisdom you wish me to accept is potentially imperfect. And my friend's well-being or misery waits upon the morrow and that questionable wisdom."

"A day, Father. A day is all I ask. At least we do not hurt the sheep or the wolf, nor does the wolf attack us. Leianna has told me Eve's story of horror on the Earth. Even men hunt men. The Creator protect us from such discord!"

He heard the anger and the thin sliver of fear in his son's voice. He capitulated, but only grudgingly. "A day, then."

Lucifer refused to allow fear to influence him.

Eve slowly worked the walnut open with her pick. But her hand was not deft and the pick slipped many times before she gained enough leverage to crack the walnut open.

Leianna was upstairs, resting on her cot, enervated by Eve's judgment, yet to come on the morrow. Michael had journeyed yet again to the Shore of the Seraphim and the Well of Being, to pray for guidance. He had left early that morning, asking for Eve's forgiveness, promising he would be home by early evening.

Eve could neither rest nor pray. She felt bereft, as lost now as she had upon finding herself trapped on Earth. The late afternoon sunlight flowed through the opened doorway, a hint of Spring arriving, but only numbness engulfed her; she couldn't feel its nurturing rays.

A shadow cut off the bright rays bathing her and the table. Eve turned her head, half expecting Michael, half expecting anyone or anything in her misery, perhaps the Hand of Judgment coming down upon her now, not waiting for the morning and the assembled angelfolk to witness her degradation.

Lucifer stood in the doorway, someone else behind him, hidden from the angle of her vision.

"Eve," he murmured and simply continued to stand there for a moment, staring at her. Then, "May Bael and I enter, my friend?" His tone was mere formality. Yet she wondered: how would they react, were she to answer *no?*

"I am weary and my heart worn," she answered him truthfully. "Will you forgive me if I want no visitors, Lucifer? But Bael, of course, may enter, for I know he comes for Leianna." She cast the young man, who had now moved beside his father, revealing himself, a sad glance. He gazed back at her uncertainly, then at Lucifer, having been himself welcomed, but not his father, an unusual circumstance, but not a rare one.

Lucifer told him softly, "Go to your betrothed."

Bael crossed the threshold and stood in the common room, frowning.

"She's resting above," Eve said.

He nodded and wordlessly ascended the stairs to the loft.

Lucifer still waited beyond the doorway. "Eve, do you deny me your friendship and your house?"

"Only my house. You can't know the turmoil within me, Lucifer. I would not wish you to know it. Leave me and wait upon the morrow when we end all this waiting for the Great One's Judgment. Then, come reprieve, pardon or punishment, I will clasp you to my breast and warm my damaged soul against your friendship in the aftermath of my trial."

"Eve . . ."

"Go now or my heart *will* break today. Leave it still intact for now, struggling to hold together. I need my solitude."

"No." He strode defiantly into the room and over to her, bending down on one knee, his arms encircling and cradling her tightly, as she sat in mute shock on the bench.

"You have broken protocol," she mumbled.

"Your own broken heart preceded it," he answered, his own tone muffled, for his lips pressed against her neck and auburn hair as he embraced her.

"Father!"

Eve pushed gently on Lucifer's shoulder. He released her, standing up. His son glared at him, and Eve saw the disapproval in Bael's eyes. Leianna, behind him on the ladder stairs, was pale, the skin around her eyes and nose reddened. She had, no doubt, been crying.

"You'd think," Lucifer commented, "a man a criminal for comforting his friend."

"Leigh Ann, wake up!"

When his son gave no comment, he added: "Or trying to protect her from a potential injustice. One long-denied by the angelfolk."

"LEIGH ANN! Oh, God, Ginnie, I can't wake her! LEIGH ANN, WAKE UP!!!"

I opened my eyes to see my mother clasping Daniel to her, while shaking me brutally.

"The house is shaking," she said. "Dad wants us outside until he checks the oil burner." She tugged on my arm again, and I felt the tremor as I stood hastily up.

And saw, through Eve's eyes, Bael across from me, on a non-existent ladder stairs in a ghostly thachka superimposed on my Earthly bedroom. My former self, Leianna, stood behind him and spoke:

"Father Lucifer, you must leave."

I gaped at my doppelganger, at her voice, so strange to my own ears. Worse yet, it felt as if I were two people in two places at once: awake in my physical body and simultaneously Eve, dealing with Lucifer, Bael and her daughter, and the chaos her actions had brought to their lives. I blinked to try to clear this dual vision, but the scene from

Old Eliom stayed layered over my mortal reality.

As Lucifer answered Leianna, saying he would leave, but that Eve should know he would fight the Creator, if needed, to protect her, a third figure materialized in front of my mortal self: Quatama.

He watched as Mother thrust Daniel into Ginnie's arms, saying: "Leigh Ann's either sick or in some sort of shock." *Now she did grasp me firmly, steering me into the hallway, Ginnie pushing ahead with the baby. The house continued rocking, and Fred's voice shouted up from the living room:* "Hurry up! Dad can't find anything wrong with the heater or hot water boiler. We don't know what this is!"

I stumbled as Miriam half-dragged me down the stairs, the scene from Eliom still playing a double bill with my suddenly chaotic Earthly life, disorienting me, making me dizzy. "Come on, Leigh Ann!" *she urged me.*

As I reached the bottom, Quatama reappeared again. "The hoop, Leigh Ann," *he said.* "The virtual reenactment hoop, sweep it from your head!"

When I gazed at him dumbly, he continued tersely: "You still wear the reenactment controller. You were pulled from the sixth plane before we could remove it. Only you can remove it now, as it has merged with your mortal magnetic field."

I mentally aimed a jumbled thought at him, which basically asked, "How?!"

"Run your hand through your hair, scalp to crown, as if straightening it."

I did so quickly. Both Quatama and the continuing scene from Eliom, and Eve's observance of it, vanished, leaving only a confused memory I didn't own nor cared about at that moment. Mother was pulling me across the enclosed porch, like a sighted person leading someone blind. The house continued its trembling. We heard something crash in the dining room, ignored it and headed out the door.

"I'm all right!" I shouted to her. "I'm all right, Mom!"

She stared at me and then down at the sidewalk. "Dear God! The ground is shaking." We ran around to the side door leading to the basement. It was locked. She banged on the wood below its window. "Bill! Bill! It's not the plumbing! It's an earthquake! Get out of the basement!"

Fred stripped off his pajama top and wrapped it around his hand. He drew his arm back and broke the glass. A neighbor, Mrs. Elsinore from across the way, ran out of her back door, scurrying over, her face pinched with fear. Fred punched shards of glass from the pane, stuck his hand in and opened the door. "Dad," he shouted, heading down the stairs, "It's an earthquake. Get out of the house."

I stood there, barefoot and shivering in my nightgown, feeling the slight tremor, worried about it worsening, as my father and Fred came out.

"An earthquake!" Dad said. "This is Pennsylvania. We don't *have* earthquakes."

"Tell that to Mother Nature," Mother snapped back. "Where do we stand? What do we do?"

The same question had been assaulting me. What if the house fell on us? What if the ground opened up and swallowed us? I felt my mortality and took Danny, wailing, from Ginnie. He calmed down in my arms, burrowing his head against my neck.

Dad took over. "Stay on the grass in the backyard, away from that concrete garage wall, while I shut off the gas."

Other lights in other houses were winking on, people awakened by the earth tremors.

Mrs. Elsinore, widowed two years ago, followed us nervously. "I thought it was an atomic bomb," she said. "I thought I was going to die and be with my Morrie again!"

We positioned ourselves on the grassy yard, my steps somewhat mincing, hoping to avoid sharp stones. The others had put on slippers or shoes. The ground beneath us suddenly stilled itself.

We waited on the cool, bumpy lawn. The night and the ground remained quiet as Dad walked back over to us.

"That definitely was an earthquake," he agreed. "I wonder what it measured seismically?"

"Can we go back to the house?" I pleaded. "Daniel's shivering. It's cold out here."

Dad shook his head. "Look, I know you're cold, and I know you're uncomfortable. The wind is making it feel colder than it is. But we need to wait a few minutes to make sure there isn't any serious aftershock."

I wrapped Danny closer inside my arms, and Ginnie hugged the shivering Mrs. Elsinore. "Thank you, Ginnie," Mrs. Elsinore said. "Lord help us. An earthquake! Here in Philadelphia! What's next?"

I said, "Nothing, I hope," and Ginnie nodded in the dusky light. I wished Dad would let us go back into the house. The late October chill prickled my skin with goosebumps. We were all underdressed.

Mother and Fred stood near us on the dew-dampened lawn. Fred had put his top back on; I hoped that he shook it out first. "Listen," Dad told us, "I'm going back into the house to check for news on the radio and try calling the police and gas company, in case the gas lines were damaged."

Five minutes later, Dad came out. "Well, it was on the news," he told us. "The quake measured 4.5 on the Richter Scale, very unusual for this area. But it looks like it's over. You can go back into the house. Get warmed up."

Mrs. Elsinore touched Mother's arm. "Miriam, I'm still a bit shaky, you should excuse my putting it that way. Would you mind if I stopped in. I mean, I'm all alone since Morrie died."

Mother covered Mrs. Elsinore's hand with her own. "Of course. I'll make a quick cup of tea for us and send Bill over to your house, to make sure there's no serious damage."

"Thank you." The lines above her brows unfurrowed. Despite her relief at our help, she looked touchingly vulnerable.

"I'll go over there now," Dad told her. "Is your back door still open?"

She nodded. "My grandfather clock must not have been level. It fell over just as I came downstairs. Scared me nearly half to death. That's why I ran out like a frightened rabbit, Bill."

"I'll set it right. You ladies go in now with Daniel before you all catch cold. Fred, can you give me a hand?"

My brother followed him across the connecting lawn to Mrs. Elsinore's house, mumbling, "Don't know how any of us are going to get up for school or work tomorrow."

I hadn't thought of the time, only the newly appreciated blessings of safety and warmth. Back in the kitchen, I saw it was past 3:00 a.m. Ginnie and I declined the offer of tea, both of us dog-tired, Daniel shifting groggily on my shoulder. We said goodnight and left Mom to comfort Mrs. Elsinore.

Upstairs, Daniel and Ginnie fell back to sleep, but I tossed, wondering how a city normally free of seismic disturbance could have suddenly been hit by a quake.

I quietly rose from my bed and gazed out the window at our front lawn, having newly developed a cautionary awareness of the Earth's power. Pieces of Mother's good crystal in the open hutch were broken, and a framed print had been jolted from the wall, its glass cracking. Luckily, no other damage occurred, at least on superficial inspection. Dad would check the house structurally in the morning. He always was a thorough man.

Standing restlessly by the front window, I saw him carrying a board from his plumbing truck around back, a temporary fix for the back door window Fred had broken. I heard brief hammering as they tacked it into place. They must have seen Mrs. Elsinore safely into her house, for a short while later, Mom, Dad, and Fred came upstairs, said goodnight and went to bed.

I remained by the window, the night silent, the house undisturbed, and drank in the peacefulness. Outside, the street lamp shone on the deserted street, bathing it in an artistic eerie glow.

Down the street, a lone man ambled into the glow of the lamp. He stopped across from my house and did an exaggerated right turn on the pavement, facing me. Goosestepping like some militia man, he crossed the street, standing on our sidewalk. He slowly raised his head and stared directly at me, despite the fact that the darkened room should have hidden me from anyone watching the bedroom window.

I squinted, trying to make out the face, frozen by this stranger's audacity. He seemed young, not very tall, had fairly long blond hair, and was dressed in casual blue jeans, shirt and a waist-length tan jacket. I would call the police if he didn't leave immediately, I thought, and then realized that I would also have to wake my parents, by which time the man would probably leave, making me look as if I'd imagined him.

I folded my arms defiantly and glared at him, half willing him to go away.

The man folded his arms and glared defiantly back at me in obvious mimicry.

I backed up, unfolding my arms, in surprise.

He did the same, copying my posture of shock.

Now I *would* call the police, even if this seemed quite abnormal. *Could* he see me?

The man was laughing now, his head thrown back, his mouth a rictus of mirth. He pointed a finger at me, sending a shiver of terror through me, then dropped all pretense of amusement, his extended arm, hand and finger the very essence of accusation.

Then something else happened that amazed me even more.

One second ago, the taunter on the sidewalk had been alone. A moment later, another, much taller man with dark hair stood behind him. He wore bizarre clothing: a tight leopard bathing thong that barely covered his essentials and a flowing leopard cape fastened over his shoulders, nothing else, and I thought: how can he not be cold? I wondered about my sanity, if I was really awake, if this wasn't a waking dream.

The dark man grabbed the shorter blond man and spun him roughly around, surprising him. The smaller man backed away. They exchanged words and angry gestures, then suddenly the first man, my taunter, pointed up at the window. The tall man looked up at me.

I could see the chiselled planes of his face, his open-mouthed excitement. And even at that distance, I knew and laid my hands against the window, as if I could break the glass barrier between us and leap recklessly to the ground below.

To be with him.

But I did no such thing. I stared down at him as he looked up at me. I mentally called out to him: *Bael! How?* And then, unable to deny my feelings: *Come to me, love!*

Azmodeus had stopped his blatant pointing. His head now turned back and forth, watching his brother, watching me.

And then Bael began to rise in the air, floating toward me.

I held my breath, filled with fright, filled with elation. I started to unlatch the window, glancing at Ginnie asleep in her bed, Daniel in his crib. Was I going insane?

Bael hovered outside the window, gesturing, telling me not to unlock it. His hand reached *through* the glass, and then the rest of him came through the window and the wall below it.

I scanned his body, head to knees, for his legs and feet appeared sunken into and hidden beneath the floor. He grinned, our faces level, and then slowly lifted. I craned my neck, following his face as he rose upward, then glanced back down at the floor. Solid-looking feet touched a solid-looking floor.

My hand reached out to touch him. He felt solid. His hand stroked and then clasped mine; he raised his other to his lips to indicate silence, and then led me from the bedroom to the hall, down the stairs and into the darkened living room.

He touched a lamp shade, and the bulb beneath it blinked on in a sudden flood of artificial light.

"What if my family wakes up?" I whispered in a rush.

"They won't," he answered, not lowering his voice in the least, his eyes examining me almost critically. "You don't quite look the same, and yet it is you."

"I'm in my mortal body," I said almost defensively.

He smirked. Perhaps mortal bodies weren't his cup of tea. I felt suddenly unsure of myself and awkward, meeting an old lover after a ridiculously long time, seeing each other fully under new and uncertain conditions. Our earlier contact had been like talking on a telephone, a voice, but no flesh, a memory and a promise, but dimensionally separated, bodies and lives.

"I should be happy," I said.

"Aren't you?" He continued studying me, critically, curiously, then seemed to be satisfied, at least accepting the changes the years had brought. He drew me to him. "Beloved."

I wanted to kiss him as his face lowered to mine, but something frightened me, making me pull back.

"What?" he asked.

"I'm nervous . . . it's been so long." I glanced down at his unconventional garb. "Do you always dress like this now?"

He laughed too loudly, making me glance upstairs. He said, "They can't hear us," puzzling me.

"But you've materialized," I said, the closest I could describe what he had done.

He laughed again, then suddenly looked upward, all trace of humor gone. He looked stricken.

"What is it?" I asked.

He continued to cast anxious eyes at the ceiling. "Quatama! He knows I'm here."

Heaven was still monitoring me. And Bael had somehow slipped past their barricade. I instinctively knew that in seconds Quatama would end this little tête-à-tête, pull Bael from me.

"No!" I cried out, craning my own head upwards. "Don't take him from me. I need to understand!"

I lowered my gaze to Bael, who stared back at me in what seemed to be awe.

His hands firmly clasped me by my forearms, drawing me closer. "Now I *know* that you still love me."

His black eyes glistened, as if tears were imminent, softening the taciturn expression he'd always worn in Eliom. He pulled me fully against him, his mouth covering my own.

And the light went out.

Darkness blinded me, panicked me, and I pulled away from him. "What happened to the light?!"

"We don't need light."

He pulled me back, lowering both of us to the rug, running his hand along my leg and thigh, drawing my nightgown up. His lips pressed hard against my mouth, his tongue flickering, searching. I gave in to the kiss, then lay complacent as his hand found my breasts, kneading them gently. He pulled my nightgown up further, then positioned himself over me, his mouth seeking a nipple. Dazed, the pleasure intense, I leaned my head to the right, staring mindlessly into the dining room.

My eyes adjusted to the darkness, and the faintest hint that something was odd finally filtered into my brain: the dining room table nearly filled the entire dining room, more than twice as large as it normally was. Its matching chairs were nowhere in sight. And upon the table, which cut off any pathway to the kitchen due to its present exaggerated size, sat a cross-legged fat figure. It began to glow greenly, becoming more visible in the surrounding darkness, until I recognized it as an immense jade statue of the Buddha.

I giggled as Bael's tongue and lips worked harder at my breast then broke away to slowly lick a trail downward. "Hey, Bael," I breathed, "I think we've achieved Nirvana."

The Buddha's serene sightless eyes began to glow and its stone lids raised. A golden light burst out of each socket, totally unnerving me. Pleasure be damned, I jumped up faster than a Jack-in-the-Box, possibly dislocating Bael's neck in the process, if he was capable of injury in his materialized state.

He raised himself from the floor slowly. I nervously smoothed my nightgown down with one hand while pointing to the glowing green monstrosity, its eerie yellow eyes fixed blindingly on us, sitting in a parody of placid meditation on the giant table.

"Quatama!" Bael hissed and grabbed my hand possessively.

"It's a Buddha," I whispered. "And what does Quatama have to do with it?"

He didn't answer me, his hand nearly crushing mine, acting like an adolescent caught at some mischief, awaiting the wrath of the snooping parent. I tried pulling my hand away, but he grasped it all the harder and pulled me back, his free hand holding me against him, unwilling to let go. "No," he said, "don't let him separate us again."

"Light!" I told him. "I need to turn on the light!" I was a strong believer in light as a protection against things that go bump in the night. How many times do people awaken from nightmares and turn on the light to dispel the lingering shadows?

I finally freed myself from his protective embrace and spun around to turn on the lamp on the end table.

"No, Leianna!"

My fingers fumbled, unable to turn on the lamp switch. "I'm out of body!"

"Yes," he agreed and sounded disappointed, resigned.

"But the table . . . the Buddha . . . I'm dreaming. That's what this is. I'm not out of body. I'm dreaming."

"No . . ."

"It *is* a dream. Else why would things be changed?"

"Leianna." He murmured my soul name again, his voice catching on a touch of despair.

Fear motivated me. The statue's eyes continued glowing, fiery yellow light issuing from its sockets. I hugged Bael in quick apology. "I'm going to wake myself up. This is a dream and I'm going to wake myself up!" I shouted, "Wake up!" and continued shouting it until my loud astral voice became a mumbling physical voice, barely audible, but pulling me out of sleep and back into the mortal world.

I opened my eyes, my body lying warm beneath the covers. Ginnie and Daniel lay quietly asleep; the rest of the house was silent.

I waited, half-hoping for Bael to psychically appear, but the roadblock was apparently back up. I thought about the dream, musing over the Buddha's appearance in it. Then tiredness washed over me, pulling me back into sleep.

I awoke three hours later, the alarm buzzing 7:00 a.m. I heard Ginnie groan as I sat up, forced myself out of bed, and pushed the alarm button off.

Daniel snoozed on, no doubt overtired from the chaos of the earthquake. Somehow Ginnie dressed and got to class. I dressed and somehow made it groggily through my workday at the hospital. Floating through my memory, as I typed the medical dictation, was the long-ago despair in old Eliom as Eve and her loved ones prepared themselves to face her judgment by the Creator, the emotions and fears the earthquake had engendered in me, and the curiously somnambulistic dream in which Azmodeus, Bael (had it truly been him?) and the Buddha had appeared.

I hoped Quatama would let a few days slide before resuming the virtual reenactment. How he had expected to complete all of the remaining events leading to the war in Heaven in one mortal night was beyond me. No matter how much he stretched time, as he seemed to insist he could, I only had one mind, and it could only hold so much per session.

Unless there was an imminent crisis brewing, of which no one had informed me, there seemed no valid reason to rush me through these reenactments with barely a spiritual breath between them.

-24-

As if he sensed my exhaustion, Quatama gave me three days respite, waiting until the weekend before calling me back to finish reenacting the events in Old Eliom.

And on the second of those days, another mystery finally unravelled itself. Terence Dearborn's missing music resurfaced.

Cecily Saraband never acknowledged receiving my letter, and Terence was never able to establish spirit contact with her, not even when he stood, in spirit form, right beside her, as he was to, briefly, less than five months after the discovery of his lost works. But the whole experience proved cathartic for him.

Terence hadn't even been with me as I arrived for work that Thursday.

Willa was waiting for me as I entered the secretarial pool, her eyes shining with excitement and, before I could so much as say good morning, blurted out: "Leigh Ann! They've found more music by Terence Dearborn. There was an article in *The Classical Forum,* a newsletter we receive. And isn't it strange, how we were wondering a while back, if he had written any other compositions?"

I blinked dumbly at her, dazed by her unexpected news.

"Oh, my," she said, "it's quite a surprise, isn't it? I'm just as excited as you are!"

"My God! When did they find it?"

"Last month. They just authenticated it. His old girlfriend had been given his piano by his parents in gratitude for all she'd done for him. Apparently she married and was moving to a new home with her new husband when the piano bench fell in the moving van. She knew that Terence had composed some new work just before his death, but she never found anything written down. The lock on the bench seat broke when it fell, and there they were: three unpublished compositions."

"She never thought to look there before?"

"According to the news item, she'd forgotten that some benches have compartments under the seat. She said Dearborn preferred to work alone and undisturbed, and she'd been undergoing grief and never thought of it."

"Oh, my," I said, just as astounded as she was, but for reasons I couldn't share with her. "Are they going to record his new work?"

"That's the wonderful part. Now you'll know why I'm so excited."

She stepped back as if to recite, her hands raised, palms outward and cupped as if to contain her surprise: "They're debuting Dearborn's posthumous works right here in Philadelphia at the Academy of Music. They're going to record them live, and Bernard Lowenstein, a guest conductor from Britain, will lead the Philadelphia Orchestra!"

"Right here." I slowly walked to my desk and sat down. "Oh, my!" Willa walked over to me, grinning at the wonder of it all. She said, "Well? You *are* going to go, aren't you?"

"What? Yes, of course. If we can get tickets. Oh, my!"

"Oh, my *what?*" Kate came sauntering in and stood with hands on hips, casting a dubious glare my way. "Lions and tigers and bears? That's all I hear as I'm hanging my coat up outside there. Oh, my, oh, my, oh, my. You havin' a heart attack, girl? 'cause if you are, you're too young." She shifted her gaze to Willa and back to me. "You two done look like cats that swallowed canaries. Plump ones at that."

Willa smiled. "New music by a composer Leigh Ann and I both like has been discovered. It's going to be showcased in town at the Academy."

"Humph!" Kate sat down at her desk and offered us a sidelong glance. "All this fuss over a little music." She shook her head.

Willa said, "A symphony, a nocturne and a sonata."

"All three!" I breathed out impulsively, but Willa and Kate seemed to consider my outburst an affirmation of Willa's words, nothing more.

I silently called out to Terence: —*They've found them! They've found them!*— He didn't respond.

"Leigh Ann, are you all right?" Willa asked.

"What? Oh. Yes. I'm just . . . just amazed. Doesn't this sound like destiny to you?"

"I don't believe in destiny. I'd call it wonderful luck or a fortunate coincidence. As for tickets, Stephanie's piano teacher, Myrna Woods, is a member of the Academy. She can reserve up to six tickets for the Dearborn retrospective in January . . . which I thought you might want to attend with us. It'll be me, my husband Robert, Stephanie, Myrna and you, if you'd like."

"What about Rob, Jr.?"

Willa paused before answering. "He's not much of a music lover. At nine, he's more interested in sports. Maybe in time . . . at any rate, he doesn't want to go with us. So you're welcome to come instead, my treat."

"Oh, no. I'd pay for my ticket."

"My *treat*," Willa insisted. "Actually Myrna's. I told her how much you admire Dearborn's music and also how you're struggling to raise your son, separated from your husband and all. I hope you don't mind. She's gone through that herself. She said to just come and enjoy yourself."

I hesitated. Willa looked at me expectantly.

At which moment, Marietta poked her head and shoulder past the entrance to the secretarial room. "Excuse me, ladies. It's past nine o'clock. Time to get working."

Kate offered our tall, elegantly dressed and coiffured supervisor a cocksure glance. *"I'm* working."

"Then Willa and Leigh Ann should follow your example. Chop, chop, ladies!" Marietta withdrew from the doorway to stride forthrightly off to her other managerial duties.

Willa grinned wickedly, narrowing her eyes and pursing her lips in mock menace. "Or off with your *heads!"*

I grinned back.

"Woman's just trying to do her job," Kate said.

I said nothing to that, sitting down at my own desk, pulling the top report from my inbox.

"She could loosen up," said Willa. "So, Leigh Ann. Are you in?"

"Huh? Oh. Yes! Thank you. Tell Myrna thank you."

"You're welcome, and I will. We'll make travel plans a few days beforehand in January."

"When *is* the debut of his new work?"

"Sunday, January 16th at 2:00 p.m. It's billed as a family concert. Great way to start the new year, huh?"

"It'll be wonderful," I agreed. "Thanks again, Willa."

"Our pleasure. Now we'd better get to work, before the dragon lady drops in again."

Kate snorted. At least, that got a laugh out of her. We actually did like Marietta and had a great deal of respect for her. When push came to shove, she proved a fair and competent supervisor. But I never had a chance, being young and easily intimidated by her stern, no nonsense demeanor, to tell her that.

I waited all day, my surface thoughts on my job, my inner thoughts expecting Terence to psychically arrive, literally floating on air. Every now and then, I'd catch an image of him in my mind, like a pleasant note sounded far away, its singer not present.

After work, arriving home, my mother greeted me as I shut the front door. Daniel rode her hip. "Well, Leigh Ann, that musical spirit guide of yours made the *Five O'clock News*. His ex-girlfriend found his unpublished music."

"I know, Mom."

"You know? Did *he* tell you? If he did, you're a stronger psychic than me. And possibly doubling for St. Anthony."

"Maybe the good saint helped Cecily Saraband find Terence's music. It seems it was an accident. She probably never did get my letter."

Fred came trooping down the stairs to the living room. "Hey, Mom. When's dinner?"

"In about 15 minutes. The meat loaf's almost done, and I have to steam the vegetables. Here, hold your nephew while Leigh Ann sheds her coat." She transferred Daniel abruptly to Fred and stomped off to the kitchen.

Fred held my squirming son, who said "Mommy," twice and held out one hand to me while attempting to push Fred away with his other. "You want to get down, Danny?"

He nodded. Fred put him down, only to watch him crawl the few feet to me and, holding my legs to steady himself, stand and demand that I pick him up. I let him ride my hip to the coat closet, then lowered him down to the rug. He rebelled. "Ub!"

"Wait. Mommy has to take off her coat." Opening the closet, I heard a skittering sound. Daniel peered into the shadowed spaces between storage boxes and winter boots. I hung up my coat and shut the closet door. Daniel let out a string of baby syllables, kept trying to open the door. I picked him up again, plunking my handbag onto the dining room table, which generally doubled as a work and study table, except on special holiday occasions, when we brought out the china and silver and ate formally. Daniel leaned over in my arms, pointing at the closet.

I walked into the kitchen. "Hey, Mom? Daniel thinks there's something in the dining room closet. An animal. I thought I heard something, too."

"That's just wonderful. We have mice again!"

"Are you okay? I mean, you seem awfully tense tonight."

She didn't answer for a minute. "I'm just tired."

Fred rummaged through our junk drawer under the laminated cabinet counter, pulling out a flashlight. He turned it on. "Never fear, Mom. I'll get the little bugger with my trusty Ever Ready. Freeze him in his tracks."

"Never mind that now. Dinner's ready. Forget the mouse and call your father and Ginnie downstairs. You can look for it later."

Fred clicked the flashlight off and set it on the counter. "Ho-kay!"

He trudged off to the living room and called.

Half an hour later, seated around the crowded dinner table, new scratching sounded, louder now, from the closet. Now Mom got up, grabbed the flashlight, and slowly opened the door, beaming the light into its interior.

Fred and I followed her, curious, in time to see a small black cat bolt from the closet and scurry into the living room.

"What was it?" Mom asked, worried. "It shot out of there so quickly."

"A cat," Fred told her. "It's hiding under the couch. I saw it go there."

"How did a cat get in here?"

Fred shrugged. "From outside."

Dad had gotten up. He walked to the couch, Mom behind him, and bent down, looking under it. "It is a cat. Probably came in when one of you opened the front or back door."

"And how did it get in the closet, Bill?"

"Same way it got in the house, Miriam."

"I would have seen it."

"Animals can be quick," Dad said. "Well, leave it alone. It'll come out when it's ready to."

Mom gave him that stubborn pout we all knew so well. "No strange cat is going to roam my house while I sit at supper."

"Suit yourself." Dad went back into the kitchen. Fred and I followed, sitting down, finishing our meal.

"A cat, huh?" Ginnie quipped. "Maybe Leigh Ann's familiar."

Dad smiled. "Probably some neighbor's cat that got loose."

I offered Ginnie a quick frown and scraped the bottom of the Gerber's jar for a last mouthful of pudding for Daniel.

From the living room, we heard Mom's attempts to coax the cat out. Finally, exasperated, she joined us. "Well, it won't come out for me," she said and finished her own dinner.

By bedtime, it still crouched in the shadows behind the couch or slunk under it when Dad tried prodding it out with a yardstick. We finally gave up, Mom fretting that it would do its business on the rug and "stink the place up" while we slept. She never had been fond of cats, although she tolerated them, for the rest of the family were cat lovers. It had been awhile since a cat had joined us. Our last cat, Talisman, a large orange shorthair, had died three years ago, dragging himself home to die after getting hit by a car. We'd found him alive but paralyzed in the front yard. The vet had to put him to sleep, and we hadn't had the heart to find him a successor. Time passed, and Mom was just as happy that we hadn't, no cat hairs or litter to clean up after.

In the morning, apparently worrying about this uninvited visitor, Mom got up first, looking for it. She found it had urinated and defecated in the bathroom tub and, although this indicated a certain neatness on the cat's part, it didn't endear it to Mom. She cleaned up the mess and looked further for the cat, intending to catch it and boot it from the house. She found it fast asleep on my bed, snuggled against me. She later said that it looked so scrawny and helpless, it had softened her heart, while not exactly winning it. She woke me gently and pointed to the small creature.

I shifted, and it also woke up, yawning and stretching as if it had always lived with us. It looked at me with deep green eyes and mewed, then noticed Mom and retreated a few steps. I extended my hand to it; it sniffed my fingers, then rubbed its lips and face against them.

"It's marking you with its scent," said Mom. "It looks starved."

I stroked it gingerly, trying not to scare it. It butted its head against my hand, wanting more, then climbed over my blanketed legs into my lap, kneading the quilt and purring.

"It certainly likes you."

"Oh, Mom, can we keep it?"

"You sound like you're five years old again, when we found Scamp. I gave in then, too."

I smiled at the cat, still working at the blanket folds. It looked up at me, seeming to smile back. "Thanks, Mom. I'll take care of it."

"Then the first job is to get it litter and a litter pan on your way home from work. It made a disgusting mess in the bathtub overnight, but at least it didn't ruin the rug."

"I'll clean it up."

"I already did. I'll go out with Daniel this morning to get some cat food, but from now on, you're in charge of its care and feeding."

Ginnie's bed creaked. She sat up, rubbing her eyes. "You found the cat?"

"It's on Leigh Ann's bed."

Ginnie got out of bed, came over, and looked at the cat. It looked at her. "You'll have to get it shots, Mom."

"I'm putting Leigh Ann in charge of everything. Time to get moving, you two. You have work and school."

"We know. What'll we name it?" Ginnie asked me. "It looks a little like that cat in Disney's *Cinderella,* except it has no white in its face. We could call it Lucifer."

I shuddered, marveling that my sister had energy enough to tease me first thing in the morning. "Not exactly my choice for a name. Besides, we don't even know if it's a boy. I wonder if . . . ," I reached out slowly and managed to pick it up without the cat squirming too much. Holding it underside up, we inspected its genitals.

"Well, so much for that," my sister concluded. "It's female."

Mom folded her arms across her chest. "Then call it Lucy," she suggested with a gruffness that said she was still unsettled by yesterday's sudden proof of the pudding that my spirit guide really existed. Well . . . empirical proof only, which should have pleased her, but didn't. The evening before, during a private conversation after dinner, Mom admitted that she'd never allowed herself to delve that closely into the spirit world. Mediumship, to her, didn't exist on a personal level: you were the protected receptacle for spiritual information, and once received and disseminated, the message no longer concerned you. No friendship, no love, just a go-between intending to help, but not intending to relate beyond the communication. A temporary job and, yes, indeed, I was breaking her rules, unstringing the psychic safety net that she insisted was so essential. Worse yet, she considered her earlier promise to me, to trust me to find my own psychic level and not interfere, unbreakable. She had swallowed the lecture that ached on the tip of her tongue and simply asked me once again to be careful.

Now she said, "I'm going downstairs to make coffee. Try not to wake Daniel and don't forget to bring home the litter and pan for Lucy." She walked softly around Daniel's crib, my son still sound asleep, and left the room.

Ginnie and I regarded the little black furball on the bed.

"Well," Ginnie said, "our matriarch has spoken. I dub thee Lady Lucy."

"I'm not too sure I'm happy with that name," I murmured, getting up and quietly opening the top dresser drawer for fresh underwear. "Not if it's a feminine version of Lucifer. That's asking for bad luck, and this poor little cat doesn't deserve it." I shut the drawer.

Ginnie opened the second drawer for her own undies. "I thought you weren't afraid of that stuff."

"I thought you *were.*"

"Not anymore."

"Why?"

We each rummaged in our closets for our clothes.

Finally she said, "I don't know. I guess I just realized it was all bunk." She looked at me. "Sorry."

"To each his own," I answered softly. "I still don't like Lucy for the cat's name."

"Mom likes it. So give it a middle name."

I thought about it, watching Daniel fidget in his sleep. "All right," I murmured. "She'll be Lucy Angelina."

"Lucy Angelina. I like that. Sounds like one of those show cats." She reached down slowly to pet the cat. It stretched and rolled on its side, enjoying being pampered. "Are you a pedigreed girl?" Ginnie cooed. The cat blinked and seemed to grin at her.

"She sure is becoming a spoiled girl. Come on, Gin, it's getting late." I finished buttoning my blouse and tucked it inside my skirt. "I'm using the bathroom first."

"Don't be long." She pulled her student nurse uniform on, as I headed down the hall.

Later that evening, when I lugged the litter box and litter home and set it up in the basement, Lucy Angelina followed me and immediately put it to good use. She followed me upstairs to be fed and then followed me from room to room most of the night. Mom thought the cat's middle name was cute. She called her Lucy Angel for short. That version stuck.

The cat delighted Daniel but was smart enough to anticipate his inept toddler lunges and swift enough to scurry out of his reach. She almost seemed to play with him, sitting nearby and waiting for temptation to build in him, then dashing a few feet away before Daniel could grab her. After four rounds of this reversed cat and mouse game, I picked Daniel up and took him upstairs for his bath. He protested until he saw Lucy Angel following us. In the bathroom, she crouched comfortably down until Daniel, miffed by her unruffled silence, splashed a spray of water that drenched me and the cat. Lucy Angel skittered out to dry herself and repair her injured feline dignity. I didn't see her again until I climbed into my own bed, glad that the weekend had arrived and my son in his crib had finally drifted off to dreamland. Then, with that sixth sense no one seems to question in cats, Lucy Angel trotted into the bedroom, jumped onto my bed and over to my side and settled down.

I stroked her tiredly, wondering why Terence hadn't contacted me since Willa broke the news of his music's recovery. But no image of Terence came; perhaps the discovery of his lost compositions had been the unfinished business he'd needed to complete. Even so, I doubted that he'd leave the mortal world behind. It hardly seemed likely or fair to have his work performed and Terence not wanting or permitted to attend their debut. No, his absence was surely due to something else. I stopped worrying over it, turned over on my side and hugged the pillow, yawning and hoping Quatama would give me another night off from reenacting my ancient lifetime in Eliom.

He did, but I still had an intriguing interlude on the higher planes.

Patrick, the dapper physician-turned-poet and Terence's master tour guide in the hereafter, called me out of body for a meeting at his house in the spirit world version of Boston.

One moment I drift into sleep; the next moment I come awake astrally in Patrick's study, a small room, almost an alcove, crowded with wooden desk, chairs and bookcases along the walls. I blink, looking around, still unused to this instant travel, like teleporting in some science fiction novel, only your point of departure is the sleep state and the means of travel seems to be controlled by some thought process. Terence sits on one of the spindle-backed wooden chairs before the desk; Patrick sits behind it.

My musical guide waves at the other chair beside his. "Sit." He looks extraordinary calm and somehow older, more mature. His blond hair combed and falling just so upon his shoulders, his serene blue eyes and his relaxed smile offsets his strong high cheekbones. His body looks trimly muscular in a flowing poet's shirt, dark jeans and boots.

I experience an emotion I'd never before felt towards Terence: desire. I'm sure he notices it. He smiles softly at me, then blushes, and I realize this sudden attraction isn't a one-way street. I sit down, too aware of his closeness, perplexed and wary.

"I *had* wondered where Terence was," I say as an opener, and to him, "Do you know your lost works have been found and will be performed in Philadelphia? In January?"

He nods. "Yes." He draws his eyes away from me and addresses Patrick. "Shall we?"

Patrick regards me, a tiny quizzical smile inching up the side of his lips. "Do you want me to explain?" he asks Terence.

"Yes. I'd prefer you do it. I'd only gum it up."

Damned if I can't feel his sexual tension; Terence positively quivers. "For God's sake, what is it you have to tell me? Something about the new compositions?"

Patrick shakes his head. "Terence has finished his unfinished business from his mortal life."

"Great. But it *was* the discovery of his unpublished musical works, right?"

The elderly guide wags his head again. "No, it was *you*."

"Me?"

"Yes. Terence realizes now that he loves you and has all along."

I nearly sputter, "But—we're friends!"

"Yes, of course." When I sit there dumbly, Patrick continues. "I believe Terence recounted his death experience to you, when he crossed over to real life?"

I nod and wait.

"I believe he recounted that I advised him of his lack of an ongoing and balanced love relationship, a prerequisite to eternal existence."

I nod again, manage to squeak out: "Yes, something like that. But I thought it was Cecily you meant. That he had to comfort her or something!"

Terence places a comforting hand on my shoulder. "Do calm down, Leigh Ann." I nearly jump at that seemingly innocent touch.

Patrick smiles beneficently, like a father about to announce the marriage banns. "You see, Leigh Ann, when Terence discovered he loved you, he knew he could not indulge his heart's desire at this time in your life."

I opt for bluntness. "Speak English, Patrick, and cut the metaphors. If this is Terence's passion and he's not supposed to indulge it, why am I feeling all hot and bothered for him?"

Terence answers me instead, with a tenderness that borders on the smug. "Well, true love *is* never a one-way street."

"True? True love? More metaphors. And I'll thank you to stop reading my mind without my permission. So what about Bael?"

He winces. "That's exactly why we can't indulge ourselves. You have to work that out. And there are all different types of *true* love. You and I, darling, we're soul twins. It didn't surface before, because we weren't ready for it."

"Then turn down the volume a bit, will you? If we're not supposed to do something about it, I mean."

"Sorry. I can't help it. Neither can you, now."

"Excuse my cliche, Terence, but this is all so sudden. So, Patrick, if Terence and I are soul twins, then what are Bael and I? Soul mates? And what the hell *are* soul twins?"

Patrick shifts in his chair behind his desk. "I believe you and the fallen angel Baelzebub are soul opposites and always were, even before he fell. Soul opposites are the epitome of the statement 'opposites attract.' You each hold qualities the other lacks and help each other to fulfill those missing traits. Soul twins are people with identical personalities; although their interests and tastes may vary slightly, their outlook on life, its goals, and their actions and reactions compliment each other. They build each other up and together strengthen one another's pathway in life."

"And soul mates? Who is my soul mate, since you know so much?"

"The term refers to someone whose relationship to another has repeated itself over a series of mortal lifetimes, working out ongoing problems and building on its strengths. It's a catch-all term, much misused by mortals. It could refer to any ongoing relationship valued by your eternal self beyond a given mortal lifetime."

"So both Bael *and* Terence are my soul mates?"

"It's really a vapid term and shouldn't be reserved exclusively for one-on-one relationships. And marriage isn't the only stage that relationships play themselves out on. Definitions like soul twin and soul opposite are more concrete when discussing relationships with eternal connections."

"Well," I say, leaning back in my chair, "at least the heavy vibrations between *these* soul twins seems to have lessened."

"I've distracted you." He grins conspiratorially. "Mind on, passion off. Except for a few, rare oddball cases I've heard of—who've scaled both heights simultaneously. Not something generally achieved by your average lover."

"Speaking of love," I say, bringing the conversation back to its original point, "*how* do Terence's, uh, feelings for me complete his unfinished business?"

"Why, because he loves you unselfishly."

I wait again; that doesn't explain anything to me.

Patrick sighs. "Young people. It's quite simple. Terence wishes to continue as your spirit guide, because he loves you and wants to help you in your mortal life. Secondary guides are not permitted to have a, umm, romantic involvement with their Earthly charges. It's too distracting and causes the guide to see things from an emotional rather than spiritual point of view. Ergo, he wouldn't guide you in a manner that was right for you, but rather in a manner designed to *please* you. That makes for very bad judgments in areas of development needing correction. Major or mature guides can both love and help their charges. Time and experience makes them tougher, more logical in determining what's right for the mortals they watch over. But Terence is inexperienced, and so was given two choices: press his suit for you as a ghost—which is difficult in itself—and let another guide take his place, thus forfeiting the privilege of officially watching over you, *or* putting his personal love for you on hold until he's learned how to guide you without his love overruling what's best for your spiritual growth."

"Geez," is all I manage to say.

"I know it's a bit confusing. Basically, Terence has chosen not to act on his love for you because he loves you, and it means more to him that he continue as your spirit guide."

I turn to Terence. "Well . . . thanks!"

Terence studies me somberly. "I'm finally willing to put my own desires aside for the sake of somebody else's well-being. I love you more than my own egotistical self. Unselfishly. Now do you understand?"

"Yes. Well," I can't help adding, "mothers do that all the time."

"Not all," Patrick says. "But those that do are blessed. And I thank you for helping him begin a balanced love relationship. As your guide, it certainly will be ongoing for him. I'm sure you'll both learn from it."

"Sure." My own emotions are mixed, mostly with relief. My own life is complicated enough without a second astral suitor breathing on my neck. But I'm also proud of Terence, putting his own wants and needs aside to officially stay by my side. I turn slightly, look at him, touched. "Thanks, Terence."

"This time you mean it. I can hear it in your voice. You're welcome, love."

Patrick clears his throat. "Now that we've finished with Terence's business, Leigh Ann, I have a message for you from Quatama. He says he will see you tomorrow night to resume the virtual reenactment sessions. And he wishes you to locate a certain book in your mortal life and read it thoroughly. It's called *Siddhartha* by Hermann Hesse. Don't try to remember it when you wake up. Quatama will guide you to it."

-25-

Terence took his noble sacrifice, to watch over me with an unadulterated heart, a bit too seriously. On Saturday morning, when I got up deliciously late, thanks to Daniel's sleeping until nine, Terence hovered anxiously around me.

When he followed me into the bathroom, I drew a sharp mental line between us. —*Terence!*—

—*What?*—

—*I'm not in here to only wash my face!*—

I sensed his grin and his chuckle. —*It won't bother me.*—

—*Terence. It will bother* me *if you watch me using the toilet.*—

—*But what if you need me? I'm your guide.*—

—*I'll call you if I require your services!*— I snapped at him. —*Out!*—

He grumbled back: —*I'll be right outside if you do need me. What if Bael comes around?*—

—*He's blocked . . . no pun intended. And he'd better not appear here* either! *Out, please.*—

I sensed him leave the bathroom, but knew he stood behind the closed door, guarding me from God knew what potential intruders he expected.

I relieved myself, wondering if his new fervor was going to prove intrusive, not to mention indelicate. Our feelings toward each other had changed, and I knew his zeal reflected his own suddenly realized love for me. Still, if sex was forbidden under his guidance contract, seeing me naked for any reason certainly wasn't conducive to serene abstinence. I also assumed that Patrick was referring to sex shared on the astral planes, when I, like Terence, also existed in whatever comprised the spiritual body. The thought of his trying to make love to my mortal flesh seemed illogical to the point of ribald humor: *Is that you, dear, or just a passing breeze that's tickling my fancy?*

Then I remembered Bael's gentle caress, months ago before his banishment by Quatama, how if I'd shut my eyes, it would nearly feel like a mortal hand stroking me.

I drove the new thought from my mind, wadded up some toilet tissue and finished up, flushing and pulling my nightgown down demurely. I washed my hands and ignored Terence as I headed back to the bedroom and Daniel, who stood up in his crib and extended his arms. I picked him up quietly—Ginnie was still fast asleep—and carried him downstairs for breakfast. Terence trailed behind me, and I wondered if my mother would pick up on his intensified presence.

It didn't take long to find out. Mom relaxed at the table, savoring her coffee, and greeted me lazily but cheerfully: "Good morning, Leigh Ann." Then she glanced past me, as I lifted Daniel into his high chair.

Mom continued to stare into space over my left shoulder. Finally, she asked, "Your musical friend?"

"He's harmless."

She paused; I could feel her mentally sniffing the air. "Yes, you're right. He's a good soul. I can tell."

"He loves me."

"Your plot thickens." She took a slow sip of her coffee. "And what about you?"

"I'm kind of fond of him," I said, pulling a ready-to-heat bottle of milk from the fridge for Daniel. "But he's my spirit guide, nothing else. The plot *unthickens,* Mom. I will be going to his retrospective concert on January 16th, next year. It seems the collective unconscious has been hard at work. My coworker, Willa, has invited me to attend it with her and her daughter Stephanie and Stephanie's piano teacher, free. So perhaps there's some purpose and connection behind all of this, but it isn't immediately apparent. As you've often taught me."

She smiled softly as I tested the milk, then gave Daniel his bottle. I poured myself a cup of coffee and brought it to the table, sitting down. "But don't worry. I'm not losing my marbles, diving off the deep end into untested waters. I promised you I'd keep my life balanced and rational, and I will."

"And I promised that I wouldn't lecture or mistrust you." She paused again, thinking, and I waited, not knowing what she expected me to say, sipping on my own coffee, until she spoke again: "I'd like to hear this new music by Mr. Dearborn that they've discovered."

"You will, Mom. They're going to record their debut at the Academy, and I'll buy us a copy."

"I do love classical music," she said. "You get your love of music from me, too. I also taught you that." She stood up. "I'll make some toast for you and Daniel, if you'd like." I nodded, and she took the bread from the refrigerator, dropping slices into the toaster. "Perhaps you have done some good, even if you only sent the idea into the beyond that his missing music should be found. The newscaster said Dearborn's musical style was comparable to Debussy and other late 19th Century composers."

"It was just a coincidence, Mom," I said, trying to keep the conversation light and *normal,* although I couldn't suppress a proud surge of affection toward Terence, lounging behind me, invisible to our mortal eyes. He sent a correspondingly warm sensation of being hugged back to me.

The toast popped. Mom buttered the slices and brought them to the table, breaking one in half for Daniel.

"Leigh Ann," she said, as I reached for a slice, "there are no coincidences, even if it seems like there are. You said it right a few minutes ago, that there's a purpose to all things, even if you can't see it right away. We are streams; we run to a great river, and it runs to a great sea. We all meet up in different combinations at different times, like waves meeting in endlessly varying patterns. Together, we're also like pieces of a huge puzzle that keeps changing the way things fit together, but its pieces still make up the whole, the big picture."

"Do we ever see the whole puzzle when it's put together?" I grinned at her mixed metaphors and chewed my last bit of toast.

"No. Only God can see the whole picture. We might as well try to see the whole ocean at once."

I swallowed the last of my coffee. "Send me up in a rocket ship. The astronauts can see it all at once."

"But they can't see waves that connect to make the whole ocean. A thinker once said everything is equal to the sum of its parts. You can know the sum and its parts of small things, but the world—what we know of it and what we don't know of it—is much too large for us to know all of its parts and their endless connections. We cannot see it, but sometimes we can feel it, the design, our place in it, and get a surer sense of our direction, which way we should go in life. But this isn't random.

"I tell you this because I survived the worst, and I know there was a purpose, a reason for my survival. It was not a coincidence. I survived to keep alive the memory of those who died, who did not leave the death camps to greet the sun on each new morning or the clouds on a rainy day. I survived to demand in my own way that the world recognize my survival and to demand that it be a better world than it was before, a fairer world, a more ethical world."

"Mom . . . ."

"I don't know if the hundreds of things I do in my life will achieve this. I cannot see the big picture, but I know that my life, its survival, has a connection to the world, to its people, and to their survival. A purpose. There are no coincidences. There is only a plan, an intricate plan, that we are all a part of, that we interact within."

"But there are choices," I said.

"Yes, there are choices," she agreed, "but who's to say they don't all lead to where we each must be, different paths leading to the same necessary goal, one path shorter, one longer, one path harder, another easier, but ending up at the same point God means you to reach. My own path was hard; then when the Allies liberated us, and I came to America, easier."

Her words made me shiver, raising goosebumps. She so rarely spoke of the Holocaust. "I think you were incredibly brave, Mom."

She got up to clear the table of our cups and plates, stopped and looked at me. "I wasn't always brave, but because I survived, you, your brother and sister, and Daniel are here. Yes, your soul could have been born to another woman, but it's not the same. You would have been a different person. And whatever God's purpose in having me survive, it's connected to you, to Fred, to Ginnie, to Daniel, and even to your father, for your father loved me and helped me to be brave and not fear the future anymore. So I now trust God and trust He will guide you, too, to fulfill whatever purpose he has mapped out for you. I've thought a lot about this since you came home, and I don't worry anymore over you. You're special, Leigh Ann, and even if you make mistakes, you'll find your way."

I quietly removed Daniel from his high chair and held him against me, feeling his solid weight, his reality, and the survival of his grandmother, which through me had made him the person he now was.

The conversation proved a high mark, giving me a clearer understanding of what my mother needed from me, both as her daughter and as her champion: to uphold ethics which had given her faith, had safeguarded her world's surviving values and regained humanity's dignity, even in the time of bitter chaos.

And I chose to champion her, because I was her daughter. Her survival and strength had given me life, gone into my life. I, too, demanded that the world better itself, that its people become more ethical and deny chaos. And like her, I had no way to guarantee how or if I could bring about any change in our world. All I could offer was my own effort, my own commitment.

Mom, for her part, became totally supportive, became my foundation and my confidant. From that day on, I could speak freely to her about my alternate existence without conditions or censure.

They say that confronting your own mortality gives you strength, lets you truly value life. My mother had learned this, and on that day, as my father, Fred and Ginnie came downstairs for breakfast, I, too, absorbed a small but potent understanding of my own mortality and a surer sense that my being here in this world was not random, and the path I walked, never exclusively of my own charting.

Mom quietly puttered around the kitchen. She cooked a full breakfast with eggs and bacon for Dad and Fred—you might say our family practiced the reform version of reform Judaism—and sighed when Ginnie insisted she was dieting, opting for a small bowl of cereal and an orange.

We munched and yacked about our mundane concerns and plans, and I suddenly felt immensely alone, a maverick trying to assimilate into a normal society. Daniel, still perched on my lap and nibbling a second half-slice of toast his grandfather had given him, giggled, all toddler contentment in the bosom of his family.

Mom brought over the half-full pot of coffee. "Leigh Ann? Would you like some more?"

"Sure." I held my cup out for her. She filled it, the simple gesture more than it seemed. She filled me with the simple beauty of my connection to her, our family, and the world.

Dad inched his own cup her way. "I'll take a little more, Miriam." She filled his cup as well.

Fred pushed his chair back, lightly holding his stomach. "I'm full. I've got to go finish this novel I got from the library for a book report. It's due Monday."

"Then you'd better get crackin'," Dad told him. "Which book did you choose?"

"Something called *Siddhartha*. It's about this Indian guy. It's also pretty short, so I figured I could read it fast."

Ginnie chewed and swallowed her last orange section, shut the nursing textbook she'd been reading, and asked, "American Indians?"

"Nah. This guy is like from the country of India, as far as I can tell. He's like trying to find himself. As far as I can tell."

Dad gave him one of *those looks*. "It *is* a short novel, and it shouldn't take you long to read. It's also a famous novel, beautifully written by Hermann Hesse."

"Yeh, I know. Some German guy. But it's about these young guys in India, Siddhartha and his friend. I forget the other guy's name."

"Govinda. And Hesse was Swiss, not German. You haven't read too far in the book, have you?"

"I only got it yesterday, Dad, from the Bushrod Library after school."

"And how long have you known you had a book report due on Monday?"

"Uh, about two weeks."

"Well, I guess you know what you have to do before you leave this house this weekend."

"Do my book report?"

"Yep. And whatsmore, I want to see it when it's done."

"Aw, Dad. What if you're out, when I finish it?"

"I have one customer to see this afternoon. I'll be home for dinner. I doubt that you'll have your report done before then."

Fred slumped in his chair. "Okay."

Mom put her two-cents in as she cleared the remaining breakfast dishes from the table. "It's a beautiful book. Take your time reading it. It still won't take you long."

"You've read it, too?"

"Yes. Like your father said, it was famous, a *literary master-piece.*"

My curiosity aroused, I asked them, "What is it actually about?"

Mom filled the sink with hot water and soap, soaking the dirty dishes. "It's a very spiritual novel. Siddhartha is seeking his higher self, learning how to best reach godhead."

Fred wrinkled his nose. "Mom, why don't you let me read the book before you give away the ending." She raised her eyebrows at him. "Well, you make it sound geeky, Mom. And I'm only up to the second chapter."

"Then go read the book." Wiping her hands and balling them into fists, she placed them firmly on her hips, obviously annoyed with him. "Do as your father says. And I, too, want to read your book report when it's complete."

Fred rolled his eyes upward and sighed. "Geez! I should've picked a book my parents hadn't read." He got up, left the kitchen to head upstairs, and called, "I hope I'm allowed a bathroom break!"

Dad called back, "Only in dire emergency." It drew a short departing snort of laughter from Fred.

Daniel wriggled down from my lap and onto the floor. Lucy Angel had come into the room, making cat tracks to her food and water bowls. Daniel toddled over to her, his hand reaching down to pet her. "Let her eat, Danny," I told him. "Here. You can help me put some more food in her bowl." I got the dry cat food from the cabinet drawer, and scooped out a portion, letting Daniel hold it with me as we added it to the bowl. Then I picked him up again to literally keep him out of Lucy Angel's hair. "You know, Mom, I still don't have a clear picture of what that book's about."

"It's better if you read it. It's not easy to explain. It's about the

Buddha. Siddhartha meets the Buddha, but it brings him no content-ment, and he leaves to seek his own way, to search for a greater wis-dom."

"The Buddha? Isn't he God in Buddhism?"

"Buddhists have a different concept of what we call God. Siddhartha meets Gotama, the Buddha, in his last mortal lifetime, and Govinda, who has been journeying with Siddhartha, joins Gotama's followers to become a Buddhist monk."

"Quatama?!" I asked, jolted.

She turned the hot water on and pulled a sudsy plate out, scrub-bing it clean. "No. *Got*-a-ma. Hesse's fictional version of the Gautama Buddha, the founder of Buddhism."

And Dad added: "He was also known as Prince Siddhartha. In the novel, Hesse recreates him, both as a young man seeking enlighten-ment and as his fulfilled self, attaining it. Why don't you just read the book?"

"I think I will. Tonight, when Danny's asleep. Fred should be done with it by then."

"He'd better be," Dad said, still miffed by Fred's deliberate pro-crastination.

"He'll be done with it," Mom assured him. "You've chided him for wasting time. Now give him a chance to make up for it." Her glance caught mine for one moment, and I knew she remembered the name I had mentioned months ago, belonging to the mysterious master spirit guide promising to protect my family during my own quest for enlight-enment. And what was it that Terence had once asked me about Quatama? Yes. I remembered. He had asked me if I knew who Quatama was. If both Mom and Terence knew, despite my mispro-nunciation of Quatama's name, that my major guide was the Buddha, why hadn't they told me? More so, why hadn't Quatama himself corrected me and explained?

I took a deep breath. "Mom, I'm going to attempt to put Danny in his playpen and hope he doesn't try to climb out. I have to get some laundry done."

Ginnie unstuck her nose from her textbook and looked up. "I'll watch him for you. I need to take a break from pharmaceutical dos-ages!" She closed the book, got up and scooped Danny out of my arms. "Saturday morning cartoons are just the change I need." She galloped into the living room with him, making him screech with laughter, then turned on the television.

"Thanks, Gin," I called to her, then went down to the basement, grabbing a laundry basket, and up to the bedroom to separate my and

Danny's dirty clothes. Terence slipped quietly into the room; I sensed some uncertainty in him. He wanted to explain; he wasn't totally certain he should be the one to do it.

I was totally nonplussed and searched for an opening line to break the tense confusion between us. Using telepathic speech, I finally ventured: —*I don't know how I'll ever get used to calling him Gau-ta-ma. I've always called him Qua-ta-ma, and he never corrected me.*—

—*That which we call a rose . . ,*— Terence suggested warily. —*He didn't want me to tell you. He said you weren't ready yet. To know who he was.*—

—*And is, I presume?*—

—*Well, yes, he's still the Buddha. But he's a good guy. You mustn't feel overwhelmed by it. He wants you to read the book, you know.*—

—*The book. Oh!* Siddhartha! *He did say, no, not him. Patrick. Patrick conveyed a message from Quatama about the book.*—

—*I know. I was there. He said Quatama would direct you, help you locate the book. It seems your brother's brought the book to you.*—

—*Apparently. Though not for the same reasons Quatama might have intended.*—

—*Fred might like it . . . though he's a bit young for it. It's a lovely book. Look, about this morning. I'm sorry if I offended you. But it's very common for spirit guides to watch over their charges in, um,* all Earthly experiences. *We're no more titillated by it than doctors attending patients, bent on making sure they're well.*—

—*It's embarrassing.*—

—*It's life. And your naked body won't arouse me. I can turn off those emotions in the physical world, being a spirit now and all. It's a bit more difficult on the astral plane when you're there, but I'm capable of being in command of my emotions there, too. You needn't worry.*—

—*Well, indulge me for now. My modesty, I mean.*—

I could picture him smiling, then he said: —*I'd indulge you in anything you want, as long as it didn't impinge on your well-being.*—

—*Fine,*— I told him. —*We'll leave it like that.*—

One worry off my mind, I spent the rest of the day between laundry and taking Daniel out with Ginnie, shopping for my son's first Halloween costume. I lingered at a little devil costume, complete with tiny red horns, a red vinyl get-up with a hood, but Ginnie vetoed it. She drew me over to a mix-and-match section in the Halloween aisle and suggested making Danny up as a magician. We ended up buying a toddler-sized black cape and top hat and a tiny magic wand. "This way you can dress him warmly beneath it if it's cold out that night," she said. Danny, of course, wanted to play with the costume. We finally diverted his attention by letting him carry the hollow plastic pumpkin we would hold the goodies he collected in as we took him trick-or-treating. He didn't quite understand the holiday yet, but held the pumpkin possessively by its little black strap, refusing to give it up as we paid the cashier. Luckily she knew its price.

Back home, I put Daniel in his playpen, where he created the game of Put The Alphabet Blocks In The Pumpkin. Fred came downstairs before dinner and showed Mom his finished book report. She read it, nodded her approval, then said, "Leigh Ann wants to read the book."

Fred shrugged, trudged back upstairs and brought the small paperback edition of the novel down to me. On the cover was a black and white photo of a statue of the Buddha, very old and damaged by cracks running through the stone. "It's not your average romance novel," he warned me wryly.

"I don't expect it to be. Did you like it?"

He thought about it. "It was okay. The ending was a little weird."

"Well, don't tell me." I opened the book up and read the first line of the first chapter —*The Brahmin's Son*—of Part One: *In the shade of the house, in the sunshine on the river bank by the boats, in the shade of the sallow wood and the fig tree, Siddhartha, the handsome Brahmin's son, grew up with his friend Govinda.*

The book mesmerized me. Siddhartha, the boy who had everything . . . looks, good family, friends, brains, respect, and a beautiful spirituality . . . suspects that these blessings are ephemeral. He decides to seek Atman, the true self that dwells beyond mortal concerns. His friend Govinda adores him, following him as loyally as a squire to his knight. Siddhartha tells Govinda that he intends to join the Samanas, wandering ascetics who practice severe self-denial to cleanse the soul of mortal corruption. But when he asks his father for permission to do so, the Brahmin is displeased and dismisses Siddhartha's request. Siddhartha stands firm, literally, refusing to move until his father accepts and understands his son's spiritual needs. For hours on end, Siddhartha waits silently. His father leaves and returns throughout the night to see his son's rigid stance unchanged. Finally, before daybreak, his father speaks to him and knows that Siddhartha will stand there unmoving, even to his own death, awaiting the Brahmin's approval, for he cannot disobey his father, even while he rejects his father's ways. The Brahmin, understanding that Siddhartha must seek his own path, gives him permission to leave, asking only that he come back, to convey what he has learned, whether he succeeds or fails in his quest. Siddhartha leaves to join the Samanas and finds Govinda also waiting to join him in his quest.

End of Chapter One. At which point, Dad came home, washed up, read and pronounced Fred's book report sound, and the aroma of Mom's roast chicken dinner, including homemade stuffing, was tickling our noses and drawing us into the kitchen. I put the novel aside and fed Daniel, while I ate with my family. Later that evening, I bathed Daniel, put on his sleeper and lifted him into his crib. He fell asleep, tired out from skipping his nap, while I put away our finished laundry. I tucked him in, covering him snugly with his soft flannel blanket, then showered and put on my nightgown. Ginnie was out, Saturday night and all, with some nursing student friends. In the quiet of the bedroom, I turned on the lamp on our dresser, fluffed my pillow against the wall for back support and continued reading, sitting cross-legged on the bed.

Sometime after midnight, I finished the book, mystified by both the beauty of the tale and how some of Siddhartha's experiences and Gotama's teaching reflected lessons I'd learned and outlooks gained. Siddhartha and Govinda had lived three years among the austere Samanas, but when hearing of Gotama, decide to seek the Illustrious Buddha and consider his teachings. Yet Siddhartha doubts Gotama can teach him something new.

The young friends find the Buddha and recognize him at once: *His peaceful countenance was neither happy nor sad. . . . his face and his step, his peaceful downward glance, his peaceful downward-hanging hand, and every finger of his hand spoke of peace, spoke of completeness, sought nothing, imitated nothing, reflected a continual quiet, an unfading light, an invulnerable peace.*

How similarly had Quatama affected me, when I first met him.

Siddhartha and Govinda hear Gotama preach, and Govinda joins the Buddha's followers. Reproaching his friend for not joining, Govinda asks Siddhartha what flaw could exist in the Buddha's teachings? Siddhartha assures him that the teachings are good, but the next day, when Govinda becomes a monk, he and Siddhartha part ways.

Before leaving, Siddhartha asks permission to speak to Gotama. He tells Gotama of his great admiration for his teachings, but that *"this unity and logical consequence of all things, is broken in one place,"* and this gap breaks down *"the eternal and single world law,"* causing *"something strange, something new"* to stream into the world.

I didn't quite understand this passage in the novel; possibly

Siddhartha found the physical world to be imperfect and not capable of the unity Gotama claimed it possessed through the universal law of cause and effect. But Gotama listens politely, agrees that Siddhartha had found a flaw in his teachings, but warns him against *"the thicket of opinions and conflict of words."* The goal he teaches is *"salvation from suffering"* and nothing else. Siddhartha, while still polite, suggests that the Buddha has reached his highest goal through means other than adopting the teachings of others: the one secret Gotama's instructions can't contain is what happened to the Buddha in his hour of enlightenment. For this reason, Siddhartha states, he must abandon doctrines and teachers and seek his own enlightenment alone, while acknowledging that Gotama has himself achieved holiness.

The Buddha wishes him well, while questioning his reasoning, and *"with imperturbable brightness and friendliness,"* dismisses him: *"You are clever, O Samana,"* said the Illustrious One, *"you know how to speak cleverly, my friend. Be on your guard against too much cleverness."*

Siddhartha sets out to rediscover himself and the world he'd earlier rejected, but doesn't return home to his father. He meets the beautiful courtesan Kamala and, in order to win her favor, finds employment with the merchant Kamaswami, to whom Siddhartha becomes a valued assistant. Even so, he has no real love for business, working only to earn money for Kamala, who alone understands him. He immerses himself in mundane life for many years until, tainted and swollen with its vices and soul-sick with spiritual restlessness, he lies with Kamala one last time, and dreams that the rare songbird she keeps in a golden cage has died. Horrified with his life, he abandons his success, leaving the town. Kamala herself has expected this and upon Siddhartha's disappearance, closes her house and retires from the life of a courtesan. She also frees the songbird from its cage, letting it fly away, and later finds that she's pregnant with Siddhartha's child.

Siddhartha, reaching the river he had crossed years ago upon entering the town, now considers drowning himself. But he hears in his soul the sacred word "Om," which he repeats and realizes that life cannot truly be destroyed. He falls into a rejuvenating sleep and upon awakening, sees his friend Govinda, who has also aged and doesn't recognize Siddhartha until he identifies himself. The friends speak briefly, then part again.

Siddhartha becomes a companion to the ferryman Vasudeva, who teaches him how to listen to the river: *"The river knows everything; one can learn from it."* The river teaches Siddhartha *"there is no such thing as time."* He finds peace with Vasudeva, until word comes that Gotama, the Illustrious One, is ill, soon to leave his last mortal life. Among those making a pilgrimage to the dying Buddha is Kamala and her son, also named Siddhartha, a spoiled and recalcitrant boy. As they near the river, a poisonous snake bites Kamala, and her son's cries for help are heard by the ferryman, who brings her and her child to his boat. The elder Siddhartha recognizes her and realizes the child is his son. When Kamala dies, Siddhartha puts all of his heart into loving and raising his son. But the boy hates him and the simple river life. When Vasudeva suggests that Siddhartha's love is chaining his son to a life he can't adjust to and returning the boy to the town and his mother's house, Siddhartha refuses, fearing his son will repeat the mistakes he himself has made in life.

When young Siddhartha runs away from his father and Vasudeva, his father goes after him, to no avail. Siddhartha finally allows Vasudeva to lead him back to the river, where the wound his son inflicted on him slowly heals. He learns to accept all of the people of the world, both the simple and mundane folk, and *"the sage and the thinker."* Still, the loss of his son pains him, until one day, seeing his aged reflection in the river, he remembers his own father. Realizing he himself left home and never returned to his father, Siddhartha confesses his folly to Vasudeva, who asks him to listen once more to the river.

He does: it teaches him that he, his father, and his son have experienced the necessary journey all people undergo in life and, therefore, all are connected, all things are connected, and never truly separated, like waves on the river all journeying onward and intermingling as they seek their course.

Realizing that Siddhartha has accepted his destiny, Vasudeva *"radiantly"* says goodbye to him, *"going into the woods,"* metaphorically *"going into the unity of all things."* And this, too, Siddhartha accepts *"with great joy and gravity."*

In the last chapter, Govinda, having heard of a ferryman *"many considered to be a sage,"* goes to speak with him, again not recognizing Siddhartha until he identifies himself. He invites Govinda to stay in his hut by the river, and the two old friends talk through the night. But when Govinda asks Siddhartha to speak of the knowledge he has gained, Govinda cannot understand his friend's answers, which he feels conflict with the teachings of Gotama. Yet, studying his friend, Govinda feels Siddhartha has reached the same pinnacle as Gotama. He asks Siddhartha to give him something he, Govinda, can understand. Siddhartha asks him to kiss his forehead. In doing so,

Siddhartha's connection with the unity of all things is conveyed to Govinda. He knows Siddhartha has become Gotama, has become the Buddha, that the positive and negative and the timelessness of eternity exist in him, and exist in all things waiting for their moment of enlightenment.

-26-

I normally can't read in bed without falling asleep, but was awake and alert as I finished *Siddhartha.* I put the book on the dresser, turning off the lamp, and lay in bed, thinking of Siddhartha's imperfect life and the ending enlightenment that gained him perfection. The idea of perfection bothered me. How could anyone be perfect in *this* world?

I heard my parents and Fred come upstairs, the sounds of their washing up and readying for bed, before I drifted off. When Ginnie came in, I woke briefly out of a dream where I sat under a leafy green tree on a sunny river bank, gazing at the glistening ripples flowing by. I listened to Gin's muted movements, the creak of a floor board, the soft whoosh of mattress springs as she undressed in the dark and got into bed. I drifted off again into sound sleep, only remembering my nocturnal meandering when Quatama awakened me the next morning after the lessons and virtual reenactment were finished.

I say nothing to Quatama at first, when my sleep-laden vision clears and I become acclimated to the switch from the mortal to the astral. I find myself sitting on the floor of Quatama's hut, the low wooden table before me. Quatama sits opposite me, also cross-legged, on the floor, Hesse's book on the table between us, a duplicate of the paperback edition Fred borrowed from the library.

"I think that you've gained much from reading Hesse's recreation of my last mortal life."

"Quatama, why didn't you tell me? Excuse me. Gautama. No Q there, is there? It's a G. I'm still not sure I'm pronouncing it right," I mutter.

Quatama smiles, genuinely amused. "I want you to go on addressing me as you always have. When I first reestablished contact with you, I thought you would not be yourself with me, would be in awe of me as Gautama Buddha. That would not be beneficial to your spiritual growth, would it? My name has not changed since we were together in old Eliom, and the stress on the second syllable and the Q sound being used in place of the G was correct then. I only wish you to know me fully now, both as I was then and as I have become since then, to know you have faith in me" (his eyes light humorously) "and possibly respect for my guidance in decisions you have yet to be confronted with. Tonight we will finish your reliving of the chaos that destroyed the peace in Eliom 35,000 mortal years ago, or Eden as your Judeo-Christian bible called our original homeland."

"But what has *Siddhartha* to do with that, other than that you lived then as a spirit master and Council member, and apparently incarnated since then and needed to reach enlightenment all over again?"

"Leigh Ann, you miss the crux of Hesse's story. Perhaps his exquisite style overwhelmed you from seeing it. Enlightenment lived within me, even in my Earthly lives; it was never lost. What I learned in that last lifetime was that the rest of my mortal brothers and sisters had the same enlightenment within them, living in them before they achieved it, as well as after they reached it."

"I'm sorry, Quatama, I still don't understand."

"Then open the book, Leigh Ann," he shuts his eyes briefly, "to Page 73 and read aloud the second paragraph to its completion on Page 74."

I find the page. At first the letters are like blurring squiggles, and I remember what Terence said about his difficulty reading mortal writing. Does the same hold true for me with astral writing? Then, suddenly, the print on the page comes sharply into focus. I look at Quatama who simply smiles back and nods. I read:

"'At times he heard within him a soft, gentle voice, which reminded him quietly, complained quietly, so that he could hardly hear it. Then he suddenly saw clearly that he was leading a strange life, that he was doing many things that were only a game, that he was quite cheerful and sometimes experienced pleasure, but that real life was flowing past him and did not touch him. Like a player who plays with his ball, he played with his business, with the people around him, watched them, derived amusement from them; but with his heart, with his real nature, he was not there. His real self wandered elsewhere, far away, wandered on and on invisibly and had nothing to do with his life. He was sometimes afraid of these thoughts and wished that he could also share their childish daily affairs with intensity, truly to take part in them, to enjoy and live their lives instead of only being there as an onlooker.'"

"Do you sometimes feel like that?" Quatama asks. "That your real life is elsewhere?"

I falter. "Sometimes."

"And that the people whom you know, possibly love, who do not know of this real life, are sometimes strangers to you, or perhaps like friends you meet while journeying to another place, all the while knowing you will eventually go home, those people only memories of when you were away from your real life?"

"Yes, sometimes it feels like that. Sometimes I feel quite alone, being me . . . being different."

"Ah!"

I babble on, disconcerted by this self-analysis and Quatama's apparent approval of it. "I also liked, when Siddhartha disappeared from the town, Kamaswami thought something terrible had happened to him, but actually something good had, because he had to leave to find himself again. And even though he dreamt that the songbird had died, Kamala really went and freed it to fly away. I liked the symbolism. I thought Kamala's pregnancy was symbolic, too, like Siddhartha had left something of himself behind in the ordinary world, but then he meets his son, and they hate each other, so I guess it wasn't."

Quatama remains silent, eyes downcast.

"Have I said something wrong?"

He raises his head slowly. "No. But you were correct the first time. Siddhartha does leave his son, as a part of himself, in the mundane world, but not by choice, neither his nor his son's. His son denies Siddhartha's path because it is not his destiny. The boy had to seek out his own path, regardless of his father's path."

"Which is what Siddhartha had demanded of his own father, the Brahmin, in the opening chapter."

"Yes. Now I will teach you something. Like Siddhartha, you felt alone, a part of the world and yet apart from it. Think on this contradiction and see that there is none. In all people exist the seed of their own godhead and at some point in time, it has sprouted and fully grown. They are enlightened and know both the intricacy and the simplicity, both existing at the same time, which holds the unity, our universe and all its worlds, together. You and they both are a part of the universe, endlessly developing and fulfilling yourselves. Yet as a Keeper, Leigh Ann, you are also a special focal point. Our Creator, through your eyes, ears, other senses and your soul watches over these other souls treading upon their individual paths toward enlightenment, achieving it and seeking again. And for these other souls, you are their focal point, through which they can spiritually see, touch and feel the unity which is God, their own enlightenment."

"Um, I'm a spiritual telephone."

Quatama laughs. "In some ways. Therefore, you must always seek to understand and have patience and love for those whose lives you touch in the mortal world and your mundane life, learning to accept their strangeness which makes them unique, and respecting your own difference, which makes you unique. That which sets you apart, Leigh Ann, is also that which sets you firmly in their midst. One hand, as they say, washes the other, despite the fact that one is left and one is right."

"But what if they don't like me? Think that I'm weird. That my beliefs contradict their own?"

"Then you must let them go their own way, while knowing all ways lead to the One . . . and have already been reached. Open the book again, Leigh Ann, to Page 109, the bottom of the page, where Vasudeva explains about time, which does not truly exist, no more so than a river could stand still to be measured at each bend."

Quatama waits as I silently read the passage, then question it. "But we do measure time. We have clocks."

"An arbitrary illusion to measure activities or the lack of them. When you reach enlightenment, you lose your illusions. One last passage from *Siddhartha,* and then we will go to the eighth physical astral plane and finish reenacting the events in old Eliom. Turn to Page 144. Look again to the bottom of the page, where it says *'time is not real, Govinda. I have realized this repeatedly.'*"

"I see it," I tell him.

"Read aloud the final lines on that page."

I read them to myself first and for some reason they scare me, but I read them softly to Quatama: *"And if time is not real, then the dividing line that seems to lie between this world and eternity, between suffering and bliss, between good and evil, is also an illusion.'*"

"Remember this," Quatama says as I place the book down on the table. He reaches out his hand, and I clasp it with my own. I shut my eyes as we travel through the illusion we call space and time. I also remember that an illusion is a misrepresentation of what we perceive to be reality.

When we thought-travel, there seems to be no movement yet no sense of solid surroundings. It feels as if I'm hanging in empty static space, except for the weight of my body and the sure grip of my hand in Quatama's. Then we arrive at our intended destination, floor once again under my feet and what I can best describe as knowing that one is *in place* again, where linear and spacial dimensions exist in a compositional structure.

"Open your eyes, Leigh Ann."

I slowly raise my lids, and I'm staring at Rosemary, who is leaning against the edge of her desk in the Aural-Visual Recall office. She's not wearing a sari this time. She has a saucy beige jumpsuit on, with gold lamé belt and a gold-embroidered breast pocket showing a dove with a small leafy branch in its beak. On her feet are gold sandals, moderately heeled.

"Smart," I say, and see her beam.

"Thanks. I'm going off-duty after I set you guys up. It's my second wedding anniversary, and I'm meeting my husband at a charming little bistro in New Italy."

"New Italy?" I ask. I notice that her short bouffant hairdo has been changed to a glamorous upsweep, topped with a shower of curls.

She smiles. "The Italian community here on the eighth plane. You'll get used to astral geography once you're back more permanently. Most transient souls still incarnating never have time to explore it fully."

"There *is* no such thing as time," I dryly inform her.

She grins. "Quatama's been getting to you, huh? Well, then, you'll still have plenty of *opportunities* to learn. For instance, New Italy is our recreation of Earth's Italy. In fact, most of the Earth has a duplicate both on the eighth and the sixth planes. People tend to be more comfortable with the familiar, whether they're staying for five years or fifty years or five hundred."

"Except for Eliom. There's no Eliom on Earth."

"No. But Earth was *supposed* to be a natural paradise with all of its creatures equally and ecologically balanced. We screwed that up."

Quatama clears his throat.

"It's just an expression, master. I suppose you want to get started, huh?" She goes to the file cabinet and extracts another accordion file, putting it on her desk. I peer in, seeing the three hoops of gold, red and dark purple, the same ones Quatama had used during our last virtual reenactment. Rosemary tells him, "I recalibrated the gold neurotransmitter to start with Eve's trial. Leianna . . . you pretty much understood from your last V-Re-E session that old Lucifer intended to stir up civil war if God didn't judge things *his* way?" I nod.

Quatama says: "He would have caused civil war if things *had* gone his way. It was his destiny to defy our Creator."

I'm still irked by Rosemary's earlier offhand remark. "Excuse me, Quatama . . . Rosemary, why did you say *we* screwed up Earth? It was Adam's and my mother Eve's fault."

Rosemary hands Quatama the file with the hoops. "We're responsible for each other, sweetie, in the long run. We all share the results, don't we?"

"It just seems a harsh judgment to blame all of us. I was just a child when my mother and uncle disobeyed God."

"Well, I'm not as smart as you, Leianna, but on whom do we blame our society's failure to reconcile Lucifer's rebellion? If *all* of the angelfolk had worked together to heal the genetic damage we inflicted on mortals, we might have finished the job a lot sooner."

"Uh, wasn't it God's choice to exile Lucifer in Hell? Did the angelfolk have any say in any of this? And how do you know you're not as smart as me?" I ask, smarting—excuse the pun—from what I perceive to be Rosemary's sarcasm.

She seems genuinely surprised. "You're a Keeper." I stare at her blankly, still not understanding what that has to do with my intelligence. "Leianna, you've seen all of eternity. At your Naming Ceremony. You hold all of the knowledge of the universe within you."

"I do?" Now I realize she meant no sarcasm.

"Yes," says Quatama, "but can she use it wisely?"

Rosemary offers us a gentle smile. "I'm betting the odds are in her favor, master." She connects with me, and I immediately know that she bases her judgment on what she takes to be my good nature. I'm touched, nearly blushing, but she switches gears, getting back to the matter at hand. "We've prepared a room on the fourth plane for you and Leianna, master. Each of the hoops recount different memories leading to the final days of the rift in Heaven, ending with Lucifer's expulsion and Leianna's own pledge to incarnate."

I ask, "How are we going to do all that in one night?"

Quatama tucks the accordion file with the hoops under his left arm. "The fourth plane is timeless. Like the river. Don't worry. We'll get you back to the right spot on your illusionary clock and calendar."

"With my brains intact?" I'm wondering how many memories are on each hoop.

"The story of your first life is almost complete. The hoops are buffered, and if you become weary, we'll take a rest period. Rosemary, I thank you once again for your help and wish you and Jordan a wonderful evening." He opens his free hand to reveal a small cube of mottled silver.

Rosemary takes it. "A music cube." She presses it in a certain way, and it plays a romantic ballad, vocal backed by a lilting guitar. "Oh, Quatama. We love this song. Thank you! 'Now The Dancing Sunbeams Play' by Joseph Haydn," she tells me. "You might have heard it as 'The Mermaid's Song.' Well, if you're all right, I'll be going now. Thanks again for the anniversary gift. Take care, Leianna."

"Happy anniversary," I say as she poofs out of sight, so fast I haven't time to blink.

"She didn't close her eyes," I tell Quatama.

"I suggest *you* still do so. You are not used to traveling free-fall in a void. I don't wish anything to disturb your state of mind tonight. We can practice modern travel techniques at another time."

I take his extended hand again, and when I open my eyes, we're in a spacious room, a well-fed fireplace before me, its flames crackling and sending waves of soothing warmth into the room, lighting its stone walls. The one to my right is partially covered by brilliant medieval tapestries, the other to my left, bare with two small windows cut into the stone, darkness beyond them.

A Louis XIII divan, all purple and gold and exquisite, faces the fireplace. To its right is a plush highback chair done in gold upholstery; to its left, a small mahogany end table with elaborate wood trim and an empty silver tray atop it.

Quatama's hand sweeps to the divan, then to the chair. I choose the chair and relax in it. He places the file box on the floor; only then do I notice that a silver-grey rug covers it, nearly to the edges of the room, leaving an outer square, slightly over a foot of grey stone showing. Quatama brings the gold hoop over to me. "Are you ready?" I nod, and he places it on my head.

The Well of Being. There had been numerous ceremonies on the Shore of the Seraphim since my Naming Day: other naming ceremonies for the hundred or so other children who had been born into our community; *Ch'llelen*, the Spring festival where we communed with our Creator and received blessings for ourselves and the Garden, that both would be fertile; the Autumn festival in which we sang our thanks for the harvest; and the holiest day of all, *Om Yahr,* when the Seraphim came, travelling across the vast waters to the shore to touch our true hearts' obeisance, to imprint it upon their hands and carry its glad tidings to our Creator.

But this day, the walk across the fields, prairies and woods as we travelled to the Well had been fearful and solemn. Nearly all of the village had accompanied my mother and her family, not only to learn of her fate, but to judge how it would affect the rest of us. Eve and I were somehow now attuned to each other, and I tried, for her sake, to be hopeful, to pray silently for the Creator's forgiveness. The weight of impending judgment, both the Creator's and our community's, and possibly punishment, hung like a stone on our backs. As we trekked down the sparse slopes to the Well of Being, despite the brightness of the day, the original burden of fear and doubt returned, like a fist descending to crush my heart. I faltered, tripping, and Bael, who had accompanied me, caught and steadied me, holding my elbow as we stared in horror at the broad circumference of the Well. No mist rose from it.

Our elders had long ago instructed us that its nebulous tendrils conveyed our Creator's most precious gift to us: our incredible longevity. On *Om Yahr,* after the Seraphim took leave of us, each of the angelfolk approached the Well, its vapors, the very breath of our Creator, sparkling out of it to envelop each man, woman and child. Now it sat starkly upon the shore, no obscuring cloud, no haze of the eternal life force emanating from its shaft. Even the sea beyond us seemed silent as its gold-flecked waves danced on the sand.

A troubled murmur passed among the angelfolk as we assembled along the shoreline. None of us dared approach the Well. Quatama led Eve and my family to stand between it and the sea. We looked out across the waters as Quatama walked a few feet farther to where the waves touched, and knelt, bowing his head.

From the crowd, four other elders emerged, travelling down the beach to kneel beside Quatama: Yeshua, Ezekial, Mirisham and Cornelius. They seemed to pray silently, then Quatama's voice rose clearly: *"Adenoy Dominey, see ha nah e.* Supreme Creator, we are disobedient to you. *See bashtay n dahney a cuwh saesha dea vohlveen dayneta.* We humbly greet you and pray that Your Great Love may find forgiveness for our transgressions."

I felt my mother grasp my hand. She let out a quick hiss of breath, whispering to herself, "Why is he blaming the people? Adam and I erred, not them!"

I heard a man's harsh "Sha!" I looked past her. My father, beside her, stood with head down and eyes closed, praying. Beside him, my Uncle Gabriel glared at Eve sternly. His eyes caught mine, softening, and he turned his gaze back to the sea.

The elders rose from their kneeling positions, standing and turning to face the people. Chamira and Eeztzu emerged from the huddle of angelfolk and stood near Cornelius, his normally cheerful rotund face now swollen and red, as if he'd been crying. Eeztzu looked toward my father, his eyes wide with sympathy. Chamira gazed placidly forward at everyone and at no one in particular, as if she waited, withholding elven judgment until the Seraphim cast their own down upon our heads. I felt her disdain for the chaos the angelfolk had wrought, yet her people had always been kind to us. Until now. No other elvenfolk had emerged from the woods as we travelled through them.

A small outcry arose from the angelfolk around us and through their ranks emerged a tawny lion on one side and a large grey wolf and a graceful gazelle from the other. They padded and trotted across the beach, converging in the middle, in front of me. The wolf and the lion gently nipped at my robe on either side, catching hold of its cloth and moving forward, drawing me toward Chamira, the gazelle bounding over to her side.

"No, no," I murmured, but Chamira extended her hand, beckoning. I looked at my mother, who looked back at me in wonder. "Go," she urged.

I went and stood beside Chamira, alongside her, Eeztzu and the elders, facing the gathered angelfolk. I saw the fear on Bael's face and held my own hand out to him. He hesitated, for I was no elder, had no way of knowing if I committed some breach in calling him to my side. But as my betrothed, he belonged with me.

When none slapped my hand down, and no one challenged me, Bael finally skimmed across the expanse of sand and stood to my left. Taking my other hand, he grasped it protectively. The wolf, lion and gazelle now faced my family and the assembled folk in front of us, but often glanced back at me with a lupine grin, a feline or bovine smile. Incongruously, they made me smile, while my heart insisted I had no right to, given the gravity of the occasion. And then a small brown bird flew in from the forest beyond the dunes, over the heads of the folk, and landed gracefully onto the lion's back. A sparrow, facing me. The lion turned its immense head enough to stare at the bird, which turned its tiny one, confronting the lion. The lion shook its head and gazed forward again. The wolf seemed to laugh at him and then stood sharply erect and alert. I, too, felt the sudden tension.

Quatama spoke again, no need to raise his voice in the silence. "I speak for the angelfolk. I cannot speak for the elvenfolk nor the animalfolk. They have sent their own emissaries, that they might be represented here, to observe and judge the outcome of the angelfolk's failure to obey our Creator."

As he paused for breath, another voice rang out, venomous with anger. "Is it *our* failure or our *Creator's* failure to afford us the right to free will and the luxury of error!" Lucifer strode forward, his wife and other sons following him, to stand, rigidly defiant, next to my mother. Bael's hand, holding mine, tightened.

Quatama answered placidly: "Our failure. Free will, which the Creator does grant us, is a privilege, not a right. It must be earned."

"By obedience?" Lucifer challenged.

"By correct decisions and choices."

"Who, then, is to decide what is correct?"

I had never seen Quatama bristle, but Lucifer's taunt clearly questioned the Creator's authority and laws. A buzz of shocked murmurs and gasps echoed among the people. Affaeteres, beside her husband, began crying silently, as if some long-pent-up dam had burst. Beside her, Azmodeus, shoulders hunched, stared sullenly, almost jealously, across at Bael, and next to him, Ashtoreth stood quietly, his gaze to the sea, his face etched with sadness.

Quatama softly said, "*You* are to decide."

"Exactly," said Lucifer.

"And then you must bear the weight of the results of your decision."

Lucifer glared at him. "A keeper of sheep, aren't you, Quatama? Frightening them into subservience with tales of the wolf." He frowned at the wolf that stood before me, as if it held some evil omen designed to destroy us.

The wolf ignored him, as Quatama answered him patiently. "Accepting faults that endanger the flock is not wise. And I am not the keeper, simply an elder ram who has seen much and offers his guidance to those who might listen."

Eve stepped forward, timidly approaching Quatama. "Please!" she begged. "The fault was entirely mine and Adam's! The people are not to blame. They failed at nothing." She, too, began to cry. "Let me bear the weight! Let me bear the weight."

"Speaking of that burden," Lucifer cut in glibly, as if this was a normal day and the conversation of little consequence, "why is it that Quatama and the other elders, as well as my son and his betrothed, stand apart from us, facing us? I can understand Chamira and Eeztzu, and the animals, but what of the rest of you? Are you free of this mysterious crime which Eve and her brother and, by some unexplained extension, the rest of us also have committed? Are *you* our accusers?"

"No," said Quatama, "we are not free of the aftermath of that crime nor are we your accusers. But we, alone, carry no blame for what occurred on the planet known as Earth."

Lucifer appeared genuinely amazed. "Why is that?" From the crowd behind and around him, other shouts of "Yes! Why?" and "Tell us!" resounded. My Uncle Gabriel turned to the shouters, a long look of fury on his face, and shouted back: "Be silent, you dissenters, or bring the wrath of the Seraphim on our heads. Even *I* will accept responsibility for my failure to stop my brother's wife from committing her willful act of disobedience to our Creator. I will accept responsibility for her brother's foolishness in joining her!"

"Then you are a fool," Lucifer thundered back at him, "an ant to be led along a path the Creator's toe pushes it to!"

Eve cupped her hands to her ears. "Stop! Stop!" But a cacophony of loud arguments had erupted among the angelfolk, pushing and bullying one another divisively, sides being drawn over the conflict.

Yeshua raised his hands, palms outward for silence. I could feel the heat, the angry buzz of the crowd, subsiding. Yeshua waited until the last querulous mutter drifted off, replaced only by the low susurration of the sea. "There is a reason why we, who stand before you, are blameless, while all of you who, excepting Eve and her absent brother, have had no knowledge of Earth, still share their misdeed. We who stand before you have attained awareness, intrinsically and extrinsically, of why their breach of our Creator's trust was so damaging, not only to the mortal creatures of Earth, but to the psyches and souls of the angelfolk as well. To understand this creates a despair for the enormity of the error, the tear in the fabric of the Creator's plans for the Earth. In despairing, the heart cries out and commits itself to correcting the error and repairing this grievous tear. In committing to healing the fabric and making it whole again, the heart gains hope and confidence and begins to seek the solution that will completely and competently bring about the repair. In completing the repair, even in the process of correctly envisioning it, we sever the burden of guilt and shame connected with the original error. We therefore feel no blame, only the plan, in time, to correct the error and put the wrong to right."

"It is a matter of awareness," Ezekial took up the thread of explanation Yeshua had started. "We are no greater nor lesser than you for having attained this awareness. You, too, shall achieve it, in time, and know when you have. Until then, both the guilt and the accusation toward the guilty will exist simultaneously within you, and you will not understand what must be done with an open heart and mind. Once you accept what must be done, you, too, will be done with guilt or blame." The people seemed to rally at these words spoken by the youngest of our elders. Ezekial, with his dark brown mane of hair and short neat beard, and deepset brown eyes, his patient gait and quiet nature, drew everyone's respect.

They called out to him.

"Tell us more!"

"Yes! Explain!"

His eyes swept over the throng eagerly awaiting answers to dispel their confusion. I, too, was confused, no matter how much I *intrinsically* understood. Yes, the only thing to do was to heal the transgression which Adam and Mother had committed, which disrupted life on Earth. And as large as that disruption might be, the importance lay in correcting its cause and its effect, not in mindless accusation or self-castigation. Yet I had no inkling of the nature of the crime nor how we might make restitution. I did know now that restitution was our Creator's choice to heal the damage. There would be no retribution, for our Creator was just and forgiving, and the weight in my heart had dissipated. But I waited for Ezekial to continue, so that I, too, would understand how the Creator expected us to make that restitution.

Ezekial said simply: "We have damaged the minds and hearts of the Earthly mortals, by altering their life force, called blood, that flows through their bodies. The damage is not visible to the eye, and yet their children and their children's children will be tainted with a defect so persuasive, it will be handed down from generation to generation throughout the duration of the Creator's plan for them and warp the future which had been mapped for them. Mirisham will explain how this came about, and why all of the angelfolk—all of us—must take responsibility for its correction."

Ezekial stepped back, and Mirisham, her black hair tied starkly in a bun, her loose white robe obscuring her figure, came forward. The only woman elder and Quatama's beloved wife, she, too, was greatly respected. Yet she hesitated, as if gauging our readiness to hear what she would say or how she might best express it. She took a breath, shutting her dark eyes, opening them, and exhaled. She spoke slowly, as if that too was necessary for our understanding. "What Ezekial calls blood can be compared to the Creator's breath as it flows through our own bodies, although ours is an open system, continually replenished and nourished by the skane within the very air we breathe in Eliom, as is all life in Eliom. The mortal bodily system is, however, a closed system. The blood flows in a line much like our traceries of life inside our own bodies, but the mortal blood line has no entrance nor exit point from the lung phalanges to the throat and mouth. The mortal blood line flows to, through, and from the heart, continually. And unlike we Eliomese, who nourish our skane traceries inside of us by inhaling the skane traces abundant in our atmosphere, the mortals have a complex internal system, in which the act of drinking and eating is not for pleasure, but for bodily survival, converting both food and fluid into energy."

Quizzical looks greeted her explanation. My mother had told only the elders, her family and her closest friends of the strangeness of life on Earth. Mirisham waited for the whispers and murmurs to abate, then continued. "It *is* a very strange system, which will be explained in detail to you later. The main crux is that their blood line and our skane traceries are very similar. Further, their reproductive system and ours are nearly identical, the only difference being that their children are completely formed within the mother's womb and expelled whole from her body." Gasps sounded from the women, my own included, having never been told this by Eve. In our own pregnancies, the life force in our wombs, which did swell slightly, formed compressed swirling energies that would become the newborn's characteristics. During birth, it emerged as a thick white cloud, pouring slowly from our birth canal. It then hovered above its mother's legs, sparkling and pulsating, until, in a sudden contraction, it congealed and defined itself, the cloud fading to reveal the newborn infant, to be clasped by its father and placed in its mother's arms.

I glanced across to Eve, mentally asking *how?* How could a fully developed infant emerge from so small a space?

There was no need for Eve to answer me. Her eyes shut tightly, and her mouth pulled back in a grimace. An unpleasant memory at best and, no doubt, painful. Yes . . . she had told me she'd died following the birth of Cahn and Ahbel, this mortal blood pouring out of her, but I hadn't understood why. A closed system it might be, but once broken, it seemed it could not always be repaired, as our own skane traceries easily were. And so she had suffered that horrible expiration of the mortal body, in the act of bringing new life into that horrid world. Now I knew how childbirth, a joyous pleasant experience for us, could cause such a fatal wound on Earth.

Mirisham waited for quiet again, and went on. "Despite the differences between the mortalfolk and angelfolk, the transgression of Adam and Eve proved something hitherto unknown. When angelfolk enter the Earthly atmosphere, their bodies undergo a metamorphosis. Their skane traceries become the mortal blood line, although certain elements they carry in their traceries, those holding the traits associated with our people, are reconstituted within the mortal blood. Inside the mortal bodies they find themselves inhabiting, once this metamorphosis is done, they are no longer purely angelfolk, but a hybrid of the angelic and Earthly. Their outer characteristics reflect the ways of the mortal soul, but their inner characteristics reflect those of our people, the immortal. Their minds and souls may be angelfolk, but their bodies are not . . . with one exception: the conjoined blood line of the metamorphosed angel turned mortal is compatible with the native mortals of Earth. Inotherwords," Mirisham said wryly, "they can mate and bear children together."

Now a subdued roar erupted among the assembled folk, an unhappy one that held a measure of distaste for such interbreeding.

"An abomination!" Lucifer shouted. "Is that what you are saying, Mirisham? That they would give birth to half-beasts?"

My mother turned to him, her eyes blazing. "My children were not *beasts!* They were gentle good souls caught in an unkind world and condemned to a piteously short life!"

"You? You—who would be good to all creatures—would, of course, be kind to them," he said, swallowing his obvious surprise.

"Nor were they creatures. Lucifer . . ." (she turned to the throng of angelfolk) "my people . . . the humans are formed as you and I are, although our Creator bestows no immortality on them."

"Human!" Lucifer snorted. "What is this word?"

"A word the Earth people use to denote their vast tribe."

"Vast?" Lucifer laughed at her and, again, toward the angelfolk as if sharing his disdain.

"Yes!" Eve stood her ground. "There are many clans; they live in many, many territories, and yet they are *all* of one people: the *humans*. They look much like us."

"Elven tales." Lucifer smiled condescendingly at her. "Of creatures pretending to be folk." He ignored the anguish on my mother's face. I knew that he understood the pain that he caused her, demeaning her Earthly children. He had been overly attentive to Eve since her return to us, following her recovery. My father had privately told me of how fond Lucifer had been of Eve, of their close friendship before and after her marriage to Michael.

But Lucifer had never acted improperly toward her. Until now.

She hadn't told him of her bedding with and bearing the children of a mortal man.

Quatama stepped between them. "There is nothing to be done about your divergent opinions for now. And Eve speaks truly: the clans of mortal man *are* many, and they are much like us." Lucifer frowned, about to speak, but Quatama spoke first. "The Creator has made them in our likeness."

He rejoined the elders and nodded to his wife, whose voice rang out over the low rumble of dissension among the gathering: "Eve bore children by her mortal mate. And Adam, still upon the Earth, has fathered many half-angel, half-human sons and daughters. These children shall, in turn, mate, and the angelic strain within them, which is stronger than the mortal strain, shall metamorphosize and adapt to the Earth's environment within its host . . . mortalkind. It shall become the dominant trait and usurp many of the traits previously intended for these humans in the Creator's original plan for the Earth, affecting not only humankind but—eventually—all other life on

Earth.

"Even we of the Council do not understand all of the mystery surrounding this. What we do know is that this will create an imbalance as the angelic strain increases out of proportion to the mortal strain, that some mortals will benefit from the influence of angelic inheritance and others will not, that some enhanced humans will use this new birth legacy wisely, while others will abuse it, bringing misery and chaos to their young world. And—we have been told by the Seraphim—the imbalance as it stands, unaltered, will one day bring events that will culminate in the destruction of the Earth." She lowered her head, as if overwhelmed and overwrought, and then lifted it, gazing left, right, then center at the folk, gauging their now-silent attention. "The Seraphim have instructed us. There is only one solution that *may,* in time, rebalance the now-mixed blood line of the mortals. If we accept it, the children of Earth may one day emerge in a unity of existence more glorious than our Creator's original hopes for them. If we deny it, not only shall the Earth be plunged into eventual chaos and sorrow, the angelfolk themselves will be touched, tainted and marred by this disruption, for our life force was the seed it rooted from."

Mirisham bowed her head again, shoulders slumping, breathing heavily. Quatama placed his arm around her, whispering to her. She nodded and stood silently beside him. He lowered his arm and turned to face the sea, the other elders, Chamira and Eeztzu also turning.

The gazelle, lion and wolf also padded behind Bael and me, facing the waves. The sparrow fluttered in the air, as Bael clasped my other hand and pivoted us around toward the sea; the bird alighted on my right shoulder. It chirped once, the only sound. We gazed across the vast expanse of the Sea of the Seraphim, waiting.

-27-

Our fear was palpable. Only once before had the Seraphim visited judgment upon us. The elders never knew what that judgment would be until the Seraphim chose to reveal it. Yet somehow I knew, if the angelfolk agreed to work toward the Earth's restitution, all blame would be lifted from our shoulders.

Chamira, who stood to my left, now leaned forward, speaking to both Bael and me. "Remember! Do not allow the link between you to be broken." She eased back and said nothing more.

The tension increased; still no Seraphim flew over the glassy sea, golden robes trailing above the waves, six wings each spread to the wind. I peered anxiously toward the horizon, but saw only the sky and the sun's reflection on the waves.

The folk behind us shifted restlessly. Perhaps the animals had caught their mood, for the sparrow left my shoulder to hover in the air near the breaking waves. The wolf, gazelle and lion trotted over to her, leaving hoof and paw marks on the wet sand.

They lined up, even the bird, facing us. A golden light swept downward from the sky, nearly blinding us and obscuring the animals. When it cleared, where the animals had been stood four Seraphim, their iridescent wings folded over their long slender backs, arms and hands. Not one word emerged from those they faced; awed by their presence, we were struck mute.

The Seraph who had been the sparrow raised her eagle's head. "I am Gehtat. You may know the name of your accuser."

The Seraph who had been the gazelle raised his ox's head. "I am Elat. You may know the name of your accuser."

The Seraph who had been the grey wolf raised her woman's head, much like our own but for her mass of silvery hair and the golden eyes through which she and the other Seraphim regarded us. "I am Seheer. You may know the name of your accuser."

The Seraph who had been the lion still had that majestic beast's proud head. "I am Chahtai. You may know the name of your accuser."

Cornelius stepped forward and said in a voice filled with wonder: "I would have told you, Illustrious Ones, that the folk have been prepared with knowledge of our breach except for its solution . . . but you already know this."

"We do," said Gehtat.

"And some would rebel," Chahtai added, "without knowing what they rebelled against."

"Change!" Lucifer shouted from behind me, for I recognized his voice. "Change stemming from an error the Great One should be able to rectify without our help *if* our Creator *is* all powerful."

Groans of apprehension sounded from the folk, but not so many as I might have expected.

The Seraphim regarded his outburst. Finally Elat answered him. "Your rebellion stems from your love for our Creator and your disappointment in being asked to share that love, acknowledging it exists in other beings beyond Eliom. You must let go of your jealousy, Lucifer, for it will cast you from the place of honor you have held in your Creator's heart."

"I beg to differ, Illustrious Ones," said Lucifer, mocking Cornelius's piety. "It is not having to share our Creator's love which disturbs me. It is the subservience, the *enslavement,* to such a Creator, being told we have choices, but knowing those choices must ultimately please the Creator. Upon what credentials is such obeisance demanded? Answer me that, Seraphim!" Lucifer came forward, striding past Cornelius, breaking our ranks. I had not dared to turn around before to look at him. Now he planted himself directly between the Seraphim and us.

Seheer corrected him harshly. "Go back to your place behind the elders. You are not without blame, Lucifer, and have no right to judge anything or anyone, least of all yourself."

"Then let me not judge, but question. How is it you appear, barring one exception and that one still retaining the vestiges of the wolf, with beastly faces? You barely resemble the Seraphim who greet us on *Om Yahr*. They, having no faces, wear cowled robes. Through those cowls, the light of our Creator scintillates with the faintest trace of angelic features hidden within. Why do you appear, in judgment over us, wearing their robes, winged but unlike them to my eyes? Are you truly Seraphim and *our* Creator's or impostors, sent by our Creator to confound us?"

After a pause, Chahtai answered. "Our robes are uncowled and our faces unobscured that you should know us fully: neither angel nor elf nor beast nor mortal. We are all and none of these. We are illusions, being composed of thought and logic, and we can *be* whatever you wish us to be."

"*Be* gone, then. Leave the angelfolk in peace, and be forgiving, as our Creator should *be.*"

Seheer placed a willowy hand on Lucifer's arm. "We will explain, but you must take your proper place behind the chosen ones."

"Is my son chosen?"

"Yes, although he has not yet earned it. In time, he will."

"Then he will stand with me."

"He will stand beside his betrothed. And you, Lucifer, shall stand beside your wife."

I felt Bael's hand slacken in my own. I didn't look at him, but thought: *Don't*. He took a step forward, wavering, then stepped back. His hand gripped mine more firmly again.

Lucifer hadn't moved, Seheer's hand still gently curled around his robed arm. She asked, "Will you return to your proper place?" He said nothing. The other three Seraphim surrounded him: Chahtai to his left, Elat behind him, Gehtat to his right, Seheer remaining before him, her hand dropping to her side.

"What are you do—" Lucifer began, then floated a foot above the sand, his hand frozen in an instinctively self-protective gesture, his mouth gaping open to his unfinished question, his body rigidly in place. Hovering in mid-air and stripped of his freedom of movement and speech, some force turned him slowly around, facing Elat. The oxen-faced Seraph seemed to grin as Lucifer rose higher and floated over my and Chamira's heads. He slowly descended to the space he had vacated, between Affaeteres and Azmodeus, his facial expression and gesture unchanged.

Bael and I had turned around, following his father's petrified form as he was forcibly removed and effectively silenced by the Seraphim. Bael grasped my shoulder roughly, as if I'd contributed to Lucifer's come-uppance. "They've changed him to wood!"

"No," I murmured, pulling myself free. "They've stilled him for stepping and speaking out of place. Look to his chest, Bael. He still breathes."

Bael stared instead at my shoulder, offered me an apologetic, sheepish glance, then looked to his father, still locked in his defiant stance. Lucifer's diaphragm rose and fell rapidly, angrily, at first, then finally slowing to normal. He stared furiously at nothing, his eyes no longer fixed on the object of his wrath. His pain and confusion saddened me, and I moved unwittingly toward him, saying, "Everything will be put right, Father Lucifer. *Please* do not worry!" My hand tingled with a desire to nurture and heal him. I drew closer, but someone gently clasped my arm: Gehtat. Her bright eagle's eyes studied me, her beak closed, almost in repose. She spoke no words, but still managed to convey her understanding of why I had approached Lucifer. She nodded me back to my own place. I returned to Bael, and we faced front again, hands again entwined. Gehtat came forward and joined the waiting Seraphim. A stillness descended.

Gehtat began. "Many of you may still wonder why we appear as we do. The faces we wear before you today represent the Earth, a young world which nonetheless has seen many necessary changes to bring it and its native species to their current place along an evolutionary span. The humans, as Eve correctly named them, were to be only a bit higher in intelligence than the other animals inhabiting the Earth. It was an experiment by our Creator: creating them in the image of the angels with a conscious knowledge of a force greater than themselves, but no direct communion with that force."

"And a mortal lifespan," Chahtai added. "They were to have no fear of the cycles of life and death, no more so than the other animals. Nor were they to seek to explain that regenerative cycle which the beasts of Earth and Eliom also experience, although your animals live longer in the Eliomese atmosphere and have an instinctive sense of the transferring process."

"As you know, all souls grow spiritually through experience," Gehtat continued, "sometimes with ease, sometimes with great difficulty and setbacks. This is true of the immortal angelfolk who advance in experience throughout their eternal span by facing challenges and learning how best to meet them, and also true of mortalfolk and animals who advance in the same manner, but use regeneration into new environments, both in body and habitat. In some ways, the mortals are less challenged, for they retain no conscious memory of their previous lives, their minds less crowded with a confusing myriad of existential references. In other ways, they are more challenged, for they have a smaller range of conscious experience to draw upon in making decisions. But both methods of learning achieve our Creator's goal. Each soul, according to its own level, whether angel or human or animal, whether flora or fauna, travels in time toward full communion with its Maker."

"And so you must not hold yourselves above any living brethren. Each form of life is loved by our Creator, and its faults forgiven as it learns," said Elat, moving forward and spreading his arms and hands outward emphatically. "You must remember this when we tell you the means to be employed in healing the damaged human bloodline. This will also eventually protect the other creatures who share the Earth. Because of the imbalance, the humans will treat them as chattel, above and beyond any valid need. Thus, we have chosen to represent these animals through our appearance today. Only the angelfolk can cure the humans of this hidden illness which Adam and Eve have introduced, which will spread, begetting evil and dissension, burdening all Earthly life. The contagion stems from the influx of angelic traits into humans, as you have been told. An imbalance will rise when some benefit while others do not, when some become strong in body and mind, while others, weak in comparison, become fodder for the fitter. The Earth and all upon it will suffer in ways the Creator never intended."

Elat stepped back, and Seheer came forward. "There is only one solution. We cannot undo the damage already done. The Creator's original plan is irrevocably altered, but a new balance can be achieved on Earth by allowing all humans to possess traits nearly at the level of the angel. Your elders have told you of the conjoined bloodline existing in the children which Eve birthed and Adam fathered on Earth. We have projected the impact stemming from this mix on far future generations. If no further influx of angelic traits occurs, chaos will eventually corrupt everything upon the planet and blight it, for the prominent angelic strain cannot die out and mortals inheriting it gain superiority over the unenhanced, with neither time nor patience to learn to use it fairly.

"The only solution for eventual rebalance is to repopulate the Earth homogeneously, all progeny born with mixed bloodlines, all having the heightened intellectual, emotional and physical traits of the angelic influx. These traits, both angelic and human, exist in their bloodline and your skane traceries and are the components which define conscious existence and direct it. They are the sparks which ignite conscious life which we call Genesis, and the components of the process of Genesis are called genes."

"It will be many thousands of years before humans or angels unravel the mystery of genes," said Elat, "yet, once understood, you will both be closer to your Creator than you can possibly fathom. For now, all you need do is commit to healing the *genetic* disruption among the humans of Earth. To do this, you must agree to leave Eliom and live upon the Earth in mortal bodies."

"For how long?!" someone, shocked beyond propriety, shouted from the throng, and a cacophony of other voices erupted with jumbled questions edged with fear.

Seheer held up her hands for quiet, her wings rustling gently. "For many thousands of years—which will pass more slowly in your dimension, for the Eliomese day and night lasts three times longer than the Earth's. It is not only the physical rebalancing of the genetic influx that is needed. You must also be as teachers, leading them to knowledge of how best to use their enhanced traits for the good of all. You must be as watchers, seeing that none, even among your own reconstituted selves, abuse the Earth and its inhabitants. You must be as sculptors, your task to mold the clay of Earth's present to a new future, when the new balance will be complete and all on Earth can live in an environment as peaceful and sound as your Eliom has been."

"And why should such a task take thousands of years?" I recognized Azmodeus's slow sardonic drawl. The Seraphim gave no answer. "I think I'm going to *like* Earth," he said, his voice rife with lewd suggestion.

Gehtat left the line of Seraphim and passed Bael on his right. We didn't turn this time, immobilized now, awed by and afraid of the immensity of the solution asked of us. Azmodeus cried out, as if in pain; we still faced front, despite the sound of a woman's ragged sobbing moan. Then all quieted as Gehtat returned to stand again beside Elat. "You will have many questions," she acknowledged. "Your elders have been prepared by us to answer them. But for now, before we take our leave of you, we will answer Lucifer's, that he may understand and cause no further disruption among his people." She looked angrily in his direction. I had never seen an angry eagle; it was disturbing: her tall form stiff, her feathered head erect, the curved beak jutting threateningly, her eyes ablaze with heated fury. All directed at Lucifer's own angry frozen visage. "You ask why our Creator cannot simply repair the damage done. If you had cultivated an unique flower, watching it grow and knowing just how it would thrive through the seasons, and if another should plant another stronger bloom beside it, and its roots crowd out and stunt your flower, possibly killing it, could you save your plant by letting it remain in that damaged environment? Would you not require that the interloping plant be forced to move and change its own environment, to save your own? And would you forgive its gardener if he or she refused to cooperate, especially if that gardener was your offspring? If the interloping plant had grown large with spreading roots and required more hands to replant it and rework the soil, would you forgive the gardener's brothers and sisters who refused to help, knowing he or she alone could no longer remove it, having grown so large, without help? How would you judge them, Lucifer?" And so saying, she drew her gaze abruptly from him and nodded at the other Seraphim.

In one motion, they raised the cowls of their golden robes to cover their heads, the folds hanging down around their faces. From within the cowls, a mist issued forth, obscuring their features, save for their golden eyes. Their four voices rang out in a melodious sweeping unison that seemed to grip us and surround us with its resonance. "The Creator visits this judgment upon Eve and Adam, daughter and son of

Deianna and Mercurius of Eliom: They, alone among the angelfolk, must wear mortal flesh continually, never to return to Eliom until the Earth is healed. The remaining angelfolk may return to Eliom for brief interludes following each mortal sojourn. But know this now, angelfolk of Eliom, that the Well of Being will never again bestow upon you the gift of your Creator's breath, which conveys more than mere continued existence, until the task set before you today has been undertaken willingly and completed. Immortal you may be, but those who disobey our Creator will find their continued existence fiercely challenged and be driven from your beloved Eliom, for none save those who love our Creator may reside within the lands of the Garden."

The four floated slowly upward until they hung, sunlight inflaming their wings and robes, far above our heads. Again they spoke in a chorus of blended voices. "We might have imbued you with foresight, as we have your elders, Chamira and Eeztzu of the elvenfolk, Leianna, daughter of Eve, and Bael, son of Lucifer, as our Creator instructed us to do. But Lucifer, in demanding the right of the angelfolk to free will, has been heard by the Great One. We do not ask for your mindless devotion, but for your reasoned judgment and honest choice upon learning all you can about your roles in the restitution of Earth. For those who choose to disobey our Creator and refuse to lend assistance, having no faith in the One's own Judgment, know that you shall, nonetheless, be watched over and cherished in your exile. You will still be beloved by your Creator, even while forced to make restitution by other means. Choose wisely."

They rose higher, wings fanning. Our heads flung back, our eyes followed their leavetaking until they were specks of white and gold against the blue unclouded sky. The specks flew off across the Seraphic Sea, glinting in the bright afternoon sun and disappearing at the horizon.

-28-

After a prolonged silence, the elders, Chamira and Eeztzu turned about, facing the people. I drew my hand from Bael's and also turned, Bael following my example but quickly reclasping my other hand. Silence continued, finally broken by Quatama. "We will go home to rest and replenish ourselves. Then we will meet again this evening in the village center."

"My husband!" Affaeteres cried out. "He is still locked in this unmoving state!"

"And so he shall be, until the Seraphim and our Creator choose to release him from it."

Our people began to drift wearily up the dunes, entering the forest.

I began following them, but Bael tugged me back. "I cannot leave my father like this, Leianna."

"What can we do? The Seraphim have chastised him."

He looked to Ashtoreth, who nodded and stood to Lucifer's right. Bael stood to his father's left. Eldest and middle sons, they lifted him and, as our families, Chamira, Eeztzu and the elders watched, began trekking up the dunes with him. Going slowly through the forest, we followed them.

They stopped several times to set Lucifer down and rest, carrying him no easy task. No one else had offered to help. I looked to my father once, the question in my eyes, but his own eyes hardened and turned away from mine.

As we neared the forest's end, the Virginal Sanctuary before us, Chamira came up to the burdened brothers, halting them. She called me over, nodded toward Lucifer, then gazed back at me.

I knew what she asked of me instinctively, but felt no vibration in either of my hands, no tingle of the healing power which every angel possessed. I had no surety if such gentle ministrations could cure an affliction born of Seraphic discipline. But then, in the little time it took to ponder this, the familiar sensation of energy began flowing through my palms, so strongly, my hands were weighted by it.

Lucifer's hands and arms still extended outward, as if to fend off a blow, and might complete their movement if he regained his agility, striking out at me. I walked behind him, ignoring Azmodeus's look of suspicion, his tensed balled fists. I placed my charged hands on Lucifer's broad back. Revitalizing energy discharged through my palms and fingers into him, yet nothing changed, even when the energy ran itself out, normal sensation returning to my hands.

Chamira approached us, grinning. "Let go now, Leianna." I did. "And stand back, child." I moved a few feet away, to Bael and his mother. Affaeteres watched her husband apprehensively and gave a sudden gasp. My eyes turned back to Lucifer; I also saw my mother and father a few yards past him, watching me, watching their disgraced friend.

A glow began to spread, emanating from his back, upward, downward and around him. He blinked. He spoke: a single syllable: "—ing!" His arms came up protectively, covering his face, completing his earlier warding-off gesture against the Seraphim. He took a deep breath, let it slowly out, then lowered his arms, his face reddened with shame and defeat.

Affaeteres came to him and embraced him, her cheek pressing his. He returned her embrace briefly and gently pushed her away. "This is not over yet."

"Father," Bael remonstrated.

"And what is this wonder before me that has chosen such a woman to wed? And how is it that you both are favored by the Creator, above Council members, her own father included, as somehow blameless of the chaos her mother and uncle have wrought?"

"That was explained, Father."

"Yes, yes. She is willing to participate in this solution. But what of you?"

"What of me?"

"Are you willing to participate? Blind and ignorant?"

"If blind because I don't see clearly, then I must repair my faulty eyesight." An edge of sarcastic irritation crept into his voice. "If ignorant, then I must strive to learn."

"Either way, you'll follow Leianna like a tottering fawn, whether you agree or disagree with her deference to our Creator and this solution," Lucifer challenged him.

"I . . . I decide what is right for myself. What is just!"

"Ah! You are a man. But what if, in making that decision, you lose your precious Leianna?"

"I will not—"

"You will," Lucifer interrupted him harshly. "I will see to it!" He stomped off, entering the Virginal Sanctuary without bothering to bow his head in prayer as was customary when we crossed its boundaries, individually or collectively. Affaeteres bowed her own head as her foot touched the prairie, then rushed after her husband, calling out to him. Azmodeus turned a sour face to Bael, Ashtoreth and me. He rose off the ground, ignoring propriety, and flew over the Sanctuary, past his mother, setting himself down beside his father. Lucifer turned to him, said something brief, and walked on, Azmodeus keeping pace with him, Affaeteres struggling to catch up.

My mother, father and the elders approached Ashtoreth, Bael and me. My Uncle Gabriel and Grandmother Deianna stood nearby. Other angelfolk, still departing, moved around and past us, asking no questions, not intruding, glancing at us, but nothing more. Ashtoreth stared out over the prairie, his parents and youngest brother dwindling in the distance. My father touched Ashtoreth's arm, drawing his attention. "That is not the Lucifer I know," Michael told him. "The man I knew would never have challenged the Seraphim nor mocked our Creator."

"Lucifer will mend this error," Eve insisted to us all. "Give him time to consider it."

Michael shook his head. "It's past time."

"No," I said suddenly, for a new vision, nebulous in content but firm in intent, gripped me. "We have all of time." But then another omen gripped me tightly, and I grasped Bael's arm, unwilling to voice it, and laid my head against his shoulder.

He held me lightly, stroking my hair. "Everything will be solved. There's no need for fear, Leianna."

"I fear for your family," said Michael. "You must not credit your father's words until this malediction he suffers from has been cleansed from his soul. I feel sorrow for your mother and for Azmodeus, tainted today by Lucifer's disobedience."

"Long before that," Ashtoreth murmured. "And your advice is well-spoken, except for one thing."

"And what is that?"

"Lucifer is still our father, and we, as his sons, are directed by the laws of Eliom to both respect and obey him."

Michael began, "But if he denies that law—"

Ashtoreth cut him off. "Do Bael and I then have the right to deny it further in responding to him?"

My father ran a hand through his cropped brown hair, a nervous troubled gesture, not answering.

"Consider the implications," said Ashtoreth. "I did not make the law. The Creator did. Lucifer has clearly challenged it. If we fight and deny our father, Bael and I have broken one of its tenets. If we defer to him, we break another, perhaps a greater one. But who is to decide which is to be broken and which to be upheld?" He glanced at

Quatama and the other elders. "Can you tell me, Quatama?"

The spirit master mused upon the question before answering. "Choices are often difficult. I can only tell you that the answer lies not in denying a law, but rather in interpreting it. Come. We must go now. There is much to discuss at tonight's gathering. Perhaps we will all decide what is best."

I stared at the other elders, standing nearby with Quatama. "Quatama?" I asked. "Where is Elijah? He wasn't with the other elders on the shore. Was he among the angelfolk standing behind us?"

"No, Leianna. Duty called him elsewhere." He walked quietly past me. The remaining elders—Mirisham, Ezekial, Yeshua and Cornelius—followed. They all knelt at the boundary to the Sanctuary, offered their silent prayers, then rose and headed home. My mother and father did likewise, as did my Uncle Gabriel and Grandmother Deianna, nodding silently at my betrothed and me as they left.

Only Ashtoreth, Bael, Chamira and I remained. "Goodbye, Mother Chamira," I said, showing her respect.

"Do not leave so quickly, little one," she said. "I have wisdom to impart to all three of you, and a witness to hear and remember it for the times yet to come."

I heard the soft rustle of footsteps upon the twigs and leaves of the forest floor. Elijah approached us, looking quite youthful with his short, curly, brown hair and peaceful brown eyes, despite the fact that he had recently become an elder. He stood beside Chamira. "Chamira's words are not her own, but she has been chosen to deliver them to you. Listen well, but hear them with your hearts first and your minds second. In time, when it is time, you will understand Chamira's words and, our Creator be willing, fulfill them."

"And remember," Chamira told Bael and me. "Remember well my words to you as we awaited the Seraphim. And you, Ashtoreth, follow your heart. The law beats there." Then, gazing at us as if from across a great void, she began:

> "When Earth once more is healed and well,
> and rebels need no more rebel,
> two shall meet, one high, one low,
> and each, the other, they shall know.
> In innocence, they spoke their vows,
> unfinished till cruel Fate allows.
> Queen of Heaven, King of Hell,
> torn apart as angels fell,
> must suffer each millennium

as war exacts a costly sum.
Queen of Heaven she shall be,
her love shall set the lost souls free.
Two sons of Hell shall woo each hand,
but only one King, by her, stand.
When all shall work to heal the rift
that sets us wide now and adrift,
then Queen of Heaven, King of Hell,
no newborn pair, we knew them well,
shall mend the tear, the thread, their love,
the Queen below, the King above.
But she, the Queen of Time and Space,
shall rise to take her proper place,
neither high yet neither low,
but where love guides her, she shall go.
And Heaven, Hell and Earth, as one,
shall share the same celestial sun,
and love shall reign and love rejoice,
and all worlds sing out with one voice.
Then faith and love shall heal our rift,
and peace be our Creator's gift.
Hope shall rule and truth shall win,
and a Golden Age begin.
And they shall sing in verse and rhyme,
that long ago, there was a time,
when Hell was born of Heaven's fears,
and Earth, reborn, wept mortal tears,
until two lovers, reunited,
many millennia past divided,
healed the rebel angels' rage,
and ushered in the Golden Age.
So shall we judge and split our sun,
folk torn in two, who once were one,
but time will spin out strong new strands,
new ties to link long-separate lands.
Our kin, once joined like threads of silk
from fabric torn but of one ilk,
will bear the future's Golden Age,
when love, not war, is what we wage."

So saying, Chamira nodded slowly to Bael, to Ashtoreth, and to me, our hearts and heads wondering at her prophecy, for prophecy it seemed, what little we understood of it. She silently took her leave of us, disappearing into the woods as we watched. We turned back to speak to Elijah, but he, too, had vanished.

"Well," Ashtoreth said, more apropos of surprise than of having anything to say. Bael and I remained silent, looking at him, looking at each other. Who was this Queen of Heaven? The dimensions in which the angelfolk were permitted to travel, including Eliom and the sky up to a certain level were called "the heavens." They were never spoken of singularly as a specific place with boundaries, where someone could act as a leader. Likewise, our usage of queen and king meant simply that: a leader. A child leading others in a game was called a queen, if a girl, or king, if a boy. It was a compliment, a sign of respect, in any given activity, such as the queen and king chosen to lead the harvest dance.

"One thing is certain," Bael finally said. "This queen and king are lovers who are destined to be separated."

"It isn't us," I insisted. "Chamira has warned us against such a thing."

"It isn't us," Bael agreed. "The lovers she spoke of were estranged countless millennia. And they seem to return to heal the rebellious angels."

"And we knew them well." Ashtoreth jabbed his finger in the air for emphasis. "Perhaps these two are coming to heal our dispute over the healing of the Earth. To bring peace to the angelfolk's bickering, father's included. Perhaps our grandparents," he said to Bael, "who have been away since Leianna's birth."

"Perhaps," said his brother. "I find it disturbing that Chamira chose to recite it to us three."

"And Elijah," I reminded him. "It sounded like one of the elven fancies, those tales they delight in telling children, theirs and ours. I wonder which of the sons won the hand of the queen?"

"Which sons?" Bael asked, sounding nonplussed.

"The sons of . . . the sons . . . yes, of Hell, although I cannot imagine what that word means. Chamira used it strangely. A king presided over it, and Heaven gave birth to it."

Ashtoreth drew the strange word out, tasting it. "Hell . . . it almost sounds like hael, our word for darkness."

Bael laughed harshly. "Why would anybody want to be a leader of darkness? How can one lead in the dark?"

"It is no matter," I told him. "Chamira's tale tells us that all will be well, that the angelfolk and the Earthly mortals will both be healed, and our Creator's plan restored to an even greater glory."

Ashtoreth smiled for the first time that day. "I hope that you're right, Leianna."

"And I," said Bael. "But these shadows are lengthening. We had best go." He clasped my hand and led me to the Sanctuary's edge, Ashtoreth following. We knelt and prayed silently, promising to hold the Virginal Sanctuary sacred, to do nothing that might alter its ancient natural landscape.

Bael and I finished and waited for Ashtoreth to complete his own prayer. His head finally rose; he stood up quietly, and the three of us traveled at a good pace across the prairie, our sandals slapping up dust where the soil lacked moisture. By the time we reached the Garden, dark clouds gathered above us and the afternoon warmth began to fade.

A sudden wind whipped my hair around my face. "A storm is coming, Bael."

"Yes. The Garden and the Sanctuary need it."

"Do you think we might be permitted to lift and fly the rest of the way to Eliom? Although this is not a time for levity, and I mean no disrespect," I added, "I would rather not be soaked and would like some time for food and rest before the people gather tonight."

Bael looked to Ashtoreth. "I don't see the harm in it."

"Nor I," Ash agreed.

We concentrated, raising ourselves off the dirt path, and propelled ourselves forward, moving much more rapidly across the cultivated fields. As we neared the smaller wood between the Garden and our village, the wind increased fiercely, buffeting us around.

"We'd best walk now," Ashtoreth shouted to us. We adjusted our thoughts to return to the required body weight and began to sink the few feet down to the ground, when a bolt of light, blue and gold, streaked out of the turbulent sky, its fiery tip crashing into the woods, the trees around its impact bursting into flame.

We gaped at the smoke, could hear the fiery crackle of the burning branches. Why had the Creator cast injury onto the land? The wind subsided, and the nearly black dome of the sky released a torrent of rain, so thickly I could barely see Bael and Ashtoreth. I cried out involuntarily. "Creator preserve us!" Bael reached out to find and hold me against him.

The downpour extinguished the fire; the trees smoldered as we entered the woodland path to take the shortest route to the village. We had never known a storm as violent as this. The sky still drove down heavy sheets of rain, creating sudden low rivers coursing along the ground, turning soil to thick mud, impeding us.

Ashtoreth shouted, nearly slipping. "What have we done to displease You?!"

And then I fell on the slick wet leaves, Bael tumbling down into the muck with me, unable to keep his own footing. "Leianna! Are you hurt?"

"Only shaken."

"Something has cut my thigh."

Ashtoreth bent down beside him. "How badly?"

"A small gash. Nothing more. It will heal."

"The rain's abating. I can see you more clearly. And what you cut yourself on." Ashtoreth held up the shard of baked red clay.

Bael stared at it and at the sodden humus he sat on. Bits of the clay, obviously broken pieces of crockery, were strewn around us. I picked one up. "A pot, I think. Broken by a child, most probably, with no adult nearby to insist that he or she clean it up."

"No," Bael said. The rain had nearly stopped, a gentle drizzle coming down now. Its contrast to the furious outbreak that preceded it amazed me. I stared at the damaged trees, their charred limbs. The fireball hurled down from the heavens had directly hit the tree before us, a huge willow, its trunk jaggedly split down to its roots, each half, leaf-top to its uprooted bottom, sagging to either side. It pained me to see it, and I whispered, "Why?"

Voices rang out before us and figures rose out of the mist: my mother and father, Uncle Gabriel and Lucifer and, yes, my friend Chloe. We had spent little time together since my betrothal to Bael. She peered anxiously at me. "We saw the Creator's fist streak down from the sky. We were afraid, your families worried, when you didn't return." Her normally animated face was crestfallen, her short curls hung damply against her forehead and neck.

"We were . . . delayed," I said, "and then the storm came and . . ."

"Why has the Creator destroyed this willow? The other trees will heal, I think, if we prune away the damage. But not this. What has it done to deserve such an end?"

"I don't know, Chloe. But I thank you for being here, for your concern, despite your fear."

Ashtoreth helped me up from the ground. Bael still sat upon it, staring at the tree, its up-ended roots.

Chloe finally smiled in that quirky manner that disparaged any and all formality, no matter how sincere. "Of course, I came, you silly bumble bee. You're still my friend, simply obsessed with this handsome fool you've betrothed yourself to!"

Bael snapped out of his reverie at her remark, picking himself up off the ground. Lucifer came forward, noticing the deep blue smear of skane on his son's robe where the sharp fragment of clay had torn through. "Your leg."

"It's nearly healed, Father. The wound's already closing. Leianna will attend to it."

His father's face visibly hardened. I wondered at Father Lucifer's sudden disdain toward me; I had not asked the elders and the Seraphim to single me out.

Bael answered Lucifer's scowl. "She is my betrothed and has done nothing to deserve your mockery."

Lucifer drew back, the venom in Bael's voice unmistakable. "You will learn," said Lucifer, as if he held the answer to a mystery the rest of us were unaware of. "What did you cut yourself on?"

Bael's hand swept toward the scattered shards of pottery. "What I earlier buried at your request, to remove it from your sight."

"Azmodeus's pot of red clay?"

My father confronted him warily. "What is this you speak of?"

Lucifer faced him unflinchingly. "My youngest committed a transgression against our laws and sought to pretend remorse, to avoid my anger and gain my leniency. He rubbed wet clay onto his face to effect the aftermath of tears. I found him out and asked Bael to bury the offending pot that held the clay."

Gabriel, overhearing, asked, "You've informed the elders of this transgression?"

"I have not."

"But you will?"

"Our world is collapsing, Gabriel, our favor in the eyes of the Creator dimmed. New creatures slightly more intelligent than animals are more valued than we are." His voice rife with exhaustion, he lifted his eyes wearily to meet Gabriel's. "You may condemn me, if you wish, but I can no longer love our Creator nor respect the law. My son will not be punished by anyone other than myself and only upon my own judgment and no one else's. Not even our Creator's. I shall challenge the Creator, whose word has been too long accepted without question. I will demand that this planet, the Earth, be left to evolve, without our enslavement as breeders, regardless of the alleged taint left by a mere two of us. I shall refuse our Creator's solution and sway others against it, in such numbers that the Great One will know we are not to be used so lightly nor our world disrupted for another lesser world."

"Then you are my enemy."

My father, his face wracked with sorrow, also spoke, but hoarsely, as if the words choked him. "And mine."

Lucifer nodded decorously to both of them. "So be it." And to Bael and Ashtoreth: "When you have seen Leianna to her thachka, return home to your own. We will travel as a family to this gathering to learn how the Creator means to abase us, by what method, and how it may be thwarted." So saying, he started back to Eliom, pausing briefly by my mother to suggest: "Join my cause, Eve, you who have already suffered on that wretched planet." We watched him walk swiftly away from us.

The rain had stopped, the sun returning, hanging low in the sky.

We trudged back to the village, Bael squeezing my hand and telling me once more that all would be well.

But Eve voiced aloud what I felt in my gut would prove the truer outcome: "Lucifer means to divide us, as surely as God split that poor willow."

-29-

I become my modern self again as Quatama lifts the gold hoop from my head and softly asks, "How are you?"

"Fine," I answer, readjusting to the present.

"Do you have any questions?"

"No, it was all pretty clear. What was coming, I mean. War."

"Yes."

"So Azmodeus was never punished."

"He was punished. The red hoop records that experience." He places the finished gold hoop down upon the table next to the purple one and picks up the red. "Are you ready to go on?"

I nod.

"Shut your eyes, Leigh Ann. It will help make the transition less jarring. The memories within this hoop begin with Azmodeus's."

He sets it on my head.

*   *   *

A wooden platform had been raised in the village center. The elders stood upon it, the angelfolk surrounding it in a rough congested circle spreading outward to the edges of the green. Unlit torches were secured to high poles at various points around the perimeter, awaiting the night. The probability of a long drawn-out gathering, possibly a volatile one, hung in the evening air.

Azmodeus relished the idea of a fight, in fact, counted on his father to provide one, if Lucifer's angry fuming at home and on the way here were any indication of how this night would go. For now, Az waited, bored and distracted, forced to listen to these elders discussing how the angels would infiltrate the mortal world for the high moral purpose of cross-breeding for genetic rebalancing.

Apparently they would not be forced to undergo the metamorphosis Eve and her brother had endured. The new method, however, to Az's ears, sounded worse. Something called *incarnation*. Whoever was in charge of planning this idiotic solution seemed more perverted than Az himself could ever claim to be, and the crowning stupidity was that the elders thought this incarnation was an *unintrusive* method. Invasion is what it was, of the most intimate kind. Az would certainly like to explore a woman's womb, but having himself reduced to a mindless essence and being stuffed into the fetus of a pregnant mortal was *not* his idea of pleasure. The thought of pushing out of that womb, being born half-mortal and possibly female in a harsh ignorant world appealed even less to him. His father was right. The angelfolk who accepted this horror were insane.

The elders droned on about a vast system of tracking the angelic souls who incarnated. An immense thachka was being built to store the records of each angel who lived an Earthly life and note what progress each made in the healing of that world. Azmodeus snorted. One mortal lifetime on that planet might be deemed bravery, innumerable lifetimes seemed masochism. These angelfolk *had* gone crazy.

Lucifer pushed his way forward, although many of the folk, seeing him coming, quickly drew away from him. He stood before the elders, above him on the platform, then bent slightly at the waist, head down, in the classic pose, requesting permission to speak.

Yeshua acknowledged him. "Say what you will, Lucifer."

Az watched his father straighten up, his head thrown back, looking handsome and in control, his eyes sweeping over Yeshua and Quatama, who seemed to do all the talking and little real explaining, not one of them answering the major question *why*: why should the angelfolk care, no, be *forced* to care about this puny planet?

Lucifer bowed a second slight deference to the elders. "May I ask when this incarnation will begin, and if all but you will be required to . . . desert Eliom?"

Elijah came forward. "I, too, will be contributing to the redemption of Earth, as will other elders, in time. Not all angelfolk will be required to incarnate at the same time. We suggest some family members go, and some stay to maintain their homes and tend the Garden. When those who have gone are returned through mortal death, then they may switch with those who earlier remained in Eliom. This will allow a rotation in which we all may help the Earth while holding to our duties in Eliom."

"And how long do we have to . . . prepare before this other duty calls us?"

Elijah looked to Quatama, who answered: "Three days. Upon completion of the Hall of Seraphic Records."

Lucifer asked him suavely, "Are the angels now forced to labor upon a monument to this folly?"

Quatama countered, "Have the angelfolk not just heard of this building a short while ago?"

A question to answer a question, thought Az. *A wily ruse.*

"Yes, we did," his father answered.

"And are the angelfolk all accounted for here?"

Lucifer's eyes swept over the vast gathering. "I couldn't say."

"I can assure you, Lucifer. We are not building the repository for the Seraphic records."

"Then who is? We've been told that the work has already begun and swiftly, although we see no such structure."

"The Seraphim are raising it. It will stand on the northern boundary of our village beyond the small forest, just before the entrance to the canyon of the winds, those which lead to other dimensions, both permitted and forbidden to us."

"That it's being built at the causeway between the dimensions is understandable. But do you truly expect me to believe that the Seraphim are building it?"

Az wondered what the point of his father's argument was. Who cared if the uppity Seraphim were soiling their hands with common labor? No doubt, they used some Seraphic trick to spare themselves the brunt of it. And who cared whether they built that monument to stupidity at the mouth of the canyon, its dimensional winds obviously the conduit to those nauseating mortal women and their wretched embryos. Neither he nor his father were going to sacrifice themselves upon those winds.

But now his father aimed a demeaning finger at Quatama. "I think you lie or are deceived." Az listened closely to his father's tone: it wasn't really disbelief, but rather a challenge, each word reeking with disrespect, including his insult to Quatama's integrity. "I cannot believe this, not sight unseen, and must view this wonder for myself. Who wishes to accompany me to verify this?! The house that will hold the record of our very souls!"

And after a short-lived silence, a trickle of voices rallied to Lucifer's call.

"I'll go!" shouted someone from deep in the crowd.

"My family would see this for themselves as well," another cried out, even as Ezekial's voice thundered out: "People! Would you doubt the veracity of the Seraphim?!"

Lucifer thundered back: "Where our lives are challenged, yes!"

Now a cacophony of yeas sounded from the diverse crowd. Lucifer returned to his family, returning the approving smirk that Azmodeus graced him with. Lucifer loudly commanded his supporters. "Follow me!" He gestured to his wife and sons to do likewise.

Az watched as his mother fearfully shook her head. Lucifer pushed her forward, speaking harshly as she faltered. "You will not stand against me, Affaeteres. Come!" His glance swept to Ashtoreth and then Bael, his eyes conveying the same demand. Az bolted eagerly over to his father, walking backwards and sideways to gauge the number of angelfolk joining them. A large crowd jostled others roughly as they made their way over to Lucifer.

Ashtoreth walked wearily behind their father, but Bael looked to Leianna, who stood with her family beside him. Az watched as he squeezed her hand, saying, "Stay," then hurried to catch up with his parents and brothers. Leianna touched her father's hand, her face turned to him, then left his and Eve's side, running to Bael. She reached him, grasping his hand and startling him.

Az grinned. Nearly half of the gathering had deserted the elders, literally backing Lucifer. They exited the village center heading north, weaving like a snake through the broad pathways between thachkas until they spilled out onto grassland that skirted the break between the village and northern wood.

Lucifer led them around the length of the smaller forest, circling it to the canyon. The village receded in the distance and disappeared from sight. Azmodeus studied the crowd behind him: six hundred or so angelfolk (a guess he felt was close to count) followed them. Pleased for his father's sake, he glanced surreptitiously at Leianna, who seemed to have joined his father's cause.

His older brother, however, was displeased by her presence. "Leianna, go back," he told her.

"No. My place is with you. Chamira plainly said so."

"Do *you* doubt the veracity of the Seraphim?"

Az relished the fact that Leianna hesitated before saying, "No."

"If you come with us, it will be believed that you do anyway. By those who stayed and by the elders."

Again, a slight hesitation before answering him. "The Creator will know the truth."

Az wanted to laugh at her piety. He temporarily left his father's side, scampering gleefully over to her. "I applaud you, Leianna of the House of Michael, soon to be of the House of Lucifer. You show good judgment in deserting those paltry kissers of the Creator's ass."

She stared sharply at him. "Bael and I will have our own house. And you will come to regret your irreverence. I desert no one, least of all our Creator."

"You are only here for Bael's sake, then?" His own eyes challenged her.

She hesitated a third time. "I, too, would see this wonder for myself," she admitted, "but only because it is a wonder, built at the Creator's command and by the Seraphim's own hands. But if Bael had not followed his father, I'd have waited with my family and the elders until we were *all* permitted to see it."

"Too late, Leianna," Az answered with mocking regret. "You cannot rationalize your waywardness in joining us. You're as guilty of disobedience to the Creator as the rest of us now, Little Miss Perfect."

She answered him angrily, snarling like a cat. "I would *not* desert your *brother!*"

"Ah, then you *have* come because of him. I misjudged you. The things one will do for love; amazing, isn't it?"

Bael swung her around to face him, but Az had seen wretched fury on her face and knew she opposed Lucifer's rebellion. He spat out his disgust. "And your own mother was defiled by the beast-men of that *Earth,*" he muttered, loudly enough for her to hear, then swiftly made his way back to Lucifer, who still grasped Affaeteres's arm, forcing her along.

Slightly ahead of Bael and Leianna, he heard Bael command his betrothed to go back.

"Too late," she answered, her tone tart and bitter, "so Azmodeus says."

Az wondered if Bael would hit her, punish her for the thick sarcasm in her voice. Perhaps Bael, having wearied of her and seeing her true nature, didn't want her there at all and would force her to return permanently to her parents.

But secretly he hoped not; her stubborn innocence always provided him with rare entertainment.

Lucifer led his followers around the last small copse of remaining woodland, where a short expanse of grass met an uneven jutting wall of high rock. It stretched out vertically and horizontally as far as the eye could see, hiding what lay beyond its summit and sides, except for a single opening the size of a large man's spread arms' length, cutting a chasm between the rock walls.

Lucifer knew, as did the others, that this path, rarely used, led to the dimensional winds, to other worlds. To Earth.

He paused midway to it on the grass, turning to his supporters. "I see no *house* such as the elders describe," he told them, genuinely angered, "nor any Seraphim laboring to raise it!"

A disgruntled murmur swelled among his dissidents. One man shouted back: "They said that it was being built before the entrance to the canyon of the winds! We have been lied to!"

"So it seems," agreed Lucifer.

Affaeteres stroked his arm, saying, "Let us return home then."

He gazed at her hand, now resting on his robe, then at her face. Her eyes were luminescent with tears, her cheeks blotched. "You are a good wife, Aff," he said, "if somewhat complaisant to others. If you wish to leave, do so. I have not examined all the stones along this path I've chosen." He turned away from her and addressed his restless followers. "There is no structure rising as a monument to folly here. Let us go down the pathway into the canyon. We'll see if anything there awaits our scrutiny. If not, we will return to the elders to tell them that they are indeed the fools!"

Leianna approached him, her face solemn, and murmured, "Father Lucifer, you will not find what you seek within this canyon."

And then another figure pushed through the querulous throng, emerged at their forefront and strode angrily over to him: Gabriel. He had obviously lifted and flown the distance to them. Lucifer had checked the crowd accompanying him carefully at intervals, for enemies within his fold. Gabriel had not been among them on their trek. Now he grabbed at Leianna's upper arm and pulled her roughly to him, while facing Lucifer. "You will *not* claim another soul for your heresy."

Lucifer remained unruffled. "Ah, then you haven't followed us to show your own good sense." He silently appraised the hot-headed twin of his once-good friend, Michael. The resemblance stopped at the physical.

Leianna twisted away from Gabriel's clutch, pulling her arm free. "Has my father sent you, Uncle, to call me back?"

Lucifer noted that Gabriel's confusion overshadowed his pious indignation. "No."

"Then I thank you for your concern, but I must be here, unless Bael chooses to return with me to the village." Her tone equally indignant, she looked to her betrothed, who met her gaze, then turned his own toward Lucifer.

Lucifer shrugged, smirking back. "Do as you must, Bael."

His second-born told his betrothed: "I cannot leave. I must see this thing through."

She answered, "I know," and taking his hand, drew him past Lucifer and Gabriel, approaching the narrow opening into the canyon.

Gabriel called after her. "Will you disobey the Creator, Leianna?"

She paused and turned toward him. "I do not disobey the Creator, Uncle. I obey a command." She continued walking through the gap between the stone barrier, drawing Bael in behind her.

Lucifer took Affaeteres's hand, his eyes questioning hers. She seemed to have regained her courage. She nodded. Together, they followed Bael and Leianna through the entrance to the Canyon of the Winds. A quick glance behind him showed Ashtoreth, Azmodeus and the others, walking single-file.

Soon the chasm trail widened, allowing three to four angelfolk to travel beside each other. Lucifer didn't glance back again. He knew that those who accepted his leadership now would remain steadfast in any trial yet to come. He cared little whether Gabriel's pious nose had led him back to Eliom or, bent by self-righteous egotism, carried him forward into the chasm.

As they traveled through this single gorge, the view on either side alternated between jagged weathered rock face, rising three to ten man-lengths, and sudden emptiness, the path becoming a bridge, vistas of more canyons and cliffs stretching out, seemingly without end. The cliffs and canyons glowed white, gold and red in the heat of a sun that hadn't set, but should have by this time. The brightness rivaled that of noonday.

Lucifer had only traveled this path twice before, the first time being when his parents had left Eliom, along with others volunteering to help a distant world at the Creator's request. So distant, the travellers had required somnambulation as their means of transport. He had watched, not without apprehension, as they had been put, by the Seraphim's mere touch, into a sleep state and lifted by the winds and carried off. They had not yet returned; no one knew when they might. And now chaos had come to Eliom, its folk forced upon a new journey, the luxury of choice denied them.

Lucifer strained his eyes toward either horizon as they tramped across one lengthy bridge, but saw nothing built by any hand, angel or Seraphim, that resembled a house. Had they been lied to? It seemed unbelievable that the elders should do so, despite his earlier rant to stir up his rebels. Yet hadn't Leianna told him he would not find what he sought? She who seemed so favored by and in favor of the Creator's dictates. Was it possible he had hit upon the truth? Or had the Creator relented, torn by Lucifer's anger and dissent, for was not *he* once favored by the Creator? Was it possible? Had their Creator changed plans, recalled the Seraphim, relinquished the command to enforce angelic servitude on Earth? Had Lucifer's voice, his denial, his stand against such bondage, been heard? Was that why Leianna, she who would never rebel, had joined them, not out of loyalty to Bael, but to witness the Creator's retraction?

His confidence grew as they passed the stone bridge, flanked once more by soaring stone walls. Sunlight still lit their way, streaming down into the gorge. Lucifer vaguely remembered that this last stretch ended in an immense, roughly circular ledge, partly enclosed on either side by the high canyon walls, these walls ending a goodly distance from each other on the far side of the ledge. The sight of the winds beyond the open section of the ledge had staggered him: a swirling nebulous vortex of many colors. Dancing, mixing, separating and merging again, they crackled with a golden energy that erupted and spent itself, only to emerge elsewhere in the splendiferous display.

None but the Seraphim could control them, draw them to the open edge of the ledge, a single color, a single wind tunnel that would lead to a specific world.

The angelfolk had been permitted, twelve long annums ago, to ride specific winds, to view Earth from a safe distance. Hanging in the void of its solar system, far above that planet, they were allowed a privileged peek at a new world. The Seraphim had somehow timed the winds to return and draw each onlooker back along the intersecting dimensional planes, catching them up and sweeping them homeward to Eliom. Lucifer had been among those onlookers, curiously glimpsing the planet, all blue, green and brown as it rotated placidly in space, a mist of white clouds circling its atmosphere. He had dutifully remained where the transporting wind had placed him and, after a short while, a glow built up around him. His wind returned and took him back. He had been impressed, the Earth a bright jewel in the black starry space. Others who journeyed to view it were equally amazed.

Too amazed. Although they were protected from the void of space, their auras generating an outer shell locking them safely inside, the angelfolk had been expressly forbidden from entering the planet's atmosphere and descending onto its surface to explore it. Eve and Adam had stupidly believed they could quickly descend to view the new world's mysterious surface and immediately ascend to their sensor positions, in time to return to Eliom. And they had ignorantly believed that the Creator would forgive their impetuous daring, that it could cause no harm to Earth or to themselves.

In a way, they had done the angelfolk a great service. They had proven that the Creator, while omniscient, was not omnipotent, that two angelfolk trapped on the planet's surface could neither be rescued nor restored, except by the planet's own preset natural laws. Worse, once trapped there, neither Adam nor Eve's subsequent actions could be controlled by the Creator, or their hybrid biological functions manipulated or altered to prevent the supposedly horrendous interbreeding. And if the Creator were omniscient, all these events had been foreseen and nothing done to prevent them and avoid the disruption in Eliom.

It all added up as neatly as a short-barreled exchange of bean pods for berries: the Creator was not all powerful, was capable of error and mistake and, while perhaps possessing greater power than the angelfolk en masse, was not an object for abject worship, but rather one for justified suspicion and potential fear. As an unchecked force capable to bending them to its will, the Creator's beneficence was a ruse, its intelligence as capable of evil as of good. A force the angelfolk must somehow break away from or keep firmly in check before they found themselves and their free will, supposedly granted them, in jeopardy. As Lucifer's had been stripped from him on the Shore of the Seraphim, leaving him paralyzed and helpless, for daring to question this beneficent Creator.

"By the Seraphim's outstretched wings!" Bael's outburst, as he and Leianna rounded the last bend, shook Lucifer sharply from his reverie. He came around the bend and saw the building covering nearly one-third of the vast stone ledge. He stood, neck craning upward, as his wife, other sons and foremost followers crowded at the entrance, all staring at the strange sight before them and murmuring prayers and questions. Those behind them, not yet privy to the sight, pushed, shoved and loudly protested the sudden halt.

"Silence!" Lucifer thundered, his voice echoing through the canyon, his command immediately obeyed. He slowly moved forward, his supporters spilling out fully onto the canyon floor, huddling together and filling only a small corner of it, the total shelf at least nine times larger than the area they occupied.

Seraphim, their heads cloaked once more, hovered at various sections and levels of the enormous edifice, the shape and structure of this House of Seraphic Records beyond anything in the angelfolk's experience. Two of the Seraphim flew down to Lucifer's contingent, landing gracefully before them.

Lucifer saw no visible building tools or materials anywhere. Yet the elaborate building stretched nearly to the top of the left canyon wall. It didn't obscure the open ledge on the far side of the canyon where the transdimensional winds still danced as brightly as a storm in the sunset. In the sky above his head, above the canyon proper, the true sun still commanded the sky where, by Lucifer's reckoning, night and stars should have been.

He could not tell which Seraphim stood before him, their faces once more a mist of radiating light. He asked them: "How are you building this, when I see no stone, wood or clay to complete it?" He pointed upward to the unfinished dome.

One of the Seraphim pointed to the swirling vortex as an orange wind separated itself from the other brightly colored winds and blew freely over the canyon. A different Seraph emerged suddenly from within the orange wind, holding a huge, clear blue stone, curved and triangular, flying it over to the dome where another Seraph hovered, waiting. Together they fit the heavy stone between golden beams. Lucifer turned his gaze back to the vortex. Three more Seraphim emerged from it, each carrying another section of the dome—weights which should have been impossible to lift in flight. The elaborate building swiftly completed, the remaining Seraphim flew down en masse, joining the two who stood before Lucifer and his rebels.

The mist of veiling light dissipated from the face of the Seraph before Lucifer. Her features now angelic, her eyes, nonetheless, were recognizable. Gehtat. "You have displeased your Creator, Lucifer, for you have shown distrust. Without trust, there can be no love."

"I do not love the Creator," Lucifer agreed. "I cannot love a being who does not let me question him or her."

"The Creator is One," replied Gehtat, "neither female nor male, your mother and your father first, before your genealogical parents, and you have shown disrespect."

The Seraph beside her bared his true face, its broad angles and bovine eyes again recognizable. "A disobedient son must be disciplined in an effective manner," said Elat. "It is plain that you have no concern for yourself, caring only to champion your errant cause, seeking your freedom from the true source of your very soul and its connection to others. It cannot be done, Lucifer."

"It can be done. I deny the Creator's hold on me. I am my own man, responsible for no one but myself, unless I choose otherwise. If others want my respect, they must show me equal respect. I am *not* beholden to this suspect Creator. I am *not* a child."

"But you are," said Gehtat, an edge of sarcasm lacing her voice. "One who would insist he is equal to his parent and would lash ignorantly and dangerously out in foolish rebellion. You threaten not only yourself, but these other children." She waved her hand, wings rustling with the gesture, toward the angelfolk surrounding him.

"No!" someone shouted, pushing through to the front of the throng, emerging between Lucifer and Leianna. Gabriel glanced quickly at her. She stared back, but said nothing.

Gabriel knelt in front of the unveiled Seraphim. "Forgive me, blessed ones. I have traveled here to protect my niece."

"And to see your enemy vanquished," Gehtat told him.

"I . . . ."

"Do not deny it, Gabriel, for you are still loved by the Creator and forgiven for this small sin of pride. But you should instead feel sorrow for Lucifer, who would raise himself to the height of his Creator. Think then of how far he must fall when he realizes the error inherent in this goal."

Gabriel, still kneeling, twisted around to face Lucifer. "Repent, my friend. Repent while you still can."

Lucifer said nothing, but as Gabriel turned back to the Seraphim, Lucifer kicked him squarely in the buttocks, sending him sprawling. "Grovel," Lucifer told him. "Grovel before them and the Creator, like the toad that you are."

Gabriel lifted himself up, glaring back with a mixture of shock and, to Lucifer's satisfaction, undisguised hatred, then angrily addressed Leianna. "Will you return home now, or do you follow that creature we once called friend?"

"I follow no one but the Creator," Leianna told him. Gabriel glanced at Bael, but said nothing more to his niece. He instead beseeched the Seraphim: "I ask that you, and through you, the Creator, forgive these angelfolk for their transgression."

Elat told him, "They are already forgiven. But Lucifer must still be disciplined, so that he will see his error and cease to challenge our Creator."

"A good father," Lucifer said, his tone even and controlled, "will free the son from constricting bonds of patriarchy, allowing him to seek his own answers to life's challenges."

Gabriel cut in brusquely. "As you have with Azmodeus? Did you not say that none would discipline *him,* but *you?*" Lucifer nodded once. "I did, but now allow him to seek his own way. I recognize the folly of my own patriarchy. I free my son to seek his own decisions on how best to deal with himself and others."

Gabriel appealed to the Seraphim. "Azmodeus has broken the laws of Eliom, although I know not how, for Lucifer has not enlightened us!"

"He . . . ," Bael began, his eyes searching out his father's.

Lucifer glared at him.

Bael continued. "My brother Azmodeus has broken the Law of Privacy. Twice."

Elat and Gehtat said nothing, studying Bael's then Leianna's face, then returning their somber eyes to Lucifer.

Fear gripped him, for the sake of his youngest, but he couldn't yield. He met each Seraph's eyes. "Misguided curiosity. No reason for harsh retaliation."

"Not only your son," said Gehtat, "but you have broken a law of Eliom. The law allows forgiveness for the first offense; it demands correction if a second occurs. Were either offenses reported to your elders?"

"I am an elder," said Gabriel, "although new to such an honor. Only the first offense reached my own and others' ears. No injured couple has come forward to claim a second offense."

Gehtat glided smoothly over to Bael. "To whom did the second offense of which you speak happen?"

Bael answered her softly. "Myself and Leianna."

Gehtat nodded pensively and returned to Elat's side, touching his hand, looking silently at him.

"But, of course," said Lucifer, "you know this, being omniscient."

Gehtat turned her head briefly to him. "We are not omniscient." She brought her gaze back to Elat, resuming their silent communication. Both Seraphim then parted, moving separately in a weaving pattern through the forty Seraphim standing guard with them. Lucifer had counted. If conflict came, even against Seraphic powers, the angelfolk, trapped between the open ledge and the narrow canyon pathway back to Eliom, outnumbered them.

Disputes were not uncommon in Eliom, but there had never been physical violence. Even for Lucifer, the thought of Seraphim and angel locked in a contest of strength and supremacy seemed impossible to contemplate.

Gehtat and Elat had nearly completed their strange promenade through the silent Seraphim. They returned to the forefront again, this time standing before Azmodeus and Affaeteres. Gehtat asked her dryly: "Does the soul of your youngest matter to you, mother?"

Affaeteres answered immediately: "Yes."

"Then you would not want it harmed."

"No."

Lucifer rushed to her side, knowing she was being coaxed into a trap. "She does not wish to see our son harmed by anyone, including the Seraphim."

Gehtat smiled wryly at him. "We will not harm him." She moved back, away from his wife and son. He noticed Az had also drawn himself backwards, no trace of his usual smirk, his eyes wide and darting, his lips pursed worriedly.

Elat and Gehtat stood there quietly, offering no further reprimand. Lucifer expelled a deep breath of relief and spoke. "We have no further argument with the Seraphim, having seen the truth of our elder's words. We will leave you now to whatever tasks we interrupted and convey our apologies for that necessary interruption."

Another Seraphic voice called his name loudly. Lucifer ignored it, taking his wife's hand, readying his exit, to return to Eliom and seek another way to thwart the madness being forced on his people. A way that didn't endanger his family. He began walking, Affaeteres in tow, Az walking beside her, past the line of Seraphim, hoping his supporters would take his lead in a solid flowing retreat.

Up ahead, two more Seraphim moved forward, blocking Lucifer's path. The haze obscuring their faces lifted; Seheer and Chahtai cut off his escape on one side, the angelfolk on the other, uncertain of their status in this confrontation and unmoving.

Chahtai's lionized visage mentally assaulted Lucifer; in contrast, Seheer cast sad lupine eyes upon him. She spoke first. "We regret that we must correct your behavior. The grief is not ours alone. The Creator also weeps for you."

Chahtai spoke, his voice resonant. "Behold the winds, Lucifer!" All heads turned to the open ledge, the turbulence of the dimensional vortex. Lucifer hardened himself for whatever was to come, willing to champion his right to self-determination even to the death, if death be the price, as long as his family went unharmed, free to make their own choices.

A wide red wind spiralled upward, separating from the vortex. It blew over the canyon itself, above the onlookers' heads, its center solid and crackling with golden energy, the fluctuating air to either side expanding and contracting. It circled above the Seraphim and angelfolk like a volatile shifting ribbon of colored light, then suddenly descended, coming swiftly toward Lucifer.

He released Affaeteres's hand, that she shouldn't be flung along with him to whatever awaited him.

The wind dipped down, soaring over his and Affaeteres's heads, and engulfed Azmodeus, bathing him in its fiery red light and lifting him up like a feather in a sprightly breeze.

"No!!" Lucifer cried out, horrified, as Az kicked and screamed inside the wind's sure grip, tossing and twirling within it as it danced, its chosen passenger buffeted about, to the waiting vortex.

Lucifer's hand dug harshly into Chahtai's winged shoulder. "Take me! Release my son! I have defied you, not Azmodeus! I have set the seeds of disobedience within him! Take me instead!"

Chahtai asked quietly, "Will you abandon your rebellion? Will you pledge everlasting faith in your Creator?"

Lucifer stared at him, feeling the wind, poised at the brink, his son locked within it, tear at his heart, scouring it of any last vestige of faith. "Yes."

Seheer began a ululating moan, the other Seraphim echoing her, until their loud high-pitched chorus became the sound of the wind. The red wind leapt into the vortex with its traveller, merging with the other multi-hued winds. The center of the vortex exploded in a shower of gold light, flaring briefly, then fading.

The vortex resumed its dance beyond the ledge, the red wind released, its prisoner en route to another dimension, another world.

Lucifer kept his grip on Chahtai, asking, "Why?!"

"Because you swore falsely."

Lucifer released him, lowering his arm. "Where have you sent Azmodeus?"

"To the Earth, to be sired by another. You may leave now, Lucifer."

-30-

Azmodeus drifted like a feather inside the red wind. The hard buffeting had ceased, but he made no attempt to reach its nebulous walls, for there seemed no escape. Through the scarlet outer haze, endless sheets of multi-colored hues sped briskly by, alternating with an empty blackness. Az instinctively knew, despite his fear, that his safety depended on his remaining within the wind.

With neither night nor day visible, time lost all context. His terror subsided, becoming a weary acceptance. He had been punished, not merely for his breach of the law, but for his father's. His father couldn't bow before the Creator. Az, too, had questioned and challenged that unknowable force.

He wondered to what fate this wind blew him, if it, too, was alive and equally conscious of him or merely a force of nature, manipulated by the Seraphims' will. After a while, he stopped caring, riding the wind peacefully, as untroubled as an unborn child safe and trusting within its mother's womb, nourished and snug within its walls.

His eyes closed, his limbs weighted by a great need for sleep.

He curled up and let sweet unconsciousness claim him.

Adam grunted as the two apprentices displayed their finished knives and axes for him on the mat. They had been with Ruh, the clan's weaponsmaker, for one year. Adam scrutinized their work for flaws and found none. He nodded at Ruh, who wore a satisfied smile and dismissed the young men. They each bowed to Ruh and to Adam, then walked off, flushed with their achievement and their master's and clan chieftain's approval.

Adam scratched at his thick yellow beard, rooting with his fingers inside of its matted hair. He found the lice and crushed it, watching as his oldest daughter approached. Bakka stopped a respectful distance away from him, lowering her head. He asked her, "Lillah?"

The girl raised her eyes as he addressed her, a shy grin playing on her lips. "The birthing has started. The wives are there. They tell me to say that the child is in the position and all seems well. The baby should be born before sunset."

Adam ruffled Bakka's hair, a special show of affection. "Tell Zinah to send you to me when Lillah bears the child, and we will go and name it."

His daughter beamed, nodding and running off to deliver her father's command. Adam grinned. Of all the lessons life on Earth taught him, the importance of clan strength was paramount. Ever since Choly's death, he treated childbirth as sacred, the clansmembers accepting his dictate that all women in labor be given respite in the birthing hut and watched over by those wives experienced in the birthing art.

The thought of his new son or daughter unleashed a memory that, in turn, filled him with both sadness and longing. He sighed as Eve's death resurfaced in his mind, followed by images of lost Eliom, the life he and Eve had led there, the loved ones and friends they had known. Had Eve returned there following death? And where had the souls of Choly and her unborn child fled to? He had no surety of any answer, only his own unproven hope.

A wave of loneliness washed over him, a need for *something* to remind him of the peaceful abode he had inadvertently exiled himself from. Some small symbol to keep the hope from fading.

The twins, of course, Ahbel and Cahn, were thriving on Zinah's milk and, being Eve's sons, left a part of her in this mortal life. But something more was needed to ease the well-hidden pain in his soul.

As he headed back to his hut, the new idea came, so obvious, he wondered that it never occurred to him before. His step became lighter, and he smiled.

So simple a solution. His newborn child would be the first to be given an Eliomese name.

The quiet of the red wind's womb ended. Turbulent shaking roused him from the depths of sleep. He tried to remember who he was, where he was, but only fear filled his mind. The walls of the wind contracted, pushing against him, pressing against and covering his soft flesh. The air about him tasted warm and wet. He began to descend, his body flowing headfirst down the wind's tunnel, its walls pushing him farther down its shaft. His heart beat wildly, his mouth and nose filled with the sticky wet warmth. He was nameless and knew of nothing but his terror at the denial of the wind to nurture him any longer, the suffocating pressure of its walls. His head was stuck, wedged between the walls. He tried to kick with his feet; he moved, but the walls moved him farther along, and the wind spat him out of it into chaos. Large shapes and sounds assaulted his eyes and ears, and he cried out in pain, spitting the remnant of wind fluid from his mouth, and cried out again and again, screeching out his horror at emerging in this strange and frightening world.

Shapes rubbed at him and wrapped him in another round wall,

its sides soft and smooth. Something held him and made low soothing noises at him. His pain subsiding, he quieted and listened to the lulling sound. But fear returned; he bawled out his terror again. The soft walls opened and pressed him to another, even smoother wall. It had a protuberance. Long shapes guided his mouth to it. He tasted it, sucking it. A new wet warmth flowed from it into him. Wetness within instead of without.

After a while, its soothing flow was like the flow of the wind before it had rejected him. It comforted him, and he slept, at peace again.

Adam knelt beside Lillah, examining the infant son asleep at her breast. The child seemed healthy. His strong cries could be heard a distance from the birthing hut as Adam and Bakka headed toward it.

Lillah looked up at him expectantly. "What will you name our son?"

He placed a finger on her lips. "Hush. I am considering." He thought of the different Eliomese names, and a new memory surfaced, of the Naming Day Ceremony he had attended for Leianna. Lucifer's wife had been pregnant and, following the ceremony, as they relaxed and ate at Eve and Michael's thachka, Affaeteres had divulged the names she and Lucifer had chosen for the coming child: Zima, if a girl; Azmodeus, if a boy.

Adam touched the sleeping infant's tiny hand. "He shall be called Azmodeus."

"What does that mean, husband?" asked Zinah.

It took a moment for Adam to remember; he no longer spoke his native tongue aloud. He had hoped to teach it to his clan one day. "It means 'he who knows the greatness of his . . . God.'"

"A good name," Lillah murmured and, allowing Zinah, her sister-wife, to take the infant, shut her own eyes, resting.

"This name is from your homeland?" Zinah guessed.

"Yes."

"Then it will bring him good fortune."

"It will bring a bit of my old world into my new world, and I will miss it less."

"Perhaps some day, if it is possible and not so far as you say, we can journey to your homeland."

Adam offered her a smile both amused and resigned. "Perhaps," he said, "but then, you would have to learn its language."

"Then my husband will have to instruct me in it," she countered, cradling the baby.

He stared at her, new hope surging up inside of him. "I will teach you," he promised her, "and any others within the clan who wish to learn it."

*   *   *

The red hoop is lifted from my head. I am no longer a newborn, stripped of all but the immediate. I am no longer its father, unwittingly giving the babe the same name it wore in its previous life. I am Leigh Ann, also known as Leianna, and I am bone-tired from experiencing, even second-hand, the trauma of mortal birth.

"Leianna?" Quatama stands there, waiting.

I look up and whisper, "I'm all right. What time is it? In the mortal world, I mean."

"Nearly three a.m. The same time it was when we began." How he knows this isn't apparent. He wears no wristwatch; no clock hangs on the stone castle walls, not even a candle clock marks the hour. "Time does not exist here, as I explained earlier. Only its illusion in space."

"I need to get some sleep," I tell him. "The heck with metaphysics."

"Your body is asleep. Your mind also will get a full night's rest. Just one more hoop, and we'll be through, your lessons from the past complete. But first, I think, some refreshments."

He wheels the small side table, which I had thought stationary, over to my chair. Beside the three hoops, the silver tray now holds a crystal decanter of an amber-colored liquid and two crystal goblets. He pours for us, and I sip mine, sweet and smooth, tasting like almonds and apples, its texture like diluted honey.

"It won't get me drunk, will it?"

"No," he laughs.

"I mean, I'm tired enough as it is. Getting born is a bitch."

"Now you know why newborns sleep so much," he says, glancing over my mild lapse into vulgarity. "This nectar will revitalize you. Do you want something solid to eat?" He waves his hand at the table: a pile of round cookies with pastel-colored sugar decorations appears on a small silver plate. They look scrumptious.

Tasting one, it reminds me of the almond cookies my mother bakes, only sweeter, like the nectar. "I'm going to get fat up here."

"Happily, no. Here, all food is also an illusion, pure energy formed in the shape of your favored delectables."

"No calories?" I reach for another cookie.

"Not the kind your mortal body stores. Everything here is made of skane, Leianna."

"Skane." I'm going to town on the cookies, they're so good.

"Skane. Energy. All energy is skane. It reacts differently in each dimension, in accordance with the necessary function of the elements it builds to sustain each environment."

The cookies are gone. "Uh, explain that to me again after I've read Einstein's theory. Right now I'm little fuzzy-brained."

"Actually, you should be feeling better."

I pause and consider my own energy level. "You're right. I am."

"Are you ready to go on? Afterwards, I promise I'll return you to your physical body at the exact moment we called you from it."

"Three a.m.?"

"Three a.m."

I smile at him, not ready to run a mile, but not wanting to prolong this another night. I retain all these memories I'm reliving and spend far too much waking time wondering what happened next. "Let's go for the finale, Quatama."

He gives me a lopsided grin as he reaches for the muted purple hoop and brings it to my head. "Another illusion," he says.

-31-

Turning their backs to the rebels, the Seraphim continued their work, flying into the rainbow winds and emerging from them to bring furnishings and other oddly shaped objects into the towering structure on the ledge.

Affaeteres had collapsed, sitting on the hard canyon floor, Ashtoreth trying to comfort her, unable to rouse her from her stupor. While Lucifer's erstwhile supporters milled nervously about, he took his wife's right arm and gestured that Ashtoreth should take her left. They lifted the lethargic woman, who swayed between them.

"Affaeteres." Lucifer spoke in a harsh rasping whisper. "You must compose yourself. We have a long trek back, and I, too, have lost a son."

Her bewilderment quickly fled. She spat each word at him, crisp and pointed as a carving knife. "You will *get* me *back* my *son!*"

He nodded once, solemnly, then turned in a slow arc, surveying his followers regally. Ashtoreth watched as his father wordlessly communicated, Lucifer's eyes sweeping over them, his visage stiff and proud, a renegade lion controlling his outcast pride.

Bael and Leianna approached them, standing before Affaeteres. Bael, as tall as his mother, brushed his hand gently across her cheek, wiping away a solitary tear trickling down it. Leianna, much shorter than either, lifted her arms to Affaeteres, who stepped into Leianna's beckoning embrace, resting her head against Leianna's. The air about both women seemed illuminated, as if dust motes were caught in rays of sun, sparkling.

The women stepped back from one another, briefly clasping hands, then Leianna, letting go, turned to Ashtoreth.

The uncanny empathy on her face was more than he could bear. He turned his own face away, afraid, should he gaze into those eyes one more moment, that he'd forget all propriety and clasp her to him in defiance of his own hard self-denial. If she really understood his feelings, his belief in his own failure to remedy this chaos in his family and in that sacred secret place in his heart, she ignored it. She took his left hand in her right hand, while clasping Bael's with her left, gave a quick appraising glance at Affaeteres and Lucifer, and began walking toward the exit pass from the canyon of the winds. Bael offered her a quizzically-raised brow, but offered no resistance, walking with her. Ashtoreth himself started to pull his hand free from hers, waiting for his parents, but Leianna tightened her grip, not letting him go. She tugged him along.

He looked back at Affaeteres and Lucifer. Lucifer met his glance, took his wife's hand and also led her toward the path back to Eliom, glancing over his shoulder to signal the others to follow.

Lucifer moved quickly ahead of his two remaining sons and Leianna, drawing Affaeteres along with him into the forefront.

Ashtoreth wondered where Gabriel was, fearing another confrontation between Leianna's stern uncle and his father. Leianna herself walked quietly along, relinquishing neither his nor Bael's hand.

As they drew nearer to the lone exit from the winding canyon bridge, the sky above them darkened. The stars and moon provided faint illumination, slowing them to a cautious pace. They moved along the final stretch, through the stone opening, and onto the field beyond.

Ashtoreth breathed a sigh as his sandals touched soft grass. His vision adjusted to the night, the northern wood a mass of shadows and shapes as they travelled back along its perimeter to the village. Time had passed normally there, the thachkas unlit, their occupants asleep, save for one.

Lucifer's followers dispersed, travelling whatever paths led to their own homes and rest. Lucifer said nothing, and no one among his supporters approached him. Whether pity stayed them or fear stopped them, Ashtoreth was glad. He basked in the silence. Lucifer continued on toward the solitary glow-lamp, a small beacon in the darkness.

Michael sat on the small wooden bench outside his home. He rose eagerly to greet his daughter, hugging her, then stared at Lucifer, at his family. He wearily asked Ashtoreth, "Where is your youngest brother?"

Ashtoreth shook his head, annoyed by the aching pressure in his eyes, narrowing them to cut off the hint of tears. He whispered, "I don't know."

"My son was taken," Lucifer said brusquely, "by the Seraphim."

Michael offered no comment, no word of sympathy. His face reflected both shock and resignation. His eyes flicked to Affaeteres, standing rigidly beside her husband, her own face an emotionless mask.

Michael finally found his voice again. "What now, Lucifer?"

"I will fight."

"You *can't* fight against the *Creator*."

"We shall see."

Michael shook his head. "It's late," he said. "Come inside, Leianna."

His daughter looked up at Bael, who bent down and kissed her cheek. "Can Bael and I be married tomorrow, father?"

"No, of course not," he answered tiredly. "The betrothal must run its appointed course."

"But there may not be time for that!"

"Come in and go to sleep, Leianna. We cannot break the law."

Ashtoreth, tears escaping despite his efforts, stuttered, "Lei-Leianna, it would be best if you broke the betrothal. F-for now." *Wilting crop! How best to say it?!* Bael scowled at him, either denying or oblivious to the danger Leianna might soon face, if she remained by his side.

"How can you say such a thing?" she asked. "Elijah and Chamira warned us against it!"

"I only mean you sh-should separate yourself from my family until—my father's dispute is resolved." He looked to Bael as he said, "If the Creator's wrath descends on us, you should not be struck by it," then turned back to her. "You don't share my father's argument, only my brother's love." *And mine,* he thought bitterly.

"I mustn't be separated from Bael, not if we're destined in some way to heal this chaos my mother and Uncle Adam caused. I trust the Creator to preserve us and lead us to that destiny. It would help us, though, if Lucifer abandoned his rebellion."

Lucifer swiftly answered her. "I cannot, but neither do I demand Bael's loyalty if he disagrees with my stance, as he seems to. No, if anything is to be abandoned, it will be the father by his second-born son, but not because he finds my cause to be unjust. You're a strong-willed woman, Leianna, and he can't abide losing you."

"We," she began, but he interrupted her.

"Yes, I know . . . you and my son are destined. Words that imply almost anything, including an illusion shared by two lovers bent on misinterpreting other words." He ignored Ashtoreth's frantic glance and wave of his hand meant to ask his father's silence on the confidence he'd—perhaps unwisely—shared with him. "Ashtoreth has told me of this chant Chamira performed before the three of you and Elijah, as if you were players in a drama about to unfold, rather than fools glamourizing a travesty to the future of the angelfolk. Take care that words you take to heart don't cloud your head." He smiled so chillingly at Leianna that Ash shivered in fear for her. Lucifer continued, obsessed. "But what was that you said to me before we entered the canyon of the winds? That I wouldn't find what I sought? Have a care, Leianna, for we all seem to need to learn that lesson."

"I only meant that *you* hoped that our Creator would bow to your demands." She turned back to Ashtoreth. "I understand your fears for me. Ash, you have to quell them, either through your own effort or your faith." And then to Bael, "Will you stay here tonight, or shall I come with you?"

"Daughter." Michael chided her sharply. "That isn't done!"

"Why? I am betrothed."

"Betrothal allows for impetuous passions. It doesn't allow for their blatant display."

"Will there be enough time, then, to trade my maiden cot for my marriage bed?"

Embarrassment and dismay flickered on Michael's face, Leianna's saucy defiance so unexpected and unlike her. Swallowing his guilt, Ash offered, "She can sleep on Azmodeus's cot. I can act as a guardian. I—I sleep in the same loft, you see."

His father's hand flew out, cuffing Ashtoreth on the side of his head, Lucifer's rage barely controlled. "Leianna is not welcome in my house. How strange that you offer to help her and Bael ignore our law, when you both faulted Azmodeus, no, condemned him for it."

Ash rubbed his ear and the scalp above it, where Lucifer's knuckles had struck. Then his mother was suddenly before him, her hand covering his, lowering it to his side, her fingers probing his ear and scalp gently. "Leianna *is* welcome in my home," she said, then to Ashtoreth, "Are you hurt?" He shook his head, ignoring the slight throbbing. Satisfied, Affaeteres confronted her husband. "You have cost me a son. You will not cost me a daughter!"

Lucifer shut his eyes tightly, grimacing, then opened them. "No, I won't. Leianna, forgive me. Do what you must."

Affaeteres touched his cheek, then asked Michael, "Where is Eve?"

"Inside. Asleep. She prayed all evening. We feared we had lost Leianna, too, when you didn't return from the canyon. Yesterday I went to your house and found it silent and unoccupied."

"Yesterday? But we've only been gone an evening and perhaps part of this night."

"No, Aff. Over one day has passed. Our people met again in the village center this afternoon. Each family chose one member to incarnate on Earth. Many others volunteered, eager to help the Creator correct the genetic imbalance." He sighed heavily. "I tried to volunteer in Eve's place. Quatama said no. She's to be exiled from Eliom and must incarnate continually . . . until the genetic structure of mortal man is fully healed and the Earth and everything on it is also rebalanced."

"How long will that take?"

"Thousands of years, they say. The elders cannot be more exact. They tell how each person's genetic pattern is unique, but that the traits they hold are subject to each person's choices in his or her life, whether angel or mortal. The Seraphim can only project the final outcome, the turning point in which the angelfolk may return home permanently to Eliom. The rebalancing, at some projected point, will succeed. Before then, challenges each incarnated angel meets and his or her response to them may hinder or help, lengthen or shorten our collective sojourn on Earth. Free will, individual intelligence, and their application can't be measured. And so I will lose a wife, and for a little while, a daughter. Leianna, Quatama asks that you incarnate."

Bael, silent until now, spoke out. "But Eve has been chosen!"

"No, Bael. Eve is being punished. Leianna and I weren't freed from this sacrifice. I offered to take Leianna's place as well. The elders prefer Leianna."

"Then Leianna has no choice!"

"She does. She can refuse, despite their preference, and I will go in her place."

"Father, when do they want my decision?"

"Tomorrow. The chosen ones and their families will be counseled by our elders. Those incarnating will be readied for their journey. The elders have been given a strange device, a rectangular stone. When held against the diaphragm, it stores a likeness of each person's traits and forms a connection to that person, reflecting that person, wherever he or she might be. Quatama and Yeshua demonstrated this, each using a stone to take the measure of the other, then separating in the crowd. Quatama's stone held Yeshua's image in the village center, showing the folk Quatama's image on the far side. We are told that distance has no effect on these stones. The elders and Seraphim will be able to track the incarnated angelfolk on Earth, even after mortal birth alters their appearance.

"And those who remain here in Eliom will act as guides to those who incarnate. The Creator has stabilized the Earth's atmosphere. We who remain here can visit our loved ones on Earth. But we'll seem like the wind, unseen and unheard by them. Quatama says that there *will* be exceptions, but for the most part, we will be invisible and inaudible, our ministrations and advice only felt and heard by the soul hidden in the flesh. The mortalfolk, whether native or incarnated, won't be consciously aware of us."

Ashtoreth pictured Leianna on the Earth, facing danger. "I'll volunteer," he told her, "and I'll find you and protect you."

His father refuted him. "No one from our family will go to Earth."

"But Leianna will go. You know she will. She won't disobey our Creator, and someone must go to watch over her. Bael and I will both go!"

"No one," Lucifer repeated. "The Earth is large, its people scattered, as Eve said. You may never come upon her, and if by chance you did, you may not know her, changed by mortal birth to resemble another." His father gave him a telling look. "You may not even know yourself. Perhaps you'll have no memory of who you once were. Ashtoreth of the House of Lucifer in Eliom will no longer exist, just another ignorant mortal until death frees you."

Ashtoreth cringed, then denied the fear and guilt which Lucifer had tried to instill in him. They had precious little time, none left for hiding a need which, by law, was not forbidden, when honorably expressed. "Bael, I love your betrothed as well as you and have since childhood. Your happiness and hers, your well-being, matters greatly to me. For Leianna's sake, you and I must find a way to protect her."

Bael said nothing, simply nodded.

Leianna approached her father, reached out and hugged him. "I need to decide, and both Bael and Ashtoreth must help me. Go in to Mother and spend what little time you have with her. Tell her that I love her."

Lucifer interrupted. "When does the actual incarnation begin?"

Michael answered slowly, his grief plainly visible. "The following morning. Tomorrow is preparation; the next day we gather before the winds on the ledge of the canyon, both the chosen ones and those they leave behind."

Lucifer nodded. "And they say our Creator is beneficent."

Ashtoreth stifled a yawn. "It's very late."

Michael, his exhaustion evident, placed his hand firmly on Ashtoreth's shoulder. "I understand. Watch over my daughter tonight. She *is* blessed, that *two* fine young men love her." To Leianna, he said, "Go with them and decide wisely, my little one." And to Lucifer and Affaeteres, he said, "Good night, old friends. Creator watch over you," before turning away, going inside, and shutting the door behind him.

At Leianna's insistence, they had pushed the three cots in the brothers' loft together. Lucifer and Affaeteres, in their own curtained alcove, gave no sign of hearing the noise.

Leianna lay in the middle, Ashtoreth to her right, Bael to her left. Sleep would soon claim them, despite their need to talk.

"How can I refuse Quatama," Leianna asked them, "if I'm needed on Earth? He wouldn't ask for me without good cause."

Bael stroked her arm. "What of your insistence that we not be parted, love? Of heeding Chamira's and Elijah's warning?"

"Chamira didn't warn us. She only recited a story of a man and a woman, a prediction of their healing this chaos we're facing now."

"Chamira did warn us, as we stood on the Shore of the Seraphim. What if we are the ones spoken of in her chant? If you incarnate, then all is lost."

Ashtoreth yawned heavily, then murmured, "She said the lovers would be separated for millennia. I don't want to lose you, Leianna." When she gently smiled at his poignancy, he added, "Neither does Bael." Her face clouded over. "This is why it's best that Bael and I also incarnate, in the hope that our souls will lead us to one another."

"There's no certainty that hope will guide us. Father said that those staying here can visit incarnated angels, can know who and where they are in their Earthly lifetimes, can help them."

Bael added, "And that those incarnated will be blind and deaf to the rest of us."

"Not all. Father implied some will not be."

"Implied. How sensitive will those exceptions be? Will they even hear a loved one's whisper in their ear, or will it sound like a fly buzzing too closely?"

Ashtoreth laughed, giddy with exhaustion. "And then we'll be slapped for all our trouble."

Leianna looked at him sternly, but the corners of her mouth soon curled up, and she giggled. "Ashtoreth, we are *trying* to *seriously* discuss this."

He smiled back at her. "A little humor will smooth your brow and help you think more clearly. As much as any of us can think." Another yawn escaped and spread contagiously to Bael, then Leianna. "I wish *our* father had not seen fit to rebel. I can understand his argument, but can't see how he can win it." He shifted onto his side, facing them, and pulled the thin woolen blanket over his body, bunching it as nonchalantly as he could to cover his groin.

He noticed that Bael made no move to draw his own blanket up, although he, too, needed to.

Leianna appeared oblivious to their bodily response to her. "I want you both to stay here in Eliom," she said, lying fully down, the glow light behind her winking out, darkness filling the loft. "Track my

Earthly life, visit me on the planet when you feel it's necessary, and forgive me if my mortal self can't see or hear you. My soul will know and welcome your presence." She fell silent, then added, "It'll only be for a little while, and then I'll come home."

"Leianna," Bael started.

"Hush," she said. "Time runs differently on Earth, three times faster. And we, the three of us, will barely age in our angelic bodies, even though I may grow old on Earth before death releases me. Eve returned to us as youthful as the day she left. Let me speak to Quatama. When I return, you and I will be married, and Ash can also ask for betrothal to me, if he still wishes it, and you agree. The law allows for that, if both husband and wife fully accept the third spouse."

Bael said nothing, but Ashtoreth smiled, his excitement building, his hope resurfacing. She did, after all, love him, perhaps not as strongly as she loved Bael, but Ash could accept her quieter, friendly love for him. He loved her back so deeply, there was nothing that he wouldn't do for her. "We'll stay then," he said, "and wait for your return. And . . . and I'd be happy to be your second husband, if Bael will permit it." In the darkness, he couldn't read his brother's face. When neither Bael nor Leianna spoke, he softly asked, "Are you asleep?"

Leianna mumbled incoherently. The need for rest had finally overtaken her.

"Sleep then," he told her.

"Ash?" Bael whispered.

"I thought you were also asleep."

"No. Nearly. How can you encourage her to incarnate?"

"If it's what she feels she must do . . ."

"I cannot abide losing her. She must not join this exodus."

"You cannot stop her."

"I can. I am her betrothed. She wouldn't allow us to be separated before, when Father rebelled, even though it made her look like one of the dissenters. Why now?"

"Go to sleep, Bael."

"Why now?"

Ash considered it. "Because she feel the Creator has requested that she go, speaking through Quatama. And she loves the Creator. More than she loves you." He shut his eyes, welcoming slumber, and left Bael to muse over this second competitor for Leianna's devotion, one greater than himself.

-32-

Eve's relief, upon being told of Leianna's return to Eliom with Bael and his family, had been short-lived. She accepted her daughter's decision to rest the remainder of the night with her betrothed in his father's house, trusting her discretion. Even the news of Ashtoreth's abrupt but respectful declaration of love for Leianna had seemed a good omen. Eve had clung to her husband, savoring the little time they had left. She and Michael had made poignant love; it had never seemed sweeter or more fulfilling. She had fallen asleep in his arms and then been awakened in the unlit pre-dawn by the dream.

In it, Leianna was mauled to death and eaten by a monstrous creature. It resembled the large striped cat they called the wamchattah in Eliom, but stood nearly three times its size with extended, viciously sharp teeth. That it attacked Leianna on Earth was plain, for her screams had brought village tribesmen armed with clubs and spears. Eve looked down upon her dead child, and while the incarnated Leianna's face had changed, her eyes remained the same. They stared blindly out, expressing her final terror before the tiger's jaws had broken her neck. Tiger . . . that was the name the huntsmen spat, after they had killed the beast in turn, too late to save their tribeswoman. And as Eve knelt and wept, her tears dropping on Leianna's upturned face, the dead woman's eyes moved in their sockets, staring at her accusingly, shocking Eve awake.

Fearful for her daughter's safety, should she incarnate now, Eve had trouble returning to sleep. Questions swirled in her mind. Had she been abrupt in her judgment of Lucifer and his harsh stance against the Earth and the angelfolk incarnating? Was their Creator forcing them to cure a defect that should have been safeguarded in the creation of Earth to begin with, so that two angels foolishly trapping themselves upon its plains, would not have caused an error that took the sacrifice of the Eliomese to remedy?

Was the Creator imperfect, as Lucifer contended? Were the folk immersed in a worship that should now give way to a call for equal say in such judgments? Eve shivered, her eyes closing in her need for more sleep.

She only knew that Leianna must not incarnate on that hostile dangerous planet. Eve had inadvertently abandoned her children, both Leianna and her half-siblings left on Earth, and now, as the Creator's judgment approached, Eve must abandon her first-born again.

This she could bear, but not the thought of her daughter forced to undergo mortality.

Eve would talk with Quatama . . . no . . . demand that Quatama allow Michael to incarnate instead . . . or better yet, that only she, Eve, should incarnate, regardless of the Creator's wishes.

Lucifer was right: they should demand the right to make their own determination, their own final judgment in matters that affected them so greatly. It took courage to oppose a god, a strength which Eve, for her own sake, didn't possess.

But for Leianna and her safety, Eve would find such courage. And the first place she would seek it was at Lucifer's house. Michael, so certain of the Creator's supremacy, might chastise her severely, but for the sake of their daughter, Eve would make him listen.

Lucifer had sardonically suggested that she join his protest. As a mother defending her child, she would.

A loud banging accompanied by muffled argumentative voices woke Lucifer and Affaeteres before the sunshaft tubing above them in the roof of the thachka played its waking beam across their faces and drew them more gently from sleep. Lucifer glanced at his wife, whose face reflected his worry. Had his disobedience already culled disciplinary judgment by the elders?

He grudgingly left the soft cot, taking his robe from the bench to clothe himself, then flung aside the curtain, descending barefoot down the stairs. Affaeteres, her robe hastily drawn about her, followed. Sounds could be heard from the second sleeping alcove. Their remaining sons and Leianna were awake and moving about.

Lucifer unlatched the upper door, opening it, cutting off a new argument between Michael and Eve.

"Good morning," Michael sourly greeted him, and Eve said excitedly, "I must see my daughter, Lucifer. She must not volunteer to go to Earth."

Michael added: "She believes Leianna will die, if she does."

Lucifer gave him a incredulous glance. "All things Earthly must die. Have you come to your senses, then?"

Eve ignored that. "She will be killed. Before her time by a terrible beast."

"How can you know this?" Lucifer asked, amused.

Michael answered with perturbed wryness. "She dreamt this."

Behind him, Lucifer heard the creak of the ladder stairs and Leianna's startled voice: "Mother, why are you and Father here? The sun hasn't even risen yet."

Lucifer unlatched the lower door. "Your parents have joined my cause. Your mother wishes you to remain in Eliom. She's dreamt that you will die violently, if you incarnate. Enter," he told Michael and Eve.

Eve stepped across the threshold. Michael tiredly said, "I have not joined your cause."

Lucifer, equally tired, acknowledged this. "You have not. But you may still enter my house, if you're so inclined."

Michael nodded, coming inside and sitting on one of the long benches flanking the table. Eve had rushed over to Leianna's side and in hurried tones told her and the others of the dream with the enormous and vicious wamchattah.

Leianna stroked her mother's arm, comforting her. "Anxiety disturbed your sleep, not a premonition. Quatama will watch over me. He won't allow a violent passage back to Eliom."

"How can you be so sure that Quatama will have any influence at all?"

Lucifer cut in, "Your mother speaks the truth, Leianna. Once born on Earth, no path you take holds any surety of safety."

"Father Lucifer . . . Mother . . . I have already decided. The people of Earth need me and others like me to right the wrong done. And you will also be on Earth, Mother. Perhaps we will meet." She paused. "Perhaps intrinsically know one another, perhaps better than we do here in Eliom." Lucifer saw the fleeting expression of hurt cross Eve's face before Leianna went on, ignoring the pain she'd inflicted on her mother. "It's been decided, regardless of your fears for the future. I will go. Bael and Ashtoreth will remain here and wait for me. Upon completion of my Earthly sojourn and readjustment to Eliom, Bael and I will marry, and Ashtoreth will declare his betrothal to us. Bael and I will accept him as a brother-husband, as the law allows us to. And we will give you grandchildren to love, one day when you finally return to Eliom, after your incarnations."

Lucifer watched as shock and dismay replaced the hurt Eve had already borne. He ruminated on the well-meaning ignorance of children, especially coddled ones like Leianna, and decided to confront Leianna on Eve's behalf. "You are prepared to leave your own children, as your mother left you?" he asked her.

"No," she answered slowly, "our children, should we be so blessed, will come after my incarnation."

"Incarnations, Leianna. This task they've set before us is expected to take thousands of mortal years. But perhaps your husbands," he waved his hand toward his sons, "can raise your offspring, at least until they, too, have to be flung helplessly upon that planet for a mortal lifespan apiece, at which point, you can resume the parental role without them."

"But they need not go," she argued. "Azmodeus . . ."

"My youngest son was exiled," he cut her off, "for his transgressions and my own against the law. The law, which you savor and quote for your own means, may take your precious Bael and Ashtoreth from you, whether they stand with me, as family honor demands, or against me. Where do you stand, Leianna? Certainly not with your mother."

She stood there, chastised, no doubt finally realizing that endless incarnations might well be required of them all, that she had no perfect answer to make the task set before them seem logical, lofty and manageable in an orderly society. She looked uncertainly at Bael, then at Ashtoreth, both of whom remained silent.

"You see, Leianna. There is no certainty at all in this grand plan of the Creator's, and no logical planting of any seeds you wish to sow between yourself and my sons. Only chaos until this mad design of incarnation and genetic balancing is completed. If it is completed. The elders have been vague on that point. And so I ask again: where do you stand? With whom do you stand? This foolish undertaking for beings lesser than the angels who are now to be fodder for the mortal beast? Or with my rebellion to secure Eliom against this madness and declare our autonomy from the Creator? Choose."

For the first time, he saw despair cross Leianna's face. She answered him slowly. "Your argument drains away the small bit of hope I had within my heart, Father Lucifer. You ask me to decide the impossible, for I want to be with my love, and Bael and I want our life together." She glanced at Bael. "But I must abide with my Creator. I cannot abandon the One who ignited the spark which lit my conscious being. And so I choose against you and for the Creator, even though I know you speak the truth. Yes, the Creator asks too much of us, far too much, even if the angelfolk, through Mother and Uncle Adam, created the problem that brings these demands upon our heads. But my intimate connection with my Creator outweighs all other loyalties, even when I disagree with these demands and consider them unfair."

"And you don't find your choice faulty? Then what of the insult to the angelfolk's long-standing loyalty and trust, including yours, in that we've been given no say in this forced incarnation, other than implicit and explicit threats to those of who dare to disagree?"

Leianna said nothing, and Michael urged her, "Answer him."

"What would you have me say, Father?"

"That the Creator is greater than all of us and we must trust such decisions and not question them."

"Even I question them, Father," she admitted, "but not presumptuously. All I can tell Father Lucifer is that I have no means to create a universe or even mold a world—not alone—and while I may one day bring life forth from my womb, neither I nor its father will be its sole creator." She turned to Lucifer now. "Your challenging our Creator is like the acorn standing up to the full grown oak. A gust of ill wind will blow you from its branch."

"Then I will root and spread my dissent into the soil of Eliom."

"That will reap a bitter harvest."

"Perhaps, but if you were given the right of dissension, Leianna, no matter how imperative the Creator insisted the rebalancing of the mortalfolk was, would you agree to incarnate?"

She tore her gaze from him to Bael and then Ashtoreth. "Yes. I would have to help my Creator."

At that instant, Lucifer disliked her intensely. She had all but stolen the souls of his eldest sons, cared nothing for the loss of his youngest, and was firmly against his stance to free Eliom from further loss. "Then I will waste no tears weeping for you, Leianna, although my sons and your mother may well grieve for you." He knew by the frown with which she greeted this remark that she already felt alone and outcast, a good preparation for her journey to Earth. In his own way, he felt equally alone and outcast, but his miasma, at least, was born of the courage to rebel. He summoned more courage and laid a conciliatory hand on her shoulder, for she was still Bael's betrothed. "But let us break bread and savor what peace remains, Leianna, your family and mine." He noticed how visibly she relaxed, no doubt believing he had forgiven her, both for opposing him and for the obvious favor heaped upon her complaisant head by Quatama and the Seraphim. "Affaeteres, would you please prepare a morning meal for us? Dissent is hard work and requires a full belly." He smiled at her; she returned it with her own small sad smile and turned toward the cooking alcove and cupboard.

Eve walked toward her, saying, "Let me help you." But Lucifer noted the hard determination in her eyes and, from their muted conversation, knew she plotted with Aff to turn Leianna from her chosen path.

Affaeteres served them fruited chumbah, the large round loaf of soft bread baked with harvest grains and raisins mixed with mashed apple pulp, and poured the sweet nectar of the apple and the grape into their cups. They ate silently at first, but then Bael began chiding his betrothed, bluntly distressed by her lack of loyalty to him. Lucifer watched as everyone but Michael and Ashtoreth harangued her to refuse to incarnate. At one point, Michael again offered to go in her place, but she shook her head, saying, "Last night you said Quatama asked for me specifically."

When Bael bristled, about to continue his argument that their marriage would be delayed until the end of her mortal days, Lucifer cut him short. "Leave her be, Bael, and stop droning on like a lovesick bee. She's made her choice. Accept it."

Bael plainly couldn't, but he quieted down, eating his own meal, peering at Leianna, who lowered her head, eyes downcast, finishing her own food and obviously upset. Bael reached across the table to her, grasping her free hand. She looked up at him, and Lucifer saw that her eyes glistened with the onset of tears. Bael said, "If this is what you must do, I'll wait for you, no matter how long it might take." She nodded, the tears brimming over and streaking her cheeks. He silently wiped them away.

Lucifer regretted her pain. He still felt a reluctant fondness for Leianna and hoped she might regain, one day, the affable and unintrusive nature he knew her to possess. The unaccountable favoritism shown her by the Seraphim irked him; it almost seemed designed to insult him, a sly initial punishment. Nonetheless, a threat to Eliom was a Council matter, not the concern of an impetuous opinionated girl. Today, while they prepared those angelfolk bereft of a backbone, he would call for an emergency convening of the Council, following the law which permitted a member to alert Eliom's governing body of any serious disruption that endangered the welfare of their community. He would speak and he would be heard and, if necessary, he would fight. As foreign a concept as that was, he and his followers were ready for that drastic contingency.

*   *   *

Unknown to most of the Council—but who knew what bees buzzed at the elders' ears?—Lucifer had been fastidiously hand-picking his rebels since Eve's return and the news of her forthcoming judgment. He had visited many of the angelfolk, sounding out their feelings on many points of law, including the breaking of the law when it impinged on self-determination, whether individually or unilaterally. He had found many angels eager to embrace the concept of self-rule, wary of an omniscient being that presupposed their needs or, worse yet, decided those needs without allowing them any valid say. The march to the canyon of the winds had not been as impromptu as it had appeared; Lucifer's contingent had been ready to rally behind him as events required and upon his signal.

He had also divided his followers into thirteen groups of 51 angelfolk apiece and had chosen specific angels to oversee these divisions, subject to his command as leader of the rebellion. Each of his subordinate commanders was as courageous as Lucifer. Each had pledged unwavering loyalty to Lucifer and embraced his cause without reservation. The Creator was about to see how far the birch could be bent down before it would snap back and crack the sky.

Moloch could be dour and had no patience for weakness, but he took care of his own, starting with himself.

Adrammelech, tall, swarthy and willow-thin, was equally determined to look out for his own and stood firmly behind Lucifer.

Nergal, dark, beak-nosed and strong as a bear was also as stubbornly certain that the Earth would never claim his kindred.

Chemosh, fair-haired and nearly effeminate in his mannerisms, regretted the turn of events that caused the Creator to cease to nurture them, all for some vile lower creatures.

Behemoth, his body a tower of flesh and muscle, hated Earth unseen, vowing that none would consider angelic souls as tools for correcting a breeding deficiency.

Dagon, thin and wily, wished those angelfolk, willing to incarnate, well, but had no intention of sacrificing himself.

Mammon, blonde and handsome, but of a girth that rivalled Behemoth, liked his comforts too well and the plight of the Earth not at all.

Belial, a nondescript weasely little man, felt the angelfolk held some complicity in the Earth's woes, but that the damage inflicted wasn't worth the remedy called for.

Thamuz, of the coal-black hair and bright black eyes, felt a responsibility to protect the angelfolk from a Creator whose love had turned to heartless abandon.

Lothan, a dark, striking-looking, well-built man, had often beguiled the women while gathering their husbands' support with his suave pointed oratory.

Phoenixious, the youngest of Lucifer's chosen, flaxen-haired and eager, had the mind of a poet, filled with images, fervor and the desire to champion the estranged, while romanticizing them.

Cimeries, black as night and possessing a coltish and lanky body, brooded over their chances at succeeding in their rebellion, but felt that no other course could be followed.

And finally, Naamah, ebony-haired and emerald-eyed, the only woman Lucifer had placed in command of a legion of followers, living alone and unmarried, swore that she would never be used, whether by man or Creator, against her will.

Lucifer had sent out word the day before the chaos in the canyon, that he, his commanders and their respective contingents were to rally this afternoon in the village center. That Quatama and his followers had chosen to meet and dispense their elven tales to the folk at the same place and time was unfortunate. Perhaps Lucifer would sway more folk to his side, after he'd had his say. He and his supporters would not accept an easy defeat. The Eliomese would not be culled like grains of wheat for another world's harvest.

As Affaeteres cleared the cups and plates, Michael, Eve and Leianna thanked them for the meal and took their leave of Lucifer's home, Bael accompanying his betrothed back to her parents' thachka.

Ashtoreth stood uncomfortably in the common room, staring at Lucifer.

"Well?" Lucifer finally prompted him.

"Does Bael know of your plans for secession, Father?"

"He knows I plan to fight the Creator's judgment. He does not know of the gathering today or its purpose. He's been . . . preoccupied."

"Do you think we can survive this?"

Affaeteres had come quietly into the room, listening to their conversation.

Lucifer asked, "If I said no, would it matter to you?"

Ashtoreth thought for a moment. "Yes."

"Then you might as well choose to stand against me, son. I've lost my youngest to a cruel demanding Being with no capacity for forgiveness. But denying me my cause will not save you from sharing Azmodeus's fate. Eventually, you, too, will be forced to endure mortal birth and life, for as long as that world permits you to live."

Ashtoreth hesitated once again, then said, "I don't see how any of us can win, no matter which side we stand on. But when Bael sees the extent of your rebellion today, that they aren't a loose undisciplined throng amassed to curiously listen to your words, but a force you've built to usurp the Council's authority, he, too, will be faced with a choice. One he will no longer be able to waver between."

"Then let him choose, as his soul leads him: to be enslaved, either by his desire for a woman or his cowardice before the Creator, or to be free of that enslavement, regardless of any loss such freedom entails." Lucifer opened the door, studying the rising sun. "This will be a day of choices for many angelfolk. Your brother and you will have to decide for yourselves which side is just and which, unjust." He gestured to

Affaeteres. "Come, wife. Let us walk about Eliom and enjoy this fine morning, just you and I. We'll forget this trouble for a short while, and your husband will lavish his attention on you." She came slowly to his side and offered him her arm; he linked it with his, then turned slightly to address Ashtoreth again. "We'll meet you at the village center at noontime. No doubt your brother and Leianna will also be there. But if you see Bael sooner, tell him that what I say to you now also applies to him. No matter what you and Bael choose, you will both always have your father's love."

He turned from Ashtoreth's anguished expression, leading Affaeteres outside as her face contorted, staving off tears. "Hush now," he said as he closed the door behind them. "No crying now. I want us to remember the joy and peace that Eliom once held. I want us to savor it, and I want us to realize that it comes with a price so astounding, it cannot be fairly bartered for."

Bael had not merely escorted Leianna back home. He'd voiced his intention of visiting Quatama's thachka before the spirit master's day drew him from it. Bael had questions concerning his betrothed and him, best asked in privacy. Did she wish to join him, as he thought she should? Leianna agreed, but asked for time to freshen herself and change her robe. He waited patiently for her downstairs, staving off her parents' curiosity as to where he stood in the face of his father's stance. He honestly didn't know yet.

Leianna had put on a rose-colored silk robe, leaving it unbelted, flowing over her breasts and the contours of her hips. Her hair, a soft cascade of auburn with lustrous highlights, was tied in back with a matching strip of silk. It looked fetching, but he preferred it loose, its curls draping her shoulders. She had dabbed her face with scented water, her cheeks rosy. The thought of losing her was painful; he suppressed it, extending his hand to her.

She placed hers in it and told her parents, "We'll meet you in the village center."

Eve and Michael stared at her silently, as if wanting to speak but unsure of what to say. Then Eve began, "Tell Quatama . . . ,"

Leianna interrupted. "What we tell him is up to us, Mother. You can't help us this way. You can't protect me, nor can Father. There are some things we have to face and resolve for ourselves."

She drew Bael gently toward the door.

"Please?!"

They both turned, the sound of Eve's anguish startling. But, for Bael, her face shocked him more. Lines were etched deeply in it, making her appear thinner, gaunter, her skin sallow, her eyes milky, as if she'd instantly aged. It seemed to him that the angelic form could return from Earth unscathed, but the cares of that world might well be scalded deeply within the returning soul. In Eve's case, fear disfigured her. He stared at her, horrified.

If Leianna saw what he saw, she gave no hint of it. Remaining calm, she spoke to Eve in a soothing voice. "When I was young, after you'd gone, I had to learn to protect myself. Please do not try to deny me that precious lesson gained, for it's kept me strong and will continue to be my strength in the future."

The ancient mask her mother wore slowly faded. Eve's features smoothed, returned to normal. She drew a deep breath, sighed it out, and nodded.

Leianna reached again for Bael's hand. Together, they left to seek Quatama. When they reached his hut and rapped on his door, he opened it, inviting them in without ceremony.

The rooms in Quatama's home were sectioned differently. The front contained a fair-sized alcove, filled with plants, pillowed cushions for reclining, a centered low table for refreshments, and a well-worn khantay, its pliant strings often plied by Mirisham to entertain the angelfolk at gatherings. Beyond that, to the left, a smaller room held prayer mats and a flower-strewn altar for meditation. To the right, the largest room held a long table, benches and the spirit masters' cooking and food alcoves. A ladder behind the food cupboard ascended to the sleeping loft.

Quatama waved toward the front alcove's cushions, that Bael and Leianna should rest upon them. When they sat, he joined them. Mirisham came in, placed a tray of fragrant hot tea on the table and, smiling at them, withdrew to the back rooms. Bael wondered how she felt about the impending incarnations. If one of each household was called to Earthly birth, then she or Quatama must offer themselves up. They had no children that Bael was aware of, yet it was hinted that she and Quatama had been married for countless Eliomese years, a mature couple long before Bael's birth. They had been spirit masters in the days of Lucifer's childhood. Yet neither Mirisham nor Quatama showed any concern for what might be their last day together for a long time to come. Were the spirit masters exempted from the rules laid out for the rest of the folk?

Quatama waved his hand toward the tea, waited until Bael and Leianna had picked up the warm cups and sipped—a tangy mint tea—then said, "You wish to marry before the betrothal time is ended."

Bael answered, "That isn't what I had in mind to ask."

"But it is what Leianna wishes. Isn't it, little one?"

Leianna nodded.

"It cannot be done. Not because of the law alone, but because it would bring Bael great anguish. Better he feels great longing for you than bitterness, feeling cheated of a wife newly united with him, then torn from him immediately afterwards."

She said nothing, but reached out and pressed her hand against Bael's. He covered it with his other hand. "My father is fomenting rebellion."

"Yes, I know. I know the extent of his dissent and the number of his followers."

"He believes what is asked of us is unfair, that the Seraphim are unfair . . . and cruel. And that the Creator's plan is unsound and shows no concern for the disruption of Eliom and its people."

"I am aware of the dissident feelings, the unhappiness which many of the folk are voicing at being called to this sacrifice." Quatama hesitated, then continued, his voice tinged with sadness. "The universe is larger than they realize, both spatially and dimensionally, and interconnected in ways not immediately apparent from our small vantage point. Time also moves at a vaster rate for our Creator than for us. This sacrifice is not only for the Earth's sake; it is also for Eliom's sake. And for others who have never set foot on Earth or in Eliom."

Bael listened, catching the inference that his understanding couldn't comprehend the full impact of *why* he and Leianna must be torn apart. "I would like Leianna to forego incarnation until after we marry *properly,* and share a *compassionate* amount of time as husband and wife. Surely whatever good she can contribute to on Earth can be accomplished later, without serious repercussion."

Quatama said one word. "No."

"No? You refuse without fair consideration of our request?"

"Your request. Leianna has not asked for this. She knows better."

Bael turned to her angrily, releasing her hand. "Do you?"

She answered in a stricken whisper. "What I know and what I want are two different things."

Bael, frustrated by Quatama's refusal, asked him, "What of Mirisham? Will she, too, be incarnating tomorrow?"

"Yes."

"And you're willing to have her taken from your side?"

"No, not willing," Quatama told him, "but I am accepting of it. We will, eventually, be reunited."

"But Leianna and I have not yet begun our time together!"

The spirit master stood up and opened the door, a blunt indication that their talk had ended. "When you love, honorably and sincerely, time ceases. It no longer exists. You must both learn this, and that love is not an excuse to deny responsibility. You and Leianna must both learn to accept this, either with foresight and graciousness or with short-sightedness and contention. The choice is yours. But however you choose, your participation in the vast tapestry of our Creator's plan will not be altered. At some point in time, the tapestry stands finished and whole. Your and Leianna's contribution to it will be the exact design a greater Hand meant you to bring to it."

Bael stood up, reaching for Leianna, helping her up. "We shall see."

"Yes, Bael, you and Leianna will see. But do not be so angry. It will not do you any good." He ushered them out. "I will say a prayer for both of you."

And Leianna said, her voice devoid of hope, "Thank you."

Bael offered no further parting words to the spirit master. Quatama had inadvertently proven Lucifer's argument. The Creator was not omnipotent and couldn't foresee, avoid or mend mistakes alone.

Bael led Leianna away from the village proper, heading towards the Garden. He would try to make her understand the danger and weakness in the path she'd chosen, and she *would* hear him out.

-33-

As if mocking his fears for the future of his people, the first hint of Spring, the season of renewal, brought warm breezes, bright patches of green and newly budded plant life in the household gardens Lucifer and Affaeteres passed. He would have liked to visit the community's Garden, to run his hand over the sprouting crops, but the sun climbed steadily in the blue and clouded sky. His followers awaited him.

He and Affaeteres headed back to the village center, other folk treading their way there, some to attend the counseling, possibly grieving for loved ones soon to be taken from them. Many wore long troubled faces.

Adrammelech, his family with him, fell into step beside Lucifer and asked, "Will we have to fight?" His family wore blue silk scarves around their necks, the same bright color as Lucifer's robe.

He slowed his pace, thinking out his answer. "Only if they force us to. They may allow our group to secede peaceably. They might bargain with us for extra help at harvest time, seeing the benefit of a larger populace remaining in Eliom, rather than depleting our numbers by one-third to one-half."

"I don't believe the Creator cares anymore about Eliom."

Maura, Adrammelech's wife, held the hand of their seven-year-old son, Marech, adding, "Or our children."

Lucifer glanced at the dark lanky child, a miniature of his father, already a head taller than most boys his age. "I question whether the Creator is the one planning this disruption. If the Seraphim are interpreting the will of this higher power, then the Creator is capable of being manipulated. If the Creator is controlling the Seraphim and, through them, us, then the Creator needs go-betweens to rule us effectively. Either way, the Creator is flawed, possibly incapable of striking out at us independently."

"And so?" Adrammelech asked.

"And so I don't intend to fight the Creator. I intend to fight the elders and the Seraphim. If necessary. Under those circumstances, I believe we might win."

"Mmn. And if the Creator should respond without help from Seraphim or elder? If your theory's wrong?"

"There's not a man—or a woman—among us who hasn't entertained that dismal possibility. They don't need me to tell them the risks. We're defying a deity whose breath, legend says, fanned the spark of our primal thought into sapient eternal existence. If true, flames ignited can be snuffed out. If so, Adrammelech, we'll die . . . as surely as a mortal, but with infinitely more honor."

Adrammelech shrugged. "I've never died before. I don't know if I'd like that. Do you think we can avoid that outcome?"

Lucifer glanced sharply at him, noting his wry sardonic grin. They had come to the sprawling green sward of the village center. People wandered about, separately and in clusters, some seeming aimless, others heading with apparent certainty toward a large, roped-off area. The crowd, milling about, blocked Lucifer's view of whatever activity went on inside it, but he could hazard a good guess.

In the opposite direction across the green, his followers awaited him, filling a good portion of the southwest perimeter. He headed for them, Aff by his one side, Adrammelech and his wife and son on the other. He heard his name called out again and again as they saw him approach. Many others wore pure blue scarfs around their necks at Lucifer's suggestion. They symbolized the blue skane running through their traceries, that it should not be mingled with red mortal blood. Their symbol of resistance. And hope for the undefiled purity of the angelic strain.

Lucifer reached his people, nodding to them, interweaving among them and encouraging them. Then he faced them and gave the first signal to his leaders, raising his left hand high above his head, then lowering it. A scurry of activity began in the crowd before him. Each of his commanders raised an arm, beckoning to their assigned followers. What had at first seemed a congested crowd now became tight-knit groups moving aside to reveal what they had previously hidden: a large square dais they'd erected earlier at Lucifer's command. Four broad steps on each side of the square led to its raised platform. Lucifer would tower above his people *and* his opposition who obviously hadn't planned for such elevation in the eyes of the folk.

Lucifer strode to the dais and mounted it. He extended his hand to Naamah, with a quick glance to Affaeteres, who stood beside the raven-haired woman. Affaeteres stared back, her emotions masked from him, as Naamah climbed onto the platform and stood near him.

Lucifer spread his arms, holding them outward as the remaining commanders of his rebellion came to the platform and stood on the short stairs leading to the dais, three commanders on three steps on each side of the square.

Before Lucifer: Adrammelech, Phoenixious and Cimeries.

To Lucifer's right: Mammon, Belial and Thamuz.

To Lucifer's left: Lothan, Moloch and Nergal.

And behind Lucifer: Chemosh, Dagon and Behemoth.

His followers clustered around them, expectant, waiting, hushed.

Lucifer, his arms still outspread, pointed palms outward in supplication. "My people, today we bring reason and self-determination to Eliom." His voice resonated in the silence surrounding him. "I no longer stand alone. You have all pledged to stand with me and have earned my respect and my thanks. We are the strongest and the brightest and the best of Eliom. We have thrown off the shackles which bind us to the Creator, subservient no more!"

"Subservient no more!" came a myriad of cries around him.

"Subservient no more," he repeated. "There is not one among us who would not be willing to love a truly beneficent Creator, one who gave us unconditional free will. But we have been offered a false bounty. We are *told* to blithely destroy our society for the sake of an underdeveloped world, a nearly savage world barely civilized. We are ordered to sacrifice our loved ones to this world. And we are forced to be responsible for carrying the weight of this world's burden, which stemmed originally from the actions of two angels. Just *two* of us! For this, the Seraphim and elders tell us we must give up our lives, our work and our families to be fodder for the fields of Earth!"

He noted with satisfaction that other angelfolk drifted toward the circle of his supporters, joining them, listening raptly. He leaned forward confidentially. "Our voices must be heard." He straightened up and turned around slowly, addressing the full circle. "We must *insist* upon our *right* to be *heard!* Unless we keep Eliom safe from such unfair disruption, all that we love will soon cease to exist. They mean to tear us from our village, our land and one another, while assuring us that the time away will be finite. But *I* can promise you: upon your return to Eliom, you will find her so distorted, she will not be recognizable. And I will not allow it!" He paused. "But as I've said, I do not stand alone, although I am proud to head this call for self-determination. I have chosen others to care for the needs and wants of specific groups of my followers, but only for the good of Eliom and never stripping them of their right to voice their own choices. I call them forward now to tell you, in their own words, why they have embraced my cause and made it their own." He stepped back and Naamah came forward.

"I am husbandless and childless by choice," she said, green eyes flashing defiantly. "My love is for the land, for the Garden. I am wed to it and call the plants nurtured by my hands my children. I will not sacrifice their well-being for the sake of another world or pay for a breach

I never committed against it. I will *never* be a brood-mother to its future generations. But I will watch over those in my care who demand the right to remain in Eliom." She stepped back, next to Lucifer.

Adrammelech, Phoenixious and Cimeries climbed the front steps and took the stage.

Adrammelech spoke briskly. "I took vows to stand by my wife, Maura. I see fatherhood as a responsibility to protect my son, Marech. Asking me to abandon them or send them into danger goes against both vow and responsibility."

Phoenixious, pale-haired, his eyes lit with the excitement of youthful quest, took a nervous step forward. "Although I am young, I believed strongly in the goodness of the Creator—until now. I cannot conceive why the Creator, if all powerful, cannot correct this *genetic* discrepancy, supposedly begun by Adam and Eve, without our puny help. The frightening prospect, my friends, is that we are not so puny and the Creator not so powerful as we've believed. Our faith and trust have been abused, and we must rethink our beliefs before they swallow us up in mental turpitude that turns us into beasts of labor without a thought for the need for autonomy, let alone individual rights!" He paused to catch his breath. Lucifer, amused, signalled Cimeries to step in, or they'd be listening to the passionate youth throughout the entire sunset.

Cimeries touched the boy's upper arm. He turned. "Oh. Too long? I'm sorry." He gave Cimeries the platform, offering Lucifer a sheepish look of apology. Lucifer grinned and winked, putting him at ease.

Cimeries waited until the titter of laughter abated in the audience, then spoke. "The exuberance of the young," he began, a smile of strong maturity softening his black, sharply planed features. Then the tall gangling man lost all allusion of humor, as if he dreaded imparting what he must. "I hesitate to speak . . . after hearing such noble passion from one whose yet untried life may be nipped before it can blossom. But the hand that breaks the branch may also be our own. Rebellion engenders risk; it can never be otherwise. 'Be brave,' I tell those under my charge, 'but also be realistic.' I stand here, knowing we may fail, and grief yet come to us. But Lucifer has declared: to live honorably, none should be our master, save ourselves. If my honor in life is denied, then I gladly relinquish life to explore this strange cessation of it called death. If death brings oblivion, then at least I die knowing I have not lived shamefully."

Adrammelech, Phoenixious and Cimeries returned to the front steps, and Lucifer waved his right hand to Mammon, Belial and Thamuz. They mounted the platform to speak.

Mammon adjusted his robe against his ample bulk and ran a hand through waves of golden hair. His full lips, almost feminine, pursed thoughtfully. His fingers hooked themselves in his belt. "I care nothing for Earth. Its hardships pose a problem none of us deserve to be subjected to. I will not give up my own life and its pleasures for someone else's blunder, regardless of the damage done. All of my people are with me on this. Let the Creator find another option beside our enslavement."

Short, skinny and plain, Belial wagged his head, his long brown hair waving. "I think, in a *very* small way, the angelfolk have contributed to Earth's genetic crisis. Perhaps we should have foreseen Eve and Adam's impetuous behavior. We, our people, might have prevented it. But we are not all-knowing, and I cannot believe that *two* of us created *so* much damage to that world's future that we must in *essence* give up being *angels* and become mortal *men* for *countless* mortal years. Something is amiss here. It cries out to be questioned." He relinquished the platform to Thamuz, a handsome man whose demeanor seemed as black as his eyes and hair.

Thamuz radiated a barely restrained anger; his voice projected it in clipped, clear tones.

"I feel like a child whose parents have said, 'Your younger brother, while playing with you, has lost a limb. Cut off your own, and give it to him.' Our Creator, who is both mother and father to us according to the legends, is being extraordinarily cruel to the children of Eliom. We are asked to sever our lives in Eliom to repair a wounded Earth. These mortals now command more of our Creator's love than we Eliomese, and we must not sacrifice ourselves to please a father who disowns our most basic needs. We must declare our own adulthood and deny forever more the need for such an authority over us!" Cries of agreement resounded through the crowd as Thamuz stalked back to the side steps, followed by Belial and Mammon.

Lucifer now motioned with his left hand to Lothan, Moloch and Nergal.

Moloch was bone-ugly: sagging cheeks, turned-down mouth in a never-ending scowl, crooked nose, and small eyes of washed-out blue. His pale brown hair, moustache and beard hung despondently. But Lucifer knew that this man was as immovable as a rock, brooking no fissure in himself or others, once he embraced a cause, remaining steadfast in his loyalty to it. Moloch gazed around at the press of angelfolk. "I've no wife and no child, but if I did, it would be to populate Eliom, hard-pressed as we are to produce new heirs for our own world. It is the Eliomese that I champion, not Earth mortals. I refuse the Creator's audacious demand. I will not be subservient like a leaf blown about by a capricious wind!"

The people cried back: "Subservient no more!" Moloch stepped back, nodding to Nergal, who held up his large hand to quiet the followers.

"Meowr!" Sensation of small feet walking on me.

Tall and thickly muscled, his rich brown hair and beard curling about his face, chest and shoulders, Nergal's large amber eyes surveyed the agitated gathering.

"Meow. Mew . . . mewr? Meowr!" I'm being pressed against by something bony but soft. "Meowr!" Pain, small pain, clawing and digging into my cheek, pulling on it, awakening me. I awake. I can see Nergal through Lucifer's eyes, the whole of the sunset village center superimposed upon my bedroom, and. . . .

Lucy Angel, Lucifer's feline antithesis, is scurrying around on top of me, butting me with her head, mewing as loudly as her small lungs allow. I feel a claw sink into my thigh, and then I smell the smoke. It's faint, almost aromatic, but not enough to make me cough or choke— yet. But something is on fire, at least smoldering in the house, and I know what to do now to break the connection with the ongoing reenactment as Nergal starts to speak, and I rub my hand wildly over my head, back and . . .

. . . forth and found myself very mortal in the middle of the night in my bedroom as the smell of smoke increased. The cat crouched near me on the bed, its eyes glowing in the light of the streetlamps coming through the window. She still mewed loudly, no doubt from fear of the smoke, but partly from indignation. My hand, in brushing across my head, had smacked her.

Ginnie came awake. "What's Lucy Angel meowing . . . oh, my God. Leigh Ann, wake up! The house is on fire! Grab the baby! We've got to wake Fred and Mom and Dad!"

"I'm already awake, Ginnie. Go get Mom and Dad! I'll get Daniel and Fred."

"Your mother and I are also up," Dad shouted from the hallway. A flashlight beam came on. He pounded on Fred's bedroom door, then opened it. I heard my brother's sleepy "Wha's wrong?" and Dad's answer: "Something's on fire in the house. Go outside while I find the source of the smoke. No! Don't turn on any lights! It could be electrical. Did you hear that, girls?" We shouted yes. "Then just get out. The smoke isn't thick, and I've got the fire extinguisher with me. Come on! I'll shine the flashlight on the stairs. Don't run! I don't need anyone tripping."

Daniel in my arms, I edged down the stairs with Ginnie and Mom ahead of me, and Fred and Dad following. The smoke had increased, but not badly enough to obscure our sight or sting our eyes. "Hey, where's Lucy Angel?" I asked.

Fred looked around. "Right by your feet."

"Pick her up," I ordered. Fred scooped her into his arms.

"Bill?" Mom called, as she cautiously opened the front door. Dad had gone toward the kitchen, flashlight and extinguisher in his hands. "You kids go outside. I'm going back in to make sure your father's all right."

Ginnie stopped her. "He told *all* of us to go outside."

"But he could get hurt, overcome by the smoke!"

"Dad's not stupid," Fred told her. "He knows how to handle these things. If he's not back in a minute or two, we'll deal with it."

No one moved. Daniel began to whimper. I held him close to me, the cold porch floor numbing my feet.

We heard a muffled whooshing sound. I started heading for the door. "My God," I choked. "Is the fire spreading!?" Mom stopped me. "No. It was the fire extinguisher. Fire crackles, explodes things. Your father must have put the fire out."

Fred rubbed his eyes. "Yeh, Leigh Ann. Fires go crackle and bang. Not *whoosh.*"

After a minute, Dad appeared in the living room, switching on the light. "Emergency's over. Miriam, that cat gets a sirloin steak for dinner tomorrow. She saved our lives." He took Lucy Angel from Fred into his own arms, petting her and babytalking the little black bundle of fur. "Yeh, I heard your big mouth, puss. You're the best watchcat this family ever had." Lucy Angel purred loudly.

Mom stroked the cat gingerly. "But what happened, Bill? What was burning?"

"Some rags in the basement caught fire, sitting in a bucket left too damned close to the gas heater. If Lucy hadn't alerted us while it was still contained and just smoldering, the whole damned heater might have blown."

I shivered, even though the door was now closed. "Why don't we get her some shrimp to go with that steak? Surf and turf. She deserves it."

"She damn well does. Miriam, we've got a mess to clean up in the back basement tomorrow. The fire's out and, thank God, we're safe now. But I want to know who left those rags down there, and what was on them."

After a silent moment, Fred hoarsely admitted, "I, uh, I was, umm, fixing up my bike." Dad glared at him, waiting. "I cleaned it with, you know, household stuff, then painted the fenders and handle bars and stuff. I didn't know the dirty rags could catch fire. I swear to God, I didn't! I left them in the bucket to ask Mom if she wanted to throw them out or wash them to use again. But I forgot."

Dad nodded. "Don't you *ever* do anything that *stupid* again. We're going to have a talk about household hazards tomorrow night and how not to burn down your house. In the meantime, Fred, you're grounded for a month with no allowance."

"Yes, sir."

"You kids go back to bed now." Dad lowered Lucy Angel onto the carpet with another affectionate pat, then he and Mom headed to the basement to survey the damage.

Fred slumped upstairs, looking dejected and guilty as hell. Ginnie and I followed, Daniel dozing off again in my arms, and Lucy Angel bounding up the stairs beside us. In the hallway, she rubbed against Fred's pajamaed legs, and he reached down, scratching her head gently. "Hey, I think she forgives me," he joked sheepishly.

To which Ginnie responded angrily, "I think the rest of us might, too, if you promise to be more careful in the future!"

"Hey, I promise, okay?" He glanced from her to me. "You know, the important thing is the house didn't burn down, and we weren't killed. But I'm already in the dog house—no offense, cat—so I'll just shut up and say good night." He went into his bedroom and firmly shut the door.

Ginnie shook her head, as if younger brothers were beyond figuring out. "Come on, Leigh Ann, let's go back to sleep."

"Thankful that we have a bed to sleep in."

"And a house with a bedroom."

She snuggled under her covers, while I lowered my sleeping son back into his crib, quietly checking his diaper. By some miracle, it was dry.

I checked the clock: 3:00 a.m. "Good night again, Gin."

"Night again, Leigh Ann."

I heard Mom and Dad come upstairs, their voices hushed, then the brief creaking of their bedsprings.

I shut my eyes as Lucy Angel jumped up, rubbed her face against my arm, and curled up next to it.

"Whoa, Quatama! What am I doing back here in this pseudo-castle drawing room? You said you'd return me to normal sleep by 3:00

a.m. and that *was* what the clock read after the fire. You do know about the fire, don't you? And I don't know what happened to the purple hoop. I had to knock it off my head when I woke up to stop those blowhards from Lucifer's crowd from confusing me and possibly interfering with my saving my own and my family's lives."

Quatama very quietly holds up the purple hoop.

"I didn't damage it, did I?"

"No."

"Oh, shucks! Well, if it's all the same to you, I'd like to go back to sleep. We can finish that memory another time."

At which point, Quatama laughs. "I'm sorry, Leigh Ann, but we must finish the reenactment tonight. As irritating as you may find Lucifer's subcommanders, you must know who they were and try to glean what motivated them."

He and the hoop move toward me. I shrink back into the chair. "You promised me I'd be back on Earth by 3:00 a.m. mortal time . . . to get my normal sleep."

"You will be."

"But it's passed 3:00 a.m. now!"

"Leigh Ann, you forget. There is no time in this dimension. You could stay here for a year and still return by 3:00 a.m., the previous year."

I sigh. "So how long will this take?" He smiles, but not humorously. I suddenly realize I'm not the only one who's tired. "Here. Give me that hoop." He hands it to me without hesitation. Obviously it's all set to continue the tale of Leianna in Eliom, which bears little resemblance to Alice in Wonderland or Dorothy in Oz, except for one thing: I want to finish these adventures and get home.

Only for me home means Earth, and for others, still living my adventure, home may very well be Eliom.

I lower the hoop onto my head, thinking *there's no place like home, there's no place like home . . . .*

Nergal raised his voice against the din. "Do you wish to hear me or prefer that I be silent?" The crowd caught the edge of sarcasm in his voice. Their voices dropped to a rustle of murmurs, then hushed. "I have a wife, Shadella, and she is with child after many years of our waiting. I feel no qualm in protesting the tearing apart of our families. We have never had commerce or communion with Earth, and now the Creator demands this disruption with no foreseeable benefit to us. To that I say, 'Pah!'" He glared at the onlookers, his head swivelling to catch as many eyes as he could, huge nose jutting out, before stepping back.

Lothan moved forward. With his rich black hair and long-lashed black eyes, his strong nose, sculpted lips and firm chin, and tall sensual build, he projected confidence. "We are not alone, are we? We stand together as a force. Some say we challenge a power beyond even our collective strength. But we must take this risk or lose all that we value, and a valueless life is dishonorable. I myself might agree to a single mortal lifetime, if I could save my wife, Tia," (he pointed to the beautiful redhead standing close to the platform), "or my daughter, Sharlan," (he waved toward the raven-haired young woman as tall as her mother), "from such hardship, but we are told that *all* family members must subject themselves to incarnation." He slowly shook his head, as if pondering the irrational. "My family has chosen to stand by Lucifer. He courageously reveals that the Creator, who does not *ask* us to undergo this chaos, but demands it of us, is not a loving deity. We must stand apart from that Creator, seeking our own counsel, making our own decisions, free to question the motives of a faceless authority." He returned with Moloch and Nergal to the left-hand stairs.

From the back steps, Chemosh, Dagon and Behemoth came forward. The platform creaked loudly under Behemoth's huge bulk. He had few graces, least of all patience. His voice thundered out over and beyond the throng of Lucifer's followers. "People of Eliom! Are you surplus seeds to be scattered upon the impoverished soil of a foreign world? We are not Earth's saviours! I will not play the studded bull to its puny cows. I also refute this demand to dismantle Eliom's future! The Creator brings this foreign cycle called death to the creatures of Earth, and when Eve and Adam's seed lifts them into awareness of this unfair trait, that future generations might rebel against it, our *benevolent* Creator asks us to *balance* these creatures, that *our* genes should sweeten the misery of their mortality with the subtle hint of an eternal life! Never! No angel who ever exits a mortal woman's womb as a half-breed will ever be welcomed in the House of Behemoth!" He stomped over to Lucifer, muttering, "Where are your remaining sons, Lucifer?"

"For now, wherever they feel they must be," murmured Lucifer. "Later they will be where I want them—beside me when I confront the elders and the Seraphim."

The wifeless Behemoth nodded sagely. "Women. They fog a young man's mind. It won't look right if they desert you for Leianna's beguiling pious smile. They should think with their heads and ignore what lies below their belts."

Lucifer said nothing. He nodded to Chemosh and Dagon, who waited with apparent uncertainty, to go on.

Chemosh nodded back, spread his slender arms and hands in a gesture of resignation, and said, "It pains me to see this day come to Eliom. I, too, believed that we, the angels, were loved by our Creator and held high in the Great One's esteem. Were we not given the Garden with all our wants fulfilled? And now we are to be torn from our homes for the sake of a flawed world with people imperfectly made in our image. Why does the One, who for ages held our unwavering loyalty, place us below these mortals, rewarding our faith by disrupting our lives and forcing us, yes, forcing us to live among them? The answer is clear: we are no longer loved. The Creator has abandoned us." He nodded to Dagon.

Lucifer's triumph, a Council elder championing Lucifer's protest, and the last to speak, Dagon surveyed the crowd patiently. The oldest subcommander, bone-thin and bald with piercing black eyes and sharp features, he brought his hands together, fingertips touching, shaping the call to prayer led by an elder. Almost immediately, the mass of dissenters touched their own hands together, signalling their readiness to accept his prayer to the Creator, yet, Lucifer thought, displaying their uneasiness as well as their unpurged fear of that deity. A murmur of dubious anticipation ran palpably through all of them. Even Behemoth raised his hands together, his face wary.

Dagon began, his voice soft but carrying well in the utter silence. "Hear me, Great One, known to us as our primal Creator! I, Dagon, an elder among your angelfolk, whose spiritual well-being I have vowed to protect, echo their cries. Betrayal and distrust rain on the children of Eliom. Your love no longer freely given, they can no longer freely worship you. Today, without apology, they refuse your call to heal the Earth. They hear a different call, one that you are deaf to: the cry of their homeland, about to be torn apart, depleted and disrupted. Who *are* you, oh, Creator, that you see no harm in this chaos you wish to inflict on us for thousands of years? *What* are you, that you make no promise of future recompense for the injury we will suffer in forcing our exile from Eliom? We must deny your Supremacy in our lives as the son leaves the father and the daughter leaves the mother, when grown, to determine their own lives. Give us, *your* children, the right of choice, even if our choice goes against you. Only then can our souls have value, for an enslaved and mindless love is worse than none. We pray that you grant our prayer."

The crowd murmured, "We pray that you grant our prayer."

"But if you don't, it is of no matter to us."

He drew his hands apart, slowly lowering them to his side, staring out over the heads of the throng.

Lucifer came to stand beside him. "We shall be subservient no more!" he shouted, and the crowd shouted back, "Subservient no more!"

"We shall shape our own world and determine its destiny," he cried, "dependent on no one!"

The air resounded with the outcry of his rebels, some louder than others. "Our destiny, our own!" called one man, a woman's voice following with, "Don't let them take our children!"

"Free will!" Thamuz bellowed to Lucifer's right side, "and not its paltry false shadow!"

His followers agitated to a frenzy, Lucifer leaped off the dais into their midst with two words: "For Eliom!"

He strode through his followers, Affaeteres running beside him, muttering, "What now? What now?"

"To the elders," he murmured, face forward, moving steadily to the large roped-off area of the green where Quatama and the others sat counseling the weak and complacent among the folk, Bael and Ashtoreth included. Lucifer had seen them from his high perch upon the platform, seen them waiting with Leianna to meet with the spirit master.

His remaining sons would never set foot on Earth, not as an angel or as a mortal!

-34-

The village green had never looked this tumultuous and congested, despite the many social and religious events Ashtoreth had attended there. He wondered if its harried appearance stemmed from the impending incarnations, like a fabric fraying suddenly from stress.

The grass had never seemed so trampled, as people flitted by on their way to find family, elders and spirit masters. Five large circular enclosures were formed by ropes affixed to wooden posts. Quatama, Yeshua, Ezekial, Elijah and Cornelius each counseled folk within them; each had one elder assisting them. Folk were lined up, snaking around the unadorned open grassland of the village center, some waiting patiently, some impatiently, in lonely silence or in conversation with others, for their time with their spirit master. Ashtoreth, Bael and Leianna stood in the line leading to Quatama.

Bael continued arguing heatedly with Leianna. "You will not go to Earth! Our time together would be nothing, our lives together minimal, if you agreed to this endless task. My father is right. This entire undertaking is cruel, and the Creator, insane. We stand in this line uselessly unless you intend to tell this to Quatama."

Her look plainly warned him against more blasphemy. "The Creator is *not* insane. How could you say such a thing?" When he merely glowered at her, she softened her tone. "There is reason behind this, even though it may seem hidden to you. The wisest among us cannot fathom the extent of the Creator's knowledge. These incarnations are necessary for the sake of a greater good. Our worlds are connected, Earth's and Eliom's, shaped by the same Hand. We cannot abandon a world in need, even if two of us *weren't* responsible for the damage that needs repair."

Her eyes searched his face to see if he understood. Ashtoreth looked away, tired of this argument, wearied by his own nagging fears for her safety. Then Bael spit out, "Is it possible for the Creator to lie to us? Is the greater good to absorb us and destroy us for this new but damaged toy called Earth?"

Even Ashtoreth, being pulled in opposite directions by his father and Leianna, and who thought of himself as open-minded, couldn't tolerate hearing the Creator accused of such deliberate dishonesty. He turned to refute his brother and saw their father bearing down on them, his followers packing the gaps between the counseling circles.

Lucifer confronted Leianna directly. "I have heard Bael's angry response to your touching naivety. What he supposes, might very well be true. Believe it or deny it, as you please. But my remaining sons will stand with me when I and my people declare ourselves exempt from these incarnations. Eliom will be protected from them. All you need decide, Leianna, is if you will stand by your betrothed or abandon him for this nebulous greater good." He ordered his sons, "Come. We'll speak with Quatama now and see if we cannot resolve this peacefully." Neither Bael nor Ashtoreth moved. Lucifer jerked his head toward Leianna. "I guarantee you she will follow. If either of you love her, vacillating over her stubborn belief in the Creator's plan won't save her. If *she* loves you, she won't abandon you. She'll at least try to see reason. Won't you, Leianna?" Without waiting for her answer, he turned back to Bael and Ashtoreth. "Now, come!"

Ashtoreth gave Leianna's arm the briefest of strokes. "My father is right. The pain from this is ripping the folk apart. Forgive me. I still believe the Creator may have good reason, but I no longer believe it's for the good of the Eliomese." She backed away, consternation in her eyes. "I'm weary," he admitted, then trudged to this father, who brusquely told Bael, "Leave her to decide alone."

"I'm sorry, Leianna. If you love me, stay in Eliom. If you incarnate to Earth, you might as well deny that love." He, too, joined Ash and their father, and also their mother now, for Affaeteres had found her husband in the crowd. She grasped both of her sons' hands, saying, "Creator, forgive us." Only Ashtoreth heard her, so softly had she muttered it. Bael, walking with his family toward the opening in the counseling circle, kept looking back toward Leianna. Lucifer walked briskly ahead of them, toward Quatama and Gabriel, who shared this circle, advising the compliant Eliomese and taking the imprint of those set to incarnate on the morrow, using the strange black rectangles to track each person.

Most of Lucifer's adherents filled the circle, spilling out of it, knocking over posts and the ropes held by them, and distorting the lines of folk waiting to speak with the two elders.

Gabriel and Quatama were seated on benches approximately halfway across the circle from each other; their current charges sat on stools before them. Now, with the sudden crowding, Ashtoreth could only see Quatama and the folk he counseled: Michael, Eve, Deianna and Mercurius. Two wooden boxes containing the dark unnatural stones rested on the bench, one to Quatama's left, the other to his right. The left-hand one held less of these tracking devices than the right-hand box.

Ashtoreth, his family approaching Quatama, came close enough to see the images of specific angelfolk, already chosen for incarnation, reflected on the stones in the left-hand box. He shuddered to think of Leianna's image, perhaps her soul, trapped in such a stone.

Lucifer waited for Quatama to acknowledge his presence. The spirit master ignored him, picking up a small hard rectangle from the right-hand box, holding it out before Eve. "I can only promise you that Leianna will be returned to Eliom following her own incarnation. She will have time to rest and rejuvenate before she is called again to complete another mortal cycle. But I cannot guarantee how her life on Earth will progress, only that we will try to guide her from afar."

Eve's agitation was apparent and painful to watch. "But what if she *is* attacked and killed?!"

"Then she will die mortally and return to Eliom. You have actually experienced this. You know that a traumatic death can be healed." Eve tightened her lips, said nothing. Quatama sighed. "I cannot guarantee you will be with your daughter. The details of each incarnation have been chosen by the Seraphim. And I cannot vouchsafe that Leianna won't undergo mortal suffering or pain. Only that we will watch over her—and you, and guide you both, whenever and wherever possible. But you, of all the angelfolk, must incarnate, Eve, as must your brother, Adam, when he returns to Eliom, be sent down to Earth again. You are both condemned to incarnate continually until mortal humanity is healed of the consequences of your and Adam's genetic breach. Now, will you allow me to prepare you?"

Eve shut her eyes, nodding weakly. Michael looked away. Ashtoreth also shut his eyes, their misery too much like his own.

Someone nudged him. He opened his eyes. His father pointed to the lefthand box, the stone within it reflecting Eve's image. Lucifer asked Quatama, "Where will these stones go, when you finish here?"

"To the Seraphim, to be housed at the canyon of the winds. Have you and your folk conceded to the Creator, Lucifer?"

"No. We come to strike a bargain with you and the Seraphim."

"I have no such authority, Lucifer. Bargain with your Creator, not with me."

Lucifer waved his hand at Dagon, standing nearby. "We already have, through our own intermediary. The folk who have placed themselves under my command choose to refuse the call to aid mortal humanity. We find it unfair and an exercise in futility. The Earthly mortalfolk are beneath the angels, and the infusion of angelic skane into mortal blood will never raise them to our level."

Quatama regarded Dagon sadly, then said, "But your dispute

does not involve those who are heeding the Creator's call. Your people are disrupting *their choice.*"

"Then we will be quick about it, and leave fools to their foolish ways. I come to you, Quatama, because you are not merely an elder, but a spirit master, and therefore permitted to confer with the Seraphim and supposedly, through them, the Creator. I tell you, that all of the Council and the Seraphim should know it, that Eliom is divided on the issue of Earth. I *represent* those who will return to their homes and lives and take no part in the Creator's plan. In return for the Creator's concession, we will agree to help wherever needed to maintain Eliom in the absence of those who are conceding to the incarnations, for Eliom will surely be depleted and the Garden suffer from neglect."

Quatama studied him, silent again, his face suffused with regret. Michael turned his head, staring at Lucifer as if awakening from a dream. "You cannot win," he told his one-time friend. "The end will come, and Eliom will fall."

Ashtoreth grasped his father's shoulder, wanting to leave, to go home, to hide. "You were wrong, Father. Leianna didn't follow us to join your protest!"

Bael scanned the circle's perimeter anxiously. "I am going to go back and bring Leianna here, forcibly if I have to."

"Yes!" The cry issued from Eve's lips. She beseeched Bael. "Stop her from incarnating!"

Other cries issued from the other half of the counseling circle, and Gabriel's voice boomed out: "The Creator will punish your irreverence!" Emotions long repressed in the folk now broke loose. Chaos erupted; restraint fled as angel struck angel, and others caught in the turmoil were pushed, shoved and knocked about. Frightened shouts and recriminations filled the sward. Folk from other circles ran toward the strange altercation, so foreign to them, to stop it. Their efforts only drew them into it, and Ashtoreth dodged a flailing arm that a woman swept toward him screaming, "Blasphemer!" The crowd pushed her past him, frenzied anger now unleashed by many, others simply terrified, shocked, and trying to escape the press of bodies. "Bael," he shouted, "we have to find Leianna!"

His brother shouted back. "She's here!" Ashtoreth glimpsed her face, pale and afraid, as the throng surged between her and Bael, nearly separating them. Bael pulled her back to him. Ashtoreth edged his way toward them, but more people swarmed around, cutting him off, disorienting him. "Bael!" he bellowed. "Take her away from here!" No answer came.

Suddenly his father's voice echoed across the incomprehensible tumult. "Stop! Don't accost them, or we play into their hands! Listen to me! It is Lucifer! Withdraw to the far side of the village green! Leaders! Remove your charges from here!" Lucifer searched the chaos for his subordinates. Ashtoreth tracked his face and torso in the melee, and then saw Gabriel approach Lucifer from behind, grab him and spin him around.

"Lucifer, who would place himself above his Creator! The Creator will destroy you and your vanity for the evil you and your followers have brought to Eliom today!" His face contorted with fury, he lunged at Lucifer, wrestling him to the ground, the crowd swallowing them from sight.

"Father!" Ashtoreth shoved hard against the knot of folk, but gained no space. He turned, searching for his mother, hoping her height would make her visible, to no avail.

The sky began to darken. Ashtoreth gazed upward and gasped. Others did likewise, and shouts of "The Seraphim!" filled the green. They came on a storm of wings, blotting out the sunlight, turning it to shade. Holding their palms downward, a mist emanated from their hands, drifting over and around the folk. As it enveloped Ash and the other quarrelers, his body became heavy and stiff. In seconds he could no longer move, a frozen figure in a multitude of frozen figures.

But his eyes still saw, and his ears still heard. A veritable dome of Seraphim hovered above them, their faces again obscured by pulsating light, or perhaps they had no features at all, only pure radiating energy, for they spoke in unison, their collective voice vibrating over the green: "We have seen and heard the events which have transpired today in Eliom. Your Creator has witnessed them and transferred that knowledge to us. We bring judgment to those who rebel against the Creator."

The Seraphim gestured, releasing some of the angelfolk from immobility. Ashtoreth was not among those freed, but in his line of sight, Gabriel rose from the grass, glowering triumphantly downward. "So, Lucifer," he snarled, "you are fallen, and I am risen in the light of our Creator!" He continued to rise, lifting into the air, puzzling Ash until he saw other angelfolk being drawn upward . . . Leianna among them. She struggled—Ash couldn't hear her words—but the Seraphic energy forced her aloft. She and the other released angelfolk drifted on the air to the left, leaving the disturbed counseling circle.

The Seraphim gestured once more, and Ash and the other rebels—for he recognized his father's supporters—could once more move and speak. But they stood isolated in the deserted circle, the compliant angelfolk ringing it, watching the Seraphim, watching their disgraced companions and kindred. One of the rebels on the far side ran toward the perimeter, seeking escape, only to meet with an invisible force, striking it in a burst of cascading white light, and being flung backwards to the ground.

Ashtoreth headed toward the fallen dissident, a dark-haired man who lay crumpled on the grass, his head turned toward the circle's edge, his arm still reaching out to it. Ash didn't know what he could do or the extent of the man's injuries, but compassion drove him to help one of his brethren. Others ran toward the man; Ashtoreth saw his father among them, Lucifer reaching the injured angel first.

His father stared at the man, then at the crowd beyond the perimeter, which the man's hand pointed to. Ash also looked and saw Leianna straining to escape the firm grip of her father's and uncle's hands, each clasping her arm, stopping her futile attempt to reenter the circle. Ashtoreth came close enough to identify the thwarted rebel, although Leianna's reaction made it obvious.

Lucifer bent down, running his hand lightly over Bael in a healing wave. Ash knelt and lent his own energy to his brother.

Bael groaned, awareness returning, and struggled to sit up, his line of sight directed at those beyond the circle. He tried to speak; a dribble of blue bubbled from his mouth.

Lucifer touched his son's lips gingerly. "Don't talk."

"Lei . . . "

"She's over there. I saw her."

Ashtoreth added, "She can't get through, either. At least, I don't think so. Some kind of unseen restraining wall separates us from her. Her father and uncle have stopped her near flight into it."

"Dohn leh her neh id!" Bael held up his hands, which had touched the invisible field, sparking the opposing thrust of energy and throwing him backwards. Burn marks disfigured them.

Lucifer called over the short but unbreachable distance to Leianna. "Bael says to stay! The barrier holds danger!"

She called back, "How badly is he hurt?!"

"Burns, his mouth injured! It'll heal! But you stay until we resolve this!" Lucifer's tone allowed no argument. It seemed to calm her. She ceased struggling. Ashtoreth said a silent prayer, grateful for her return to common sense, before realizing the incongruity. Nonetheless, he was still glad, and prayed once more to the source of this contention, knowing full well he was asking the Creator for lenience with nothing to barter in exchange.

He heard the rustle of wings once more above him.

The Seraphim converged, alighting on the green, magnificent

winged messengers, towering over the recalcitrant angels.

With Ashtoreth's support, Bael managed to stand again, and drew forth his own healing energy, half-wondering if that most important trait still existed in the rebels, or if the Creator had stripped them of their regenerative power. He felt the familiar tingle run through his body, his pain diminishing, his jaw and teeth becoming whole again. Soreness still remained, a mere inconvenience compared to his earlier pain. He placed his hand upon his brother's. "Thank you."

"You are well again?"

"Greatly improved. At least we aren't in total disfavor. Yet."

"Father will champion us." Ashtoreth warily eyed the silent Seraphim interspersed among Lucifer's followers. "Why don't they speak?"

Bael had no answer, but he felt no fear, only regret that his world had tumbled into an impossible situation with an unacceptable solution. He glanced toward Leianna, watching him in return. He smiled wearily and turned to his father. "Where is Mother?"

"Somewhere among the crowd. We were separated. Perhaps she prefers it this way at this moment."

"She loves you, Father. She's been loyal despite her misgivings."

"I know that and, regardless of how it might appear, I still love her. But I can't allow her fear and confusion over this travesty to cloud my own judgment."

Ash asked, "Should I go look for her?"

"In this crowd of hundreds? She'll find us and we, her, eventually. No, I want you and Bael here beside me when I confront the Seraphim."

Bael studied his father's opponents, their featureless faces glimmering within the cowls covering their heads, their wings folded at rest, their hands clasped before them. They stood absolutely motionless, as if they slept standing up. "Their behavior is puzzling. They make no move to confront *you.*"

"Fine," Lucifer murmured. "Then we'll use the hiatus to build up our morale and prepare our defense. They may not be ready to speak, but I'm certain that they'll listen to every word I say. I intend to make each one count."

Both the leaders of the rebellion and their charges were divided and partially obscured by the tall Seraphim. Bael knew that they had effectively separated his father's followers, both bodily and emotionally. No doubt, Lucifer, too, saw this ploy, for he raised his voice, his anger and the silence lending it volume. "My people! There is an energy field ringing this circle, cutting us off from the rest of the green and retreat! This energy field holds danger! Make no attempt to leave the circle, but seek to form our own inner circle around these motionless Seraphim! Subordinate commanders! Position yourselves along this inner circle with enough space between yourselves for those angels under your command to find you and regroup!" There was a rustle of movement as Lucifer's subordinates moved out of the jumbled mass of Seraphim and angels and formed the staggered inner circle. "The rest of you now! Find your leader! Do this quietly now, and avoid all conflict with the Seraphim!"

The remaining followers began snaking and weaving their way outward. The Seraphim, as rooted and silent as trees in summer heat, did nothing to hinder their retreat. Lucifer, Ashtoreth and Bael also edged cautiously backward until the tingle of energy from the invisible field halted them. The tingle felt palpable, Bael noted, a deliberate fence, trapping them inside. He was thankful that his betrothed was safely beyond it, her fate slightly less uncertain than his own.

The inner circle swelled, becoming solid with the dissident folk. To Bael's eye, the tableau before him resembled the rings of a tree exposed in a storm: the outer ring of compliant angelfolk, the inner ring filled with the rebellious, and the core thickly packed with the Seraphim. *No good will come from this,* he thought. He was already missing Leianna, sure that he and his father's followers would be flung to Earth, as Azmodeus had been. Perhaps he would meet Leianna there, when she incarnated, even if that life obscured the memory of their eternal identities. Perhaps their love would surface despite that. One good thought to cling to.

Ashtoreth touched his shoulder, breaking his reverie, pointing to their left. Affaeteres moved cautiously along the few yards of space remaining between the clustered followers and the Seraphim, her eyes scanning the folk anxiously. Lucifer walked quickly toward her, calling her name; they closed the gap between themselves, embraced and walked slowly back to their sons. She gazed at Bael. "I saw you fall. Are you injured?"

"I healed. We can still regenerate."

She nodded. "One good thing left to us. But what now, my husband? Do you plan to fight the Seraphim? They frighten me, so unmoving, their faces hidden from us, masked by light, like glowing embers in the cooking pit, a pretty sight that equally may warm or burn us. Speak to them, Lucifer. Tell them your followers simply need time to debate and weigh the Creator's request, for it came too fast upon us. Tell them, Lucifer; I know you can right this. I have faith in you." He raised his eyebrows at her. "I do," she insisted. "I have no choice, but to. Now."

"Then stand with me now, wife, and pray to the Creator that, for once, we are given respect as creations with minds of our own and judgments to make without coercion."

Lucifer extended his hand. Affaeteres grasped it. Together, they faced their sons, Lucifer saying, "Forgive me, if all of our efforts fail."

Bael tersely replied, "We stand with *you,* Father."

Ashtoreth nodded stiffly, silently. Lucifer favored his eldest son with a poignant smile, then offered Bael a more regretful one. "Forgive me, if I've torn you from your Leianna."

"We would have been torn apart, regardless of your actions."

Lucifer gazed up at his wife, tears staining her cheeks. "Forgive me, if I've brought you pain, all for the pleasure of loving me."

She smiled at him. "If love brings pain, better than a loveless pleasure. My vow is intact, Lucifer, and where you go, I will follow or seek you there, if separated."

Lucifer stroked her wet cheek. They shared a brief but touching kiss.

Bael turned, peering through the invisible barrier. Leianna still waited beyond it, Michael, Gabriel and Eve standing near her. She watched him mutely, but her face bore witness to her wretchedness. He couldn't bear to return her gaze, turning away as his father spoke out, his voice carrying well over the green.

"Hear us, Seraphim, you who represent the Creator! Those among the angelfolk whom *I* represent surround you. Look upon their faces. We are not merely an extension of a greater power, beholden to that power's commands with no forethought to our own needs. We understand the Creator's desire to repair the world called Earth and its inhabitants. We simply disagree with the manner in which the Eliomese have been asked to involve themselves in that repair. We cannot believe our Creator would force a reluctant hand, for all honor and strength would be forfeit in whatever gesture or help that hand produced under duress and coercion. We offer instead to lend our hands, hearts and minds to the maintenance and well-being of Eliom, while those angelfolk who *choose* to incarnate on Earth are absent. We will work the Garden and see that it flourishes, even if we must strive twice as hard to complete the tasks of those angels called to Earth. We will comfort those angels remaining, whose loved ones are gone for the duration of a mortal lifetime.

"All this we offer, wishing neither to conflict with those who agree to participate in the mortal rebalancing nor to engage in an unsavory conflict with those who once were held high in our estimation and warmly in long-established friendship. And so we ask, will you, and through you, our Creator, accept our heartfelt offer, resolve this dispute, and allow Eliom to survive whole and undivided? Speak, Seraphim, and tell all of Eliom of the Creator's *merciful* justice, trust, acquiescence, and understanding, that we are freed from control, coercion and subservience. Carry our fair request to the Creator."

The Seraphim made no reply, silent as stone.

"Speak, I implore you. Tell us we are heard, for we cannot accept the silencing of our collective voice, and will speak out evermore, until we *are* heard!"

The Seraphim gave no sign of hearing.

Bael could stand it no longer, turning back to meet Leianna's stricken gaze. Torn apart, separated, Chamira's warning wasted, the prophecy a lie.

And then the sky above them darkened, the sunset of spring turning grey with a strong quickening wind and wintry chill.

Lightning streaked through the sudden turbulence, and the voice of the Creator spoke through it, thundering out over the screams of the stunned angelfolk. —*WE HAVE HEARD. WE HAVE HEARD THE ONE CALLED LUCIFER. WE HAVE HEARD THE ONE CALLED DAGON. WE HAVE HEARD ALL AND SEEN ALL AND KNOW OF YOUR DISCONTENT.*—

"Then grant us our self-determination!" Lucifer shouted against the gale.

—*WE WILL. THE ONE CONSECRATED TO US HAS TURNED FROM US, BUT HIS WORDS ARE HEEDED. WE WHO ARE YOUR PARENTS SHALL LET GO OF OUR CHILDREN. YOU MAY STAND ALONE. YOUR COMPLIANCE SHALL BE CHOICE ALONE, YOUR OBEDIENCE OR DISOBEDIENCE YOUR CHOICE ALONE, AND THE CONSEQUENCES ENGENDERED ONLY BY YOURSELVES AND THEIR REPAIR EFFECTED ONLY BY YOURSELVES. YOUR BLIND AND MINDLESS LOVE IS NOT OUR DESIRE. YOUR UNTETHERED SOULS HAVE VALUE, EVEN WHEN YOU STAND AGAINST US, AGAINST OUR VALUES IN CONSTRUCTING THE SALVATION OF EARTH.*—

"Then we are freed?! Freed to return to our homes, our families and loved ones?!"

The clouds that were not mere clouds thickened and roiled above them, a brightening building in its center above the rebels. The faintest of hopes lit itself within Bael, like a fluttering candle that might or might not go out. "Leianna," he whispered, as if her name might keep the flame alive.

—*YOU ARE FREED, BUT YOU AND THOSE YOU SPEAK FOR MAY NOT RETURN TO ELIOM.*—

The flame died.

—*WE HAVE CHOSEN A NEW REALM TO TEST YOU IN YOUR INDEPENDENCE. YOU WILL ANSWER TO NONE BUT YOURSELVES, AND YOU WILL DEPEND ON NONE BUT YOURSELVES. WE WILL GRANT YOU YOUR IMMORTALITY AND YOUR HEALING ABILITY, BUT ALL OTHER CHALLENGES YOU FACE MUST BE DEALT WITH INDEPENDENTLY OF US.*—

"Bael!" The cry came from Leianna. He left his father's side and moved as near to the energy barrier as he could. Leianna had already approached it, far too closely, the force that separated them lifting her hair in flying waves that sparked ominously above her head.

"Go back!" he shouted.

"No! I love you! Creator, hear me!"

—*WE HEAR YOU, LITTLE ONE.*—

"Let down the barrier. Let me be with my beloved!"

—*WE HAVE OTHER TASKS FOR YOU.*—

"We cannot be separated! Chamira says so!"

Bael watched her in stuporous amazement, wanting to force himself through the barrier, to risk all injury to reach her and clasp her to him, denying grief its sting.

The lightened center of the cloud swirling above the rebels widened; the dark fringes boiled into black night over the rest of the folk.

Leianna screamed: "Do not take him from me! We cannot be separated!"

—*YOU WILL NOT BE.*— The voice of the Creator spoke calmly. —*YOUR HEARTS ARE BOUND. THOUGH YOUR BODIES AND MINDS JOURNEY WHERE THEY MUST THROUGH THE TAPESTRY OF TIME, ALL IS AN ILLUSION. THE FUTURE WILL TURN INTO THE PAST AND THE PAST INTO THE PRESENT.*—

Leianna's eyes, boring into his across the invisible wall, told him what he already knew. They were going to be taken from one another. The Creator's logic was not their own. Only they would feel the loss of years and mourn, and although the Creator promised reunion, Chamira's prophecy now made sense. The lovers within it were separated for thousands of years. "No," he moaned.

"Please!" Leianna cried. "Let me through the barrier!"

The Creator didn't answer her, addressing Lucifer instead and the rest of the dissidents. —*PREPARE TO JOURNEY. WE ARE NOT*

OF YOUR MIND, BUT WE ATTEMPT TO COMPREHEND YOUR MIND, REDUCING OUR OWN, TO UNDERSTAND. THUS WE GRANT YOUR PLEA AS WELL AS WE CAN ACCOMMODATE IT.—

"Wait!" Lucifer called out. "Grant me the answer to two questions, and then we'll face this exile to this realm, for in truth, we will not deny you the honesty of our argument against involvement with Earth."

—YOUR HONESTY OR INTEGRITY ARE NO LONGER IN QUESTION. WHAT ARE YOUR QUESTIONS?—

"You said we may not return to Eliom and that we must journey to this distant realm, which better suits our request to you. My people will see this as punishment. How long will our punishment last before we can return to Eliom and benefit her and her Garden in the ways I've described? My son, Azmodeus, will no doubt return here when his forced life on Earth is through, and he will find his family gone."

—WE DO NOT PUNISH YOU. WE RESPOND TO YOUR REQUEST IN THE MANNER THAT BEST SUITS YOU AND WHICH REMOVES YOUR DISRUPTIVE FORCE FROM ELIOM. THIS IN TURN BEST SUITS OUR PLAN FOR THE EARTH AND THE ASSISTANCE OF THE ELIOMESE TO CORRECT THE TEAR IN ITS GENETIC FABRIC CAUSED BY TWO OF THEIR NUMBER. THE LENGTH OF YOUR RELOCATION IS EQUAL TO THE LENGTH OF THE MORTAL GENETIC REPAIR.

—YOU HAVE ALSO DISPARAGED THE MORTALS, BELIEVING YOURSELF AND THE ANGELFOLK SUPERIOR AND WORTHIER OF OUR LOVE AND CONSIDERATION. YOU ARE TOO PROUD, LUCIFER, TO PRESUME THAT EACH WORLD IS NOT EQUALLY DESERVING OF OUR LOVE. FUTURE GENERATIONS OF MORTALS WILL SHARE THE TRAITS OF THE ANGEL, AND AS THE REBALANCING CONTINUES, MANY WILL ATTAIN THE RIGHT TO ASCEND TO THE HEAVENS AFTER MORTAL DEATH, ENDING THE EARTHLY CYCLE OF MORTAL BIRTH AND DEATH. ELIOM WILL BECOME A HAVEN ALONG THAT PATH, WHERE GUIDANCE CAN BE OFFERED BETWEEN THOSE CYCLES AND AT THEIR COMPLETION. BUT SHOULD WE HAVE RENEGADES, WHO ACT IN THE MANNER BENEATH OUR LOWEST EXPECTATION, WE MAY CHOOSE TO SEND THEM, AT OUR DISCRETION, TO YOU FOR CORRECTION. IF YOUR SON, AZMODEUS, IS AMONG SUCH FAILURES, WE WILL RETURN HIM TO YOU.

—UNTIL SUCH TIME AS ALL REBALANCED EARTHLY

SOULS ARE WORTHY OF ASCENSION TO ELIOM . . . OR UNTIL ONE SOUL WHO IS TRULY A CHAMPION OF ALL FOLK CREATED BY US AGREES FREELY TO CARRY THIS BURDEN YOU HAVE PLACED UPON YOURSELF FOR YOU, ELIOM WILL BE FORBIDDEN TO YOU AND YOURS.—

Lucifer glanced quietly at Affaeteres and Ashtoreth, then looked toward Bael and then Leianna beyond. Bael wondered if his father knew he had lost Eliom in gaining their freedom from the Creator? He turned sadly to Leianna. Her eyes questioned him. She had finally moved back, away from the strange field cutting them off from one another. He called out to her: "Do not despair, my love! I will find a way back to you. I promise you this! I will find you and make you my wife!"

"Bael!" She came toward him, the energy field catching at her hair and robe.

"No! Go back. I do not want you hurt!"

She hesitated, her uncertainty plain, then moved obediently back.

Lucifer called out to his followers: "Do you still wish to stand with me?!"

From across the circle, a woman called: "Have we any choice?" Numerous followers cried to the Creator for forgiveness. Their voices finally stilled. Silence returned. A new voice rang out among those in the inner circle: "Subservient no more!" Bael recognized it as Nergal's.

"Subservient no more!" Behemoth bellowed out, raising a hue and cry among the followers, echoing Lucifer's motto.

But where and to what do we follow him?, Bael wondered. He returned to his father's side. "The Creator has granted us two questions, Father. Ask where this new realm is, so that Leianna will know something of it and try to seek us there. The knowledge will at least comfort her."

Lucifer studied him as the tumult of shouts from the dissidents faded, then raised his head to the glowing center of the storm. "We find your logic cruel, but we will stand proud and determined before any fate you cast for us. But we would know the nature and motivation of a Creator who frees us at such cost. It is said that you are all powerful, that you created the eternal flame from which we all sprang. We have been taught that you exist as a singular entity: the One, Creator of the Universe which extends beyond Eliom and beyond our knowledge. Why is it then, at this crucial juncture, that you speak of yourself plurally, as if more than one Creator existed? Are you One or many?"

—I AM WHAT I AM. WE ARE WHAT WE ARE. YOU ARE

WHAT WE ARE, AND WE ARE WHAT YOU ARE.—

"You speak in riddles! Answer me fairly!"

"Father . . . "

"Be quiet, Bael."

The Creator remained silent, the scintillation above them pulsing. Then, —*WE ARE BOTH ONE AND MANY. I ADDRESS MYSELF PLURALLY TODAY BECAUSE I AM IN ALL OF YOU AND IN THE EARTH AND ITS CREATURES AND IN THE PLACE YOU MUST JOURNEY TO AND IN THE WHOLE OF THE UNIVERSE, WHICH SHALL BE AFFECTED BY THE MULTIPLE DECISIONS OF THE ANGELFOLK IN TIMES YET TO COME. I RESPOND OMNISCIENTLY SO THAT THE SOULS OF ALL THAT ARE INVOLVED WILL CARRY A PORTION OF THAT WHICH HAS EVOLVED TODAY, AS IT BLOSSOMS FORTH, FURTHER EVOLVING TOMORROW. YOU ARE PLURAL IN YOUR RESOLVE AND DECISION. WE SPEAK PLURALLY. IF ONE OF YOU DOES NOT INVOLVE ANOTHER IN YOUR DISCOURSE, I WILL SPEAK TO THAT ONE PRIVATELY AND RESPOND INDIVIDUALLY. THE EVENTS TODAY ENTAIL MY GRANDEUR.—*

Silence in the circle again . . . the motionless Seraphim . . . the anxious rebels . . . the angelfolk who heeded the Creator waited breathlessly as the pulsing above Lucifer and his followers quickened and a blinding light poured down upon them and the Seraphim.

The Seraphim awoke from their stupor, their wings unfolding and fanning the air. They flew upward, hovering, and then converged upon the dissidents, lifting each one in a firm hold, ignoring shouts, screams, flailing arms and sandaled feet kicking futilely against the air.

"NO!!!" Leianna's voice.

Bael twisted in the hard grasp of the Seraphim, searching for his betrothed, and saw her reach out to the barrier, hands and arms extended, lifting into the air as she attempted its breach.

Sparks ignited about her as she pushed into the energy field.

"Don't, Leianna! Don't!"

She was nearly halfway through it, flames leaping about her, her hair engulfed as the Seraphim flew higher into the golden light above with the struggling rebels. "Please, Creator! Stop her! For her sake, whom you love, not for mine! I cannot bear to see her hurt!"

The barrier dissipated in a violent shattering burst, flinging Leianna back towards the crowds of remaining Eliomese. Bael cried out as her body struck the ground and lay there, twisted and seemingly lifeless. "LEIANNA!!!!"

The rebels were pulled into the core of the pulsing cloud now, into a brightness that nearly blinded him. He struggled to see Leianna—Quatama, Michael and Eve surrounded her now. "Heal her! Oh, Creator, heal my beloved."

He could no longer see. The light robbed him of all vision. He felt formless, as if his body itself had been stripped away. Sensation seeped away.

He had two fleeting thoughts before losing all consciousness. He wondered if the Creator had destroyed them, rather than exile them. And he thought of Leianna, but as a warm and effervescent flame burning brightly, soothing him, however briefly.

-35-

Quatama wipes a tear from my cheek as he removes the purple hoop.

"I was crying."

"Yes. Do you need a refreshment before we finish?"

"No. Let's get it done. I didn't know I could cry in this dimension."

"You've just relived a great deal of sorrow—your own and others." He holds out the hoop. It's no longer murky; it glows and sparkles with the deepest amethyst.

"Wake me when it's over," I say and take the hoop, lowering it onto my head.

They peered down at me as I awoke on my cot in the sleeping alcove: Michael, Eve, Deianna and Chloe. A sparkling healing aura surrounded my body, its tiny silvery stars winking on and off as they rotated about me.

My grandmother's face receded. "Mercurius! Go get Quatama. She's come awake!" Then she hovered above me again, along with the others, all babbling endearments and reassurances, a cacophony of sounds that ran together in my ears. I listened mutely.

Mercurius entered the alcove with Quatama behind him. Quatama held a night lamp before me, moving its light, studying my reaction. I followed its wavering illumination, but still said nothing. A great exhaustion gripped me. I closed my eyes again, wanting to sleep.

"Leianna."

I opened them, gazed quietly at my spirit master.

"Do you know what has transpired?"

I opened my mouth; my lips felt dry and cracked. "Bael. Gone."

"Don't make her speak," Deianna said sharply. "Her face is still badly burned."

"It is healing," said Quatama. "She'll be fully recovered by morning." He smiled wryly at me. "Be thankful your hair has regrown. You were as bald as a newborn bird."

I smiled, despite the discomfort in my jaw and cheeks, and lifted my hands to touch my hair. They were red and cracked with blisters. My smile faded. "My whole . . . body?"

Quatama nodded. "You were badly injured, your robe and sandals burnt away."

"I remember pain. I wanted to die, like a mortal, rather than . . . ."

Michael stroked my hair. It felt short and tough under his touch. My scalp tingled, but didn't hurt. "Don't say such things, my little one."

"Why shouldn't I? You, more than any of the others, should understand."

"Yes, daughter, but I never wanted to end my existence. To do so would deprive me of all hope."

"She didn't *really* want to die," Deianna cut in.

"No," Eve agreed. "She wanted to reach her beloved. And someday you will, Leianna. We heard what the Creator told you."

I returned my gaze to Michael. "Father? Why didn't you go to Earth to seek Mother?"

"It was forbidden, Leianna!"

"But you loved her! How could you have borne such obedience? It *is* cruel!"

After a moment's silence, he said, "I had you to care for. And it was better for one of us to be lost than for both of us to be lost. It was hard, very hard. I had to learn patience. I had to be strong. Patience lent more strength. Strength allowed me to accept the need for continued patience."

Quatama passed his hands over my body, strengthening the healing aura. "You were given a great gift, Leianna. The Creator spoke to you directly to assure you of your future."

The aura glowed more brightly, the tiny sparkles lulling me. "I need to sleep."

"And yet you refused those words, attempting to cross the barrier and share Bael's fate. Thus you would have been lost to us, as well as your betrothed. The Seraphim would not have allowed you to journey to the new world of the exiled rebels, but the barrier might have destroyed you. Sleep now, little child of the light, and heal fully. But while you sleep, reflect on one thing: the Creator destroyed the barrier, before it could destroy you. You are most important to our Creator, and tomorrow you must prepare yourself to incarnate, as the Creator has asked you to."

"I will *not* incarnate!" Tears finally claimed me, welling up and spilling over my cheeks. "I need to *grieve.* Would you have asked this of Father, so soon after losing his wife?"

Quatama took my swollen hand gently in his own; the pain in it receded. "I do not ask this of you. The Creator does. Sleep now. I will return in the morning."

He released my hand and, with the same gentleness, wiped away my tears.

"Please, Quatama. Tell me where they have taken him." He did-n't answer, just stared at his dampened fingertips. "Please, Quatama. I need to know where Bael is."

He shook his head. "I myself do not know exactly. Perhaps the Seraphim will tell us. But where he has gone, you cannot follow. It is not your path. But think on this as well: your path is not solely your own. The Creator walks it with you. Therefore, it does not only deal with you."

He passed his hands once more over me, then nodded to my par-ents and grandparents and left the alcove. Michael followed him, their footsteps treading the stairs to the floor below.

My mother watched me mutely, as if she had no comforting thought to share with me. Deianna looked disgusted and muttered, "It is no matter. It is no matter. All will be righted." Chloe stood quietly beside them now, her expressive face subdued.

Only Mercurius seemed calm and reflective. He pulled a stool over to my cot, sat and leaned toward my ear, as if planning to whisper a great secret into it. "If the wind is blowing hard about you, Leianna, and there is no shelter you can hide from it in, it's best not to fight it. Pushing against it only saps your strength, and the wind, which must blow as nature dictates, will not be affected one wit by your futile struggle. If you wish to win over the wind, you must walk in the direc-tion it travels." I frowned, but he ignored that. "If it shoves you along impatiently, trying to trip you and knock you off balance, lean away from such wily gusts, counterbalancing them. But travel with it, not against it. When it has blown itself out, you'll have saved your energy and equilibrium and can travel refreshed along a path of your own choosing."

Deianna came over to him. "You're tiring the girl."

"No—I'm teaching her." He kissed my cheek and got up. "Deianna, I am also tired and must myself incarnate on the morrow. Although our romance has not always been consistent, and despite our never marrying; we have shared a life, two children and a grand-child, making me regard myself as a partial husband to you. Will you allow me to spend the night with you and warm me against that wind?"

My grandmother placed her hands on his thin shoulders, rubbing them softly. "You old pushover. I suppose I owe you something for each time I bristled over your complaisant ways. Why did you go and volunteer for incarnation anyway?"

"I've always said that the best way to get a job done is to do it." He slid his arm around her formidable waist. "Goodnight, Leianna. Rest and heal. Your body *and* your heart."

"Grandfather? Are you afraid?"

"No. Apprehensive, yes, but that will keep me alert, if the undercurrent of my eternal self emerges in my new mortal form. Ask me how that fared when you see me again in Eliom."

Deianna bent and kissed my forehead. "Goodnight, my little one. We'll return to see you in the morning." An uncharacteristic tear escaped from her eye.

"Thank you, Grandmother."

She nodded gruffly, pursing her lips. She and Mercurius turned back to Eve and embraced her, Deianna saying, "Be brave, my daughter. All will be made right," and to Chloe, "It's late, young lady. You should be home with your own family. Would you like us to walk you there?"

"Just let me say goodnight to Leianna, now that I know she's recovered."

"We'll be waiting downstairs."

"Thank you, Deianna. I'll be down momentarily."

My grandparents left the alcove. Only Eve and Chloe remained.

Chloe sat on the stool beside me. "I also incarnate tomorrow. Perhaps we'll meet and be friends on the Earth. Unless you still intend to refuse."

My tears returned, spontaneously, choking me, running into my nose and mouth. I raised my right hand to wipe my face and stared at my arm and wrist, but not because they were now free of blisters and the skin smooth again. "Where is my betrothal band? Was it—?"

"No." Eve came over. "It survived the barrier intact . . . but changed." She withdrew it from a fold in her robe, slipping it over my hand and onto my wrist. "We removed it. Quatama felt it might interfere with the healing."

The band, created from the golden sand of the Shore of the Seraphim, still held its luminous color. But the minuscule ridges and bumps, its smoothly polished but strange texture, had softened and rehardened into an unblemished surface. Its sleek gold captured the faint glow of the night lamps more brilliantly than it ever had before.

Chloe ran her finger along the band. "It's more beautiful than before."

"Bael also touched the barrier," I said. "I wonder if his band underwent this change?"

Chloe took my hand, lowering it to my side. "I . . . I think you should heed your grandfather's words . . . and Quatama's. We've seen the price of rebellion . . . although I don't think the Creator would be as harsh towards you. I'm your friend, and while I'm only one person and don't pretend to understand it all, I do believe the Creator wouldn't demand this of us, if it wasn't necessary. If that means Bael and his father were wrong, so be it. Hate me if you must. But I wouldn't want to lose you, too."

"Oh, Chloe!" I lifted my hands, begging her comfort. She embraced me carefully, cradling my neck and head. I leaned against her and cried out my sorrow until my tears subsided to a trickle and my grief to a dull ache in my chest.

When my sobs ceased, she murmured, "I've got to go. Your grandparents are waiting downstairs, and my own family needs me. Promise me you'll be brave?"

I nodded into her shoulder.

"I have faith in you, Leianna. You'll do whatever is best!" She kissed the top of my head and gently untangled herself from my grasp.

I managed a weak smile. "Thank you, Chloe."

She smiled back and left the alcove.

Only Eve remained, her face blotched, her eyes, reddened.

"I've made you cry, Mother."

"I've had my own sorrows. Yours reminded me of them." Eve folded her arms across her chest, hugging herself hesitantly. "I have no right to say anything to you, but I think you should consider what Quatama said: that this is not only about you. I know you fear you've lost Bael forever, but forever is a long time, especially for us. And in that context, what you fear may not be true.

"I love you dearly, Leianna, although my foolishness in what I've done makes me feel unworthy of the right to be loved back by anyone. Perhaps in the mortal world, if we meet, I'll be able to make up for that foolishness. Until then, your mother asks that you forgive her, and if you can't, at least not hate her."

My grief was too fresh to answer her honestly, and so I said nothing.

She nodded, more to herself than me. "Your father is waiting downstairs for me. He asks that I ask if you'll incarnate on the morrow and . . . please the Creator. He needs to know what tomorrow brings."

"Why doesn't he ask me himself?"

She offered me the weariest of smiles. "He has feelings, too, Leianna. He's been hurt no less than you have. Your father often seeks solitude to deal with those feelings."

"Tell him . . . tell him I will incarnate. Whatever is required of me to end this tragedy and be reunited with Bael."

Eve wiped away new tears. "I'll tell him."

"Mother?"

She turned back, silent but expectant.

"I can't find it in me to forgive you yet, but I don't hate you."

"Thank you," she whispered. "Perhaps in time." And went downstairs to my father.

When Quatama arrived the next morning, I had fully recovered my health. He brought the smooth, black, tracking stone and embedded my image within it. I held it in my hand, watching me watching myself, my betrothal band dangling from my wrist. "What will become of my band, if I wear it into the wind when it lifts me to this new life?"

"Clothing will dissipate. In the case of a spiritual object, it will integrate with your immortal soul. Your eternal body will wear it unseen, hidden within the mortal flesh that serves you in each lifetime."

"And if I should take it off, leave it here?"

"We will keep it safely for you."

I ran my finger along the sleek gold of the transformed band. "I'll wear it. Is it true, when I return to Eliom, that I'll be naked?"

"Yes," he said, obviously amused, "but unlike your mother's first return, your soul will be intercepted at the canyon of the winds in the great hall which the Seraphim have built. You'll awaken in your eternal body in the privacy of a recovery room, new garments provided for you."

"And will I remember the mortal life I've left?"

"Yes, although after many of them, you may have less recall of the earlier ones."

I nodded. "How many times must I incarnate?"

"I do not have that answer for you, Leianna."

"Do the Seraphim?"

"Possibly. I do not think we should ask them, though."

"Why not?"

"There are some things it's best not to know. Not right now. Are you ready to go? Your family is downstairs, waiting."

I played nervously with the belt of my white Spring robe. "In just a little more time, Bael and I would have been wed. Quatama?"

"Yes?"

"Will it hurt? The wind that carried Azmodeus off . . . seemed a harsh wind."

He smiled. "No, Leianna. The wind that carries you and the others of your and their own accord will be gentle."

"Our own accord. Tell me, Quatama, if I had refused, what would have become of me?"

"We would have waited until you understood the necessity and agreed."

"And if Lucifer and his family and followers had quietly refused?"

"The same. But they never quietly declined to incarnate. They rallied for insurrection against the incarnations, Earth and the Creator."

We descended the stairs to my family: Eve and her father Mercurius, who also would incarnate; her mother Deianna and husband Michael, who would not.

"How will it feel?" I wondered. "Incarnating."

"I have been told," Quatama said, "that incarnation feels like this: a long sleep in which you dream a long dream of another life. Your dream plays out in a reality so vivid that you also sleep and dream within your dream, and glimpses of your original life murmur in your mind, filling it with hints of longing for that life. But only when mortality releases you, and you awaken from the dream, do you know which was the dream and which was the reality."

Mercurius grinned at him. "It sounds fascinating!"

"May you greet each new day of it so positively," the spirit master told him. "Let us go. The Seraphim are waiting."

I trod the same pathway to the canyon of the winds that I'd walked along with Bael when his father stirred his rebellion. The sun seemed to shine brighter, and the distance to the ledge seemed shorter now as we entered the wide canyon, walking with others traveling there to incarnate.

The winds had undergone a startling change, no longer swirling freely in varied colors beyond the ledge, no one waiting by its edge to be lifted and carried off.

The winds gusted into and out of high conduits, immense tubes of a clear material attached to the upper floors of the immense Hall of Seraphic Records, those records which would tell the stories of our Earthly lives and their progress in the rebalancing.

The tubes jutted over the ledge into open space, the winds entering and exiting them in a steady orderly stream. Rays of sun glinted on the tubing, throwing colored light about them, blinding the eye in a rainbow scintillation.

Angels and Seraphim came and went from the building. Two, large, round columns composed of smooth white stone supported an overhang of the same material before huge, polished, wooden doors, opened to the flow of folk.

Quatama smiled at our astonishment. "A wonder to behold, yes?

Come inside."

He led us into the building, down long corridors with rooms with doors, up stairs much wider and longer than any I'd seen before, stairs that changed direction as you traveled higher and led to other halls and rooms. Both folk and tall Seraphim passed us, the ceilings high and accommodating. The faces of the angelfolk reflected an array of emotions: dazzlement, calm, resignation and sorrow.

Chloe's mother passed me blindly. I turned back and touched her arm. "Sarah?"

She stared at me blankly for an instant. "Oh. Leianna. Do you incarnate, too?"

"Yes. And Chloe?"

"Gone. She said you were ill."

"I've recovered, by the graciousness of the Creator."

She hung her head. Nearly as youthful-looking as her daughter, sudden loneliness etched lines of weariness into her face.

"You miss Chloe already."

"And my husband as well."

"Demi, too? But they asked only one incarnation from each family."

"He requested this." She attempted a weak smile. "He worried for Chloe and hoped to be near her somehow. No doubt he'll insist on it again, when my time comes. Until then, I'll wait for their return."

Eve, watching and listening, said, "God bring you strength, Sarah."

"God?"

"The mortal word for Creator."

"No doubt we'll all know that word soon enough. Thank you, Eve. Creator strengthen you also." She gave my mother a look of unintrusive sympathy, then turned slowly, continuing on her way.

I walked on with my family and Quatama. "Chloe said she hoped we'd meet," I said, but no one else spoke as Quatama opened a door in the third floor corridor.

A huge circular room stretched beyond it, crowded with angels and Seraphim, folk hugging one another, saying their farewells, the Seraphim still faceless, their features obscured by the light emitted beneath their cowls.

Clear high cubicles of the same material as the wind tubes stood against the far wall of the room. Through them, I could see an opposite opening that seemed to extend briefly into the wall itself. A wooden table with many wooden boxes on top was placed beside each cubicle.

The cubicles seemed one solid seamless piece with no doorway leading into them. Yet several of the angelfolk stood inside them, the Seraphim outside them. A mist filled the cubicles. The folk within floated in the mist, their bodies curling in a circular posture. The inner opening dissolved. Bright winds blew softly into the cubicles, surrounding the incarnating angelfolk and carrying them off through the outside tubing, now visible, to the Earth and their mortal birth-mother's womb.

I asked, "Will they sleep?"

"Oh, yes," Quatama assured me. "The mist is forgetfulness."

Each Seraph held out one of the small, black, tracking stones and pressed it to the clear unbroken wall fronting each incarnation cubicle. The stone glowed briefly with a golden light. The wall disappeared, leaving an outer opening; the inner opening closed up. Each Seraph put the stones in a box on its table.

Mercurius sighed. "So many tracking stones. How will they *keep* track of them?"

"There are rooms for archiving them," Quatama answered.

"Such small stones. Will they record each mortal lifetime?"

Quatama nodded. "I have been told a strange thing. The Seraphim say the stones will grow and that the knowledge within them is contained by a system of numbers."

"Then I shall be accounted for," joked Mercurius. "Are they ready for us now?"

Quatama gestured to a Seraph standing by an empty cubicle to our left. It nodded. "Yes. Will you be the first, old friend?"

"Yes. I think I shall lead the way."

I was afraid, afraid of the mortal world my mother had described, suddenly afraid of her ill-omened dream of an Earthly beast ending my Earthly life. I feared to show my fear, that it would mark me as unworthy in the Eyes of the Creator. I turned my face away from my family, gazing off to my right . . . and saw Persea, a child of four I often helped watch during the last harvest. She stood before an incarnation cubicle, chattering with the Seraph who bent to hear her, her smooth brown skin dimpling as she talked, her brown eyes flushed with excitement, while her mother Darnia and father Ahrial looked fondly on.

The child lifted her pudgy arms to them. They lifted her up, kissing and hugging her, whispering endearments I couldn't hear.

Then they lowered her down. She entered the incarnation cubicle.

"In the sacredness of the Sanctuary, Quatama! They're sending Persea to Earth and remaining in Eliom."

The child heard me, my shout picked up by her keen ears. She left the cubicle and walked over to me, followed by her parents. "No, Leianna," she said, "my parents are going to follow me. We're all going to help the people on the Earth."

"Persea . . . you're so young!"

Darnia quietly explained. "She asks that we do this." She showed no resentment or reproach at my outburst, her expression and tone serene.

Ahrial said, "We chose this as a family."

Persea tugged on my robe. "Don't worry, Leianna. We'll be back. I'll play with you again."

She took each of her parents' hands and drew them back to the waiting Seraph. Darnia smiled back at me over her shoulder.

Persea reentered the cubicle. The Seraph pressed her tracking stone to its side. The cubicle glowed, its clear material extending and covering the front entrance seamlessly again. The mist came, lulling Persea to sleep. And then the wind came, carrying the child away to her chosen duty.

The Seraph pressed Persea's stone to the front of the cubicle. It glowed. The cubicle opened up once more for the next traveler. Darnia reached up to kiss Ahrial deeply, then stepped inside it.

Quatama softly touched my arm. "Have you seen enough?"

"Yes, but I have one last concern. When I attempted to reach Bael and was injured, I saw nothing more of the rebels' expulsion from Eliom or its aftermath. Many of the rebels cried out for forgiveness. Were they granted it? Did any remain after . . . ?"

"One . . . who was not truly a rebel."

"Who was it?"

"The infant within the womb of Shadella, Nergal's wife. The Creator drew the babe from her, fully born, as the Seraphim carried the child's parents into exile. We found her lying asleep on the green."

"Poor child!"

"The Creator could not allow an innocent to suffer for a wrong she never committed. Sarah is caring for her."

"Chloe's mother?"

"Yes. It will help assuage her grief and loneliness, now that Chloe and Demi have incarnated. We've allowed her to name the girl. She chose the name of Rinah."

"She Who Walks in Sunlight."

"Yes, that is the sacred meaning of that name. And now, is Leianna, who is She Who Seeks the Farthest Star, ready to begin her journey?"

I nodded. "Yes."

"Good. Mercurius and your mother have been patient. And a fourth friend, who has suddenly asked to incarnate solely to be near you and has been granted her request." He waved his hand to Chamira.

The silver-haired elven woman smiled tenderly at me. "We cannot have you alone on the Earth, bereft of protection. You may not know me as Chamira, but I will be there with you to keep you safe from harm." Her grey eyes refused all argument.

Surprise left me nearly mute. I whispered, "Thank you," no longer afraid.

Mercurius gave Deianna a lingering kiss. "I go now to seek a great adventure." He hugged Eve. "Your mother speaks the truth. All will go well in the end." And to me, "Remember to walk with the wind and not against it," as he entered the cubicle. Moments later, Mercurius rode his own wind to his new life.

Eve, who was my mother and yet nearly a stranger to me still, clung to Michael. He held her tightly, promising he would wait for her through all eternity, if necessary.

I thought of Bael's promise to me.

Eve finally drew away from her husband. She hugged her mother, who returned the hug fiercely, but for once said nothing.

Eve approached me hesitantly. "Lei-Lei?"

I looked at her; an infinite sadness filled my heart. "Mother, I do forgive you."

Her weariness fled, her face glowing and beatific. "I do love you, my sweet daughter, and someday will find a way to prove that I do."

She reached out to me. I allowed myself to move into her embrace. Tears stung my eyes. "Mother!"

"I'll be back," she murmured, and stepped into the cubicle. Moments later, she was gone.

The incarnation cubicle stood empty. I turned to Chamira.

She grinned at me, an amused elder. "You go on ahead. I'll be right behind you."

I smiled and suddenly felt weary, but peacefully so. I embraced my normally taciturn father, whose tears dampened my forehead, and hugged my Grandmother Deianna. "Help Father, please, until I come back. I don't want him lonely." She nodded and, fighting her own tears, turned away. "Quatama? Watch over me as best you can."

"I will. You and Mirisham."

I gazed at the betrothal band I still wore. "If Bael should return somehow . . . ."

"I will tell him to wait for your return, Leianna."

My own tears broke through as I stepped into the cubicle, and the Seraph pressed my tracking stone against it, closing it. I turned to the Seraph. The light emanating from its face, hiding it, cleared. Chahtai smiled back at me, his strong leonine features wordlessly conveying his sincere but somewhat wry confidence in me.

A soft pink mist surrounded me, bringing on irresistible exhaustion. I curled up, shutting my eyes.

As Quatama removes the purple hoop, I know that the tears I cried so long ago have been recried as I sat here in this astral castle reliving these last memories of old Eliom. I wipe the delicate moisture from my astral face.

Then I notice the child on the divan, her smooth brown cheeks and nose dimpling in the most impish of grins, her soft brown eyes twinkling with secret mirth. I stare at her, at the little blue robe she wears, the tiny sandals. Her hair, a mass of black curls, hangs over her forehead and dangles on her neck.

"Hello, Leianna. I told you we'd be back."

"Persea!"

Two other people materialize behind the divan: short Darnia and tall Ahrial. "Hello again," Ahrial says. And Darnia says, "Hello again, Leigh Ann Elfman."

Her face changes subtly, and now I recognize the friend and co-worker I greet each weekday. "Willa!"

"Yes, that is who I am on Earth these days."

"And Ahrial?"

He laughs. "I'm between incarnations. Darnia's on her own. Besides, as Willa, she has a mortal husband. Wouldn't want to interfere with that."

"Aren't you jealous?"

He seems to find the idea of romantic jealousy an odd concept. "No. Love is love. Why should I be?"

I shrug and change the subject. "Persea . . . you're still a child?"

She grins again. "Not really. I grew up between incarnations. We may be immortal, Leianna, but even *our* children grow up into eventual adulthood. Quatama just thought it would mean a lot for you to first see me as I once was. This is what I look like now." The four-year-old disappears; a slender comely teenager dressed in jeans, tee shirt and sneakers appears.

"You're beautiful, Persea."

She laughs. "That's what all the boys tell me."

Darnia/Willa clasps my hand. "Don't mention this to me in the mortal world. I'm a very devout Catholic, you know, and such things are rarely discussed there, let alone admitted to."

"I understand."

"Oh, there'll always be moments when the truth peeks through, but for the most part, the world isn't ready for such admissions."

"I know that all too well, Willa . . . Darnia."

"So many lives, so many names."

We hug, Ahrial, Darnia who is Willa, and Persea, and say goodnight.

I'm once again alone with Quatama. "So," I ask, "that's it?"

"Yes. The reenactments are complete."

"Thank you for stopping that last one before I underwent birth again."

He laughs. "You've undergone that many times."

I sigh. "And so, nearly 35,000 years ago, the angelfolk changed the genetic code of Cro-Magnon man."

"And committed ourselves to the development of this extraordinary change. We gave modern man his eternal soul."

I stare at him.

"We worked long and hard with humankind to evolve it, bringing greater ingenuity, adaptability and the sacred gift of creativity. But Adam's efforts to civilize mankind were somewhat delayed. Farming and the Neolithic Revolution—the New Stone Age—didn't begin until 8,500 B.C."

"Is the rebalancing nearly complete?"

"Emotional and spiritual evolution is still ongoing."

I sigh again. "I miss Bael."

"Ah, yes. I did promise you that we would remove the restrictions, when you were ready."

"I'm ready, Quatama."

"Then you are free and may rediscover one another now. But tell him I am still watching over you and expect him to respect you as an individual, who has matured over the centuries. He may find you changed, but those changes can be a delight and not a hindrance, if he views them in a positive frame of mind."

"And will I find *him* changed?"

"I'll leave you to discover that. And now, my dear, I'll return you to your longed-for rest, but with one more thought to ponder. Do you remember the first of the memories you viewed?"

"My Naming Day, when I spoke with God?"

"Yes, but recall the conversation between Michael and Lucifer as you lay in your cradle."

"They were discussing . . . their own parents . . . something about the elders being called away to help another new world."

"Yes. Do you recall when Michael said that these elders would return to Eliom?"

I shake my head.

"In 35,000 years."

"Oh, my!"

"Yes. Two events intertwining, and you and many others are important to their outcome."

"But when will the 35,000 years actually be completed?"

"In the 21st century."

"Oh, well, we've got at least 30 years to go."

He smiles whimsically at me. "But time does not really exist, and all things in time are relative." He takes me by the hand to the stone windows. Outside the castle, stars gleam in the night sky. "So many worlds," he says, "so many worlds. It's 3:00 a.m. Go home and enjoy your reward."

And I awoke in my mortal body in the silence of my bedroom, the clock reading 3:00 a.m. exactly.

-36-

I lay in my bed, Daniel asleep, curled on his side in his crib, Ginnie sound asleep in her own bed. Images from the reenactments flickered like scenes from old movies in my mind, keeping me awake.

A light in the living room came on, filtering upstairs and into our bedroom. I got up quietly, walking softly down the darkened hallway, clutching the bannister. Peering downward, I heard no sound, no indication of any other family member being up and about.

I padded down the stairs as noiselessly as I could, trying to steel myself for the unexpected. On the last step, I could see the couch in its entirety. Despite my bravest efforts, my mouth dropped open. Only the fear of waking the entire household stopped the scream that normally would have erupted.

Bael sat there, a portrait in black—hair, eyes, tee, jeans and boots, his expression reserved. Ashtoreth sat beside him, golden-haired and handsome, clothed in brilliant white, also wearing jeans and boots, but topping them with an open-necked shirt with long flowing sleeves; nearly as tall as Bael, his emerald eyes seemed to drink me in. And next to him sat—Terence, all in blue, jeans, shirt and sneakers, and looking irritated.

My heart pounded wildly, not because I was afraid of them, but there are certain reactions upon *seeing* ghosts for the first time. It's one thing to mentally commune with them. It's another to walk smack into them in the middle of the night, although Bael and Ashtoreth technically weren't ghosts. "I'm dreaming again!!"

"You wouldn't bloody well be this afraid," Terence snapped, "if you were. A little, perhaps, but not this scream-your-guts-out fear. No one would have heard you, by the way, if you had."

His surly attitude annoyed me. "Then this is a dream, if no one upstairs hears us talking downstairs."

"Not so," Terence said and clammed up, giving no further support to his argument.

"Leianna, you're out of body," Bael muttered, equally nonplussed, and Ashtoreth added, "You're astrally projected," the only one speaking in a pleasant tone.

"This body feels awfully solid," I told Ash.

"That's because you're close to your physical body and in the physical world. We're actually in your family's house."

"And how, pray tell, did you turn on the lights?"

"We didn't."

I peered at the bulbs in each end-table lamp: unlit.

Bael pointed upward. Near the ceiling, numerous round globes of light floated. He said, "We brought our own."

Terence leaned back, folding his arms. "Can we get this over with?"

I plunked myself down on the rug before the lot of them, tucking my nightgown under my legs. "What is going on here?"

Ashtoreth leaned forward. "Negotiation, Leianna." He jerked his head toward Bael. "He can't just carry you off to the Kasbah. There's a lot more riding on this than the consummation of a betrothal promise made centuries ago. We need your approval before it can happen."

"Before *what* can happen?"

"The Alliance."

"The alliance," I repeated, totally lost.

Terence straightened up, sighed heavily and said, "The Alliance between Heaven, Earth and Hell."

Bael added, "Mostly between Heaven and Hell. Our father doesn't want it."

"Our father?" I asked.

"Our father who art in Hell, Leianna. Where do you think our gracious Creator sent us for rebelling?"

"I had a vague idea."

Terence stood abruptly. "Leigh Ann, you don't have to do this."

"Do what?"

"Enter into a political marriage."

"I believe Bael and I were betrothed for love."

"Yes, well, that was then. This is now. You've both changed, I should think. You might want to reconsider."

"I believe the term Quatama used was that Bael and I should *rediscover* each other."

Terence plopped down on the couch again. "Do you want to?" he asked in an incredulous voice. "You know who he is now, *what* he is."

"He's Bael. My betrothed."

"You've got quite a *lot* of discovering to do, Leigh Ann," Terence said and, folding his arms again, gave the ceiling an exasperated glance.

"I believe the prophecy—" They all leaned toward me. "—meant that Bael and I would be reunited in 35,000 years and could finally marry." They all leaned back.

Terence glanced nastily at the other two, as if they'd deliberately mimicked him. "I think that it's a bit more complicated—and optional—than *that* scenario."

"Terence, I believe you're jealous of Bael."

Ashtoreth looked so woebegotten with silent heroics that I had to add: "And Ash, I think that *you're* still in love with me."

They all stared at me.

Terence exploded: "That is the stupidest drivel I've ever heard. I am *not* jealous of that horned toad from Hell."

Bael grinned, obviously finding a great deal of mirth in that description. "Rrr...ibit!"

Terence glared at him. "Oh, *stop that!* Some prince of the Netherworld!"

"Oh, lighten up," Bael countered. "You are jealous, not that it'll do you any good. She's mine and has been for centuries. I expect to claim her, and no one else gets to stake a claim in that particular territory."

Ashtoreth cleared his throat.

"I never agreed," Bael told him, "to an additional relationship."

I held up my hand for attention. "But I did."

"It was only discussed, nothing more. And I'd think you would want to start with the man you promised yourself to. Instead, you're kissing up to this half-cocked composer." I noticed he didn't mention Ashtoreth, only Terence. "I can see you're attracted to him."

Terence bent down toward me with a confidential air. "Leigh Ann, could you please tell these two that I *am* your spirit guide and therefore permitted to advise you?"

"He's my spirit guide and therefore permitted to advise me."

Bael snorted. "And I will be your husband, your allegiance to whom will override any others you've known."

"Excuse me, Bael. When do you expect to become my husband?"

He eyed me warily as if it were a trick question. "As soon as you agree to it."

"And where do you propose we go to get our marriage license?"

"We won't be married on the mortal Earth. The marriage will take place in the astral dimension, existing outside of your physical world."

"Then I think we have a problem. You're missing a major requirement demanded of any husband I have, while I'm alive and well on this Earth."

"What would that be?"

"You can't take out the garbage."

His furious sneer slowly curled into an amused smirk. "Are you telling me you need to wait until you've completed this mortal cycle?"

"I'm telling you I need more time to understand what's happening here in the present, before deciding anything."

He spent scant seconds considering it. "Fine. But until you've come to a decision, you will pledge your allegiance to me."

I smiled. "Bael, you're not the flag."

His smirk turned to a grin, and he laughed. "Which flag? By the laws of Eliom, we are still betrothed."

"Eliom has changed, and so have I."

He fell silent. Ashtoreth slid off the couch, onto his knees, and clasped my hands in his own. The gesture was romantic and powerful. "Leianna, there is so much more at stake here than Bael's ego and your need for a man capable of removing trash. There are conflicting ideologies that need to find a common medium before they separate completely, causing worse disruption in this corner of the universe. There are souls that have been lost to darkness and have forgotten how it looks to see the light of day. There are souls who have seen it and their loved ones in it and then were imprisoned in our realm, some by their own ignorance, but some through our coercion, for which I am ashamed. They, too, have been separated from their loved ones, who couldn't follow them to our depths, who were lost to them. The parts you and my brother will play in this prophecy—should it come to pass—isn't only one of lovers reunited. Together, they're also the catalyst that brings about the redemption of Hell, reuniting it with Heaven, and freeing its lost folk, both angelic and mortal."

He slowly, reluctantly, let go of my hands and stood up. "Terence, if you're going to guide her, be aware that any marriage between her and Bael—or me, for that matter—has vaster implications and responsibilities than the mere satisfaction of romantic ardor."

I stood up as well, agile as a gymnast in my astral body. "Excuse me, you guys, but if I represent Heaven and Bael represents Hell in this potential alliance, and we're supposed to set some kind of an example to the opposing sides of this alliance, wouldn't our love for each other become an obvious beacon in the night? Metaphorically? I mean, like braving the differences and all that?"

Now Bael stood, towering over me, at least six foot four. He leaned emphatically toward me, like a teacher about to correct a wayward student. "Among those holding power in Hell, Leianna, only a handful are for opening *any* dialogue with the dimensions of Heaven. The rest still hold angry grudges stemming from their exile, and trust no one from the upper planes. You would be viewed as an interloper at worst, or as a bit of unfinished business I chose to settle in my favor at best. The latter *scenario*," (he glanced at Terence, who remained seated) "would entail my claiming you and taking you below as my *obedient* wife. They would expect nothing less of me as heir apparent to my father's empire."

"Your reputation's at stake, huh?"

"I'm telling you this, because I could not treat you subserviently. But, of all the women in Hell, you would be expected to be kept forever in your place, a prize won back from our defeat at the hands of the Seraphim, a hostage to placate the hierarchy's eternal bitterness, a gem to be kept under glass and gloated over rather than admired."

"I don't think I like that scenario."

"Then we must play this game most carefully." He addressed Terence. "I have no intention of ever allowing her to be harmed, alliance or no alliance. Time may well have changed us in other ways, but my feelings for her remain the same."

Terence regarded him thoughtfully. "I want to believe you, but you *are* known as the Prince of Lies."

"A title bestowed on me by fools. What better way to discount any attempt by me to tell the truth than to deny that I can, and smugly validate their own arguments as inviolate?"

"I've always thought that sounded a bit one-sided, that old Lucifer and his gang never got to plead a fair case on Earth. Still, church conditioning leaves a large mark on a poor mortal's brain. I'll take your bid for trust under advisement. I also love Leigh Ann; I'd like nothing better than to take her to my own Kasbah. And it's real love; we spent a few years developing it. But as her guide, it's got to be acted on platonically. Rules. Maybe someday those rules will change. Until then, my jealousy doesn't matter. I'm here to advise her, not control her. I love her, yes, but I won't stop her from expressing her love for you or some other bloke." He glanced up at Ashtoreth. "You know, they take a dim view of jealousy on the upper planes. Monogamy exists, but it's not a law, only a popular option. Relationships enhance the people in them and serve their purpose, whether during the Earthly cycles or afterwards in the heavens. But jealousy isn't put up with. The beloved's happiness is what matters; a bloke's or bird's possessiveness is his or her own problem."

Ashtoreth said, "It sounds much like the laws of old Eliom."

"Well, yes, you can't run around abusing relationships or using people. But it's more open than I expected. Eternal viewpoint, I suppose. The reason I brought it up is to let Leigh Ann know I understand. She has to work things out with Bael." He looked up at me. "But I want you to take it easy, girl. Indulge your heart, if you must, but keep your eyes opened and your hearing sharp. God knows where this'll all lead to, but I'm part of the upside team whose job it is to lead you in the right direction."

"What direction is that?"

He stared at me. "I don't know yet. It's never been tried before, this alliance business, but *our* Powers That Be have put it on their agenda." He stood, fished in the pocket of his jeans and brought out a gold key hanging on a golden chain. He slipped it over my head to dangle against my nightgown. "You hold Bael's hand and hold the key in your other hand. It'll transport you both to a pleasant house on the sixth astral plane. It's your house, Leigh Ann. Quatama secured it for you. Wear the key on your astral body at all times. No one but you can use it. You can entertain whomever you want in your astral home, or go there alone to relax, if you'd like. But I have a pretty good idea of how you'd like to use it tonight." He said that last bit as if he'd accepted it and possibly empathized with me.

"Terence? How does time flow when you're out of body on these other astral planes? I know Quatama arranged it so that the reenactments were conducted outside of time in the fourth dimension. But how about now? I have to get some sleep tonight, even if it is Saturday night."

"Sunday morning, Leigh Ann, 3:05 a.m. on Earth to be exact. And it's still 3:05 a.m. in the astral dimensions, but time moves three times slower there, a ratio of three to one. We don't really judge time the way you do in the mortal world. We just have more of it. Five minutes have passed since you woke up, fell back to sleep, became astrally conscious and came down here. But for us, if we judged time by your standards, fifteen minutes passed."

"So, if I spent what seemed to be three hours in my new house, only one hour would pass here."

"Yes, that's right. And when you want to come back here, just shut your eyes and think of yourself returning to mortal sleep. Your astral mind will send you right back to your mortal body without awakening it. Unless you want to wake up, to try to remember your astral experience. Then tell yourself to awaken after rejoining the physical form." He paused. "Sometimes it works. It hasn't always, when I've suggested it to you."

I decided not to ask him what we were doing *when* he suggested it. "Whoa! That's a lot to remember."

"Don't be nervous. If you have a problem, call out to Quatama or me, and we'll help you." He looked toward Bael. "Just remember, love." Then back to me. "Take it slow." He bent slightly and kissed me softly on my cheek. "And I believe that's my cue to cut out."

A sparkling silvery cloud seemed to emanate from him and about him. Then he was gone, the space he occupied startlingly empty.

I blurted out, "My, that was quick!" Bael and Ashtoreth grinned at me, and Bael said, "A world of wonders awaits you, my love."

Ashtoreth bent over and kissed my other cheek. "The offer to help goes for me as well, should you need it and Quatama allow it." He started to disappear in the same manner that Terence had.

"Wait!"

He reappeared.

"I just wanted to tell you it's . . . it's good to see you again."

He smiled. "We'll talk. I'm sure." And quickly faded in a swirl of silver.

"Well," I began, then stopped. I felt a sudden weight on my right wrist, staring down at it. The sleek gold of my betrothal band encircled it.

The right side of Bael's mouth twisted up in a quirky half-smirk. He lifted his hand; he now wore his matching band. "Alone at last. And whatsmore, it's *authorized.*"

"Heaven-stamped with cautious approval," I agreed.

"So."

"So. Umm, Bael?"

"Yes?"

"It's been awhile for me."

"35,000 years."

"Whatever happened to 'It's been four thousand years . . .'?"

"Oh, that. That doesn't count. A stolen night in time in Phoenicia. You thought you had been visited by a god."

"I believed all that then, huh?"

"Actually, you thought the gods were cruel. Until I appeared in your garden. And then you were too amazed to say anything, simply submitted to me—quite willingly—and kept your opinions to yourself."

A brief thrill of memory surfaced and washed over me. "One doesn't argue with a god." I actually lowered my eyes, then forced myself to forget that long-ago passion. *That was then*, I silently told myself, *and this is now.*

"Have you changed that much," he asked, "that you can't abandon yourself to passion?"

"Not completely. I just want to follow Terence's advice. But if we've been in touch, so to speak, sooner than those 35,000 years, then how can we be the lovers in Chamira's prophecy, the ones spearheading this alliance business?"

"One night of unbridled sex doesn't count. I knew I still loved you, but my anger was unrelenting. I intended to persuade you to descend into Hell with me, to demand that you abandon Heaven. And Heaven thwarted me, punishing my arrogance, when I sought you on the following night. Quatama, or whoever was monitoring you at that time, strengthened your defenses that night, blocking all pathways back to you. One night of pleasure cost me hundreds filled with anguish. It made me value you even more, knowing I could not extinguish your light. I also realized I would destroy the thing I loved most in you, if I did."

"Bael? Do *you* think we are? These lovers in the prophecy?"

"I don't know. I know no more than your cranky guide Terence. I live in the present. I have always lived in the present. Let the future take care of itself."

"But Quatama says the 35,000 years will be reached in 2001, the 21st Century. And that the elders who left Eliom for some mission in another galaxy or star system, when we were babies, will also be returning. To Eliom. Quatama had me review that memory. The elders left the night before my Naming Day. Your grandparents—Lucifer's parents—were among those who left Eliom to do the Creator's work elsewhere. Their names weren't mentioned, though."

He gazed at me thoughtfully. "Their names are Othorah and Ise. My paternal grandfather and grandmother. My maternal grandparents, Marcellus and Venea, also lent themselves to that endless mission. My father never spoke of when and where they might return."

I held up the golden key in my right hand. "Perhaps I should take *your* advice. Live in the present, as honestly as I can, and perhaps the future will turn out all right. Would you like to see this new house of mine? If the future turns out the way *we* want it, it may be yours as well someday."

"I am still condemned to Hell, Leianna, and barred from Heaven."

"Well, apparently you've been given a reprieve up to the sixth physical astral plane." I held out my left hand to him.

He looked like a condemned man freed from the noose as he grasped my hand, tightening his fingers about mine.

"Won't Lucifer be jealous," I said as my parents' house disappeared.

A wonderful wild kaleidoscope of streaking colors flash past us. I keep my eyes open during the three or four seconds of the astral journey, refusing to be intimidated by the transdimensional canvas we travel within. By the fifth second, the colors slow and begin to take on shapes. By the sixth second, we find ourselves on a quaint cobbled street with picturesque townhouses reminiscent of the American Colonial era. Tiny walled gardens peep over high fences between the rows of houses. The sun is setting, bathing the street gold and pink.

"Which one is mine?" I wonder, then look up at him brightly, only to see rivulets of silent tears running down his face. "Bael?"

He remains mute for a moment or two, then says, "Look at the key. Perhaps there's some indication."

I study it. "There's a number. Thirty-three."

He walks over to one of the townhouse doors. "This one's thirty-one."

Two houses down, we find thirty-three, all red brick and white shutters fronting the three stories. Flower boxes are attached below the first and second story double-paned windows; the only flowers I recognize are late-blooming mums. The front door is a polished cherrywood. I fit the key into the lock, and it opens easily.

We step inside to a charmingly furnished front room leading to a dining room. To our right, carpeted bannistered stairs lead to the next floor.

Bael shuts the door and locks it. Then he goes ballistic, scooping me into his arms, his mouth finding and nearly crushing mine. After a minute of shock, my own emotions rise to the occasion, and all hell breaks loose. One of its inhabitants and his betrothed are in heaven.

-37-

Afterwards we snuggle against each other in the second-story, front bedroom, a small globe lamp illuminating our corner of the room, the rest in shadow.

"Bael?"

"Umm?" He nestles closer to me.

"Do you realize what a tremendous responsibility we inherited when Eve and Adam procreated on the Earth? We bestowed humans with an eternal spirit."

"No, we imbued them with a soul. Spirit is something all living entities have, mortal or immortal. The spirit is akin to building blocks to create systems of life. The soul is akin to the architect, mapping out the life which spirit provides us with. The soul is the master of spirit. It gave humanity a rank just slightly below the angels. And it's why my father seeks to trap them in his realm after they die. Their souls possess the angelic genes of Eliom, the homeland he was driven from."

"Thirty-five thousand years ago. A tragedy followed by a gift beyond comparison to early man. Was there some event, some historical moment, that lit up the Earth when the angels incarnated and mingled their genes with the mortalfolk's? And does the soul reside inside our genes?"

"One question at a time, dear. I'll try to answer the second first. You know what DNA is, an extensive code containing the traits that living entities possess. Some are extreme to the individual. Some are common factors among a given species. The angelic DNA, now also a part of mortal man's DNA, contains the code that allows the immortal soul to survive past mortal death, triggering an immediate transfer to an astral state of spirit. This state of being is directed and controlled exclusively by thought, a command center which can exist outside of the material elements, yet recreate the illusion of a material world. Mortalfolk commonly call this command center the mind. An endlessly creative tool and a blessing, first bestowed upon the angels, and then, through the events you relived, accidentally upon the mortals by Adam and Eve's disobedience and deliberately through the angelic incarnations to spread that gift equally among the mortalfolk."

"But is the *soul* in the DNA code?"

He hesitates. "The blueprint for the soul is in the DNA, from what I understand. But the soul is . . . you . . . the self you create." He grins sourly. "Ask Ashtoreth. He's more scientifically minded. Or go find some DNA specialist on the upper planes. That's the best I can explain it."

"All right," I say, running my finger over his jaw line. "What about my first question?"

He laughs. "Oh. The cataclysmic event. That's easy." He closes his eyes, enjoying the light massage of my hand on the back of his neck. "For 100,000 years before we came, homo sapiens lived primitively, hunting and gathering and only creating the most rudimentary of tools. Following the incarnations, after about 2,000 years of producing angelic-mortal hybrids into mankind, humans became more aware of their environment, more observant, and began evaluating the world around them in ways they never conceived of before. Their creativity evolved. They portrayed their world in paintings on the walls of their caves. They searched for greater understanding of that mysterious higher power and began to visualize it in carved figures, most commonly the pregnant mother goddess." He pulls the blanket up, covering our shoulders, cradling me inside.

I sigh and curl closer to him. "I still don't understand why you and I are so important to such an immense undertaking as the spiritual evolution of humanity. We're just two lovers who got stuck on opposite sides of an age-old battle. There must be wiser, more experienced people—than me, at least—to play this diplomatic role for the upper planes, representing them in this alliance."

He strokes my shoulder. "I think you underestimate yourself. Perhaps they know of strengths and abilities within you that you, yourself, haven't recognized. I wonder how many of those will surprise me. But my father has also questioned your being asked to represent Heaven and has his own theory concerning your involvement."

I pause, unsure if I want to hear it, but curiosity wins. "What is it?"

"That the heavens want to free humanity from my father's tactics, to stop him from further corrupting them to evil acts. Since asking nicely wouldn't work, he believes Heaven intends to bargain with him, and somehow you're a bargaining chip."

"I can't see how. Not when they've already allowed us to be together. Your father's not sentimental. Letting us marry wouldn't make him open up Hell to Heaven's interference."

"I agree. He doesn't know what Heaven's up to yet, or how you fit into it. But he's determined to find out. And he absolutely distrusts you."

"The feeling's mutual." I pull away, bristling. Bael draws me back, holding me tightly, shushing me, trying to calm me. "I'm sorry,

Bael, but I mean that. Once, ages ago, I looked up to him with respect, but before that lost age was over, he treated me abominably."

"My father, since then, has specialized in abominations and other unsavory delights. But he won't harm you. He's promised me that much. He simply won't trust you."

I squirm out of his embrace, troubled. "I have to go soon. I don't even know how long we've been here. What time is it on Earth?"

He turns over and points to a modern clock on the dresser. "I noticed it briefly when we came in. It seems to track the mortal hour."

I squint at its illuminated dial. It reads 4:15 a.m. One hour has passed on Earth. But here, that hour has stretched to the equivalent of three lazy hours, making love and talking. "I should go home."

"I'll go with you. Maybe you can't normally see me when you're awake, but you know you can feel me to some extent." He gives me that smirk again, then softens it. "I'll hold you until you fall asleep again. And protect you."

"Do I need protecting?"

He considers it wryly before answering. "Probably not. But if you do, I'll be there."

I kiss him gently, get out of bed and pick up the astral version of my nightgown from the floor. "I didn't dress very properly for travel, did I?"

"You can create whatever clothing you want to astrally. Surely your Terence told you that."

"Uh, yes. He did. But we're going right back to my parents' house, so it's not really necessary."

"Leianna? Have you been in contact with your immortal parents? Michael and Eve?"

I slip the nightgown over my head and pull it down. "Not officially. I had a major spirit guide named Emmett, whom I'm almost certain was Michael in another guise. But he never admitted to it, and I haven't seen him for at least a year. Quatama seems to be running the show now, priming me for this alliance stuff. As for Eve, no. There's been no contact with her. I don't know where she is."

Bael stands up and jeans, tee shirt and boots appear instantly on him. "Strange. Leianna, one other thing has been bothering me. When you took my hand to travel here, why did you say my father would be jealous?"

I hesitate, trying to remember, thinking it out. "Because you returned to the heavens, or at least a part of them, first. And because love paid your ticket."

He nods. "You're right. He will be jealous. And he'll seek to use this new status that you've secured for me to his own advantage."

"Bael? Don't let them separate us again."

"I won't." He reaches down and lifts me up, my legs dangling over his left arm. "Ready?"

I blush and giggle. "I'm going to try to remember this. How did Terence say to do it? To shut my eyes and tell myself to return to my body, but wake up immediately afterwards. Okay." I wrap my arms around his neck and give him a lingering kiss that begs for more. Some other night. "Ready." I shut my eyes and think: *Back to Earth and my mortal body and wake up!*

My eyes opened, my head creasing the pillow of my bed. Ginnie slept on. Daniel slept on. The clock read 4:20 a.m., and I remembered everything.

Something brushed softly against my lips. I grinned maniacally, but then another, more familiar sensation came. Getting out of bed, I tiptoed down the darkened hallway to the bathroom, shutting the door and switching on the light.

I pinched myself firmly to make sure I was back in my physical body.

There are needs, beyond sex, that mortals must relieve and couldn't wait to convince Bael to leave the bathroom.

I sensed him leaning cavalierly against the sink as I answered nature's call.

—*It's not like we haven't been intimate, Leianna.*—

I was in no position to argue.

-38-

My mother knew immediately, but, of course, no one else in my mortal life saw Bael and Terence shadowing my every footstep, both separately and together. They kept their rivalry to a low sneer. If they hadn't shown that restraint, I would have told them off or called for higher help. The distractions of clairvoyance had to be ignored, taken in silent stride, or dealt with firmly, if you wanted to stay sane. My mother taught me that. Now she eyed me incredulously, obviously bursting with questions, but saying nothing, honoring her earlier agreement to trust me.

Late Wednesday evening, Daniel tucked into his crib and asleep, my father, sister and brother were watching a movie on TV in the living room. I found Mom alone and reading in the kitchen and sat down across from her. "Don't you like the movie, Mom?"

She placed a marker in her book, shutting it. "I don't care for police dramas. We can talk if you'd like."

"Umm . . . about what?"

"I'm not prying, Leigh Ann."

"I know, Mom. You've kept your promise. And I've kept mine."

"You seem to have your feet firmly on the ground," she agreed.

I smiled softly. "And my head in the clouds?"

Her own smile was wistful. "Yes, but you also seem to have that under control."

"I do, Mom. Honestly. And I'd like to tell you all about it. But first I need to ask you for a serious favor."

She riffled the pages of her paperback, then stopped and looked at me. "You can ask, but we can't talk of psychic things tonight. The others could walk in on us, and your father is still upset about the fire. I'd like us to have more privacy, so that you'll feel at ease and not be interrupted. We can talk this Saturday, after breakfast. Your father will be out on calls, Fred is going to a football game, and Ginnie's going to her friend's bridal shower at noon. We'll have a good three hours all to ourselves, you, me and Daniel. Enough time for our mother and daughter heart-to-heart."

"That's fine, Mom, but I still have to set one condition."

"Ask."

"Well, the story may go against some of your own theories and beliefs. I want you to promise to keep an open mind and not be judgmental, at least not aloud. You can make comments and ask questions, although I may not have all the answers yet. You can even give advice, and I promise to consider it. But no matter what you hear, promise you'll still let me make my own decisions and handle things my own way. Unless I ask for your help."

She gazed at me quietly. "Honey, I've already made you that promise. It hasn't changed."

"Okay. Saturday, then. And Mom?"

"Yes?"

"Perk a large pot of coffee that day."

"Sounds like it's going to be quite a story."

"I'll bet you've never heard anything like it before."

She laughed lightly. "I have secrets inside of me that I've never shared with you, Leigh Ann. You might find them just as strange. Perhaps I'll tell you one or two on Saturday, if they're relevant to your own revelations."

"You mean there are some things we should keep to ourselves?"

"Oh, there are always things that are best kept to ourselves," she said. "It makes life much easier."

The one other revelation that touched my mortal life—that Willa was the incarnated angel Darnia—was never mentioned aloud by Willa or by me. We worked alongside each other and Kate, discussing our jobs, families, musical interests including the upcoming orchestral debut of Terence Dearborn's recently recovered compositions, but never murmured one word about psychic matters. The only change I noticed was a warmer camaraderie between us, but aside from our plans to attend the concert together with her family in January, we lived separate lives after office hours.

And perhaps because the tale of old Eliom and its modern implications was too huge to hold privately within myself and not doubt both my sanity and its logic without holding it up to another trusted person for sharper inspection, I told it to my mother on that Saturday over numerous cups of hot coffee. She listened quietly, our only interruptions switching Daniel from his high chair to his swing with various toys to keep him happy. I finished up with the quaint house on the sixth plane. I left out Bael's lovemaking, but recounted his concerns about Lucifer's cold dismissal of my diplomatic credentials and his belief that I was a pawn to be bartered and nothing more.

My mother took another sip and put her cup down. "Have you told me everything?"

"Everything I could think of."

Her face took on a serious mien. "Then I must tell *you* a story you've never heard. Although I've told you that Heaven and Hell were only states of mind and didn't exist in the simple-minded way people portray them, I never admitted that they, nonetheless, were real dimensions with their own social structures and governing bodies. I wanted to protect you, Leigh Ann, and so I told you they existed only in the minds of those who believed in them, and those people could free themselves from Hell, simply by changing their outlooks and attitudes about themselves and their world. This is a half-truth, meaning it is true, but the rest of the truth was deliberately withheld. I apologize for leaving out the other half, but I wanted you to center on the first half: that you control your own eternal destiny, both mortally and immortally, and not some priest or rabbi handing you the most popular fear or hope about the afterlife." She paused to refill her coffee cup. "Do you understand?"

"I understand why you withheld it, but not what you were protecting me from."

Daniel threw his plastic jangle keys onto the kitchen linoleum. Mom picked them up and gave them to him. "You think this is a game, Danny, throwing your keys down on the floor. But you shouldn't throw the things you love away. Someone might not be there to get them back for you." I waited for him to fling them down again, but he bounced in his swing, studying his grandmother intensely, then stuck one of the keys in his mouth, chewing quietly. Mom turned her attention back to me. "I'm afraid to say what I have to say."

"Just say it, Mom. We'll work through it, whatever it is."

She nodded. "Okay. This is my last lifetime." She paused. "I've had many more than you." She paused again. "I am Eve. Or was."

I stared at her dumbfounded. Yes, they were both petite and red-headed. But the Eve I recalled from the reenactments was fragile, not the paragon of devoted strength I knew my mother—Miriam Elfman—to be. Yet now she hung her head, averting her eyes.

"Mom?"

She slowly lifted her head and met my gaze. "Yes, I know, you've told me your story. What proof do I have that I'm not imagining that I'm this Eve you spoke of."

"There's that yardstick you've taught me to use. All right, then. Let's measure it, and see if it fits. Do you have some memory as Eve which I haven't told you, that might mesh with what I've relived? There were quite a few details I didn't mention. Try for something specific."

"All right. Let me think. And then I'll tell you why I never admitted the whole truth to you, including my acknowledging you as

Leianna."

"You couldn't have known that. Not until today."

She shook her head vigorously. "I knew. I knew when you were in my womb. My memories also came from dreams, making me face the woman I once was, the life she lived, and the trouble she and her brother caused. But the trouble turned out to be a blessing for mankind, as you say, at least mostly a blessing. Let me think. What memory of my own might coincide with one you relived, but haven't mentioned." She drained her coffee cup, looking suddenly nervous. "I'm thinking."

"Look, Mom, if you can't come up with something, I'll still believe you. Why would you say such a thing, if it wasn't true?"

Her face took on that old dictatorial expression that she always wore before lecturing me. "Corroboration is important. It may not be scientific proof, as the skeptics always say, but it's better than purely subjective belief. Logic is all we have as a buffer, people with our strange talent, to guard against crossing into the darker side of the mind. Logic allows us to reflect on our experiences and put them safely within their proper psychological boxes as we live our mortal lives, without their undue interference." She stopped, her eyes thoughtful, mouth slightly opened. "Reflections. Boxes. During the angelic exodus, the Seraphim had boxes of shiny, black reflecting stones. The elders had somehow captured the essence of each soul into these stones. The stones could track us, our true selves, no matter where we were, even on Earth in a different body! Do you remember anything like that?"

"Yes, Mom. Now I'm glad I didn't mention those details, not that I understood the mechanics behind those stones." There'd been so much to tell, when I came to the story's end, I finished it briefly with the rebels' exile and the incarnations of Mercurius, Eve, myself and Chamira. The only details mentioned were the immense, newly built Hall of Seraphic Records, the canyon of the winds, and the red wind that had carried Azmodeus off. "Mom? Do you remember how we incarnated? I mean, the procedure the Seraphim used."

She seemed lost. "They used the stones."

"Yes, but how?"

"My dream of this was sketchy. Some of it disturbed me very badly, because it reminded me of the rumors about the death camps. The rumors which were true."

I realized—suddenly—why it reminded her of that. "Tell it to me, Mom. We'll make the fears go away." *Dear God,* I thought, *she's been punished enough.*

Still, she hesitated. Then she took a deep breath and let it out. "There was a glass enclosure. You stepped inside it, and the Seraphim somehow closed it with your stone. The glass box filled up with—gas, and you went to sleep. Until you were born on Earth."

"Not gas, Mom," I said softly.

"No?" She seemed very afraid, the memory reflecting another, truly terrible.

"No, Mom. It filled up with the interdimensional wind, lulling you to sleep, and suppressing your eternal identity until you completed your mortal cycle."

"Forgetfulness." She wiped away tears that had escaped.

"Yes. Can you think of anything else . . . earlier? During our life in Eliom?"

She sighed, sitting quietly, pensively. I waited, patiently, glancing at Daniel. He had fallen asleep in his swing, his chest rising and falling rhythmically.

Finally, she said, "I wasn't there for most of your life."

"I know."

"I can only remember two things right now. One was a small ball you liked to play with. It changed colors as you held it. You were very young, perhaps two or three years old."

I nodded. "A skane ball."

Her face brightened. "Then you relived that memory."

"Not exactly. The memory from my Naming Day showed Ashtoreth playing with that ball. Eve—you—gave it to him when his parents came over for the Naming Day celebration." I laughed. "He was the cutest three-year-old. Bael was barely a year old, and he was jealous. He wanted the ball."

Mom smiled, a hint of sadness still in her eyes. "Then I'd say that's a match. Different memories, but the same pretty ball. We must have gotten it for our newborn daughter. Leigh Ann? Have you seen Michael on the higher planes?"

"I'm not sure, Mom."

She nodded, more to herself than to me. "I haven't seen him either. My guides tell me that he's well and has asked about me. We weren't permitted to incarnate together, you know."

"No, I didn't."

"Well," she shrugged, "we couldn't. It's all right. I love your mortal father—Bill—very deeply."

"I know you do." I grinned. "And jealousy is frowned upon on the higher planes. Mom, is Dad—I mean Bill—one of the incarnated angels?"

"Now that's a question I truly don't have an answer for. You know he doesn't believe in any of these things."

"You could find out."

"That would be a breach of his trust and gain me knowledge I could never share with him in this world. An invasion of his privacy, too. Even if I wanted to know his spiritual history, the guides would never permit it."

"I stand corrected. I guess we'll just have to love him unconditionally. What was the second thing you remembered?"

She smiled more warmly, relaxing. "It probably wouldn't be helpful. It's a fragment of a dream from my first life on Earth—the one Adam and I found ourselves trapped in when we trespassed on the planet."

I sat up straight. "Actually, Mom, I relived part of that life as *you*. Tell me about it."

"Another sad memory. In the dream, Adam and I are both naked after we transform into mortal flesh. Our clothes have disappeared, and we're embarrassed. We find some bushes with large thick branches and fashion a sort of bush-skirt around our front and back." She caught the gleam of laughter in my eye. "No good, huh? Sounds too much like a bunch of fig leaves?"

"No, go on. But that's not sad. It's funny."

"Wait. Adam and I are both very tired and starting to feel hungry. The rough land hurts our bare feet and walking is hard. Then we come upon a band of hunters, and I am horrified by the dead animal they carry. A deer, I think."

"No. An antelope. Mom, don't go on anymore. I know the rest." I got up, walked around the table and embraced her in a tight protective hug. "I love you, Mom. It's good to be together again." Tears stung my eyes, wetting her cheek.

"Oh, Leigh Ann, you've forgiven me!" She wrapped her arms around my back, returning the hug fiercely. "Oh, my Leianna. Thank God, you believe me."

We drew apart, slowly, reluctantly. "Well, Mom," I said, "your measuring stick proved pretty accurate."

Mom asked me not to interrupt her until she was finished speaking, as she made another pot of coffee—which later kept us up half the night—and told me why she'd held back half the truth from me, and what she had protected me from.

"When I was in the concentration camp," she began, "I was so sick. Many of us were. There was lice and vermin and illness all around us. Then, one night, I had the first of the dreams of Old Eliom. I thought I had dreamt this beautiful dream to keep my mind sane, to give me hope. The dreams were always happy ones, of you and Michael, of days in the sun tending the Garden and nights of quiet contentment. The memories of Earth and my return to Eliom and Lucifer's rebellion came later, when I was in America. In that way, God comforted me, while imprisoned in the camp. Only good dreams came to me then.

"But time passed slowly, and hope became harder to sustain. I couldn't sleep and lay in a stupor, and then I floated out of my body. I thought I had died, but my spirit drifted through the barracks and over the camp. I floated through the night clouds, and night gave way to day. I found myself in a sunny meadow, and a small dark-haired man in a simple brown robe met me there. He told me that I hadn't died, that help would come and free me from the Nazis, that I would heal and live a good life. And then he said, 'One day, tell your daughter of this dream, Eve.' He called me Eve, the same name I had in the beautiful dreamworld of Eliom. And he said, 'We will reunite you with your daughter Leianna in this life, your last mortal lifetime. As she grows, help her to understand her spiritual power, but also to rely on and treasure her mortal skills. One day, she will need both to help her world.'

"Then he stroked my head, and he and the meadow faded. I awoke in my bunk, filled with a strange new hope. A week later, the GIs liberated the camp, and my health slowly returned. I came to America and met and married your father.

"The dreams continued, but now they told me the rest of the story. Then I became pregnant with you, and in my seventh month, I had a different dream. Lucifer was in it. He shouted at me, telling me he should not have championed me, that he had lost the war in Heaven, but he would win the battle for Earth. And he pointed to my stomach and said, 'That opinionated, stubborn little bitch will not change things. Say one word to her of Eliom, of Bael, or of us, say one word of the chaos you created that resulted in my downfall, and I will send my followers to dog her every step, to torment her and cloud her mind until it breaks and madness is her only reality. Don't thwart me, Eve,' he said. 'There will be no Alliance. They have flung me into Hell, and I will torment their precious mortals forever!' And then he gazed at my swollen stomach with such hatred, that I feared for your unborn life and prayed frantically to God. And God heard me, because I awoke shivering in the dark next to Bill.

"I was afraid and angry, but my anger outweighed my fear. I had no idea what alliance Lucifer meant. I only sought to protect you from his hatred. I decided then, if you developed these spiritual powers, which the gentle man in my earlier dream predicted, I would help you use them fearlessly, to measure whatever fruit they bore, sour or sweet, with a yardstick made of logic and common sense. I would teach you that the universe was larger than the petty ideology of a Hell in conflict with a Heaven. And that the Creator of our universe and all of its dimensions gave us two precious gifts that we might understand and cope with life wisely, wherever it led us: our free will and an eternal soul capable of directing that will toward the greater good.

"All we need to do to direct it toward the greater good is to refrain from doing evil. I know you will ask me how do we know which acts are good and which are evil, and if I say, by judging them by God's standards, you will ask how can we know for certain what God's standards are? But I say, you can know this, because we are all a part of God, and all we have to do is *ask*. When all mankind learns how to ask the right questions and get the right answers, everyone will be working for the greater good.

"One day my original sin will be paid in full. All the souls in Hell will be freed, and Lucifer will be out of business. This is why God agreed to let mortals keep their eternal souls rather than letting that trait go extinct. Humanity will be balanced and exist to serve the greater good. But until this occurs, always remember that no one can rob you of your free will or your capacity to do good. Not even Lucifer. They are God's gifts and cannot be taken from you."

It was nearly 3:00 p.m.—it was getting to be a habit, lessons finishing up in the third hour. My mother seemed exhausted. I felt pretty wiped out, too, and my stomach was queasy from all that coffee. Mom kept an eye on Daniel, still napping, while I ran upstairs to the bathroom.

When I returned to the kitchen, she was heating his bottle, and Daniel was bouncing in his swing. "Perfect timing, kid," I told him, lifting him out and checking his diaper. Still dry. Mom tested the milk, handing me the bottle. "Thanks." I positioned Daniel on my lap and fed him.

"Are you all right, Leianna—Leigh Ann?"

"You're going to have to watch that, Mom. I'm okay. It feels a little weird, psychologically, I mean."

She leaned against the table conspiratorially. "Leianna sounds enough like your name that the others will think I'm using a pet version of it. Just don't *you* call me Eve." She grinned and shook her head at the wonder of it all.

"Speaking of names, Mom, how did you come to name me so closely to my eternal name? Was it because Quatama—that was Quatama in your dream of the beautiful meadow—mentioned it? I mean, you've always told me you named me after Vivian Leigh and Ann Miller!"

"I did name you after those talented ladies. But, yes, the memory of my lovely dream daughter, and the similarity of that name to hers influenced me. And, yes, I later came to realize that the dark-haired man was Quatama. But I couldn't mention any of this to you, not if I wanted you to grow up strong and independent. I knew, when the time was right, that you would someday learn of all this. It simply wasn't my place to tell you, but rather the High Council's."

"The High Council? What's that?"

"I've told you before. You've forgotten. Look, Danny's spitting up. Here's a towel. Let him have a good burp."

She draped the wash towel over my shoulder, and I leaned Daniel over it, rubbing his back gently. He responded with a hearty baby belch, then looked at me, a lopsided grin on his face. "Ma!"

"Yes, I am," I told him and lifting him up, slid him into his high chair, offering him his bottle again. He took it, sucking noisily. "All I can remember you saying is that the High Council is made up of higher spirits."

"Elders, Lei—Leigh Ann. Quatama is one of them."

"Oh. Well, maybe it's a later version of the elders who made up the Council of Eliom, the governing body from the reenactments."

"Yes! That is the origin of the High Council today."

"Well, they obviously felt it was time."

Mom sat down across from me. "Look, sweetheart, I'm glad, in a way, that you and Bael have been reunited with Heaven's approval. But I'm sure they want you to be as cautious as I do. Bael may still love you, but you don't know what influences the dark realm has had on him."

"Then I'll lead him to the light."

She didn't say anything. She didn't have to; her eyes challenged my blithe certainty.

"You've taught me well, Mom," I said, "and Quatama said we're being monitored."

She nodded, and then we heard the front door open and close.

Fred came walking brightly into the kitchen. "Well, we won the game." He unzipped his jacket and hung it in the closet. "They tried to defeat us, but when you're good, man," he spread his hands expansively, striking a pose, "you're good!"

Late that night, keyed up from caffeine, Mom and I folded our laundry in the basement.

"Never breathe a word of what we discussed to Dad, Fred or Ginnie, Leigh Ann," she said. "I know you might be tempted to confide some of it to Ginnie. Don't. You'll only put a painful burden on her, wondering if . . . to her way of thinking . . . we'll come to our senses ourselves, or if she'll have to find mother and daughter accommodations at Friends Hospital."

Friends Hospital is the historic mental healthcare facility in Northeast Philadelphia. I had no wish to join its patient load. "Ginnie does believe in some of this mystic stuff," I told her, "mostly in the reality of evil and the need to guard against it. But she thinks the rest of it is bunk."

"Then leave it that way. She also believes in angels. She's told me so. That's enough to protect her. You and I had to share this knowledge. Ginnie doesn't need to know it. Neither does your father or Fred. I intend to keep this alliance from spilling into our family's waking lives."

"It won't. At least, not openly. Quatama promised me that our mortal lives won't be disrupted. But, Mom? I think Ginnie is Chloe."

"Chloe?"

"A girl I was close to in old Eliom. You don't have memories of her?"

She shook her head. "I'm sorry."

"Don't be. 35,000 years ago is a long time. She was at my side when I recovered from injuries inflicted on myself when I tried to reach Bael during the rebels' expulsion. You were there, too. And the next day, you passed Chloe's mother in the Hall of Seraphic Records and stopped to comfort her."

She shrugged and lifted the filled laundry basket. "I never had any dreams about this Chloe and her mother. But even if Ginnie is Chloe, let it silently strengthen your unity with your sister. Only silently, never aloud."

"Understood."

"Good." She started up the basement stairs.

I followed her with my own basket. "Fred seems to have made himself a den down here." Across from the stairs and against the far wall, he had placed an old legless sofa, a standing lamp and a stereo turntable on a scratched-up nightstand. Speakers sat on the floor on either side. A stack of records rested under the nightstand.

"Yes. It's his hide-away. Come on. I'm finally starting to get sleepy."

I trailed behind her, my own exhaustion creeping up on me, to our bedrooms. We quietly stashed the baskets in them and said good-night.

The stacked clothes could be put away tomorrow. Ginnie and Daniel snoozed in the blissful land of Nod as I washed up and crawled into bed, so tired that I didn't bother to sense any nearby spirit or put an aura of protection around myself. As my head creased the pillow, a hard electric shock pierced into the center of my back, causing a sharp arching spasm. I put an immediate white light around me, Gin and Daniel, then swivelled around, angry and alert, mentally calling out to both Terence and Quatama, and belatedly, to Bael. Passing my hand through the air above the bed, I felt for any traces of hostility, but whatever had been there was now gone.

And then I sensed Bael, saw him standing anxiously on the side of my bed. —*Are you all right, Leigh Ann?*—

—*Yes.*— My suspicions were aroused, love or no love. —*Who did that to me?!*—

—*I don't know. It wasn't me. I heard you call out, and I answered. It certainly wasn't a friend. Quatama approved my investigating it. Whoever it was is probably from my realm and left before I arrived. It won't happen again. I'll see that you're protected, not only by the upper planes, but by my own personal guard.*—

I yawned. There hadn't been any lingering injury to my back. —*Can you trust them?*—

He snorted. —*It happened once. It won't happen again. Go to sleep, my cranky beloved.*—

I felt him lay down on the bed beside me, a phantom, but one who was unquestionably there. The edge of the blanket slid almost imperceptibly up over me, covering my exposed shoulder, tucking me fully in. I turned my head to stare at it, now unmoving, then cuddled deeper under the blanket, against the space I knew he occupied. His one arm circled me protectively, resting against the covers. Within his invisible embrace, I shut my eyes, drifting off into an uneventful sleep.

Halloween fell on a Sunday that year. Ginnie and I took turns carrying Daniel, his small magician's cape tied with a double knot, his little top hat tied around his chin with a black shoelace we'd drawn through holes poked in each side of the hat. He kept throwing down the tiny magic wand, but held on possessively to the strap of his plastic pumpkin. The other costumed children romping from house to house fascinated him. He pointed at everyone and copiously used his favorite new word. "Look! Look!"

"I see, Daniel. That's a ghost, and that's a mummy."

"Mommy?"

"No, sweetie," Ginnie told him. "You'll understand when you're bigger. Look, Danny, there's a cowgirl . . . and a princess."

He squirmed restlessly in my arms. "Down!" At ten months, he could walk totteringly. I lowered him to the pavement, but Ginnie and I took each of his hands firmly. He let me share his right hand with the pumpkin. There was no taking that away from him.

We went up two blocks on the right side of the street, then turned around, working our way back on the left side. The pumpkin basket nearly overflowed by the time we reached the last house. Ginnie held Daniel, and I held the pumpkin, bribing it away from him with a lollipop. He sucked on it as we rang the last doorbell and gaily cried out, "Trick or treat," holding up Daniel for inspection by our neighbor and the pumpkin for the treat.

"Well, that's it," I said as we came down the steps of the house.

A teenaged boy walked slowly down the street and stopped in front of Ginnie, Daniel and me, looking at us. A beautiful youth with golden blonde hair waving down to the edge of his shoulders, a thin contoured face and deep blue eyes, he glowered at me. I stared back, recognizing him, but my mind wouldn't believe it. It only saw a cocky teen, dressed in typical jeans, tee-shirt, sneaks and open ski-jacket, a boy not much younger than Ginnie. One with an obviously crummy attitude.

Ginnie was just as teed off by it. "What's your problem?" she snapped at him.

He turned and studied her, his eyes hot and calculating. "I've got tricks you've never been treated to before, sister."

Ginnie tapped my shoulder lightly. "Take Danny, Leigh Ann." I bundled him into my arms, holding him against me, the Halloween basket dangling at a precarious angle near his legs. He twisted around, grabbing for it. "Me!" he said. I told him, "No!" and backed away from the surly youth, who laughed and leered at us. "Hey, Danny boy, I'll bet you don't know the real meaning of Halloween. 'Cause candy is dandy, but sex is sweeter. Helps you grow big and strong."

Ginnie quietly took the filled pumpkin out of my hand, letting me get a better grip on Daniel. Both her hands lifted, balled into fists, clutching the pumpkin as if she intended to use it, if necessary, as a weapon. "This is a decent neighborhood, kid. We don't need perverts in it. Go home to whatever cave you crawled out of."

He laughed again, a short snorting sound. "Funny you should mention home." He swivelled his gaze to me like a snake, his eyes burning, blue flames that hurt my own, making them ache, forcing me to blink. "You would come back," he said venomously, no other word for it. "You just would! I'm warning you. You're not welcome where we are, so don't go by one besotted ass. There's no cock so hard, it can't be cut down to size, if his brain's gone soft."

I tugged on Ginnie's coat arm, edging toward the curb. "Look, you don't know us. You're obviously mistaking me for someone else." Get across the street and head back home. Four houses up. Safety.

"Oh, I know you." He moved slowly past us, heading for the intersection. Away from us, but with a sideways gait, his face craning backwards, watching us intensely. "You would come back! You would come back to interfere! Well, bitch, we're ready for you." He gave me a hateful, twisted parting glance, turned the corner and kept going.

We crossed the street quickly, walking briskly home.

"Leigh Ann, who the hell was that?"

"I don't know, Gin. Just some nut."

"I think we should call the police."

"It wasn't that serious, Gin. Just let him crawl back into his cave."

"But there are kids out there, still trick or treating. That guy could be dangerous. He's obviously sick, and he certainly *acted* like he knew you."

I shook my head. "Mistaken identity. Look, call if you want to and give his description. But don't have the cops come out. He didn't actually hurt us, just mouthed off. I don't want Danny's first Halloween ruined."

We reached the open door, the outside light and lights within shining warmly, protectively.

"Oh, all right. I'll just call and report the incident. Ask them to patrol the neighborhood."

We went inside and told Mom and Dad of the strange, foul-mouthed teen. Mom threw a questioning glance my way as Ginnie went into the kitchen and dialed the local police district. Ten minutes later, she came back into the living room. "They said they'll have a patrol car cruise the neighborhood, but they think it's an isolated incident."

Mom and I were sorting Daniel's candy, while Dad attended to the trick or treaters. Daniel kept grabbing for the loot. Mom opened the wrapper of a Hershey miniature, inspecting it. She gave it to him. "Here. No more tonight. Then it's bedtime for you, young man." He stuffed it into his mouth, reaching for more.

I scooped him up, out of temptation's way. "Okay, kiddo. Time for your bath and *ah-ah-baby.*" I told Ginnie, "Whoever that kid was, I don't think he'll come around again."

"He was rude and lewd. And he seemed to hate you. What makes you so sure he's gone?"

"Because he's obviously not from our neighborhood, and I have no intention of visiting his. And if I see him again and he mouths off, I'm going to slug him."

Mom eyed me incredulously, a small doubtful smile creeping onto her lips. Dad responded, an edge of both pride and sarcasm in his voice. "That a girl, Leigh Ann. And then we'll haul your ass out of jail when he presses charges."

The front door opened as he said this. Fred came in, dressed as a vampire, complete with fake blood running down his cheeks and chin, and fake fangs. "Who's going to jail?"

Mom got off the rug, holding the sorted box of candy. "No one. Someone started trouble with Leigh Ann, and she says she's going to knock his block off."

"Can I watch?"

"No. How was your party?"

"Cool. Hey, Danny, vant a bite?"

Daniel gaped at him, then looked at me. "Don't worry. It's just your goofy Uncle Fred—I mean, Rick."

"I vill bite you, too, if you don't ged id right," he said.

"Uncle *Rick* is a ham on Transylvanian rye tonight."

He went over to Mom, peering with exaggerated interest at the small box of goodies she held. "I vill seddle for a piece of candy instead, den!"

I nodded to Mom.

"Just don't eat it all. It's the baby's," she told him. "And go upstairs and wash that red stuff off your face. I don't want it smearing on the furniture or sheets."

Fred gobbled down one of the larger chocolate bars, then bowed low, unfurling his cape. "Your vish is my command. Gooooot night!" Swirling the cape back around him, he bounded up the stairs, Dracula ascending to his sanctuary, our laughter, his applause.

The doorbell rang again. Dad answered it to another chorus of

"Trick or treat."

I started upstairs with Daniel. Ginnie followed, helping me get Daniel bathed, changed and to bed. She picked out a warm sleeper, while I dried and rediapered him. I put it on him, gave him a kiss and lowered him into his crib. The excitement must have tired him. Instead of standing against the bars and protesting, he curled on his side, laying down, waiting for me to cover him. I drew his blanket snugly around him, then turned off the overhead light. "Night-Night, Danny."

Ginnie reached over the bars to stroke his hair. "Night, sweetie." While she did, I called forth a protective white light, bathing the room with it.

We left the door slightly ajar and started downstairs. My sister asked, "Did you mean that?"

"What?"

"That you would slug that kid if he started with you again."

"Yes," I told her, no trace of doubt in my voice or mind. "If it came to that."

"That's pretty courageous. I mean, I'd fight if I *had* to, but I'd probably try to get out of it some other way."

"Well, I don't like confrontations either, Gin. But I'm not going to have anybody intimidating me. Not if I can stop it before it starts."

"That's still pretty brave. Just promise me you won't do something stupid, if you do run into him again."

"I won't do anything stupid, okay? But I won't put up with it, either. Someone can *ask* me to do something. But nobody gets away with *telling* me what to do. It's my life," I told her, "for better or for worse."

Although my rational mind tried to insist that it had all been a coincidence caused by a deranged and confused teenager, my psychic instincts told me differently, that Azmodeus had deliberately materialized to threaten and harass me. Despite my brave front, I was more than slightly unnerved. The comforting thought of scientific limitations on what we considered psychic contact seemed suddenly and severely impinged upon, and my sense of safety plummeted down around the freezing mark.

I washed up, put on my nightgown and robe, checked on my sleeping son, then came downstairs to read the Sunday *Inquirer,* pulling out the comics section. Something funny to lighten my mood.

Fred came into the kitchen as I waited for the kettle to boil. "Hi, Rick." It still sounded strange, calling him that, but hardly the strangest thing in my life. "Nearly didn't recognize you without your fangs."

He offered a wide toothy grin. "Filed them down."

"Hey, Fr—Rick?"

He grinned again. "It's okay, sis. If you're not used to it. I can answer to both names."

I breathed a mock sigh of relief. "Thank you."

He poured himself a glass of apple juice. "So what were you going to ask me?"

I lifted the whistling kettle off the burner and poured myself a cup of tea. "Oh. Just wondering what records you have in your basement den."

"Lots. Crosby, Stills and Nash. Grateful Dead. Earth, Wind and Fire."

"Folk rock."

"That. Other stuff. You can listen to them, if you want to."

"Actually, I was going to ask to use your record player. Mine was somehow broken on Dad's truck when he and Richard moved our stuff back here from Queens. My own records arrived intact, though."

"You can use mine. Sure."

"I mean tonight. I just need a little time to myself."

"That's okay, too. What's going on with you and Richard, anyway? Are you still getting a divorce?"

"Yes." I had started proceedings in September, having saved the money for the lawyer's and master's fees. Richard and I were going for irreconcilable differences, and he wasn't contesting it.

"That's too bad."

"No," I told him, "that's good. When you discover you've made a mistake, run, don't walk, to the nearest exit."

"I don't know. I think you ought to review it first. You know, learn from it, to make sure you don't do it again."

I raised my eyebrows at him. We hadn't told Fred the whole story: the VD, the other woman, the scanty support for Daniel. "Don't worry, Fred. This is one mistake I'll never repeat."

I took a flashlight upstairs and rooted through my records in my closet, pulling out a Peter, Paul and Mary album. Mom, Dad and Fred were watching TV; Ginnie sat at the dining room table, hunched over a nursing textbook. "Call me if Danny wakes. I'll be in the basement, unwinding."

Mom nodded, waving me on my way, then returned her attention to the movie.

Ginnie's nose stayed buried in her book.

In the basement, I started the record on the turntable, then curled up cross-legged on the old broken sofa. I leaned back, shutting my eyes.

The folk trio's songs relaxed me. It felt like old times, when I was single, times I could never go back to, but I could savor a taste of that freedom.

It was 9:00 p.m., at least two hours before bedtime. I wanted the quiet. I wanted to meditate. There were so few minutes of stillness in my life now.

I would also have to somehow seek out Quatama tonight, to ask for his guidance concerning Azmodeus's impromptu and angry materialization earlier that evening. I was sure Quatama knew of it already.

"Leigh Ann?" It was a whisper, a low male whisper, and it didn't match my father's or brother's voice. I kept my eyes shut. I recognized the voice, but balked against another challenge to my rationality. *I'm awake now, dammit,* I thought, *Don't do this to me!*

"Leianna." His voice was firmer now, but still soft spoken, just slightly above a whisper. "I know that you're awake. The veil between the dimensions can be pierced on Allhallows Eve. Open your eyes. There's nothing to fear."

I raised my eyelids.

Peter, Paul and Mary wondered where all the flowers had gone. I wondered how Bael could be standing there, three-dimensional, solid and in living color, in front of me.

My mouth went dry. I swallowed, painfully.

This certainly was *the* night for apparitions.

The song ended, the needle slid to the end of the LP. The phonograph arm lifted, traveled backwards to its rest and, clicking into place, turned the record player off.

I heard footsteps in the dining room above me. They sounded on the kitchen linoleum, and Mom called from the top of the basement stairs. "Leigh Ann? Who's down there with you?"

I couldn't answer. All I could do was stare at Bael. But I could think.

Oh, hell, I thought as she came down the stairs.

-40-

"Who's here with you?" Mom repeated. She didn't recognize Bael from the back, a trim, tall stranger with black hair.

Bael pivoted slowly, allowing her to see his face.

Her eyes shone, seemed larger; she seemed to have difficulty placing him. "Leigh Ann, who is this?" She seemed afraid to ask him directly, breathing shallowly, standing very quietly at the foot of the stairs. He seemed content not to answer her, either waiting for her to recognize him or for me to jog her memory.

Oh, sure, I thought, *I'll just say: Don't you remember, Mom? This is my dark spirit, Bael. My long-lost love of my eternal life.*

Bael took a step forward and held out his hand. "I'm her dark spirit, Bael. The long-lost love of her eternal existence." He still kept his voice low. "I just thought I'd pop in, since the corridors between our dimensions left their doors unlocked tonight."

"Allhallows Eve," she whispered, then lapsed into some Yiddish, something I hadn't heard her do in years and couldn't understand. But Bael apparently could.

He turned back to me. "Your mother's experiencing shock. She wants to know what sin she's committed, that the evil should torment her. Talk to her, Leianna."

"What should I tell her?" I hissed. "That you've crossed the safe metaphysical line she's set for herself and her family? That you can't stay for dinner? That you don't belong in this world?"

Anger darkened his face. "No more than Azmodeus, who accosted you tonight? I deserve a warmer welcome from you, Leianna."

"The rest of my family could come down here any minute. How are we going to explain you?"

"I've taken care of that," he said drily. "They're in a sort of stasis, their minds riveted to whatever activity they're engaged in."

"Fred and Dad to the TV, Ginnie to her textbook."

"Yes."

"So why was Mom overlooked?"

"I wanted to meet—or rather see her again. My father requested it." He turned back to my mother. "Hello, Eve. You look surprisingly similar, as does Leianna, unless my memory is playing *trompe l'oell.*"

She moved slowly across the floor, as if entranced, and lowered herself carefully down beside me on the sofa, shivering despite the warmth of her knit sweater and corduroy slacks. "You have broken a rule of my household." Her voice came out ragged, the words forming themselves into staccato clumps of sound. "Angels, ghosts and demons may not interfere with the mortal responsibilities of my family or myself. You have overstepped your boundary, Bael, and must leave."

"Aren't you even the slightest bit curious about my father's message for you?"

She rapidly shook her head. "Leave."

I lightly touched her shoulder, worried by her glassy-eyed expression. "Mom? Bael, I'm sorry if I wasn't the perfect hostess." I looked up at him, no sarcasm in my expression or voice, just serious concern that I wanted *him* to take seriously. "Next time I'll bake a cake complete with Halloween decorations. In the meantime, I think Mom's right. You've got to leave and release the rest of my family from whatever you've done to them. By the way, have you bespelled my baby as well?" My eyes flashed the question.

"No. Innocent minds are protected from such coercion. Beware of what you teach him, Leianna. I am not the last word on how well he is protected."

"I know you're not," I said pointedly, relieved. "Regardless of what I feel for you, I don't want anyone messing with his head. He also might wake up, need me. Say what you came to say, Bael, then go. You have to keep my mortal world safe and sacrosanct."

Mom turned and stared at me. "Balanced . . . emotionally balanced."

"As you've taught me," I assured her.

She nodded and looked at him expectantly, as if ready to hear what he had to say.

He nodded back to her, and I realized that he could hear our thoughts as clearly as our words, although we hadn't the same advantage.

"I know when you've been bad or good," he said, joking.

"But only when you're around," I countered.

"Not always." He let his response lie, ambiguously. "Eve, my father rescinds the threat made to you while you carried my beloved in your womb this second time. Quatama has enlightened her with or without your confirmation. Lucifer can no longer lay the blame for her awakening on you. He also knows that you were not totally responsible for his downfall, although he harbored anger for centuries over your refusal to join him after he'd championed you, fighting the Creator's judgment. But his main concern now is this proposed alliance and Leianna's possible role in seducing me into it."

Her color back to normal, not quite so pale against her auburn hair, my mother breathed deeply, then said, "Are you saying no harm will come to us at Lucifer's hands or those of his minions?"

"I can't speak for all of the hierarchy. There are those who vow to stop this alliance at all costs, including my father and Azmodeus. But my father has sent this promise: he will not permit any harm to come to you or your family, for the sake of your ancient friendship, which he once treasured. This is not to say that he won't thwart any attempt by Leianna or her mentors to force changes on his realm."

I asked, a bit sarcastically, "Who wants to go to his dark old realm anyway?"

He responded with just the subtlest hint of amusement. "Some of the Netherworld is quite beautiful, Leianna. We've worked hard over the centuries to make it alluring." He paused, as if hesitant to say what next came to mind, then continued. "There is a beautiful garden I created in the courtyard of my private quarters. None may enter the garden without my permission, and few see its extraordinary night blooms. It is my sanctuary, where my memory of you and of Eliom is kept alive."

Somehow the thought of that garden frightened me, as if the love and sorrow that had sculpted it might steal my soul. I lowered my eyes. "I'm sure there are other spots in your world, Bael, that are less appealing."

He didn't argue.

Mom glanced wearily at her watch. "It's ten o'clock. I promised Leigh Ann that I wouldn't tell her . . . how to act. But if she wants you to stay until . . . this astral doorway closes . . . ."

"Midnight," Bael told her. "The start of All Saints' Day."

She nodded again. "You have to let me go upstairs to the rest of my family. And then you have to lift the spell that you've placed on them. And Leianna—Leigh Ann must be very careful if you remain down here. Speak in whispers. If you hear someone coming," (she looked at Bael) "you must leave. You can leave, can't you, by means other than *our* doors?"

"I can dematerialize. Instantly. I won't jeopardize Leianna's mortal . . . cover." When Mom looked at him dubiously, he added, "You have my promise. I will not be seen or heard by the rest of your household."

She got up slowly. "Then allow me to return to my husband, son and other daughter. Leigh Ann?"

"I'll be all right, Mom."

"If Danny should wake, I'll come and get you."

She went to the stairs and then froze, gazing upward. Footsteps descended the stairs, a pair of sneakers and bluejeans coming into view. I held my breath. Mom backed up, allowing the rest of the person to reach the bottom step. She turned and glared at me, more angry than afraid, as if to ask *Who, now?*

Terence looked at her, at me, at Bael, then addressed me sheepishly. "Well, I wasn't expecting your Mum to be down here, you know."

Mum said, a bit sharply, "Leigh Ann?"

"This is Terence Dearborn, Mom," I explained, realizing it wasn't any explanation.

"Nice to meet you, Terence, but we really have to cut this short. I have to get back to my family upstairs, Bael's going to wake them up and then be *very quiet* with Leianna, and *you* have to leave."

She waited for his agreement.

Instead, he said, "Just one minute more, Leigh Ann's Mum. That last part, about Bael being very quiet with Leigh Ann, that's why I'm here. And don't worry, no one saw me come in. Bael, time's up. Violation of Astral Code 914. Blow the girl a kiss and say goodnight, then fix it up like Mum said, and we'll go."

Mom folded her arms across her chest, studying Terence. "I think I like this one."

"Thank you."

Bael folded his own arms and struck a pose exuding sarcasm and challenge. "Astral Code 914?"

Terence dug in his denim jacket's pocket—he certainly favored that material—and pulled out a small book bound in what appeared to be brown leather. He riffled through its pages until he found what he wanted (I wasn't totally sure it was what *I* wanted). "Astral Code Number 914," he read with a slight flourish. "Guidelines governing astral entities materializing on the mortal plane are as follows: a. Physical Contact—Under no circumstance shall physical contact between a conscious mortal person and a materialized spirit or other astral entity subject to High Council jurisdiction be permitted without a waiver signed by that mortal person's spirit master and preparation of both that mortal person and that materializing astral entity to avoid deleterious effects, both during and following contact." He pointed the tiny handbook at Bael. "You haven't got a waiver, you haven't been prepared. You don't make contact."

Bael countered, "I'm not subject to High Council jurisdiction."

"Oh, ho, ho! You are *now*. Look, mate, I'm doing you a favor, saving you quite a bit of face. If you had tried to put the make on our little Leigh Ann before I got here, well, let's just say she's protected, and you would have been yanked out of here without so much as a toodle-loo!"

Bael frowned; it matched his James Dean dark dude outfit. "I'm her betrothed. What possible damage could I do to her?"

"Aside from the psychological side effects, while she's trying to get on with her Earthly life, you could possibly impregnate her."

"Pregnant?!" I yelped. "You mean, like physically?"

"Yes. It's happened in the past. And it's not a pleasant ride for the woman, explaining the baby or raising it. When it lives." His face became guarded. There were definitely other things he wasn't mentioning. I surmised that they'd be unpleasant.

"Terence? I can't get pregnant on the astral plane, can I?"

Again, his face was guarded. "Uh, not physically."

I took that as a no. "Then, Bael, as much as I'd love to have you hold me in this world, we shouldn't break the High Council's rules, not when they've been so good to us as far as our having an astral relationship. I mean, like the house on the sixth plane." He stood there, giving me an I-am-not-happy-about-this look, definitely nonplussed, so I said simply, "You have to leave. What good is it anyway, your being physical for a few hours one night a year? I mean, I'll never be able to wake up the next morning and *see* you beside me. Not in this world."

His expression softened, looking less teed off. He seemed depressed and defeated.

"Well, you *have* to see the psychological hardship it puts on me. You could never really share this life."

"There are ways," he said, then told Terence, "You win. This time."

"Don't take it so hard, mate. You've already scored quite a few points. You don't want to go screwing up those gains." His tone held a warning, clear and caustic. "Are you ready to go? It's nearly eleven, and Miriam and Leigh Ann have to get back to their mortal lives."

Mom said, "He has to undo whatever he's done to Bill, Fred and Ginnie. You promised," she told him, although that wasn't what he'd promised her.

Bael looked at her with all the wariness of a man being confronted by his lady-love's mother. "The spell of fascination will be removed the instant I—and Terence—leave here."

She nodded. "And Terence, you seem to have left part of that rule about contact unread."

"Oh, it goes from a to g, but a's the only one we need, right now." She looked unconvinced. "The rest, umm, deals with non-contact materializations and also appearances of fringe entities. You know, silkies and other were-persons, elves, fairies, gnomes and such."

Bael snorted. "Since when were *they* under angelic jurisdiction?"

Terence stared at him. "There's been changes, mate, since *you* were in the Garden. But they're not, I mean under angelic rule. The code book," he held it up, "was created as a joint project, between many astral species. We all worked together to live in harmony and all that and not get in each other's way. Each group has its own elders, you know."

"Yes, I know. Leianna, I will seek you out later, reduced once more to being your invisible man."

I said nothing, just met his eyes, the hurt in them.

Terence shoved the little code book back into his pocket. "Well, then."

"Terence?" Mom smiled shyly at him. "Leigh Ann played me your music. It's quite beautiful."

Terence blushed. I'd never seen a spirit blush, but it was Allhallows Eve. He didn't look ghostly at all. "Thanks."

He looked good.

"Hey, Terence," I said, "I'm glad they found your lost music."

"Yes, well, I've got you to thank for that as well."

"We don't know that. It may have been an accident, sheer luck, Cecily's finding your lost compositions. She might never have gotten my letter."

"Well . . . thanks anyway." He turned back to Bael. "Ready, mate?"

"Yes. Oh, by the way, your music's pretty good."

Terence gaped at him, as surprised—and pleased as I was. "Oh, *ho!* Well, thank *you.*"

Bael shrugged. "Leigh Ann has good taste in music and men." He pronounced my mortal name *Ley-hahn,* as if it were a shortened version of Leianna.

"On that *note,* I think we'd better go."

"Wait!" I said. They both looked at me. My eyes drank them both in. "What happened tonight . . . it doesn't normally happen on Halloween?"

Terence shook his head.

"Then, unexpected as this was, it's sort of special. And I believe someone owes me a kiss blown my way."

Bael offered me a half-smile. "I would rather have planted it upon your lips, girl." He slowly brought his index and ring finger of his right hand to his lips, pressing them together, then cupped his hand and blew softly across it in my direction. My own lips tingled and a shiver ran down my body: neck, back, bosom and groin, a delicate and delicious ache.

Terence sighed audibly, quickly bussed the fingers of his left hand and blew it to me in one quick breath. "Later," he said. "You first, Bael. And keep in mind we're being monitored."

Bael studied him, his own face a placid mask with a slightly sardonic twist to the lips. Why did I think he looked as if he were about to cry? He faded from sight and then was gone completely. I couldn't detect his presence and suddenly felt alone and bereft.

Terence shook his head at me. "Leigh Ann, it's for your own good. And, by the way, love, this won't happen again. Seriously against the rules without a waiver." He looked at me, as if *he* would drink *me* in, and then he, too, faded.

I slowly took the album off the stereo and slipped it back into its sleeve and cover. "We'd better go up and check on everyone."

My mother nodded tiredly. "Where can I request that they *don't* get a waiver?"

"It's okay, Mom. We're back to normal."

She laughed nervously. "Normal. We'll have to work on that, won't we?"

We started up the stairs.

"Are you all right, Mom?"

"Yes, as much as I can be. Are you?"

"I can see why they have Astral Code 914."

That broke the shaky surreal cloud around us. Humor always helps.

"Thank God for Astral Code 914," she said, and we smiled wryly at each other, a conspiracy of two.

In the dining room, Ginnie yawned over her nursing book. In the living room, Dad and Fred looked up at us. The TV movie had just ended, the credits running up the small screen.

"You missed a good show," Dad said, "yakking with Leigh Ann."

Ginnie ambled into the room, book clutched against her, and yawned again. "That was the best study session I've had in a long time. I don't know why, but even with the TV on, I could really concentrate."

Daniel slept through that night, but I didn't, waking up a few minutes shy of 5:00 a.m., Monday morning, from an astral event that culminated with Quatama's welcomed intervention.

If you face my parents' house from the street, a path loops around to the right from the base of the front door steps, continuing past the porch. The path travels under a trellis with white rose bushes and leads you to our side patio with a long strip of garden with a red rose bush on your right. On your left is the side door leading up to our kitchen or down to the basement. The concrete patio you stand on between the garden and the house is painted red and cracked in spots. Past the house and garden, the path winds to your left, to a yellow rose bush, our driveway and garage. We have a large expanse of backyard lawn behind the house and side patio. A white picket fence separates our backyard from that of the house behind us on the next street. Tall bushes line the left hand driveway. The right side of the lawn flows into our neighbor Mrs. Elsinore's lawn.

In my dream, I found myself standing alone on the side patio. My nightgown swirled as a wind stirred the air around me. I was barefoot, but couldn't feel the concrete beneath my feet. It was dark outside, the sky a purple black, in the early hours of the morning before dawn brings its light.

And then I notice the plants in the side garden. The roses and tiger lilies never bloom this late in the Autumn, yet they leaned toward me, a riot of flowering colors, as if inviting my inspection. I moved closer, the fragrance of the roses intoxicating.

I touched their delicate, velvet, red petals and leaned closer still to take in their scent. A bee crawled out of the partially closed bloom. I quickly edged backward, wary. It flew from the bush, hovering in the air, then disappeared into the darkened expanse of lawn. I peered at the backyard, suddenly wondering why I was standing outside in my nightgown, and why the patio, house and garden were faintly illuminated when the backyard was obscured, a black toneless wall.

The texture of that wall now changed, shapes visible within it, first trees, then bushes, then another pathway leading further into it, none of which existed in our real lawn. I knew then that I was out-of-body and was standing at the threshold of a portal.

This was not my true patio and garden, but a duplicate created to set a scene and lure me beyond it.

I knew where that portal led: to Bael's Dark Garden within his father's realm. I also knew he had created that garden for me, believing that someday I might be trapped in that realm of my own accord and in need of some soothing reminder of Eliom.

The Dark Garden lay beyond the path, pulling me toward it. I already stood on the outer fringe of the portal, at a juncture between dream and reality. I knew Bael had told me truly: a beautiful gift created by love awaited me, just a few steps forward into the darkness. The Dark Garden called to me, its shadows whispering endearments, beckoning as if it possessed arms flung wide, lonely and waiting, waiting too long and nearly touching its elusive inspiration.

I knew that no harm would touch my eternal soul if I answered that call, but I also knew, an instinctive knowledge, that immeasurable harm would come to my physical body and mortal life. All these things I knew, and yet I knew nothing, picking up on bits and pieces of the truth, unaware that they were being rearranged in my psyche to create a web too sparkling with the sweet taste of dew for me to avoid becoming enmeshed in it. Even knowing that danger lay before me, desire for the garden pulled me toward it, like an alcoholic toward a glass of excruciatingly fine wine, its bouquet tantalizing and irresistible.

I inched toward the darkness, all efforts to resist seeping away. What was mortal life compared to such ungodly beauty? What were mortal ties compared with passion of this magnitude?

"Leianna."

The voice, soft-spoken, stayed me from the darkness, a foot away. Its allure . . . the garden it promised to lead me to . . . slowly faded. I turned around, feeling an irrational regret.

Quatama stood next to the rose bush, dressed in his simple brown robe and sandals. He broke a full red bloom off from its branch and held it out to me. It glowed in the astral night, and my heart ached for it.

I walked over to my spirit master, accepting the rose, noting it had no thorns.

"From Bael," said Quatama, "a symbol of love. He tried to transport himself here, to stop you from entering the darkness, but found no entry that didn't repel each attempt."

"Heaven blocked him?"

"No. The Netherworld set up a field of resistance, powerful enough to thwart its second-in-command. Those who were responsible obviously wished to remove you and the threat you pose to their power. They sought to control you, to imprison you as a hostage in their realm."

"*You* got through."

"Those who have no wish to control cannot be controlled, Leianna."

"I'll have to learn that."

"Yes. Bael called out to me, knowing the danger, but we were already monitoring you." I gazed at him, amazed. Quatama seemed so small, so unassuming, yet he had side-stepped the combined efforts of God-knows-Who in Hell.

"Yes, I side-stepped it," he said, hearing my thoughts. "I did not win or lose against them, neither took from them that which was theirs nor gave to them that which was not theirs. Such is the key to opening many locked doors. But we do know who to thank for their attempt on your life."

"My life?"

"Yes. You might have died, had they succeeded. You might have suffered immediate death, but more likely would endure a sudden mental breakdown ending with your wasting away. There is very little hope for recovery when a soul is trapped in spiritual darkness by its own selfish desires."

"Selfish?!"

"Who were you thinking of, Leigh Ann, when the Dark Garden drew you to it?"

"Bael."

"No, Leianna, you were thinking only of satisfying yourself, regardless of anyone else."

I stared into the blackness beyond the patio, seeing it for what it was: ugly and deceitful. No garden of delight lay beyond it.

"They would have taken you," Quatama continued, "but not to the garden Bael cultivated for you, which you desired to see. They enlarged that desire within you a hundredfold. You placed no one and nothing above that desire. And thus they used it against you. A trick. And you allowed them to."

"Thank you." There seemed nothing more important to say than that. "For saving me."

"You're welcome. You have learned from this experience. I can tell." He smiled then, but I remained silent, embarrassed at being upbraided by my spirit master and deserving it. "Let us leave this place, which is not your home, but a sham created to fool you. Our wayward friends are still not satisfied with losing their quarry." He pointed to the darkness, movement within it, forming faces and bodies standing just beyond the patio. I recognized Azmodeus at once, and Mammon behind him. I peered at the others, uncertain of their identities. "Do not fear. They cannot cross over the threshold. You must come to them of your free will, or their magic cannot hold you."

Quatama held out his hand. I sucked in breath, about to speak to the leering damned, but Quatama said, "No." I took his hand, turning away from my would-be kidnappers.

The kaleidoscope of dimensional light burst into colorful patterns around us and seconds later congealed and resolved itself into a meadow bathed in soft shades of early sunrise. Dawn, but where? I sensed no timelessness as it existed in the higher planes. Bael stood in the tall grass with his back to us, hands clasped behind him, head lowered and shoulders slumped as we arrived.

"Bael!" I felt moist dew-kissed blades beneath my feet as I ran to him.

He turned, his face filled with relief, and hugged me fiercely. "You're all right?"

"Yes. Where are we?"

He smiled, not quite up to his characteristic grin, it seemed. "On Earth, in a spot that's private for now."

I held out the rose, still fragrant, still blooming. "Will you keep it for me? I can't bring it back to my parents' house."

He took it from me. "I'll take it to your sixth plane house and put it in a vase. With Quatama's permission."

Quatama regarded us patiently, then nodded. "She'll be awakening soon, Bael. Tell her what you must."

"Tell me what?"

"What his opponents hoped to accomplish, and how to guard against such interference in the future."

Bael stroked my arm, bending down on one knee to bring our eyes level. "You must learn how to deal with the law of attraction, Leigh Ann. There are two mind-states a psychic entity can use against you. One is desire. The other is fear."

"How do I stop that?"

"By being in control of those two emotions. Knowing when it's beneficial to experience them and when it's to your detriment."

"'Quatama said those who don't wish to control can't be controlled."

Quatama responded. "I meant that wishing to control others, even for what you believe to be good reasons, is a subtle acknowledgment of their right to control you in return. It is better to teach by example than coercion, which often leads to confrontation, subterfuge and violence. It is why I stopped you from speaking to Azmodeus and Mammon, but I implicitly let you know you had a choice. You chose to follow my advice. What Bael speaks of is, of course, self-control, which should not harm you if you carefully examine what should or should not be controlled within yourself. But no one can control you against your will. Think on that. Even if they think they have, they have failed, if you haven't agreed to being controlled."

"Desire and fear," I repeated.

"Yes. Do not allow others to use these emotions against you. We are still monitoring you and will continue to do so. But we would prefer that you develop your own defenses in both your mortal and astral lives."

Bael said, "You also need to know that Az and his supporters intended to cast suspicion and blame on me, when your soul went missing and your mortal body sank into madness or death."

"Uh . . . couldn't you have gotten me out of it? I mean, wherever Az and his gang intended to take me?"

They both stayed silent for a moment or two. Then Bael stood up. "I would have eventually found you in my realm and returned you to the upper planes, for your own sake and to prove my honesty. But your mortal life would be ended. The Alliance most probably would be ended."

"You have not yet learned enough to correct a mistake of that magnitude," said Quatama. "For this reason, we protect you from your own ignorance. But with experience, you will be able to reverse errors in judgment with minimal disruption to your lives."

I wondered just how much experience that would take. "In the meantime, I'll keep my eyes and ears open to these tricks, and if I think I'm sinking in the mud, I'll call out to you guys."

"Exactly."

"We'll pull you out," Bael assured me.

"Umm, Bael? You've been using both my eternal and mortal names. Have you come to terms with my mortal life and my need to give it equal attention?"

He seemed confused. "Yes, but I am not calling you by your mortal name, not in my mind. The little or shortened version of your angelic name is Leiann. It sounds nearly the same as your mortal name."

"Convenient," I said and wondered how much of our lives was left to chance. "Except when your younger brother blocks you. How are you going to handle that? He seems to have set himself up as your adversary."

Quatama answered for him. "We are monitoring Bael as well, when he is within the Earthly or higher planes. We will assist him wherever we can. Neither he nor Ashtoreth are alone; they are protected by and important to Heaven, having agreed to act as our representatives in Hell as we work toward healing the rift born out of the ancient war in Heaven."

"The Alliance," I said. "But when they're in their own realm, not your jurisdiction? Are they in danger?"

Bael quickly answered for himself. "Beloved, my own powers are vaster than you realize, as are Ashtoreth's. Az and Mammon caught me off guard as well, but only because they drew power from *you,*

Leianna, while under their control."

"From me? What power?"

"You are a Keeper, Leiann, and God-protected. Your power is greater than my own, but in succumbing to the glamour they created from your own desire, they were able to siphon your power and use it against me. All without your knowledge while the glamour was upon you. But Az and the others have no such power on their own." A wave of frigid anger emanated from him, psychically chilling me. "I will deal with them when I return to the Netherworld." For a moment, he seemed a different man, cruel and vengeful, nearly despotic. I stared at him, and Quatama shook his head slowly. Bael regarded him with hard eyes. "Do not presume to tell me how to run my kingdom, Quatama. You have no knowledge of Hell's intricate politics."

Quatama met his gaze with calm certainty. "The mountain won't come to you. *You* must approach *it*. I suggest you tread carefully."

I yawned. "Gotta climb it. Long way up. Maybe we should take our time." I yawned again. "God, I feel fuzzy."

Quatama lightly touched my forehead. "Your mortal body is awakening. Bael, give your betrothed a kiss and bring her home."

Bael lifted me in his arms, bent down and kissed me. "Thank you for trusting me," he told Quatama, who nodded and said, "Remember, Leianna," as colors flew about me, Bael's arms wrapped tightly around me.

Then blackness of a gentler sort as my eyes opened and adjusted to my bedroom in the early morning stillness. I lay there, sensing Bael near me, but he didn't interrupt my solitude as I pondered all I had experienced.

Then I noted the time, thankful I had two hours left before the alarm rang. I snuggled back under the covers, feeling safe and grateful for it.

Bael, in spirit and invisible again, rested beside me, the slight pressure of his arm on my shoulder, tangible.

I slept undisturbed till seven and rose to face the day strangely refreshed, grateful to be alive and determined to stay that way until my purpose on this Earth was fulfilled. Whatever benefit Heaven and Hell might derive from this alliance, Earth also had to be involved beyond the completion of humanity's genetic rebalancing. I was one of its Keepers, and I suddenly knew what my duties as a Keeper entailed.

We held the Earth together, patching up rifts in its tapestry through some special process in our minds and our souls. We healed its hurts, helped its children to endure pain and loss and go on, shared their joys and triumphs, and put an aura of protection around this pretty blue and white ball in this solar system.

And in view of what had almost happened in the night, I finally understood *why* the Alliance was not just about a fallen angel and an incarnated angel.

A Keeper is like a surrogate parent for Earth, acting with the Creator and as the Creator's agent. The Alliance was part of the Creator's new plan for the Earth. The plan might fail. It might herald a new beginning. We held the outcome in our hands, all of us.

I was once told, should I need help, to seek out other Keepers. Many years would pass before I met one. But we all worked silently and separately together, like the spokes in a wheel that, while never fully touching, keep it turning.

-41-

On Thanksgiving, 1971, it rained. I remember arguing with Richard on the phone over whether he could take Daniel to the Gimbel's Parade in Center City. The temperature was fairly mild, in the mid-forties, but the thought of Daniel outside in the dampness catching cold made me veto the idea. Richard came over at 2:00 p.m. that afternoon to spend time with his son and share our holiday meal. Mom invited him. "He's still the baby's father," she insisted. "It would be cruel to exclude him."

I was scheduled to go before the master in December and hopefully our divorce would be granted and finalized. Richard wasn't fighting me at all on that or challenging my retaining custody of Daniel. I supposed I could give in to a few dinners together while Daniel was young.

One problem with having a secret astral life, your mortal existence takes precedence. If anything, you have to work harder at it, keeping it uncomplicated and avoiding conflicts. Doesn't always work, but you try, because the more you separate the two, the saner you stay.

The same goes for divorcing spouses. Richard had asked me, once, if I wanted to try to make the marriage work. He seemed both relieved and lost when I said no. I almost said yes. The prospect of raising a child alone, for the most part, would be a challenge. Would I fail Daniel in some way, depriving him of an intact, two-parent, home life? But my instinct kicked in, and I stuck to my decision. Richard now only came around to see Daniel, but aside from that, we dropped all pretense of love, barely managing friendship.

In March, 1972, over a year since we had come home to Philadelphia, the divorce became final. I changed my name legally back to Leigh Ann Elfman, although my son remained Daniel Warren.

But the last months of 1971 were rough. My father wasn't crazy about Richard sharing our turkey and pumpkin pie, but he kept it to himself, acting reserved but polite to Richard. I wondered what Dad would say if he knew Bael and Terence were there? The fine thing about invisible lovers and friends is that no one else usually knows they're around. The rotten thing, as I told Bael, is that you can't invite them to the party unless everyone else is drunk or stoned. Neither of those altered states appealed to me, so I was stuck maintaining my rigid dividing line.

Two other events before New Year's Eve created friction between Richard and my father and caught me in the middle. Richard received no invitation to Fred's Bar Mitzvah on December 18th, his actual birthday. Dad felt, under the circumstances, Richard and I were no longer a couple. I agreed and, for once, so did Mom. Ginnie understood, and Fred said he understood. When Richard called the Friday night before, to ask if he could visit that Sunday with Daniel, I asked in turn if I could drop Daniel off at Richard's parents' house on Saturday morning instead, the day of the Bar Mitzvah. If not, we had a neighborhood girl willing to take the job.

Dense silence filled the phone line, then Richard said, "I meant to ask you why I wasn't invited."

"Well, we're getting divorced, Richard."

"So?"

"Richard, it would be a bit awkward."

"So it's like you get on with your life, I get on with mine?"

"Yes, except for jointly raising Daniel."

"Well, thank you for that much."

It was my turn for silence.

I hadn't seen my father enter the kitchen, my back to the archway. He tapped me on the shoulder and gently took the phone out of my hand, speaking into it. "Richard, this is Bill. You should be happy that Leigh Ann has *anything* to do with you, even for the kid's sake, what with your sleeping around on her and being a half-assed provider. So stop complaining and be a good father to your son, if you can. As far as Fred's Bar Mitzvah is concerned, it was *my* decision to leave you off the guest list, not Leigh Ann's." He handed me back the phone, his face slightly red from anger. "You're divorcing *him,* kiddo. Don't let him get away with playing the victim." He grumbled to himself as he went back to the living room.

I put the phone to my ear. "Richard?"

"Did I ever tell you your father is a control freak, Leigh Ann?"

"The world is full of them," I said. "Well, are you going to watch Daniel for me on Saturday, or should I hire a babysitter?"

"Why can't I watch him at your house?"

"Out of the question," I said, adding, "It's my father's house." My frustration rose to a new level as I sensed Bael's arrival. *Oh, great,* I thought, *two men expecting the impossible.* "I'm sorry, Richard, but it's either yes or no. Yes, you'll watch him at your house, or no, you won't. Answer in monosyllables."

He laughed, a bit caustically. "I'll say one thing for you, Leigh Ann: you're witty. Yes. What time are you going to drop him off?"

"Early. Nine o'clock. Ginnie will drive us over. Then we have to be back at the synagogue by ten before they finish the regular prayer service. They'll switch from the prayer books to the Torah at ten-thirty. Mom and Dad have the honor of opening up the ark, and Dad and others will read passages from the Torah. Then Fred is called up to read a passage appropriate to his birthday."

"You don't even understand Hebrew, Leigh Ann. Do you have to be there so early?"

I sighed. "Ginnie doesn't understand Hebrew either, but it's disrespectful to show up later. We couldn't embarrass Fred and my parents like that."

"Fine. I'll get up early. I'm about to become your ex-husband, but I still have my uses, huh?"

"Richard, I really am sorry, but he's your son, too. I'd help you if the situation were reversed."

He snorted. "Fat chance of that, Leigh Ann."

Bael stroked my shoulder lightly, sending chills through me. —Stop that,— I thought frantically. He did. "Richard, just what is that supposed to mean?"

"That the courts normally don't give custody rights to fathers."

"Umm, that's true, especially at Daniel's age, but later on, when he's older, we might work out a joint custody arrangement. And in the meantime, you do get visitation." I thought: What more could you ask for, under the circumstances.

"That's very generous of you, Leigh Ann."

"Cut the sarcasm, please? Just watch Daniel for me tomorrow?"

"Fine. What time will you be picking him back up? I might want to go out Saturday night. There are a lot of women out there who do want me around."

I ignored that. "That's no problem. The synagogue service ends at noon, and the luncheon starts at one. It'll be over at four. We'll pick Daniel up by five. Okay?"

"Fine. Maybe you can bring one of your ghosts as a date. Maybe old Bill approves of ectoplasm."

My hand gripped the phone. "That's hitting below the belt."

He listened to my angry silence, then said, "Okay, I take it back. I was just joking, Leigh Ann. I hope you don't take that psychic stuff too seriously. People have gone off the deep end with it."

"You don't have to worry about me, Richard. I'm a rational, hard-working woman, and I intend to stay that way."

"Good." He didn't quite sound like he meant it.

"And my Dad doesn't believe in the supernatural."

"Give the man a gold star."

"Richard, please, I don't want to fight."

He paused again. "Okay, Leigh Ann. Neither do I. I'll see you to-morrow morning at nine."

"Thank you," I said and meant it.

"You're welcome," he returned. "Bye." He hung up.

Fireworks avoided, I went upstairs to shower and wash my hair.

Bael followed me. —*At least that ex-fool of yours is perceptive. I will be with you during the festivities.*—

I paused on one step and asked telepathically: —*Will they let you in a House of God?*—

—*Yes, under these new circumstances.*— He added with a touch of derisive humor, —*I've no doubt that some of the higher plane folk hope I'll learn from the experience. As if I hadn't already undergone* Barugh Nahtel, *my own dedication to the Creator, as a boy.*—

I vaguely remembered the private ceremony Eliomese children underwent in their seventh year. I said uncertainly, —*As long as they don't mind. But you will be unobtrusive, I hope.*— A touch of regret fla-vored the thought. I wanted him beside me; I knew I could never ac-knowledge it publicly.

I sensed his amused smile. —*Of course. A gentleman never makes a scene.*—

The next incident that nearly set Richard and Dad against each other came at Christmas, one of the few times when I sided with my ex-husband. Richard showed up on Thursday, the night before Christ-mas Eve, with a four-foot, fake evergreen, shiny red ornament balls and a gold-tinsel garland, blithely ignoring the fact that my family, no matter how reform in our beliefs, was still Jewish. He kept a beatific smile on his face as he set up the tree in the dining room, fitting the branches into the wooden trunk held upright by a plastic, three-pronged platform.

My father came over to him, obviously mind-boggled, hands on hips, looking down at him. "Richard? What are you doing?"

"Putting up a Christmas tree."

"Did it occur to you that we don't celebrate Christmas?"

Richard looked up at him from his kneeling position, disgruntled. "Of course, I know *you* don't celebrate it, Bill. But Leigh Ann, Daniel and I do. Damn, these last three branches aren't fitting in the holes right."

My father's mouth clamped shut. He took a quick breath in through his nose and opened his mouth, simultaneously letting it out and saying, "Leigh Ann is Jewish," his face reddening.

I jumped into the foray. "Dad, it's okay. We're just celebrating the spirit of the season."

"You *knew* about this?"

"Uh, no, but what's so wrong with Danny having Christmas? It's a lovely time of year. It promotes peace and good will among men."

Dad took another angry breath and let it out. "Jews support peace and good will throughout the entire year. We don't *need* a special day."

"Dad, I'm not saying that Judaism isn't a good religion or that I'm turning Christian. I just think it's harmless fun. You know, Santa Claus and silver bells and all. And Richard is Catholic. Even if he doesn't believe in it, it's still part of his tradition."

"Then, fine. Let him have the Christmas tree over *his* father's house."

I gave up the ghost of Christmas Present, realizing that my father bore wounds from his and my mother's past that would never separate the religion behind the holiday from the message of hope and joy it sought to convey to our world. I couldn't argue with him. Jesus may have been okay, but some of his so-called followers throughout history had reeked of cruelty and intolerance toward the Jewish people. "Richard, forget it. It's asking too much of my family."

By this time, my whole brood surrounded us. Mother, holding Daniel, stared at the tree and ornaments, saying nothing. As Lucy Angel came over to investigate, batting the lower branches with her paw, Ginnie bent down and picked up the shiny gold garland, saying, "Oh, I don't know. Just for the baby, it might be okay. Just for fun."

Fred, newly Bar Mitzvahed, scratched his head. "Uh, I don't think there's any law in the Talmud that covers this, guys."

Richard threw down the ill-fitting branch. "Well, the tree's defective, anyway. Forgive me for trying to give my son—and you—a little holiday cheer. I mean, it's just a little tree."

Mom put her hand onto Dad's shoulder.

He turned to her.

"I am the one who should have the most say about this. My family, many of my friends, they all died at the hands of people calling themselves good Christians. Many others died, too, and their killers weren't good Christians. But there *were* good Christians who helped save many of the Jews from slaughter. These Christians risked their own lives to aid our people, thwarting the Nazis, and doing what they felt was decent and right in the eyes of God. They didn't distinguish between the Jewish God and Christian God; their bravery and courage led them beyond these distinctions. I believe that's what Leigh Ann wants to honor at this holiday, that universal spirit of brotherhood that ties us together despite the evil that exists."

Dad sucked in and let out a third exasperated breath. "So what do you want us to do, Miriam?"

"I want Richard to realize that we don't celebrate the religion, but that we are willing to celebrate the good will among decent men. You understand this, Richard?"

"Of course."

"Then let Leigh Ann and Daniel have this little good will tree. With it, we'll honor those who were saved and the good Christians who saved them. The tree is a symbol of life, you know." She hugged Daniel to her. "The boy is going to grow up with both heritages, anyway. All I ask is that he grows up to be a good man."

Richard gazed up at her, his expression surprised and subdued. He whispered, "That's beautiful."

Dad nodded gruffly. "All right, then. You can have the tree this year, as a tribute and symbol of that unity."

"Uh, Bill, I still can't get these branches in. Have you got something to widen the holes with?"

My father sighed. "Fred, go downstairs and get the drill out of my tool box."

And so we had Christmas that year, although it was a small celebration with gifts only for Daniel. Richard brought them over the next night, after our son was asleep, then clinked a glass of Mogen David wine with me in a toast to peace and good will between ourselves, and wished me both a Merry Christmas and a Happy Hanukkah, our Jewish holiday which had already come and gone. Then he left at 10 p.m., promising to return early the next day, Christmas morning, to pick Daniel up for his own family's holiday celebration. The Warrens had invited me, but I politely declined. Richard accepted my refusal without a single wisecrack.

I washed up, put on my nightgown and came downstairs to stare at the little tree. Ginnie had made a tin foil Star of David and attached it to the top branch. I thought of Mom's reason for allowing us to have the tree and wondered if our world would ever be free of the evil, if good men would always have to risk their lives to triumph over it. I thought of Jesus and hoped that no follower of any religion would ever use their faith again to hurt other people. As excuses went, it was the worst, blasphemy against the Creator.

—*Oh, Leiann, you are naive.*—

I felt Bael's arms encircle me from behind.

I didn't answer him. I didn't agree with him, and he knew it.

It was my duty as a Keeper to hope and to dream, to spread my own featherweight gospel, to silently and secretly be that spoke in the wheel that jointly helped keep the world going.

Bael was a part of that, despite his skepticism. He would have to champion me in whatever responsibilities came my way or risk losing me. And risk my losing him. After a chasm of separation—35,000 years, I doubted either one of us would risk such a thing.

Such were my thoughts as I gazed at the tree, at the brightly wrapped presents for Daniel underneath it. Bael made no further comments, and my mother, passing by to the kitchen, asked, "Are you all right, dear?"

"I'm fine, Mom." I followed her into the kitchen and sensed Terence standing beside the refrigerator.

Mom looked at me and nodded in his direction.

"I know," I told her, and silently asked him, —*What's up?*—

He answered, —*Quatama would like to see you tonight.*—

I smiled, my back to my mother as she cleaned the counter. —*I'll beam up as soon as I'm asleep.*—

He nodded, my mind's "eye" seeing him clearly. He was dressed all in white tonight, shirt, pants, belt and boots. Even his blond hair seemed lighter. —*Merry Christmas, Leigh Ann.*—

—*Merry Christmas, Terence.*—

Mom, rinsing out dishes in the sink, giggled.

I grabbed a towel to dry and whispered, "What's so funny?"

"Didn't you hear Bael? He mimicked Dickens."

"Huh?"

"He came in, and in a little high voice said, 'God bless us every-one.' I don't think he's quite used to all of this."

"Merry Christmas to you, too, buddy," I murmured, making my mother grin.

Bael laughed, the sound echoing in my mind and filled with the tender sort of tolerance one reserves for small children and pets.

It was nearly midnight. I dried the last plates and glasses, gave Mom a hug goodnight and went upstairs. I heard the shower running in my parents' bathroom—Dad getting ready for bed. Fred was in his room, his door shut, muted sounds coming from his birthday present, a small television all his own. Ginnie was still out, attending a Christmas Eve party at one of the nursing school dorms.

I snuggled into my bed, the wine making me drowsy, and slipped into sleep.

Timelessness returns as my soul, my true self, glides long dimensional corridors connecting with Quatama, being drawn to him like metal to a magnet.

I arrive, and Quatama is there awaiting me, but I'm not where I expect to be. We're in the dining room of my astral townhouse. Terence wheels a beautifully ornate tea trolley in from the kitchen. Another younger-looking man is seated at the dining table, also dressed in the brown robe of a spirit master. He looks very familiar with his long light hair and peaceful demeanor. He smiles at me as Terence serves us tea and cakes.

"Thank you, Terence," I say, while studying the stranger and thinking he looks a little bit like the depictions of Jesus, which can't be right.

Terence distracts me, tapping my shoulder and waving his hand toward the tea trolley. "Do you like it, Leigh Ann? I had it made for you, using my skane points."

"I thought it was your tea trolley."

"No. This one's much finer, fancier. It's my official thanks for your help in finding my music."

He's so convinced that I helped, I decide not to correct him. "It's beautiful. Thank you."

He sits down next to me, having set himself a place there. "You're welcome."

Quatama and the other spirit master sit across from us. I suddenly realize who the unknown guest is. "Yeshua!"

"Yes. How are you, Leianna?"

"Uh, changed! Terence, this is Yeshua. He officiated at my betrothal to Bael." Terence stares at me strangely. I turn back to Yeshua. "You still look as young as ever. I always thought it was remarkable, your being an elder. I mean, you didn't look much *older* than us." I blush at my own silly pun.

Terence continues to eyeball me. "Uh, Leigh Ann? You're being honored here and don't apparently realize it."

Quatama holds up his left hand, palm outward. "Don't force her understanding, Terence."

My handsome secondary guide sits straighter. "Sorry."

I frown at him and Quatama, then tell Yeshua, "You know, when I couldn't at first place you, I thought for an instant that you were Jesus, whom some people say was really a mythological figure from the lack of historical evidence. Did he ever really exist? I mean, the upper planes are Heaven, and no one's ever mentioned him or his being a big mahoff here. Some of the Christians seem awfully sure of themselves, which is going to be very disappointing for his good followers. Or is there more to the story?"

Terence coughs as if he has something stuck in his throat.

Quatama answers patiently, "I, too, am considered a legend by some. But, yes, Jesus did exist and still does."

Yeshua smiles, his eyes crinkling. "His followers may find that some of their doctrine may not fit his or Heaven's reality. But I don't think the good souls who have asked me to intercede for them will be disappointed."

I gape at him, but not speechlessly. "Oh, my God!"

He laughs, a light wind-chime laugh. "How do you mean that, Leianna?"

To say that I'm flustered doesn't cover it. "I'm not invited to tea with the son of God every day. But you're Yeshua, I mean you were Yeshua, and now you're Jesus. Oh, my—I don't know what I mean."

"It's all right, little sister. I was and still am Yeshua, which is both Eliomese and Hebrew for Jesus."

I gaze warily at him. "Uh, I have to tell you something honestly. I don't believe in vicarious atonement or virgin births. Umm, I'm Jewish."

"Yes, I know."

Now Quatama is laughing. "Old fears are surfacing, Leianna. Yeshua does not expect you to have the same needs and beliefs as those who created Christianity out of his life and teachings. You must realize you are different from most ordinary mortals?"

"Uh, yes, but there must be others like me."

"Many," Quatama agrees, "but none quite like you."

"But there are other Keepers. God told me there are other Keepers."

Yeshua leans forward. "Yes, there are. For each century, three are born, for each millennium, thirty."

"Were you one?"

"Yes. And for each millennium, one of the thirty Keepers leaves a permanent mark on the world until the following millennium, when the next Keeper chosen for that distinction will carry on his or her predecessor's work." His eyes look directly into mine.

I point to him and then point to myself. Body language is all I can manage at that moment.

"Yes," he says.

I look at my tea. It must be getting cold. As soon as I think that, steam vapors up from it. I lift the cup, take a sip, set it down. "Umm, I don't have anything—any talent—that especially qualifies me for that job."

Yeshua slowly shakes his head from side to side, his eyes sad, his smile sympathetic. "You have a vision. It hasn't been fully developed yet, and how could it be? The vision is so vast and requires the insight and acceptance of others who will benefit from it. But one day, you will find the way to express it properly, and others will reach out and embrace it with joy."

"Something that will change the world?" I ask, becoming more than a little frightened.

"Something that will allow mankind and the Earth they are shepherds over to continue to grow spiritually and evolve . . . to become as our Creator envisioned these creations."

"But I can't be doing anything revolutionary, Yeshua. I have a son to think of."

"As you once did before," Yeshua answers tenderly.

A long-hidden memory surfaces that I choose not to comment on, one I can't bear to think about, but our eyes lock again in a measured mix of sadness and love. "That was then; this is now," I tell him. But I vaguely worry about all those Catholics praying to her, if it's true.

"She hears them," Yeshua/Jesus assures me. "There are certain souls who exist like a rare diamond, unaware of their many facets, unconscious of how their light radiates in many directions."

Fear sends me rushing for the refuge of humor. "And I thought it was tough leading a physical and astral dual life." I wonder if I can hyperventilate in an astral body?

"Don't worry, little sister. I won't let anyone crucify you."

"They have other methods today."

He remains silent for a minute, then says, "Your mortal life will be quite different from my own as Jesus of Nazareth."

I turn in my seat to face Terence. "Terence, can you believe this?"

"Well, yes. I've known about it for some time. But don't get all uppity on me, Leigh Ann. Like He said, your life is going to be different."

"Different times, different messages," I quip. "Thank God. Here I thought I was going to be *holy!*"

It must be the way I deliver that line. All three of them break out in hearty laughter, gales of laughter tinged with love. When they calm down, I ask, "So what do I do now?"

Quatama lifts his tea cup and takes a sip, then smiles a smile that almost matches the serene smile on the statues in Buddhist shrines. "You do what Yeshua did, when I handed him this gift two millennia ago. You live your life as your heart and soul guides you to, expressing your gift as the Creator guides you to."

Something clicks inside my mind, a rather simple calculation. "I can do that. But if you passed the baton on to Yeshua—Jesus—in the first year A.D., then who did Yeshua pass it to in 1,000 A.D.? Because the same person would be handing it to me in 2,000 A.D., and I get the feeling he or she's not here." I tilt my head toward Terence. "You?"

He chortles, grinning. "No."

Quatama answers me. "The timing is not exact to the start or finish of a millennium. I myself lived in the middle of the first millennium B.C. But you are right. Another held your theoretical baton, moving mankind forward in his own way from 1,000 A.D. to the present. But he did not choose you anymore than I chose Yeshua."

"Then who does the choosing?"

"The Creator, of course."

"And who was my predecessor, and why isn't he here?"

"He chose not to be. He felt it might influence you incorrectly to know who he is, that you have far too much already to digest within your mind and heart, and far too much yet to learn before you can comprehend his influence upon the world without preconceived prejudice."

"It doesn't sound as if he has much faith in me."

"But he does," Quatama insists. "Both I and Yeshua agreed with him. It is not essential that you know his identity right now."

"Fine. So I go forth and just be myself, and somehow I'll add to the building blocks of history which you guys helped to erect."

"Yes," Yeshua says, and Quatama adds, "If it makes you feel better, Moses was my predecessor."

I smile with just the slightest hint of chagrin. "I assume I'm the first woman on the job."

"No," Quatama says, "but we speak of times even farther back in prehistory. You would not recognize her name."

"It's about time you opted for a woman's touch again," I tell them. "What with the way this world's been going, I think I'll borrow my motto from the Sixties: *Make love, not war.*"

"That will be a fine beginning," Quatama agrees and then lapses into thoughtful silence. There is an air of anticipation running between him and Yeshua and Terence, as if they know what he is about to say and are wondering about how I'll take it. Another revelation? It can't be as extraordinary as what they've just confided to me. Quatama finally says, "Your celestial father Michael, before he last incarnated, asked that we reveal his Earthly identity to you on the day that you learn your full destiny." Now I wait expectantly and wonder why Michael would want me to have this knowledge. "He is your son Daniel."

My brain seems to freeze and for a few seconds, I can't focus my eyes or speak. It feels like I'm caught in a familial time warp: father, son, son, father. Doesn't match. Yet I know it does, and I know why mortal people are better off not knowing certain details of their past lives. "My baby?" It's a shocked whisper.

Quatama nods. His eyes are gentle, understanding.

"Does . . . does *he* know? Does Daniel know?" As dumb as that sounds, I must ask or forever wonder if my son is viewing me as his mortal mother or his eternal daughter.

Quatama smiles. "No. And you must never tell him of it. He may be told, should a serious reason arise, of your Eliomese past, but you must never tell him the person and part he played within it, unless such knowledge comes to him without your revealing it. This also applies to your mother Miriam, who now knows she once was Eve. You must not tell her that Daniel is Michael. Mortal lives have their own sacred ebb and flow. The current should not be disrupted." I nod, still a bit shaken. He sits straighter. "When you awaken on Earth, your memory of this conversation will be muddled."

"Vague," Yeshua says. "You will remember that you've been chosen for some great honor, and that Daniel may be Michael reborn, but you will also tell yourself that you are misinterpreting it or imagining it."

"Denial," I say. "Doubt."

"Yes," he says. "A mortal safety valve to protect your emotional balance as you grow and learn and create your legacy."

"To stay sane," I bluntly suggest.

"Yes. Your own mortal life has its own ebb and flow and cannot be disrupted. At least, until such time when you feel ready to reveal yourself. Or are compelled to."

"Quatama, what has all this got to do with the Alliance?"

He shrugs. "I believe your contribution may have something to do with the reformation of Hell and the healing of lost souls. This in turn may have an impact on world religions and mankind's interfaith communication."

"Sounds like a job for Superwoman." I yawn. "Tomorrow morning, people will be celebrating your birth as Jesus, Yeshua, and the promise they believe your divinity gave to the world."

"I have often been touched by that," he says quietly, "but I have always preferred that they follow my teachings. That is celebration enough. What can a birthday celebration or worship as a divinity mean to me if they don't value my words or seek a life that reduces the burden mankind placed on my shoulders?"

I have never allowed myself to dwell too much on what Quatama and Yeshua told me that night. The rest of that remarkable tea party went on in hushed tones. They did tell me that Michael had asked to be permitted to share my last mortal lifetime, and his wish had been granted. It only made me love my baby more, knowing such a fine soul was within him, now a part of him.

-42-

My eyes fluttered open. Fingers of dawn light crept through the window blinds of my bedroom, but no sun yet. I saw a fleeting peripheral movement, a flash of white. Then it was gone, but I sensed Terence sitting on the wooden radiator cover, his legs against the metal grillwork below.

—*Christmas morning,*— I told him. —*So will someone tell me what last night was all about? I don't think I'm remembering it quite right.*—

—*You're someone special, Leigh Ann.*— I "saw" him jerk his head up and to his right, suddenly startled. I sensed Bael standing there. Terence frowned at him. —*Can you give a bloke some warning, mate?*—

Bael regarded him drolly, then sat on the bed. —*What you are, Leianna, is a Millennial Keeper. As you were in your first incarnation.*—

The memory becomes more focused. —*I'm supposed to do something, something of value to my world, something to leave behind after I'm gone. But what?*—

—*Don't worry about it,*— Bael advised. —*Tomorrow will take care of itself.*—

—*Terence? Can I tell him about Michael?*—

—*Nobody told me you couldn't.*— His mental tone held a touch of doubt. —*He'd eventually hear you thinking of it.*—

Bael asked, —*What about Michael? You told me you haven't seen him.*—

—*That's because he's incarnated,*— I told him, —*as my son Daniel.*—

Bael stared at my son, asleep in his crib. —*Lucifer will want to know.*—

—*The baby's protected,*— Terence added.

Bael regarded him with chagrin. —*My father wouldn't harm the child if he could. He and Michael were once trusted friends.*—

I thought of that friendship we all once shared. —*Bael, is your mother still with your family?*—

—*Yes.*— He paused. —*She's somewhat changed. The perpetual dusk and night of the Netherworld has soured her and made her brittle. The well of her tears has long since dried to dust.*—

—*She knows of us?*—

—*Yes, and she fears for you, no matter how much I assure her of your safety.*—

—*I don't understand. Am I in danger?*—

He hesitated. —*Not in the way she fears you are. You'll never undergo what she suffered through. I'll see to it.*—

—*Poor Affaeteres.*—

—*Someday, if you could see her . . . your presence would do her good.*—

—*Can she visit the higher planes?*—

—*No . . . not yet. Ashtoreth and I are the first to be permitted access.*—

—*Then perhaps I could be taken . . . down below.*—

Terence jumped in. —*No, Leigh Ann. That's forbidden. We have to work out certain, umm, terms and conditions.*— His tone was firm, no argument allowed.

—*Then instead tell your mother I send my love. And I'll work to free her from the darkness.*—

Bael remained silent, but vestiges of the complex emotion he tried so hard to hide from me came through, a mixture of hope, gratitude and abject despair.

The strangest sensation overtook me. I felt myself reach out with my astral hand—while my mortal one lay placidly on the bed—and pat the top of Bael's hand where it rested on the blanket. —*It's all right,*— I told him. —*It's going to be all right.*—

He almost looked offended. —*Go back to sleep, Leianna. I won't disturb your rest.*—

—*Do you want to go to my astral home?*—

—*No. I have to leave. Attend to certain responsibilities. In my father's . . . in my realm.*—

Terence said, —*You've spent so much time astral, Leigh Ann, preparing yourself to understand your own responsibilities, why don't you give yourself time off, let your mind rest, too? Sleep fully. I'll watch over you, love.*—

I smiled wistfully. Being watched over. The phrase conjured up all the nurturing and comfort of a fairytale childhood. —*Thanks, guys.*—

I felt Bael lean over and a soft sad pressure caress my lips. Then he was gone.

Terence smiled poignantly. —*Sleep,*— he said. I did.

By the second week of January, bitter cold returned to the city. Willa worked out arrangements for me to attend, for free, the debut of

Terence Dearborn's recovered compositions, thanks to her daughter Stephanie's music teacher, Myrna Woods. Myrna lived in the Olney section of Philadelphia, much closer to my parents' home in Oxford Circle. Since she held the concert tickets, and Willa and her family lived in West Philadelphia, Myrna agreed to pick me up at noon on Sunday and drive us down to the Academy of Music. Willa, her husband Robert, and Stephanie would meet us in front of the Academy at 1:30 p.m.

The discovery of these previously lost works had excited the music world. Although I wasn't knowledgeable enough to understand why certain compositions were treated as serious classical music and other pieces as lighter works, Myrna assured me that the three rediscovered compositions assured Terence a lasting measure of fame.

The weather turned extremely frigid on January 16, 1972, the temperature getting no higher than the middle teens in the day and sinking toward single digits later that night. But the sky remained clear of snow or rain, a beautiful day despite the cold.

Myrna arrived on time, ringing the doorbell, allowing my mother to draw her into the warmth of our house to meet my family. She wore a knee-length, blue woolen coat and sleek black boots. Her black hair was shoulder-length and loosely curled, and she had pleasant, dignified brown eyes, a petite nose and mouth, high cheekbones, and a smooth brown complexion. She looked about five years older than me.

After quick introductions and a goodbye kiss to Daniel—Mom was babysitting until Richard arrived to take over—I bundled up, and Myrna and I left, driving over to Roosevelt Boulevard and then onto the expressway, heading downtown.

"I don't know much about the different forms of classical composition," I admitted as she drove. "I'm basically a novice who enjoys what she hears, and that's it."

"It's not all that mysterious," she said. "Take the three works we'll be hearing today. One is a sonata, which highlights one or two instruments, such as piano and violin, and has three or four contrasting movements. Another is a symphony, a longer, more complex work, composed for an orchestra. It starts off with a sonata, which is usually the first of four movements. The others can be a scherzo, which has a light and playful melody, or a rondo which—how can I state this—has a theme which repeats itself. There are other forms, but I won't confuse you further with them right now."

"And what's a nocturne? It sounds like *nocturnal,* things related to the night."

"Exactly, Leigh Ann. It's a musical piece with an evening or nighttime theme, often lyrical and haunting."

That last description reminded me of Terence's absence. I had mentally called out to him several times that morning and received no response. Once again, at a special moment in his life—one related at least to his mortal life—he had disappeared on me. I turned my attention back to Myrna. "Musical composition sounds fascinating but complicated. Is it hard to learn?"

"Can you read music?"

"Very, very slowly. I can play the guitar, though."

"A budding Segovia."

"Not really." We had turned off the expressway, exiting onto Broad Street in Center City and heading south. We circled around City Hall and continued past Locust Street and the Academy. Myrna turned right at the next light and then left into the parking lot. The attendant gave her a ticket, directing her to a parking spot. She pulled into it, turned off the ignition and put the ticket in her handbag.

"You know, Leigh Ann, if you want to further your musical studies, there are quite a few guitar studios and good teachers in the city."

"I've been thinking about it, but right now, I just want to get on my feet, once my divorce is final. I can't live with my parents forever. Daniel and I need a place of our own, and that's my priority."

"I understand. I assume Willa told you that I've been through what you're going through?"

"Yes."

"I have a six year old daughter and a ten-year-old son. Their father and I were divorced when my youngest was three."

"That must have been rough."

"It was. But we worked things out. If you're willing to work hard and set your eyes on a goal, you will, too. Just take it one day at a time, and take time for yourself and your son. No matter how minimal that time might be, it's important."

"I appreciate your advice. And I can get in touch with you through Willa, when I have time for guitar lessons again."

"When you're ready, I'll find you a good instructor. Right now, we'd better get going. Willa, Robert and Stephanie must be freezing if they're waiting outside."

"I'm ready. Oh, by the way, I'd like to pay for our parking after the show. Since you paid for my concert ticket." I got out of the car, locking the door behind me.

Myrna locked her own side. She wore a pleased expression. "I appreciate your thoughtfulness. Why don't you pay half?"

"Okay. You just don't know how much this means to me."

"Oh, I know." She didn't elaborate. I didn't pursue it. We walked down Broad Street to the Academy of Music.

Willa, Robert and Stephanie were waiting inside the doors, a much warmer choice. I greeted Willa, hugging her, and was introduced to Robert, a tall trim man with a burnished mahogany complexion, short black hair and striking eyes in an angular face, and to Stephanie, a slender girl with her father's eyes and dark brown hair done up in a crown of curls.

We entered the theater, gave the attendant our tickets, received our programs, and were directed to our seats. As we walked down the aisle, the majesty of my surroundings, the red and gold decor and the crystal chandeliers above, lent an aura of romance and glamour.

We were seated in a boxed-off section midway from the stage. It held six chairs. I remembered Willa saying that Myrna could reserve up to six tickets. Willa's son, Rob, Jr., had opted not to come. I wondered who would have the last seat as we filed in: Robert, Willa and Stephanie, then Myrna, then me. The seat to my right remained empty as the theater darkened and the red velvet curtain was drawn to reveal an orchestra arranged on the stage, spotlights on the musicians and their guest conductor, Bernard Lowenstein.

I sensed movement to my right and looked over, half-expecting to see a late concert-goer claiming the seat. No one was physically there. Terence sat down. —*Sorry, I'm late.*—

I thought, —*You certainly are!*—

—*Shh!*—

Mr. Lowenstein, an older man with a shock of silver hair, spoke to the audience. "We are here, ladies and gentlemen, to honor a young composer lost to us in the prime of his life. A year ago, only one recording of Terence Dearborn's musical works existed, music with a lilting beauty, that conjured stories for listeners of all ages. Now, to the music world's delight, three new compositions by Terence Dearborn have been brought to light by his former fiancee, Cecily Saraband-Rogers. Mrs. Saraband-Rogers is here with us tonight." He motioned to a woman in the front row orchestra seats, who stood, turned, and nodded graciously. "We are deeply grateful to Mrs. Saraband-Rogers. And so, we hope you will enjoy the debut of Terence Dearborn's final legacy, which we will be recording. We begin with his seductive nocturne, *By Starlight Possessed.*"

I am not an orchestra musician, not much of a musician at all, so bear with me in my description of Terence's music. The nocturne began with a sigh of violins that seemed to start and stop, start and stop, sounding almost like wind waving through tall tree tops in a fitful night. Then a low wind instrument, possibly an oboe, blew a plaintive sustained note through the violins. It changed to a staccato flurry of notes, and then the melody came, an alluring whimsical song, as if the stars were calling out to their lovers. The other orchestra members joined the lilting voluptuous dance across the night sky, and somehow I could imagine the stars swirling, beckoning, drawing the human dreamer forth to decipher their mysteries and conquer them. But the richly lyrical crescendo made it plain that the stars had conquered us and would forever hang in the night sky, their fiery brilliance beyond our ultimate control, demanding our respect. The nocturne ended with a high sweet farewell of harmonious flutes, the clear cold sound of an xylophone-like instrument and the sighing violins.

After a stunned moment of silence, the audience began its applause, rousing and sincere, my hands adding to the generous tumult. When it quieted down, Mr. Lowenstein introduced the sonata, which Terence had whimsically titled *Where My Soul Has Flown,* a lighter work, featuring a delicate combination of violins and harp. Listening, it evoked images of flight across cloud-flecked mountain tops, birds wheeling and swooping in the air, and then switched over into melancholy, as if his soul had fallen from its carefree bliss. Now buffeted about in a storm-cloud sky, a clarinet cried out at the loss of the peaceful motif, the violins pleaded for resurrection. The harp created rain falling in quickening torrents, then slowed as the storm abated. Other instruments picked up the theme of the sun's return and soul's delight, reminding me somewhat of Ferde Grofé's *Grand Canyon Suite,* which also ended with a triumphant crescendo.

Bernard Lowenstein stepped to the mike again. "The last work is the ambitious and beautifully rendered *The King of Elfland's Daughter.* Based on the master fantasy novel by Lord Dunsany, and Terence Dearborn's tribute to him, this symphony tells of the story of Alveric of Erl and Princess Lirazel of Elfland."

He stepped back, and a woman in a floor-length, long-sleeved red velvet dress came on stage, standing behind a podium to my left.

"The Lord of Erl has sent his son, Alveric, to enter Elfland and win the Princess Lirazel as his bride," she intoned. "The people of Erl wish for magic to reenter their lives again, but the borders of Elfland have receded farther and farther from the mortal world. They would have a royal marriage, uniting Erl and Elfland. To overcome the magic of Elfland, Alveric is given a sword of thunderbolt iron by a witch. Alveric abducts the princess, bringing her to Erl, and they marry." She paused. "The first movement: *The Sword And The Quest.*"

I listened, entranced, as royal trumpets blew, and a processional began the orchestral rendering of Dunsany's novel. When the witch made the sword, thunderbolts and lightning crashed, the kettle drum very much in use. Then a softer refrain began as Alveric entered Elfland to woo his intended, ending in a rousing march, presumably Alveric and Lirazel's return to Erl and their wedding.

The storyteller continued: "Lirazel gives birth to a son, Orion, but the King of Elfland calls to his daughter. A magical wind of swirling leaves enters the castle and spirits Lirazel away, blowing her back to her father's realm. Alveric finds his wife gone and his young son left behind. The second movement: *Lirazel's Return.*"

The movement began on a romantic happy note, but soon turned sad and melancholy. The wind and leaves that carried Lirazel back to Elfland were portrayed in an alluring playful measure, perhaps the scherzo form Myrna had spoken of. Harp and violins lent the magical mood. The music grew darker as Alveric discovered Lirazel's reabduction by her father. The movement ended on a sad note, the harp repeating earlier strains. I wondered if these represented their abandoned child.

—*Yes,*— Terence said, the first time he'd spoken since shushing me. —*Orion was a little boy, barely past his toddling days.*— Then the lady in red spoke again, and Terence quieted.

"Alveric begins searching for Lirazel, becoming older as years pass and the borders of Elfland recede farther away. He gains many followers who travel beside him. Among them are two lunatics, the only men who remain when all of the others abandon Alveric. Alveric ages, his youth consumed while seeking an entrance into Elfland. He ultimately discovers that to cross over the magical border, he must give up the magic of his sword. He relinquishes its magic. The threshold of Elfland appears before him. The third movement: *The Great Search.*"

The violins held prominent sway, and the wind instruments set a counterpoint harmony to a recurring refrain of longing, perseverance and fading hope. It built slowly, like a dirge, then increased in power, the volume rising. The madmen seemed to be represented by swirling flute notes, Alveric's sudden realization that the magic sword thwarted his search, by swift violins, and the discarding of its magic by flute and drum. Then the harp and violins again wove their beautiful sounds together, becoming the glorious reappearance of Elfland.

The orchestra paused as the storyteller finished the tale. "As Alveric attempts to step across to Elfland, his two remaining followers, the lunatics, stop him, afraid that their own mad dreams will be dwarfed by the dreams of Elfland. As Alveric presses through the bor-

415

der and blows his hunting horn, they drag him away and through the wasteland where Elfland has receded. But Alveric's despair, the single note of his horn, has touched the heart of Lirazel in her father's timeless kingdom. Lonely for her husband and child, she cajoles the King of Elfland into using the last elven rune to join her husband's realm with her own kingdom. Her father, knowing change must come, even to Elfland, grants her wish. Elfland flows over into Erl, engulfing it in a glowing tide, uniting the two realms into one both magical and mortal. The fourth movement: *The Last Magic Rune.*"

Wind instruments again took precedence as Alveric was held back by the madmen and pulled along through the wasteland left by Elfland's retreat. Against their low mournful notes, harp and violins returned, and the single long note of a horn blew Alveric's despair to Lirazel. The entire orchestra, swelling majestically, created her plea to her father to employ the last rune. His agreement may have been the slow build-up of the kettle drums against that rich, flowing musical entreaty. And then—with a crash of drums—the orchestra broke into a lush finale, reaching an ecstatic height as Elfland flowed into Erl, becoming one with it, fulfilling Alveric's quest, reuniting the lovers, their families and their worlds forever.

One heartbeat of silence and then the applause thundered up to the stage. In a slow but steady wave, the bulk of the audience rose to honor both composer and musicians. The moment was as magical as the elven realm.

Bernard Lowenstein bowed to us and then waved his hand to encompass the orchestra. The applause continued enthusiastically, then finally subsided. We sat down. Mr. Lowenstein held out his hand toward Cecily. "I would like to call Mrs. Saraband-Rogers to the stage." She rose, walked to the left side steps and was escorted to him. "My dear, you will always be owed a debt of gratitude by the world of music."

Terence still sat silently beside me. In my mind's eye, I saw tears brim in his eyes, running down his cheeks. —*Go up on the stage!*,— I told him. —*Even if they can't see you, acknowledge them. Take your bow! Thank them for their applause.*— He didn't budge. —*Terence, it's your triumph. You deserve it, and I'll know you're there.*—

Cecily took the mike. She was dressed in a conservative blue dress-suit with a white ruffled blouse peeking through the top and blue heels. I couldn't remember if Terence had told me her hair color at the time they'd lived together; now it was dark auburn, done up in a sleek French twist. "I wish that Terence Dearborn could have been here today to hear how beautifully his work was performed. I appreciate Mr. Lowenstein's kind words, but I am simply glad that I discovered the missing compositions, hidden in a compartment beneath the seat of Terence's piano bench. The world is richer for their discovery."

Terence rose, literally in the air and over to the stage in seconds. He stood beside Cecily, calling her name, as the audience applauded her. An attendant walked on stage from the wings, bearing roses, as Terence faced the audience and spoke to whomever could hear him. I hoped I wasn't the only one. —*I thank you for your wonderful response to my music. I would also like to thank Leigh Ann Elfman, for she, too, contributed to the recovery of my work. But, most of all, I thank you for taking my music from me. For I realize that is the only true worth I have as a composer, when you absorb my music into your own hearts and lives and make it a part of you, allowing that part of me, of the man I was on Earth, to live on through you. No greater gift can ever be given, no greater honor. Thank you for accepting my legacy. Without you, I have none.*— He bowed slowly and humbly, as the audience continued its applause for Cecily, smiling her appreciation of the dozen, long-stemmed, red roses. Terence disappeared from the stage. I felt him beside me again.

His hand found mine and clasped it tightly. Our triumph, our special moment.

That night, I had a hard time falling asleep. Bael, Ashtoreth and Terence were there, keeping me silent company, listening to my mind remembering snatches of musical refrains from the concert, simply basking in the knowledge that I, in my own small way, had helped bring something wonderful to my world.

It was well past midnight, the house dark, quiet. —*You know? I think I love all three of you, guys. I think I'm in love with the whole world.*—

I sensed Bael's wry raised eyebrow, Ashtoreth's gentle empathy, and Terence's smile of contentment as he said, —*Patrick wrote a small poem honoring the debut of my recovered works. May I recite it to you?*—

We offered him our silent attention.

—*I am an empty vessel until you fill me with your unison,*— he murmured, —*a lonely song until you add your harmony. Now share your world with me, and we, who were separate, become one.*—

I pulled my blanket more snugly around me. —*It may take a lifetime to discover who I am and what I'm meant to contribute to my world, to know how I can best share it.*—

—*Usually does,*— Terence agreed. —*Then I'll stay with you until you're old and gray and accomplished, until you shed your mortal cocoon, little butterfly.—*

Ashtoreth whispered, —*And then we take you home.—*

—*Will you love me when I'm aged and wrinkled?—*

Bael reached over and stroked my cheek. —*You will never grow old, Leianna, my Sleeping Beauty. I will cut away the thorns and give you only smooth-stemmed roses. I will subdue the dragon and make your palace a safe place to awaken within. I will keep you forever young and rouse you with a kiss to greet the future as my bride.—*

I smiled. —*Sounds like a fable.—*

—*Legends are often based on truth.—*

Terence butted into this tender conversation. —*Even would-be legends need sleep. Come on, Leigh Ann. We'll miss the party Patrick's throwing for me, if you lie awake all night.—*

I shut my eyes, drifting off on waves of sleep like a boat on a river. I could only navigate this dual life one day and night at a time.

Only God knew where it would lead me.

The End

www.ingramcontent.com/pod-product-compliance
Lightning Source LLC
Chambersburg PA
CBHW020635020726
47494CB00001B/204